BOLT

BOLT SAGA: VOLUME ONE
PARTS 1 - 2 - 3

ANGEL PAYNE

This book is an original publication of Angel Payne.

This is a work of fiction. Names, characters, places, and incidents either are the product of the author's imagination or are used fictitiously, and any resemblance to actual persons, living or dead, business establishments, events, or locales is entirely coincidental. The publisher does not assume any responsibility for third-party websites or their content.

Paperback ISBN: 978-1-947222-45-8

BOLT

BOLT SAGA: VOLUME ONE
PARTS 1 - 2 - 3

ANGEL PAYNE

WATERHOUSE PRESS

TABLE OF CONTENTS

For Thomas...
my incredible superhero,
every single day.

BOLT

PART 1

PROLOGUE

REECE

She's got the body of a goddess, the eyes of a temptress, and the lips of a she-devil.

And tonight, she's all mine. In every way I can possibly fantasize.

And damn, do I have a lot of fantasies.

Riveted by her seductive glance, I follow Angelique La Salle into a waiting limo. A couple of friends from the party we've just left—their names already as blurry as the lights of Barcelona's Plaça Reial—wave goodbye as if she's taking me away on a six-month cruise to paradise.

Ohhh, yeah.

As an heir to a massive hotel dynasty, I've never wanted for the utmost in luxurious destinations, but I've never been on a cruise. I think I'd like it. Nothing to think about but the horizon...and booze. Freedom from reporters, like the mob that were flashing their cameras in my face back at the club.

What'll the headlines be, I wonder.

Undoubtedly, they've already got a few combinations composed—a mix of the buzz words already trending about me this week.

Party Boy. Player. The Heir with the Hair. The Billionaire with the Bulge.

Well. Mustn't disappoint them about the bulge.

As the driver merges the car into Saturday night traffic, Angelique moves her lush green gaze over everything south of my neck. Within five seconds my body responds. The fantasies in my brain are overcome by the depraved tempest of my body. My chest still burns from the five girls on the dance floor who group-hickied me. My shoulders are on fire from the sixth girl who clawed me like a madwoman while watching from behind. My dick pulses from a hard-on that won't stop because of the seventh girl—and the line of coke she snorted off it.

Angelique gazes at that part with lingering appreciation.

"*C'est magnifique.*" Her voice is husky as she closes in, sliding a hand into the open neckline of my shirt. Where's my tie? I was wearing one tonight—at some point. The Prada silk is long gone, much like my self-control. Beneath her roaming fingers, my skin shivers and then heats.

Well...shit.

If my brain just happens to enjoy this as much as my body...I sure as hell won't complain.

Maybe she'll be the one.

Maybe she'll be...more.

The one who'll change things at last.

Even if she's not going to be the one, she's at least *someone*. A body to warm the night. A presence, of *any* kind, to fill the depths. The emptiness I stopped thinking about a long damn time ago.

"You're magnificent too," I murmur, struggling to maintain control as she swings a Gumby-loose limb over my lap and straddles me. What little there is of her green cocktail dress rides up her thighs. She's wearing nothing underneath, of course—a fact that should have my cock much happier than it is. Troubling...but not disturbing. I'm hard, just not throbbing. Not *needing*. I'm not sure what I need anymore, only that I seem to spend a lot of time searching for it.

"So flawless," she croons, freeing the buttons of my shirt down to my waist. "*Oui*. These shoulders, so broad. This stomach, so etched. You are perfect, *mon chéri*. So perfect for this."

"For what?"

"You shall see. Very soon."

"I don't even get a hint?" I spread a smile into the valley between her breasts.

"That would take the fun out of the surprise, *n'est-ce pas?*"

I growl but don't push the point, mostly because she makes the wait well worth it. During the drive, she taunts and tugs, strokes and licks, teases and entices, everywhere and anywhere, until I'm damn near tempted to order the driver to pull over so I can whip out a condom and screw this temptress right here and now.

But where the hell is here?

As soon as I think the question, the limo pulls into an industrial park of some sort. A secure one, judging by the high walls and the large gate that rolls aside to grant our entry.

Inside, at least in the carport, all is silent. The air smells like cleaning chemicals and leather...and danger. Nothing like a hint of mystery to make a sex club experience all the sweeter.

"A little trip down memory lane, hmmm?" I nibble the bottom curve of Angelique's chin. It's been three weeks since we'd met in a more intimate version of this type of place, back in Paris. I'd been hard up. She'd been alluring. End of story. Or beginning, depending on how one looks at it. "How nostalgic of you, darling."

As she climbs from the limo, she leaves her dress behind in a puddle on the ground. It wasn't doing much good where I bunched it around her waist anyway. "Come, my perfect Adonis."

Perfect. I don't hear that word often, at least not referring to me. Too often, I'm labeled with one of those media favorites, or if I'm lucky, one of the specialties cooked up by Dad or Chase in their weekly phone messages. Dad's a little more lenient, going for shit like "hey, stranger" or "my gypsy kid." Chase doesn't pull so many punches. Lately, his favorite has been "Captain Fuck-Up."

"Bet *you'd* like to be Captain Fuck-Up right about now, asshole," I mutter as two gorgeous women move toward me, summoned by a flick of Angelique's fingers. Their white lab coats barely hide their generous curves, and I find myself taking peeks at their sheer white hose, certain the things must be held up by garters. Despite the kinky getups, neither of them crack so much as a smile while they work in tandem to strip me.

I'm so caught up in what the fembots are doing, I've missed Angelique putting on a new outfit. Instead of the gold stilettos she'd rocked at the club, she's now in sturdier heels and a lab coat. Her blond waves are pulled up and pinned back.

"Well, well, well. Doctor La Salle, I presume?" Eyeing her new attire with a wicked smirk, I ignore the sudden twist in my gut as she sweeps a stare over me. Her expression is stripped of lust. She's damn near clinical.

"Oh, I am not a doctor, *chéri.*"

I arch my brows and put both hands on my hips, strategically guiding her sights back to my jutting dick. I may not know how the woman likes her morning eggs yet, but I *do* know she's a sucker for an arrogant bastard—especially when he's naked, erect, and not afraid to do something about it.

"Well, that's okay, *chérie*." I swagger forward. "I can pretend if you can."

Angelique draws in a long breath and straightens. Funny, but she's never looked hotter to me. Even now, when she really does look like a doctor about to lay me out with shitty test results. "No more pretending, *mon ami*."

"No more—" My stomach twists again. I glance backward. The two assistants aren't there anymore, unless they've magically transformed into two of the burliest hulks I've ever seen not working a nightclub VIP section.

But these wonder twins clearly aren't here to protect me.

In tandem, they pull me back and flatten me onto a rolling gurney.

And buckle me down. Tight.

Really tight.

"What. The. *Fuck?*"

"Sssshhh." She's leaning over my face—the wonder fuckers have bolted my head in too—brushing tapered fingers across my knitted forehead. "This will be easier if you don't resist, *mon trésor*."

"This? This...*what?*"

Her eyes blaze intensely before glazing over—with insanity. "History, Reece! We are making *history*, and you are now part of it. One of the most integral parts!"

"You're—you're batshit. You're not forging history, you bitch. You're committing a crime. This is kidnapping!"

Her smile is full of eerie serenity. "Not if nobody knows about it."

"People are going to know if I disappear, Angelique."

"Who says you are going to disappear?"

For some reason, I have no comeback for that. No. I *do* know the reason. Whatever she's doing here might be insanity—but it's well-planned insanity.

Which means...

I'm screwed.

The angel I trusted to take me to heaven has instead handed me a pass to hell.

Making this, undoubtedly, the hugest mess my cock has ever gotten me into.

CHAPTER ONE

EMMA

One year later...

The executive offices at Hotel Brocade are always a fun place to be, but they're even more exciting when the boys in the reservations bay are trying to kill each other.

"Bam!"

"Kazow!"

"You're dead."

"Not if you're dead first."

"Yeah, right. Because your spleen on the ground isn't an indication I got you first, huh, crap-for-brains?"

Ahhhh. Nothing like the sounds of cybergeeks in full slay-or-be-slain mode, a special perk of working the six p.m. to four a.m. shift. When splattered spleens are invoked, I know it's time to finish up my break and get back to work. Let nobody say the new girl didn't learn the important lessons fast.

Thank God.

Because I really need this job.

I swore I'd cut off my right nipple if I got this position. The left one too, though thankfully things never came to that. I intend to keep my nipples *and* the job by being the hardest-working person in the building.

This job is what finally got me out of hell.

Okay, Orange County hasn't always been hell. It just took a dive that direction once Dad got his massive promotion to VP at an international conglomerate with a massive campus in Irvine, thrusting our family into another income bracket—and the stratosphere of vanilla-flavored snobbery.

AKA hell.

But I've escaped. I'm no longer part of that world. I've finally begun a life filled with more than hair appointments, yoga classes, and fretting about the carb count in my morning muffin.

I intend to stay here.

This job is the key to truly beginning my life.

I arrive back at my office, a proud smile erupting as I take in my view. Twinkle lights glow in the olive and palm trees surrounding the pool area. Banks of tropical flowers flutter in the gauzy night breeze. A few people are enjoying the hot tub across the deck, quietly laughing and talking, but there's nobody in the bigger pool, so the water is reflected as lazy aqua swirls against my office window. The scene is stunning, even at night.

God, I *really* love working here.

"Well, good evening, Miss Emmalina Crist."

I smile toward the source of the greeting issued in a musical accent from my office doorway.

"Good evening to you too, Miss Neeta Jain."

Neeta folds her arms and grins. "The warriors of Geekdom have you cutting and running for the sane side of the building again?"

I laugh, slightly nervously. Neeta is dressed nearly the same as me, in a dark skirt suit with a satin blouse beneath, but on her the look is sleek and glam, while I feel like the girl playacting at adulting. Which is ridiculous. I'm nearly twenty-four now. I landed this job on my own. Paid for this suit with my own money. It's not dress-up. It's mine. This *life* is mine.

I can do this. I can do this. I can do this.

I intend to keep repeating it, in my heart and on my lips, until I really believe it.

For now, I push aside how her waterfall of dark hair and perfectly kohled eyes remind me of the pretty but plain world for which I still feel like the poster child.

"It's all right," I assure her. "Wade and Fershan deliver when it matters most. Their guest satisfaction scores are among the highest for the Reservations Department. As long as they're Prince Charmings for the public, I don't care if they eviscerate each other a hundred times tonight."

She laughs softly while walking toward the window. "Excellent point." But her composure jolts the second she pivots toward my monitor. "And speaking of excellent points..." Her jaw goes slack. She drops into my chair. "Look at the glory of *this* one."

I move behind her, curious about what's caused her to gawk. Every staff computer is programmed to boot up into the guest-room online menu so we stay aware of any technical issues. In addition to local attractions, there's a live feed of local news features cultivated for the maximum relevance to our guests, though the feature is often more valuable for us. Our downtown location puts us in the thick of it during major emergencies—which could be anything from a six-plus magnitude earthquake to a diva breaking a fingernail en route to an awards show—so the constantly changing feed has become an essential compass.

Right now, Neeta expands the compass with eager

swiftness. I won't be surprised if her throaty gasps and dreamy sighs develop into drooling.

"Glory?" I mean every note of my fascinated echo. I need to see what's turned her from worldly and sleek to stuttering and adolescent.

Once I step around and view the screen, a frown takes over. "A convenience store robbery?" I thought I'd be helping her ogle the hottest hunks on some movie premiere red carpet. "Okay, even the OC peasant isn't getting the appeal." I wonder if we need to change the feed to another station. Last time I checked, stories like this didn't fit *any* of the Richards Resorts "R's of Hospitality." *Relax. Revitalize. Renew.*

"A *thwarted* convenience store robbery." Neeta jabs a red-tipped fingernail in emphasis. "And look at the god who did the thwarting."

"God?"

"God."

I peer closer at the feed. It shows the same basic news-chopper view of the little store like so many others in the city. Semi-busy street intersection. Palm trees. Geraniums planted in the median. A couple of parking spaces and a bike rack out front. Posters for beer and lottery tickets in the front window. A neon sign: Yes, We're Open. There's nothing special about the police presence either. A pair of cruisers with lights flashing, turning the area into an ironic urban disco.

"I really...don't see what's so..."

But then I *do* see.

The screen changes, showing cell phone footage timestamped from forty-five minutes ago. Looks like amateur stuff captured from across the street from the store. The cell owner's commentary can be heard, captured along with the images.

"Damn. What assholes would rob Santa Claus?"

Sure enough, the store's proprietor is a sweet old guy who probably volunteers as Saint Nick around the holidays. I wouldn't believe any less, though right now he stands behind the counter wearing a Go Dodgers T-shirt. Though the leader of the hoodlums has drawn a gun, the man reaches for them like Santa trying to reason with a pair of Jack Frosts with matching bleached Mohawks.

"That sweet man," Neeta murmurs. "I'd be on the floor in a puddle of terror."

"You mean like her?"

The cell phone shot pans wider to include a woman no older than us cowering on the floor. Bad guy number three, just noticing her, stomps over for the grab.

But he clutches at nothing but air because the woman has...levitated.

At least five feet. Straight into the air.

"What...the..."

"Right?" Neeta gasps as the girl starts to scream. "That's not even the best part."

"There's *more*?"

I barely get the words out before the poor woman starts to gently float toward the back of the store as if being carried by some invisible divinity. There's five feet of empty air between her and the floor and a discernible black line scorches the linoleum along the terrified woman's path to safety.

"How...is...that...?"

"Right?" Neeta repeats.

"No," I blurt. "*Not* right. How the hell is that even possible?"

"They say he does it with massive electric fields," Neeta responds. "Though how *that* works is still anyone's guess."

"He who?"

"He...him." She declares it as if heralding Eros himself, just as another man appears at the left of the video. That's barely an exaggeration. The figure to which she's referring could double as the god in a movie. He seems to appear from nowhere, as ceiling lights burst and shower behind him, like he's descending from freaking Mount Olympus in a fit of rage. Damn good way to describe what the guy's mood looks like too. His strides are wide. His arms are an A, framing the air on either side of his body. His fists look like brutal coils at the end of muscled ropes. And holy shit, do I mean muscled. Having a tennis star for a sister means I actually know the name of every striation in the human arm, though rarely am I able to recall them while *looking* at them. His legs present the same fun game, and don't get me started on his abdominals.

On second thought, go ahead and get me started.

All of that is encased in an outfit I can only describe as motocross meets rock god. The black leathers are so tight he should look like a pretentious jackass but weirdly doesn't. His getup has flexible fabric insets of some sort which cushion his glorious body in all the key places he needs to move. He even wears kick-ass boots—if that's what they can be called—evoking black ops or SEALs, pieced in a crisscross up to his knees.

He's part ninja, part ultimate fighter, part thundercloud—and a hundred percent captivating.

I can't rip my stare off him. He seems to uncoil power like a live electrical wire—but with an insane body.

Truly insane.

"Holy...shit." I finally summon the bandwidth in my brain to breathe.

"Nothing holy about what I'd love to do to that guy." Neeta snorts. "Whoever he is."

"What do you—"

Eros-ninja-thunder-dude interrupts my question, stalking toward the robbers and planting his feet the same width as his fists. He lowers his head as if he's saying something, and it earns him a triple hoodlum rush—which he answers by raising both fists and spreading his fingers until they're strained wide. In another universe, I'd expect spider webs or fireballs to fly from his palms. In this one, there's only a tangible but invisible shudder through the air that acts like a three-way punch striking the robbers.

It's as impossible to comprehend as the levitation trick on the woman, but it's the truth. Neeta's gasp, in tandem with mine, tells me she thoroughly agrees. We're riveted as the hero lifts his arm a little higher and flings it as if throwing trash away—which is very likely what he's thinking too—as the hoodlums scatter into the air like a wind-tossed trio of used slushy cups, flying twenty feet before crashing into the drink coolers at the back of the store. They stick there for a few seconds, bawling in terror, before plummeting along with the glass to the floor. Whoever's taking the cell footage provides a perfect flash of commentary.

"Yeah! Dude is takin' care of business!"

I'm faintly aware Wade has scooped up his cyberguts long enough to wander in our direction. At the sounds of our reactions to the video, he scoots in behind us. "Fersh!" he shouts. "Get over here. It's him."

"Sure as hell is." Every syllable out of Neeta is just sultry.

"Him who?" I demand as Fershan dips his head, baring a smile that's brilliant against his dark skin.

"Dude," he repeats, shoving Wade's bony shoulder. "You're right!"

"Him *who*?"

"Nobody knows," Neeta supplies.

I glance back at the monitor. "Wait. Are you serious?" My scowl becomes a gape. "Is *he* serious? Is he really wearing a mask?"

Okay, not a big one. It's like the Maserati of masks. Sleek and black and subtle, fitted like a tight blindfold across his upper face but with eyeholes. I can't tell a lot from the angle of the video, but the eyeholes look like rectangles, almost making him look like a wavy-haired hipster with designer glasses. But instead of skinny jeans and a cardigan, he rocks custom leathers and weird-but-hot ninja boots.

"I think he's pretty serious," Wade responds as the ninja thunder god pivots, grabs a couple of extension cords off an endcap, and makes his way to the back of the store. Next to the hanging cords is a rack of mini flashlights, which all start to blink as his hand passes near.

"What on..." I whip a startled glance at the guys. "Did you see—"

"Yep," they answer in unison.

For the next thirty seconds, we only see the store owner glancing furtively toward the spot where weird electro man flung the bad guys, though the cell phone owner illuminates with his play-by-play. "Boss is usin' those cords to tie those slimebags down. Yeah, man. That's the way."

When the video feed is filled with red and blue lights, the man in the Maserati mask snaps up. At once, hunk-god rapidly strides toward the front of the shop like a man on his way to save the world. Which, at this exact moment, doesn't seem like an exaggeration at all.

Despite his near blur of speed, he's mesmerizing. When he's in the shot, my sights focus on him alone. I'm nervous but attracted, almost feeling like I'm on a first date—pretty lame, considering I haven't exactly logged a ton of those—but the symptoms are the same.

I'm sweating.

I'm throbbing.

I'm aching.

In all the worst places.

"Holy...wow."

The reaction tumbles out before I can stop myself.

"Aha. OC finally figures it out." Neeta's sarcasm saves me from having to summon a fun comeback to Wade's and Fershan's shouts.

"Is he gonna do it?"

"C'monnn. He has to do it!"

"Do what?" I ask.

"*Please*," Neeta drawls. "He's totally going to do it."

"Do *what*?"

The guys bellow in victory as the hero on the screen checks on Santa Claus, spins away from the counter, drops into a stance similar to a competitive runner on the starting block...

And disappears.

"What...the..."

The store fills with flying paper, slushy straws, and condom packets—in short, anything that can easily be tossed around in a strong wind.

A revelation sets in. He didn't disappear. He just left so

fast, that was what it looked like.

Fershan and Wade launch into a leaping high five. "Gotta bolt!"

I want to join Neeta in chuckling at them but am trapped in stunned mode. I do manage to blurt, "Excuse me?"

Excitement adds to the ruddy flush on Wade's face. "It's his whoop."

"His whoop?" I echo both syllables with slow caution.

"Like his war cry," Fershan interjects. "It distinguishes him. Puts his unique stamp on shit."

"Because that outfit and the mask don't do that already?"

"Easily copied," Fershan asserts. "But the whoop is unique. Nobody can say it like the original." His gaze twinkles. "Every self-respecting superhero has one."

My scowl disappears—to make room for my gape.

"Okay, whoa. Are you guys telling me—"

A shrill bell cuts me short. The door to our offices, locked at night, sets off the sound when someone uses a fob to open it. The security measure isn't all that safe, though, because most of the time we ignore the alert. The only people who have fobs are supposed to have them.

Tonight, that's not the case.

Wade, Fershan, and Neeta snap their heads up in matching alarm. Before I can question their paranoia, they're hustling like someone's just yanked the fire alarms on every floor of the tower.

"Damn it," Neeta hisses.

The guys add earthier expressions.

"Hey." I sprint as fast as my heels will allow, catching up with them. "What's going on? Somebody want to fill in the new kid?"

"Shit," Wade blurts as if I haven't spoken. He darts a frantic look at his buddy. "He never uses this entrance."

"He who?"

Fershan swallows. "Unless he's spying on us."

"He *who*?" They'll have to acknowledge me eventually.

Neeta rolls her eyes. "His last name is on the letterhead, guys. He's not 'spying.' He's checking up on the business."

I stop so hard my toes turn to jammed stubs in my pumps. *His last name. On the letterhead.* "Holy crap."

My stunned gasp has justifiable cause. The only person I'd never expected to meet, even if I worked days instead of nights, is the same man who approves my paycheck every two weeks. I've heard enough about Reece Richards to figure that much out and to use it as the springboard for my discomfort now.

Okay, yeah, I'd known about the guy before landing the job—though only through thirty-second mentions on glossy entertainment news shows and his paparazzi-favored face on every magazine in the grocery store. The Richards family's gorgeous youngest, known as much for his unconventional business ideas as for his unrestrained sex drive, had only gotten wilder after college. At some point, he stepped into some shit pile so deep, he was banished here, ordered to run the family's West Coast hotels from LA.

Needless to say, I don't expect to meet a happy guy.

Honestly, I wonder if I can get out of meeting him at all. I won't even have to lie about the stack of work I just left behind—and the fact that the news feed is still running on the monitor doesn't hurt either.

Who the hell am I kidding?

All I can think about is watching that robbery footage again. If my rampaging libido doesn't already dictate it, Wade and Fershan's insane claim sure as hell does.

Superhero?

They're joking.

They have to be.

Even if the man can toss electric pulses, levitate people, and go zero to light speed in three seconds, that doesn't make him a freaking superhero.

Then what *does* it make him?

I'm forced—saved?—from contemplating that further as the air shimmers with new energy.

Okay, *energy* might be pushing it—but I'm not sure what other label fits this crazy surge of feeling. Is it a quickening? Full-blown anxiety? Leftover thrills from the excitement of watching Maserati Man? This feels like more. As if every ion in the air has been plugged into a cosmic supercharger.

"Mr. Richards. What a pleasant surprise!"

Higher.

Power.

Neither word does him justice. Even strung together, they barely do the job.

Reece Richards is nothing I expected.

And everything I need to fear.

It's not just the physical stuff—though, holy wow, that's the obvious place to start. It's all there, just as I remember from the magazines. The gray gaze so deeply set, the irises resemble midnight. The nose so bold and masculine, it could only be paired with a lush, elegant mouth. And those plush curves are set into a jaw of such sharp angles, I wonder if it's as alluring when clenched. That's all before getting started on his hair. And yes, his hair is really worth the attention. I know this because no matter what, I've always gawked twice at the man's photos just because of those dark-auburn waves.

But like I said...that's only the beginning.

His beauty—there really is no other way to say it—is the thinnest nick on the surface of what it's like to look at him. Experience him. Is the air buzzing? Are my breaths xylophoning my ribs? Have my nerve endings been punched to a higher resonance?

Presence. Aura. Mystique.

All words I've heard before—and thought I understood.

And never have. Not really.

And that leads back to the wanting. And the fear because of the wanting. As in, already fighting visions of what it'd be like to leap at the man, wrap my thighs around his toned hips, and fit every inch of my needy cleft along his swollen—

"Miss Jain. Good evening."

His acknowledgment to Neeta, followed by similar greetings to the guys, is delivered in a voice as powerful but silken as an ocean wave on the shore. *His voice.* At once it worsens—and heightens—my fantasy. Now, as I mentally jump him, he's rasping like that in my ear. Saying illicit, erotic things... Things I haven't allowed myself to think of doing with a man in a very long time.

Ride me harder, Emma.

Things I can't—I won't—allow myself to think now.

I want to be inside you, Emma.

Not. Now.

I'm going to fuck you deep, Emma.

Not with a man like him.

But all I can focus on *is* him, standing there with his tall, graceful body filling out that dark-navy suit and matching tie, the fit so perfect my stare can't help but wander...

Everywhere.

Yes, even down there.

Oh...wow.

His bold, hard elegance is so *not* a disappointment.

Stop.

The dictate echoes through my head in Mother's voice. Appropriate. Too damn much so. What would she think if she were here? And why does this man himself seem to read every nuance of those thoughts as they seize my mind—and be just as tense as me about them?

"Good evening yourself, boss." Wade scoots forward and eagerly pumps Richards's hand. Though Neeta barely masks her horror about the familiarity, the "boss" himself seems mildly amused. "Deciding to slum it with the commoners for a bit tonight?"

A ripple of confusion crosses Richards's brow. "Of course," he says slowly, as if reading Wade's lips and guessing at the meaning.

Neeta, still more rattled than I've ever seen her, pushes out a huff. "Mr. Richards doesn't have time for *slumming it.*" With a look drenched in apology, she clarifies, "He's here to collect the weekly reports, of course. And has extended the honor of doing so in person."

It's difficult to interpret Richards's new expression. Relief? Surprise? Both or neither, the angles of his face are beyond riveting. "Right. The reports." His voice is almost a question, though the words don't seem to match.

He pivots toward me, and our eyes lock. I open my mouth, but there's nothing. I wonder if it'll ever be capable of sound again. Especially when he appears to lean closer, as if there's something we should say to each other. How did a blade of lightning find its way through the concrete jungle outside to zero in on my swimming, careening senses?

The room tilts, forcing me to an inescapable conclusion.

The lightning...is him.

I suck in a breath. He does the same. He seems puzzled. Angry. Maybe neither. What's he feeling? Why can't I figure it out? I *need* to figure it out. The need is urgent, pinging harder and harder at me...

What the hell is he doing to me?

No. What *isn't* he doing to me? I feel like my sex drive is jammed into a light socket, and I never want to rip it out again—even when Fershan rushes over, wrecking our moment. "It's not yet eleven, Mr. Richards. We can't have the weeklies ready for you until after midnight."

Neeta backhands his shoulder before turning on the charm for Richards again. "What he means is that we'll get to work on them right away for you, sir. We've tricked the system forward in the past for forecasting, and I'm sure this time—"

"No." The man's interruption is calm but commanding as he realigns his posture. "Midnight's not that far away. Just have someone bring the report to the penthouse when it's ready."

"Of course, Mr. Richards. Enjoy the rest of your evening, Mr.—"

The *whump* of the closing elevator doors serves as her conclusion. After two more seconds to confirm the elevator is really carrying the boss away, Wade and Fershan erupt into brutal snickers.

"'My, what a pleasant surprise, Mr. Richards.'"

"'Your wish is my command, Mr. Richards.'"

She jerks an eyebrow Wade's way. "'Slumming it down here, Mr. Richards?'"

"Hey." He ticks the air with a forefinger. "He laughed!"

Fershan snorted. "As much as a guy like that can laugh."

"A guy like that?" I can't help the accusing edge in my echo.

Wade chuffs. "C'mon, Emma. You know what I'm talking about."

"Not sure I do." I'm able to replace the indictment with confusion—and mean it.

"Of course you do," he counters. "Dude probably bought an airline and banged three flight attendants before breakfast this morning. When that far on top of the world, who needs humor? Laughing is a time burner, you know?"

Neeta smirks. "Perhaps he just knows the value of a good smolder."

"A good smolder?" Wade grunts. "Or a bad brood?"

Their round of laughter isn't the reaction I expected. When I step back, flustered, Neeta gently grabs my shoulder. "It's all right, Emma. You don't have to pretend for us. That you didn't feel it?" she supplies when my frown deepens.

"Seriously?" Wade volleys. "Even a corpse would feel it."

I jerk out of Neeta's hold. "Feel *what*? Honestly, *what* are you guys talking about?"

They fall into silence and exchange glances, as if concurring I've just sprouted a second head. And then Wade breaks it to me gently. "The guy's weird, Emma."

Yeah. In all the most incredible ways.

But that isn't how Wade means it. One glance at the color staining up to his light-ginger hairline and I know it.

"The last time I checked, 'weird' wasn't a crime."

Fershan smacks a hard facepalm. Neeta exhales with meaning.

"You're saying that right now because he's got you by the hormones." Wade's astoundingly gentle about that one. "And that's all right. He's made of money, manners, and damn good genetics. But once all that wears off, you'll start agreeing with us."

"He's got me by the—" I interrupt myself with a grunting laugh. Is he serious right now? Holy shit. He's serious. They all are. "I may be from the boonies, Wade, but I'm not fourteen. My 'hormones' aren't your business—or anyone else's."

Fershan steps in. "Of course," he mutters. "We weren't implying they were. We've just been here longer, and know the situation better, and ask you to consider all that."

"As you trash-talk your own boss?" I retort.

"As we speak the truth as we know it." He exhales roughly. "You've been here less than a month. We were waiting for you to get more settled in before speaking to you about Mr. Richards's...situation. He's not the person you think he is, Emma."

I flash a sardonic look. "No kidding."

"You must listen to me." He grabs both my shoulders. "He's...not right, Emma. The man the media has glorified isn't the one running this hotel. He's..."

"What?" I'm tired of feeling like the one kid on the science team who hasn't seen the dissected frog. "What the heck *is* he? Spit it out, Fershan."

He compresses his lips. "He's just...strange, all right?"

"*Arrgghh*." I toss up both hands and whirl away from all of them. "No," I finally snap. "It's not all right."

An hour later, I don't feel any differently. If anything, my feet are planted deeper into that mental sand, mostly because of confusion. How have I perceived things so differently than

Neeta, Wade, and Fershan? I've only known them for a couple of weeks, but they've seemed sensible and smart—at least until tonight, with all their talk about a superhero on the streets and a wackadoodle boss in the penthouse. That being said, there's no way to disremember the surreal experience of coming face-to-face with Reece Richards. The charged air and the electric presence, sucking out my breaths and telescoping my vision.

Who's really going nuts here?

And do I want to pass up a chance to find out?

My psyche fires off the question as the printer in the next room starts spewing the weekly reports.

And my whole body answers with three sweeps of decisive action.

One kick. Pump number one is off.

Second kick. Pump number two meets the same fate.

Motion three—a ninja-quiet sprint over to the printer and a surreptitious swipe of the contents in the tray.

Before another minute is up, I'm in the back-of-house elevator, jamming my shoes back on and stabbing the button marked P.

Preparing myself for weird.

No. Hoping for it.

CHAPTER TWO

REECE

"You've raised 'idiot' to an art form tonight, haven't you?"

Thank fuck it's a rhetorical question. I'd start to worry if this asshole glaring back at me from the penthouse's dark glass had anything to contribute to the conversation. I'm not in the mood to talk, anyway—not even to my own reflection. There are bigger things to worry about.

Much bigger.

As if the point needs clarification, my cock punches against my pants. Right on cue, for the hundredth time in the last hour. Or is it the two hundredth? Does the answer matter? As the residual electricity in my system keeps recirculating through my blood, the torture becomes sheer hell.

I grip the armrests of my desk chair and rear my hips, seeking relief from the ache. No use. I'm as hard as a bull and ready to screw my fucking pen cup. But that'll bring ten point five seconds of relief before the torture surges again, twice as hot and three times as painful. The pen cup probably wouldn't ever speak to me again either.

And *there's* Karma's bitch-slap of the day. Because she can't let *any* day go by without getting that tidbit of a reminder in, can she?

I deserve this.

No matter how many Santa Claus shop owners I save between now and my deathbed, it'll be the same.

I deserve this.

Exactly *why* did I have to grow a conscience? This new asshole I've transformed into is way more trouble than the old one. Especially when my idiot factor is added into the equation and I choose to go saving Santa's slushies the same night the weekly reports have to be reviewed.

I just pray to God, or whatever deity is choosing to listen to me these days, Neeta doesn't let the new girl bring them up.

Damn. *Damn.*

The new girl.

No. Not a girl. She's a woman, as my traitor of a body reminds me in flashback mode, booting up a vision of her lush curves, white-gold hair, and big aqua eyes in time for my next slam of an erection. I groan, struggling to banish her to my subconscious. I can control that or my hard-on. My system won't allow both.

I opt for keeping my cock in my pants and letting her run wild through my memory.

Her.

Her who?

I couldn't get my shit together to even ask her name. Maybe that's a good thing. Because even if I hadn't been battling a thousand extra watts in my bloodstream, what was I supposed to say? *Hi there. I'm Reece. No, you haven't been transported to another planet and had the equilibrium sucked out of your skull. That's just me. Wanna grab sushi sometime?*

The erection starts to subside. "Thank God," I mutter toward the ceiling. "Really, man," I add, taking my first full breath in what feels like days. "I mean it this time."

Finally, I let my hands stretch over the armrests and peer at the veins still throbbing inside them, glowing in some tone between milky white and quicksilver and pulsing in time to my heartbeats, making me look like a goddamned Christmas display. Wouldn't that be the irony of the year? The prodigal son of the Richards clan, invited back for holiday cheer as the Yule tree. *Pass the eggnog, Pops.*

I turn my right arm enough to glance at my watch. Just after midnight. With any luck, there'll be an unexpected hit of calls on the team downstairs, and they'll be too busy with check-ins, pillow requests, and noise complaints to pay attention to the weeklies. This crime-stopper hangover needs another half hour to flush its way completely out of my system. I'm almost there but not close enough.

I force myself to sit up straight. I fish into my desk drawer for the spare elevator keycard. Locking the penthouse against staff elevator access will be as easy as swiping the thing. I only need a few minutes more...

And Karma, with her sick humor, picks that moment to send the damn elevator up.

I throw the card back into the drawer while gritting out the F-word. The gears in the elevator shaft whoosh and glide, and eventually the car dings at the landing outside the office.

I take another full breath. It wouldn't be *her*.

After the exercise in awkwardness that was my meeting with the Scooby-Doo night crew earlier, Neeta will make certain it's not. The woman fought hard to add this new one to the team, so she'll want to keep exposure to the Big Bad Wolf to a minimum for now.

Or so I tell myself.

Force myself to believe.

Because believing anything feels a lot like...

Hope.

Hope suddenly fulfilled, with brilliance making me grip the desk once more, as the doors slide open.

And she steps out.

And quickens the air.

And quickens *me*.

Like nothing I've ever experienced before. Like no *one* I've ever met.

So much more than I ever thought possible.

More.

No. Goddamnit, that's not possible. Didn't Angelique force-feed me that juicy tidbit clearly enough?

But the woman's presence doesn't let up on the wallop. Literally, my heart rate doubles. The lightning in my blood sizzles before shooting between my thighs, making my ass clench and my hips jerk. It's agony, but it's no longer hell.

It's fucking heaven.

At once, the suspicion hits too. *Don't trust this.* What's wrong with this? I'm not supposed to get heaven. I had my turn at a damn good life and was too huge of an entitled prick to spend a second being grateful for it. I don't get heaven now. Hell's my only reward, and I can only pray it comes sooner than later.

Don't trust it.

But as she takes steps closer on those sky-high heels, file folder clutched to her chest and eyes widened as she takes in the suite, I can't help but enjoy her magic. I even savor it. Isn't that what wolves are supposed to do when baby bunnies wander into the lair?

"Hello?" She clears her throat and stops to smooth her

jacket and skirt with her free hand, drawing my attention to her graceful curves. Her breasts are high and full, her ass a sweet bump in the skirt. And her legs, especially in those shoes...

Fuck. Me.

I imagine those shoes digging into my back. Then my shoulders. Then the back of my head...

"Hello?" the bunny repeats, her voice like silk. "Ummm... Mr. Richards? Anyone? I've—er—brought the weeklies, and—" As she pivots toward the windows, she cuts herself off with a gasp. It's so quiet up here—seventy stories up from the city—I'm able to hear her whispered follow-up. "Holy *shit*. Is that China?"

"Not quite."

"Oh!"

I bite the inside of my lip to keep from laughing as she nearly leaps like a bunny—only the joke's on me as she wobbles in those precarious heels. I lurch up, jabbing my hands into my front pockets to hide the glowing tips, but see I don't fool her with the "casual" approach. She looks me over, head to toe, her gaze bold and probing and unafraid.

Jesus.

When was the last time somebody stared at me without fear in their eyes?

I don't want to analyze that answer right now. I only want to enjoy the effects of it. The need to move closer to her, even as I feel the danger of her. The fire she ignites deeper in my fingers. The heat she causes to swell to the very tip of my cock. The awareness she opens in all my nerve endings.

Still, I manage to get out, in a tone as suave as how I *used* to sound, "Easy, Velvet. I'm just here for the view too." Only it's sure as hell not the cityscape stretching outside the window.

"My... My name's not Velvet."

"Probably not." I only move my gaze. All the way across the creamy angles of her face. "But it fits." *Velveteen Rabbit.* The book had been one of my favorites growing up. Gerta, my au pair, read it to me so many times. *What does it take to become real...?*

The bunny in front of me now says nothing. She presses the folder tighter to her chest—but I know arousal disguised as decorum when I see it. The recognition draws me closer to her, even though she stiffens and thrusts a stiff hand between us.

"I'm—I'm sorry, Mr. Richards. I'm just going to restart this train and hope I don't wreck it this time." She jogs her chin up, beaming a smile I can only describe as adorable. "Emmalina Crist. It's a true honor to meet you, sir."

Yeah. Adorable. And now, impossible. If I shake that gorgeous hand, she'll wonder why my fingers look like glow sticks and my skin feels like an electric fence. She'll never look at me with such open trust and honor again.

She'll never see me as human again.

So I put on my own masquerade. I give her fingers and their light-pink nails only a casual glance and step back with an air of moneyed asshole before jerking my head toward my darkened office. "You can leave them on the desk, Miss Crist. On your way out."

The edges of her mouth fall, but the optimism doesn't dim from her eyes. "Of course." She sidesteps me—undoubtedly, at last, sensing what everyone usually does. The air molecules that just aren't "right" around me. The freakish "force field" that'll soon have her beelining for the desk and making hurried excuses to leave...

Any second now.

I can only hope.

And dread.

"That desk?" She lifts a tentative finger. "In there?"

I almost laugh. Humor is the heart of pathos, right? I'm sure as hell not going to cry in my milk about giving this woman the creeps from being near me. From what I can tell, she volunteered to play delivery girl on the reports. *Curiosity can kill bunnies too, Miss Crist.* "Unless you want to drop them on the other one?" I murmur. "In the bedroom?"

Her gaze flares. She's not too innocent to miss *that* lob of inappropriate—which baffles the fuck out of me too. I've logged more than my fair share on the bridge of the *USS Man Whore* but have never moored the thing at the company dock. What the hell has made me lose my mind now?

"Does that room have a better view than this one?"

That. Right there. *That's* what made me do it. This woman. This pure, sparkling, open, awe-filled creature, taking my obnoxious overture and turning it into something completely different. Something funny, even sexy. The realization is all my dick needs to surge on board once again, making me clear my throat and turn from her—back to the shadows from which I originally emerged.

"Does that matter?" I'm not sure what I mean by that, only that it'll keep her here a few minutes longer.

"Of course it matters." She follows me in, her steps becoming more confident. "A desk in the bedroom doesn't make sense otherwise."

"Because bedrooms are strictly for romance?"

"Well, they're not for desk-type sh—" She cuts herself off again. "Desk-type *things*." She shakes her head in what can only be a silent self-punishment. "And I'm stepping way out of line again." She lifts a fast wince to where I now stand, between the desk and the all-the-way-to-China view she loves so much. "So I'll just...ummm...drop these here and... Well, good night. *Oh, good night!*"

Her repeat is a full-out shriek as her "casual toss" of the file turns into a different event altogether. Near as I can determine, her shoes are the traitors. She loses balance on one, causing her to overcorrect with the other, but twists that ankle too. She lurches forward, but the file hasn't left her grip. In one impressive burst, every page of the weekly report is now a white flurry in the air, dancing with each other before landing across the desk and at my feet.

"Shit, shit, shit, shit, shit." No self-editing for her this time. She keeps it up, scrambling to grab each page, clearly clinging to the hope of collating them again.

I should tell her to stop. I should reinforce how pointless her cause really is, with fifty-plus pages of data in eight-point font. I should reassure her it'll be easier to recycle this mess and simply reprint the report.

I should. But I don't.

Because fate has given me a bonus gift, and I'm not about to waste it.

Because watching her reminds me of beholding something like the Eiffel Tower or the Taj Mahal for the first time. There'll never be another moment full of all my wonder and none of my breath—

Grabbing me by the center of my balls.

Seizing. Then gripping. Then pounding.

Not even the Eiffel Tower pulled *this* shit.

I clench back a groan. Barely. I reconsider restraint as Miss Emmalina Crist leans across my desk, stretching for a piece of paper on the corner. The woman's ass is a work of art—a canvas I imagine painting with streams of my come as she reaches for her own orgasm instead of some stupid spreadsheet...

"Shit, shit, shit, shit." Yep. She's still at it. "Guess everyone knows who goofed off in charm school, right? How much lamer can one person get?" She pushes back to her feet, only to hurry around to my side of the desk. "Well, the idiot is going to make this right," she blurts. "I promise."

With that, she drops again. To her knees.

Shit, shit, shit, shit. Guess it's *my* turn now.

"Miss Crist—"

"Wow. It's all over the place back here."

"Miss Crist—"

"I know, I know. I should've binder-clipped the pages. This won't happen again, I promise. *I promise.*"

"It's all right," I mutter. It's *unreal*, my brain growls back. No. It's completely nuts. This, from the guy who just put three assholes behind bars using electromagnetic bursts and a handful of extension cords. But if the angel fucking Gabriel had descended in here ten minutes ago prophesizing I'd be standing here in the shadows, trying to talk a woman up from her knees while my erection all but throbbed in her face, I'd have laughed him back up to the cloud of crack from which he'd descended.

Last time I checked, the angels knew to leave me alone.

Which means I'm really all alone here. In the dark. With this woman. And her hair and her skin and her curves and her frantic little mutterings, filling the air with an energy I can't comprehend...

Filled with everything except fear.

What the hell?

Why isn't she afraid of me?

Yeah, I'm damn sure she's not.

If I've become an expert about anything since being turned into a walking diode, it's what fear smells, tastes, looks, and feels like. I've experienced it in some form, big or small, from every person on the planet forced to interact with me since those months with "Doctor La Salle" and her gang of torturing freaks. Emmalina Crist is a lot of things right now, but scared isn't one of them.

A realization I refuse to let go.

A treasure I refuse to relinquish.

A woman I refuse to resist.

No matter how wrong it is.

No matter how high Karma sets my payback price.

EMMA

Weak, weak, weak.

The word pinches my psyche worse than the damn shoes on my feet. Both are reminders of how I have nobody to blame for this humiliation but myself.

Weak.

I had to go and wear the platforms to work, believing the advertising that sold them to me in the first place. I'd be glamorous, sophisticated. I'd at least *look* like I belonged at a job in the big city.

Weak.

Glamorous and sophisticated? Look how long they'd lasted from the moment Reece Richards walked in the office door. My massive case of stupidiotic was compounded by this lame excuse to see him alone.

Weak.

And now I must be a lunatic too—or at least I have been since the second he emerged from the shadows looking better than the view. And the view is *really* damn impressive...

But holy hell, this man. At this moment. His tie is off. His glasses are on. Why the hell is he the only man on earth who looks better in glasses, not the other way around? The bold black frames are lined in silver, making his eyes seem to glow as he exhales hard and stares down at me.

And stares.

And stares.

Right past the noticeable swell between his legs.

The ridge seems to surge toward me now, beckoning with heat that washes across my whole face. Then swelling as I let out heavy breaths of my own, all too aware of how the air has changed between us. Of how it's now *charged...*

Oh, my God.

I want him.

Not just with gee-it's-been-a-long-time-for-me lust.

With singular, groundbreaking, life-altering need.

I want him.

Worse than I've ever craved a man before. The desire tears at my muscles, burns at my blood, pounds in every cell of my sex. The papers in my fingers start to rip from my grip—but if I let them go, I know damn well what I'll reach for instead.

"I—" My voice sounds foreign to me. A light year away. Achingly intimate. "I... Maybe I should just—"

"Just what, Velvet?"

Velvet. He had to go and say that. Using *that* rasping demand of a tone.

"I should..."

I should go. You're my boss. I need this job. This is wrong. This is so right, it's terrifying.

Just for a second, I need to succumb to the rightness. For one mindless moment, I can no longer resist the terror. I let my mind leap over the cliff of my propriety. Fate hasn't brought me to this exact unreal place at this exact unreal time only to be slapped down by a dorky bumpkin from the OC who can't take a massive cosmic hint.

It's just one moment.

Just him and me.

Drawn. Desiring. Surrendering.

The force pulls my head over. I slide through the inches separating my face from his body, brushing my nose across the seam over his crotch. He groans softly. His whole body jolts. The fabric tautens. He changes the moan to a hiss while I draw in a deep breath. My senses swirl from his heady scent. His cologne, metallic and smoky. His arousal, musky and thick. Is the fabric under my nose getting damp?

I want to know.

I need to find out.

I press closer.

His new rumble consumes the air as it plummets down over me, tempting beyond the line we're still just dancing on. Unbelievably, there's still a sliver of room for turning back. We're in silent agreement on that, our muscles tight and our breaths shallow, waiting for the other to leap to their senses and declare this the really bad idea it is...

But it doesn't feel bad.

It feels...

I can't even try to fill in that blank. Nor do I want to.

I just know I don't want it to end. Not yet. *Please, not yet.*

"Miss Crist." Nor does he. His growl, vibrating from a place deep inside him, is my verification.

"Mr. Richards?" I'm not sure if the whisper is a question or a supplication. Maybe both. I revel in how his zipper stretches beneath my lips. He's so big, so hot—and I'm so amazed. I'm on my knees in front of a man but have never felt more powerful in my life. This is beyond anything I've ever thought of doing to anyone. Beyond anything I've ever dreamed.

"Shit."

His husky burst is like a caress to every trembling inch of my body, every clenching corner of my sex. My hips roll, driven by raw instinct, struggling to alleviate the ache in my core. No. It's not just an ache. It's an instinct, stripped and primitive, twining my every cell to the energy he's heightened since I first felt his eyes on me. It's unbelievable. Unbearable...

And now, unavoidable.

He knows it too. I feel it in the harsh spasms of his muscles. In the growling effort of his breaths. In the energy vibrating so potently between us, I swear the air nearly glows.

Wait. It *is* glowing.

Brighter still, as he stretches his elegant fingers across my periphery, reaching into my hair. Why do each of his nailbeds look like lit fireflies?

"Eyes. Here."

He enforces both syllables by twisting his grip into my hair, the right hand, then the left, compelling my stare straight ahead. I'm consumed with nothing but his crotch once more. The pulsing ridge. The magnetic heat.

"Miss Crist?" It's not a full question, though inflected enough to prompt mine.

"Mr. Richards?"

"Do you want this?"

I wet my lips. "Yes. Oh, yes."

"So swift," he murmurs. "So eager. Yet you don't even know what I want to do to you with it."

I dare a glance up. His face, encased in lust, will be the centerpiece of my memories for a long time to come. "Will you tell me?" I purposely bite my bottom lip. "If I ask nicely?"

His jaw clenches so tight, a pulse ticks against his stubble. He pulls harder on my scalp. "Nice has nothing to do with what's happening here, Velvet."

Freaking. Hell.

Just like that, he throws open the lid to a new space inside me. Gives rise to a creature worthy of his electric erotic power. A woman I hardly recognize as me—but wholly, happily embrace.

"Then shut up and just show me."

CHAPTER THREE

R E E C E

Could I have prayed for her to say anything better?

Could I have dreaded she say anything worse?

Show me.

She has no idea what she's asking for. Fuck. I have no idea what she's asking for, though I can claim the advantage of an educated guess. My four-women-a-month life is a distant memory now, but my dick hasn't forgotten that playboy's needs. Fine-tuning the art of jerking off has brought some revelations—like the fact that I can now see my jizz, glowing like nuclear waste, as it swirls down the shower drain.

Christ.

How am I standing here, even thinking of exposing this magnificent creature to that danger?

I'm not thinking. At least not about her. Because once again, it's all about me. Guess the saying is true. Once an asshole...

"No." It's a scream in my brain but a grate on my lips as I weather the conflict. The woman at my feet interprets the sound differently. Her stare, huge and dreamy and lusty, confirms it. I'm a fucking wreck, and she's an aroused rabbit thinking I'm opting for some coy bid at nobility. I don't know whether to laugh or rage, until both options are ripped away by Emma herself. She reaches to unfasten my pants with purposeful twists of her fingers and a delectable as *hell* swipe of her tongue along her lips.

One quick release of my top button, and my cock takes full advantage of the extra breathing space. As new blood rushes to my groin, harsh air grunts into my throat. It becomes a full growl as she drags her fingers down the seam of my crotch.

"*Fuck.*"

Velvet rabbit? What the hell was I thinking? She's a seductress, those big blue eyes the gateway to her temptation, softness and light beckoning me to give up, give in, give over. *It's all right*, she seems to whisper to me. *It's all good. It's so good. It's going to be even better once you're inside me.*

No.

Yes.

No.

A gust of wind whumps the windows at my back. A blast of lust fills my cock, turning every motion into torture...and her warm breaths into unbearable teases. With limp surrender, she releases the papers in her grip. They smack to the floor and fan apart, forming a crisp bleached carpet for our dirty, debauched acts.

Corruption I need to end. A goddess I need to let go.

But I can't. *I can't.* Her desire is like a new drug. Her surrender is my new sanity.

I hang on tighter—to bring her face even closer.

She parts her lips, but doesn't stow her tongue. With that wet pink softness helping her effort, she runs her sweet, perfect mouth up and down my hardening ridge. There's not a trace of hesitation in her movements. Not a single waver in her low, needy moan. She's a gift. *My* gift...

Which is why I have to make her stop.

Which is why I can't.

"Unzip it," I command in a soft growl.

I won't let her go too far. I'll give her just a taste. I'll stop before she swallows anything. I'll let her lick until the precome returns, and then I'll pull out and—

"Wow."

Her rasp, so sincere, is joined by her wondering stare as she palms the bulge beneath my briefs. It comes close to being the goddamned sight of the century—close because *that* honor goes to what she gives me in the next second. With a sweet little sigh, she dips in close enough to nuzzle me again. To inhale me...

"Mr. Richards?"

I'm grateful for her soft query. It forces me to focus. To coalesce brain matter into words. "Yes, Miss Crist?"

"You're wet."

Fuck the hell out of me.

Which is so *not* going to happen, even if the effort kills me.

And wouldn't that be fate's ultimate joke? The player turned freak, throwing himself at petty thieves and thugs in the hopes of taking a stray bullet to his gut, instead put down by his wayward dick. *Step right up, folks. Come and get your poetic justice riiigght heeere.*

But for now, I'm alive. And that means forming words. *Remember those, moron? Get the words out. Keep the come in.*

"And are you?"

She narrows her gaze. Breathes harder. For an incredible second, I can see down her blouse. She's wearing a dark-pink bra under the matching satin blouse. I wonder if the nipples under it are a similar hue. Are they tight from my demand? Have they become erect berries centered in puckered areolas?

"Am...I...?"

"Wet." I all but snarl it out. Maybe if I talk like a monster, she'll comprehend I am one. "Are you wet too, Miss Crist?"

She shivers. I prepare to watch the fear creep into her gaze, but only clear blue curiosity returns my scrutiny. "I...I think I *am*."

"And that surprises you?"

She furrows her brow. "I suppose it does."

And just like that, my dick fills with new lightning. What the hell? All she's done is touch me through my underwear—but it's enough. Holy fuck, *more* than enough. I'm so hard, it's turned into throbbing physical pain. My balls are pounding thunderheads. My shaft is a Tesla coil, pent-up electric spears with nowhere to go.

"You should check."

Her gaze widens. "I should...what?"

"Check." I nod curtly, enforcing the mandate. "You heard me. Do it, Emmalina. Pull your skirt to your waist, drop your panties to your knees, and put a finger in your pussy. Then tell me if you're wet."

For the first time, uncertainty clouds her face. Perhaps a little fear. Has she finally grabbed the clue? Realized I'm *not* the lonely Heathcliff up in the tower? That Neeta, Wade, and Fershan are right to be freaked out by me? That *she* should be freaked out by me? But I search her face again and see none of that. I think she's just hesitant about obeying me—about seeking her pleasure in front of me. But I remain implacable. She *will* obey.

"You... You want me to—"

"Touch yourself." I massage her scalp. "Yes."

"While you watch?"

"Every fucking moment."

She twists her lips. "Said the Big Bad Wolf to Red Riding Hood?"

A growling chuckle spills out. *Good Christ, little girl. You have no idea what's in my dark forest.* Still I snarl past my smirk, "What big eyes I have?"

"What beautiful eyes you have."

So much for laughter, even the growling kind. The reverence in her voice... *Fuck.* Now I'm just as awestruck in return, wildly wondering where this amazing creature has come from—and why the fuck that even matters. Not when all I care about is her obedience to my demand.

"You're stalling, Bunny." I splay my fingers wider against her scalp. "Do it now. Your finger in your pussy. Watching you will bring so much pleasure to me."

She turns up a tentative smile. "I...I like that idea."

"Fingering yourself? Or bringing me pleasure?"

She tilts her head. Her eyes flicker, conveying the true thought behind her answer. *Where the* hell *has she been hiding my whole existence?* If I'd known a woman like her existed, I'd never have given Angelique a second look. So much about my life would be different...

"Both, I suppose," she finally answers. At once, my smile widens.

"Very good answer, sweet beauty. *Christ*, you're making me so fucking hard."

My filthy narrative is the right flip to her switch. She even kicks up a bigger smile while bunching her skirt north of her waist, though it vanishes the moment her panties drop the other direction. With one more glance to ensure I'm still serious about my order, she slides one hand south...

Bringing heaven to the seventieth floor.

Heaven, in her guttural gasp of sheer arousal... In the soft drop of her head against my fingers... In the heady musk of her on the air...

Arousal I need her to tell me about.

Heaven I can experience through her.

If just for a moment...

"Tell me." Focusing on the words helps me keep control—at least in the parts where it matters. I focus on their syntax, along with how it aches to push them from my locked teeth, but even that's barely enough. Witnessing her arousal brings on more of my own. It's fucking near intolerable...

"You... You were right."

Her voice, now husky as whiskey, rolls through me in the same way. She brings torment and salvation together, a pleasure-pain I crave but resist. "About what?" I jerk on her hair, forcing her to stare up at me. "Say it, Emmalina."

She swallows. Dear *fuck*, so gorgeous. "I'm...wet," she stammers. "So damn wet."

"Good girl." At my praise, her skin flushes, her lips fall open, and she drags in heavy air. Dear fuck. She's my complete undoing. The freedom of how she looks at me, offering herself to me... It's like a bolt cutter on some lock inside, a shackle that's been so heavy for so long, I'm not even aware of it anymore. Not until this moment of getting to throw it free, celebrating with a new command for her.

"Now show me."

For a moment, she's confused again. "Show...you...?"

"How wet you are." I dip my head toward her fingers, which still massage between her creamy thighs. In the same instant, inspiration hits. I push down the front of my briefs far enough for my balls and shaft to spring free. If she only gets a taste, I'll make sure it's a damn good one. "Drench your finger with your arousal and spread it over me—here."

I watch without restraint as she obeys without question. Her touch is full of fascination and adoration as she slicks her juices along my flesh, even taking time to trace over the larger veins, which pulse as if they're going to explode right off my shaft. I'm just as spellbound. Her hair turns into a glowing halo under my fingertips. Her gaze all but worships my cock. And the perfect O of her lips reaches for my tip like a choirgirl about to take communion.

And holy God, do I want to give it to her.

But *she* gives before *I* can. Takes me in, surrounding me with her mouth, displaying the whole fucking universe to my senses in one stroke of heat and warmth and wetness. She sucks me deeper, tightening and expanding that cosmos at once, filling it with the echoes of my mindless moans.

Mindless. That says it all. My thoughts have vanished. Logic, or whatever I thought I possessed of it, is gone. I'm nothing but desire and ache and need, every electron of my body zooming to the crux of my thighs, the length of my cock, the perfection of her mouth.

A groan careens through my head. It's edged in conflict, and for a second I wonder why.

You can't do this.

You could kill her. This could kill her. She's not the one who's supposed to die.

It's me. I'm the one. And I *am* dying already, my chest locking down air with every new effort at restraint. Before I can control it, a spurt of precome erupts out. I force my eyes open, watching her throat convulse on it, praying like hell I haven't scalded her for life...

Her gaze goes wide.

She keens in shock.

Shit. Damn. Fuck.

She goes down on my dick like a kid given candy for the first time. Confirms I'm not imagining it by lifting a stare full of brilliant blue arousal before going back to work as if it's fucking Godiva.

"Holy sssshhh..." It's all I'm able to get out before she pulls me in so hard my balls collide with her chin. "Emma... lina. *Fuck. Yes!*" My amazement is totally real. I'm not hung like an elephant, but my cock is built like the rest of me, length instead of girth, meaning that despite the number of women I've known biblically in my life, getting deep-throated has been a rare and incredible treat.

And never, *never* as good as this.

No. Forget good.

This is...transformative. An all-access pass to another dimension. My blood converts into light ropes. So good. *So good.*

"Christ!"

My consciousness blares. My senses blaze. I fist my hands in her hair until I drive her harder, fucking her deeper and rejoicing in the sweet compliance of her deep, needy moan.

I can't stop.

I can't think.

I can only feed her hunger. Sate my lust. Lunge and push and fuck and need...

And *need*...

Until my balls squeeze tight. My lungs seize on air. My brain turns to toast.

And my universe becomes her.

My life pours into her.

It's the best orgasm I've known. And the worst agony I've ever felt.

I'm killing her. I'm killing her.

"Fuck." I finish with a helpless choke, a mix of ecstasy and remorse—who knew I'd ever be putting *those* two in a mental test tube—as the heat keeps sizzling through my cock and spurting into her. She answers every drop with a wanton moan, even grabbing my hips when I try to pull away. She's a creature possessed, and I'm ripped to shreds about stopping her. The last meal of her life is a throat full of my come, and the woman is damn near thanking me for the experience.

I will never leave the depths of hell after I die.

Which may be sooner than I think, because she keeps sucking my dick as if her erotic buffet won't end until she has my blood as well as my seed.

At last, with a harsh hiss, she releases me.

At once, my knees give out.

I plummet next to her, still gripping her head. Damn good thing because I can force her to look at me. To see the apology, too late to do any good, in my eyes.

"I'm sorry." I kiss her desperately, hating myself more as my dick jerks from the taste of myself on her lips. A snarl rips up my throat as I yank away. "I'm so damn sorry."

Her forehead crumples. "Why?"

I struggle for the right words. *Because you sucked my cock so well, I forgot my own damn name. And, oh yeah, I also forgot about the band of lunatic scientists who turned my blood into electricity a year ago, meaning I just turned you into—*

What?

What *have* I done to her?

I have no answer for that—just as I have no words for what starts to happen to the woman in my arms. Only now do I realize I've harbored some dark fears about what to expect if this ever happened—and the reality before me doesn't match any of them. The lightning fire in her eyes, the ruby tint of her lips, and the sensual flare across her cheeks aren't anywhere near the horror of a woman in the last moments of her life.

"Emmalina," I croak in place of kissing her again. "Emma," I revise, daring to stroke her cheek. After the climax, my fingertips have returned to their normal color. "What can I do? How can I—"

Her high gasp cuts me off. Her body jerks, and she falls against me. I lower to my haunches, letting her sag sideways into my arms. She slides a hand under my shirt, scoring my abdomen in time to her spasms. The second her bare ass lands atop my spent cock, she turns into a ball of sensual slithers. What the *hell*? Is this what death throes look like? I've seen a lot of shit for a guy three years shy of thirty, but a dying person isn't one of them.

"What can you *do*?" She laughs, taking me from mystified to disturbed—especially as she grinds her backside harder atop my cock. "Haven't you already done it?"

I rest my forehead against hers. "Fuck. I'm so—"

"Proud of your handiwork?" She ropes both hands around my back and digs her nails into my shoulders. Her eyes dilate, the pupils huge islands in cyan seas. "Well, you should be."

I narrow my own gaze. "I..."

"You want to hear me say it, Mr. Richards? Fine." She gulps hard. "I never thought it could be like this. I never thought *anything* could be like this. Happy now?"

I guess I would be—if I knew what the hell she's talking about.

Like a physical punch, comprehension hits.

As soon as I shove aside my guilt long enough to look at her. *Really* look at her.

The pulse in her neck, throbbing wildly. The needy huffs of her breaths. The subtle swivels of her hips...and the light dew of sweat along their inner curves.

Holy fuck.

My jizz isn't killing her.

It's getting her off. From the inside out.

For a second, I just stare harder. Then release a sound of such wild incredulity, it comes off as an arrogant snort.

"Oh, aren't you clever?" She stabs the words at me with a turned-on grin, though the look fades as more arousal jolts her.

I preface my reply with a smirk that feels so fucking good. "Clever?" I drawl. Yeah, I'm dicking with her. Because I can. Because I'm so full of joy right now and can't dance on the ceiling about it. I much prefer watching her pleasure from this prime seat. "Miss Crist, I'm not sure I know what you mean."

"The hell you don't." She laughs until the invisible arousal stabs her again. With a fierce punch, she arches her hips higher. "Ohhh!" Her nails burrow deeper into my shoulders. I let out a dark snarl, welcoming the pain.

"Tell me," I order. "Don't hold back, Velvet." *Because you just turned my hell into complete heaven.* "I want to hear it all."

She responds with an extended cry, coinciding with her new contortion. "Lower," she finally gasps. "It's... It's flowing lower."

"Toward your pussy?" When she nods, I dictate, *"Tell me,* Emma."

"Y-Yes. T-Toward my pussy. So hot. So intense. Shit. *Shit!* You bastard. You amazing, dazzling b-b-b..."

"Yessss." I tuck a hand under the roll of her skirt and press my fingers over her abdomen, picking up on the movement she's describing. Her skin is hot, tingling. Her body is alive, trembling.

"There," she confirms, arching up toward me again. "Now there...and there. Oh, shit. It feels so—"

"*Words*, Emma." I need them. I need to know every damn detail about this. I'm a caveman who's just discovered fire but now needs the instruction book for the blowtorch.

"C-Can't," she rasps, thrashing her head against my arm. "So much. So m-m-m-m..."

"Then you'll show me." I run a hand down, pushing against her inner thigh until her most wicked fruit is visible. "Yeah. Just like that."

She breathes harder, the coral and pink layers between her thighs like a rose in a rainstorm, fluttering as lightning strikes their core. I've never witnessed anything more incredible. What guy gets to see every moment of a woman's climax from a viewpoint like this? The clenches of her ass. Her glistening pussy lips clutching around her tight dark slit. The sweet swell of her clit, all but glowing like her hottest ember.

I lean in, gripping one hand into the valley between her torso and thigh, and spread her a little farther. I can see every shimmering drop of the cream she squeezes from her trembling core—now blended with the milk she just drank out of my cock.

"Holy. Fuck."

I rasp it.

She screams it.

I watch, entranced, as she falls apart in my arms—again and again and again.

And again...

Every time more of my fluid hits her tunnel and her clit, she's flooded with fresh ecstasy, taking her through wave after wave of wordless pleasure. Every time, I'm taken to a new high by the incredible creature in my arms. How all of this hasn't Tasered her trust and passion is beyond my comprehension but not my gratitude. She may be the one on her fifteenth climax, but I'm the fucker celebrating the biggest win of the night. I'm holding a gorgeous woman in my arms, watching her lose her shit because of me. I'm mindless, weightless, infinite... A feeling I never dreamed I'd know again. A nirvana I'd written off a long damn time ago.

But now isn't the time for that morose mental path.

Now is about a lightning strike named Emmalina Crist and learning more ways to make her feel good. After what I've just witnessed, I'm not exactly sure how that miracle will be accomplished but am open to exploring the possibilities.

Wait a second. Open? No. *Open* is for trying new food or looking at a new avenue of auxiliary revenue for the hotel. I'm not *open.*

I'm obsessed.

I follow the path of her sated sighs, soon learning she likes circling caresses along the length of her arm. Her groans deepen as I curl my other hand to comb her brilliant blond hair.

After a few minutes filled with nothing but her soft groans, she murmurs, "Mmmm. That feels so good."

I lean over and kiss her forehead. It feels so good, so right. I do it again. Then question myself. *Was* that right? I've never been a postcoital cuddle muffin or whatever the fuck they call it. It's always been easier to live up to the infamy of my media nicknames, all serving as convenient red carpets to roll out before ushering my bedmates right out the door.

But the carpets are still rolled up. The excuses, all gone. No. They've been blasted into obliteration—though not by the force of the lightning in my veins. They've been turned to dust by the woman in my arms. By her artless passion, her captivating honesty... This astounding blend of her and me for which the word *chemistry* feels like a goddamned insult.

She feels right.

Better than right.

She feels fucking *great*.

And no way in hell do I want her anywhere near the door.

Which is why I inhale with determined meaning and answer her with what sounds like sappy pillow talk, but for once I truly mean it. "A lot more where that came from, Bunny."

She snaps open her eyes, and a giggle spills off her delectable lips. "Now I *know* I must be dreaming."

I frown. "Why?"

"Because the mighty and mysterious Reece Richards just called me *Bunny*—after getting me off so many times, I lost count."

I quirk my lips. "So, I assume it's a good dream?"

She smacks at my chest before sighing again. *That sound.* If Guinevere and Cleopatra sighed like that, no wonder Lancelot and Mark Antony went willingly to their ruin. "Hmmm. If you must know..."

"Yeah." I kiss her forehead. "I must."

"It was *very* good." She curls closer, looking languid and gorgeous. "I just don't want to wake up."

"Then don't."

"Not an option." Her forehead furrows. "I mean, with all due respect, Mr.—ermmm..."

I'd laugh if her uncertainty wasn't so damn palpable. "Why don't you just call me Reece?"

She blinks. Then again. Clearly she's wondering if this is the point where she wakes up from her dream. Her quixotic smile returns once I dip down and take her lips in a lingering kiss. Damn. She still tastes like passion, mixed with a lot of silken woman. I want to sample her deeper, so I do. Once the soft, slow tangle of our tongues comes to a reluctant end, I realize my face is tight with confusion. I'm nearly thirty years old and only now I am experiencing the best kiss of my life. Some worldly golden boy.

"Hey." Her gentle prompt breaks me out of my funk. "Are you okay?"

I twist a sarcastic smirk. "Isn't that my line?"

Her look mimics mine, only she's a lot more adorable. Her champagne-colored lips mellow into a soft pout as I finger-comb her hair again. The stuff is incredible. I'm fascinated by the strands of gossamer, which glow even without the help of my penlight fingers. I could run my touch through them all night.

Her sleepy grumble tells me I might have the chance.

"Reece?"

I grunt in approval. That's so much better than *Mr. Richards.* "Hmmm?"

"You need to stop that."

"Stop what?" It's tinged with a tease.

"That." She tries to bat my hand away. "I have to get up. I have to...go back."

"Back where?"

"Work." She whimpers, attempting another drowsy protest. "The... The work people. They'll be—"

"Fine." I massage her scalp deeper. "They'll be just fine without you for a while, Emmalina."

"Ohhhh." Yeah, she really likes the head rubs. "You're not playing fair."

"Of course I am," I press my lips to her forehead. "I'm just better at the game than you, sweetheart."

"But this has nothing to do with games."

"I said they'll all be fine." After brushing my lips down to her mouth—I can't keep myself from touching her and don't even want to try abstention—I stress, "I'll take care of it, Velvet Bunny."

Little tremors shake her form, the motions of a giggle without the sound. "Velvet Bunny." She droops her face against my chest.

I don't say a word until her breaths lengthen and her body slips into the lazy curves of sleep. Only then, as I lift her from the floor and carry her into the bedroom, do I let my mind echo with her whispered word, letting it part the curtains of my memory. A new passage from my treasured childhood book filters to my conscious—and slices into my chest.

Once you are real, you cannot become unreal again. It lasts for always.

Always.

It resounds so deep, I rub my chest after sliding Emma beneath the comforter.

Always.

Fuck. I'm weaving way too much symbolism into this shit. It's just a stupid childhood memory of a word that never meant much to me—not that it should have, in my world of all-for-me-all-right-now gratification. After Angelique and the Consortium got their hands on me, I compelled it to mean even less. A concept I couldn't and wouldn't accept.

Monsters don't get to have *always*.

And nothing has changed about the monster I really am.

That means this gets to be my always. Moonlit peace. Depths of midnight. A starscape and a cityscape, their silent beams radiating the room. But none of it as beautiful as the person at my side, sleeping through satiation from our passion.

She consumes my attention as I stretch beside her, tracing fingertips along her collarbone and shoulder. She tremors a little and turns toward me.

"Sleep, Bunny," I murmur. "I'll watch over you, sweetheart."

For as long as this *always* will let me.

CHAPTER FOUR

EMMA

Some dreams are just better than others.

But this one's a freaking Big Mac of better. With extra cheese and secret sauce.

So damn good, a lot of the details climb out of the sleep fog with me. I swear I can still smell Reece Richards on my skin, smoky and spicy. I can feel the lingering warmth of his climax on my throat...and everywhere else.

Everywhere.

I roll to my side, twisting the bedcovers against my pussy, moaning into my pillow as the sensitive surfaces swell to life...

As if I really did climax over two dozen times for the man last night.

As he did nothing but watch.

Impossible.

But so wonderful to think about.

I trail a hand down and slip my fingers beneath my panties. The world beyond my closed eyelids is still too bright, meaning there's time for at least a quick fantasy before prepping for work. This time, I'll be awake for it too. *Yessss.*

I roll to my back and kick the covers free, letting the room's warmth drench my skin. I get rid of my panties in an equal hurry, luxuriating in the softness of the sheets and pillows—and do I mean *soft*. New fabric softener for the win. My discount cotton sheets suddenly feel like thousand-thread Egyptian stuff, and I'm Nefertiti in the middle of them.

With a fantasy pharaoh filling my mind's eye.

His stare, silver and charged. His face, striking and bold. His body, proud and etched. *Oh, that body*. His chiseled torso pulls my stare in, and I push heavy air through my chest as I trail the gaze of my dream-self down to the best part of him.

Oh.

That.

He's magnificent. Undaunted. So unafraid to show me how his cock wants me. I'm not even bashful about using the word *cock*.

My sex clenches as I trail my fingers down, finding the most tender part of my clit. As I stroke those sensitive nerves, my mind blooms with an image of his stalk, long and gleaming and erect...

And delicious.

Oh *yes*. That too.

As if my dream is actually a memory, I relive every moment of pulling him inside my mouth. All the way down my throat. He groans, amazed that I take him so deeply. Even I'm astounded. Somehow, his come has cauterized my gag reflex. I'm able to suck his cock all the way inside. Deeper and deeper...

He grows inside me. Bigger and bigger...

He fucks my mouth. Harder and harder...

I release a sigh. Spread my legs. Dig my heels into the bed, thrusting my pussy into my hand. I moan, rubbing faster. Trying, with urgent need, to keep up with what the dream does to my blood, my nerves, my sanity.

Needy gasps tumble off my lips.

His hungry snarl tangles with them. A beautiful sound... only now it seems so real...

Too real.

I force my eyes open. Every muscle in my body stops. This isn't my little bed nook at my studio apartment. I'm in a room twice that size, in a bed my whole kitchen could fit into, set on a platform overlooking everything between the Brocade and the Pacific Ocean. Golden sun spills over all the buildings, streets, and cars before glimmering on the sea along the far horizon. Just as distant but just as real is a memory of this room by night...from the vantage point of Reece's arms.

Reece.

He'd asked me to call him Reece...

I'd agreed...

In the same giddy haze I find myself now...

And never want to leave.

Especially as the man drops his sweats—the only thing he's wearing—and kicks them aside, stepping onto the riser and bumping his knees to the bottom edge of the bed. If I didn't just shudder with ten kinds of new arousal, I'd seriously start wondering about the dream angle again. But *holy shit.*

"This is real." I finish the thought aloud, needing to hear myself speak it. "*You're* real."

"It is." His gaze heats. "I am." He slides one hand around the base of his erection. As he strokes that mesmerizing length, his body tautens into amazing lines of muscle. "And you are. Thank *fuck.*"

At once, I start moving too. Any fragment of uncertainty or insecurity is scorched by the spell he casts on me. Is the air sparkling? And if it really is, why am I not surprised? It's him and that bizarre but beautiful force field of his. He ignites my blood and electrifies my pussy in the same incredible second...

A moan spills out before I can help it. *Shit, shit, shit,* this is good. And bad. And wrong, but so very, very right. Dear God, what this man and his body and his energy do to me. Every inch of my intimate triangle cries out now, demanding attention. I writhe against his incredible sheets, shameless in my lust. My thighs start to ache. My nipples pucker, painful and pulsing.

It all gets worse—and better—as he hikes both knees to the bed and scoots his way toward me.

"Spread for me, Velvet."

Velvet.

That wasn't a dream either. I shouldn't be so damn happy about that, but I am. I shouldn't be reveling in any part of this, but God help me, I *am.*

I'll return to real life after this. After one more little indulgence.

With that promise to fate filling my mind and a surrendering sigh on my lips, I obey him. My attention is rapt as he widens his pose, scraping my inner thighs with his knees. The coarse hair covering the sinewy muscles of his legs is a turn-on plunging my lust to primal levels. *Take me. Please.*

He keeps fisting his erection. Up and down, steady and sure, bold and demanding. His strokes correspond to the force of his stare on my body.

"You're so fucking beautiful." The words rasp from between his locked teeth as he leans over, bracing himself with his free hand. "Just looking at you like this... Feel what it does to me."

My gasp twines with his groan as his hand halts on his cock. The muscles in his arm constrict, aiding the extra hard squeeze he gives just under the purple mushroom at his tip.

The slit in it brims with a liquid pearl—a drop he aims directly over my clit. We both watch that gleaming bead, hovering... teasing us...

"Oh," I croak. "*Oh*." When I lift my head, his stare awaits, severe as a dagger and slicing me just as deep. I'm not nearly so sure of myself. Of any of this. Will that liquid, pumped from that wicked place inside him, have the same effect on me as last night? Will it feel as good on the outside of my pussy as it did from the inside? I can barely force my brain around the questions, let alone my lips.

His mind and mouth aren't so hesitant.

"You want it, Velvet?"

I shiver from the electric caress of his voice. "Y-Yes."

A corner of his decadent mouth kicks up. "Then you have to say it."

I gulp hard. "I—I want it."

"Say it all. *What* do you want, Emma? And *where* do you want it?"

I groan.

He smirks.

"Please...Reece..."

"*Say it.*"

"I... I want your come. Right here. In... In my pussy."

He squeezes, and his liquid drips into my shivering folds.

I shoot to the stars.

The orgasm hits hard and fast. My eyes blaze wide. A scream spirals up my throat and is consumed by Reece's brutal kiss. I give him the sound with open abandon, too shocked and aroused to fight his sweeping, searing attack. His tongue is the center of my world, a life raft of reality in an ocean of unthinking ecstasy. He groans hard in response, the sound emanating from his core as he drips again onto me, making me burst again.

"Ahhhh!" I shriek while breaking away to search for air and logic and what's left of my sanity. "What's going on?" My plea shoots toward the ceiling. "Wh-What the hell are you doing to me?"

The cherubs sculpted into the corners of the crown molding have no response for me. But the man between my legs sure as hell does. He's everything they aren't: full of motion and passion and wicked, wild intentions firing like quicksilver in the depths of his focused stare.

"Doing to you?" he echoes, grabbing my face to angle me for his deep, hard kiss. "Everything I possibly can, Miss Crist. Every*where* I possibly can."

REECE

"Yes, Mr. Richards."

I'm not sure what turns me on more, the formality she automatically returns to or the submission with which she does. Everything this woman does and says has my cock surging with magma. The pressure builds like a volcano about to explode...my lightning, clamoring to announce my storm. Her surrender, open and generous and perfect, is all I've been waiting for. Her passion, real and unbound, is all I've dreamed of. And never thought I'd ever have...

I slide my hips forward, impelling her legs to widen for me. I aim my aching dick toward her willing entrance, ready to take her pussy with one full push—but stop myself. Fuck. Twelve months of imposed celibacy, and I've really gone as stupid as a teenage virgin.

"Damn it." I lower my head and push up a little, breathing hard. Our foreheads are pressed together, so I feel her puzzled frown at once.

"Wh-What's wrong?"

Shockingly, I'm able to grunt out a laugh. "No condoms."

"Wh—" She huffs. Stares at me harder. "Are you kidding?"

"Wish I were." I raise my head a few inches more to study every adorable line of her scowl. "And you don't believe me."

"Would you, if you were me?"

Damn good point. *Probably not.* But hell, I want to change her mind. Right here, right now, I want to give her all the real answers for trusting me. As in, I want to tell her everything. All of it. For just once, for just this woman, I long to come out of the shadows. To trust *her* with everything. The whole truth, from beginning to end, exactly as it happened last year.

Out in the foyer, there's a loud chime.

Emma starts. I break away, springing off the bed.

"What is that?" Anxiety fans her tone. Before I can stab both legs back into my sweats and throw on an old T-shirt, she's clutching the cover to hide her breathtaking nudity.

"Stay here." I curl one knee to the bed, grab the back of her neck, and slam an adamant kiss to her lips. "We're not done yet."

Not by far.

I shut the bedroom door and clear the hallway into the foyer just in time to plaster a professional smile on my lips. It's enough of a reply, at least for the moment, to the questioning gaze in the pretty face of the woman stepping off the elevator.

"Miss Jain. Good day. What can I do for you?"

EMMA

"Shit, shit, shit, shit."

I rasp it at least twenty more times while peeking through the crack in the door at Reece and Neeta. I've dragged the comforter off the bed with me, certain Reece has simply gone to sign for a package or something. But now I'm gaping at my boss, who stands there with *her* boss, less than ten feet from where I flailed and screamed like a porn star last night. While *he* watched.

Yeah. I've finally realized it wasn't a dream.

And no, I'm not thrilled about that fact anymore.

Especially because I can't see if Reece had the time or inclination to clean up after our debauchery last night.

And holy wow, what debauchery.

I let my head drop into my hands and succumb to a nearly silent sob. This is fate's version of sarcasm, but it's not funny. I've finally escaped the OC, gained freedom, independence, and a great job, only to risk it all because I got horizontal with my tantalizing god of a boss—who, by the way, also happens to be the most amazing lover on the planet.

And no, I don't need to sample the rest to be sure of that.

My attention rivets back to the discussion in the foyer. Neeta's talking about me—and looking pretty stressed about it. *What the hell?*

"...can't believe she fell ill like that so fast." Her hair catches the sunlight coming through the same bank of windows that caused my holy-shit-is-that-China gawks a few hours ago. She's dressed in the same suit she wore for last night's shift, making me realize it isn't as late in the day as I first thought, though she still looks as fresh as the moment we first clocked in. I'm not sure if I admire her or hate her for that, especially as she executes a classic toss-toss of her ebony mane. The move would've likely preceded a sweet and worshiping smile at Reece if the subject matter weren't my health. I can't even blame her. Reece is, as Wade and Fershan would phrase it, "clickbait for the chicks' sake." I'm not sure of that definition, but it's close enough to "freaking hot" that Neeta's subtle flirtation is no-brainer obvious.

"Stomach bugs can be capricious," Reece responds diplomatically. "Which was why I insisted on calling a car for her. She wasn't in any condition to drive."

Neeta's head jogs to the side. "She told you that?"

I'm tempted to restart the shit-shit-shit litany as Reece takes a second to consider her question. I'd have thought a man who spent more time on nightclub couches than conference calls would be better at bluffing, not worse.

"Not in so many words," he finally says, re-earning his master bullshitter stripes. "She wasn't really in the mood to... talk."

Neeta's forehead pinches. "Oh. I see." Though I wonder if she really does—another instinct I'm unable to verify, since she clearly forgets the thought behind it once Reece folds his arms, returning to pharaoh mode. The move—so arrogant it can only be pulled off by a man of his glory—stretches his clothes across his muscled limbs until Neeta defaults into flustered-and-faltering mode. I don't blame her. I'd be doing the same—if I weren't so preoccupied with wanting to brain the man.

"Well, then." She readjusts the shiny red purse on her shoulder. "May I be forward and ask if she followed up with you...to let you know she got home all right? I normally worry because she insists on taking the train home, but if you had a driver take her—"

"He called after the drop-off. Told me she got in fine."

I swallow hard. The easy undertones in Reece's voice are gone. He's lying through his teeth and not happy about it.

It's so time for *shit-shit-shitting* again.

Instead, I let the comforter drop and dart into the bathroom, hoping beyond hope he somehow brought my—

Yes.

My suit has been placed onto a couple of hangers that dangle from the side of a door to the connecting bathroom. As I shimmy into my skirt, I fling a longing gaze to the palatial setup of the space. Roman tub with jets. A shower so big it has a seat. A little vanity area with a mirror lined in adjustable lights. In a little side room, there's a toilet with an electronic bidet extension.

I'm thiiiiis close to letting the skirt fall in the name of honoring this bathroom by having sex in it, but then Reece's voice bleeds through the door beyond the bed. He's still uncomfortable about the charade for Neeta's sake—a pretense *he* propagated, I might add—but I'm not about to sit around and extend the fib any longer.

With a few twists, I reattach enough of the buttons on my blouse to get out of here without flashing the world. The effect is better once I get my suit jacket on, especially because there's no time for the twelve-point procedural of putting on my bra. It, as well as my panties, can be his souvenirs for the blue-ribbon debauchery.

Hell.

Debauchery.

No way will I ever be able to hear that word again and avoid remembering last night's precious, perfect, mind-altering version of it...

Or the man who gave all that wickedness to me.

The man I now have to escape at all costs. No matter what. I need this job.

I. Need. This. Job.

Not just keeping it. Thriving in it. Excelling at it. Showing Mother and Lydia and everyone else at the club that "little Emma" *is* capable of succeeding in the big, evil city. That *their* checklist for happily ever after doesn't have to be mine. That not everyone on the face of the earth measures success with a house that sleeps thirty, a car that transports ten, and a passport that's stamped in Paris, Milan, and London.

My checklist is bigger.

So much bigger.

It starts with this job. And does *not* include shacking up in the penthouse with my boss.

I need to get out of here. Now. Before he finishes chitchatting with Neeta. The second her elevator returns, he'll be back in here, frying my resolve with his raw sexual presence and his outrageous force field magic.

Outrageous.

Yes.

That's what this all was. An outrageous out-of-this-*world* aberration that must seriously, definitely, never happen again. Meeting that goal starts with getting out of the pharaoh's lair. *Now.*

I creep to the door on the other side of the room, praying it leads to a back corridor of some sort. The front elevator that brought Neeta up isn't the only way into this place. Reece himself usually gets up here via the private elevator in back, which is located somewhere along this side of the tower.

I crack the door and sneak down a short hallway until I enter the kitchen. Still a good sign. The back elevator is also the service elevator for the suite, so direct kitchen access makes sense.

I step across a polished black wood floor and through a culinary spaceship made of glass and stainless steel. Side-by-side ovens, a fully stocked wine cooler, and a coffee bar nearly induce me to another orgasm—okay, so maybe I do miss a few creature comforts from the golden land—but there's no time for more than a few drops of drool right now. I need to locate that back elevator.

Ding ding ding.

A small anteroom also turns out to be the landing for the elevator. I pad across it and stab the call button for the car. "Please, please, please," I whisper, hoping the car is already parked at this level, but since Reece came up in the main elevator last night, I have to wait while the system brings it up.

Thankfully, the gears work fast. Not so thankfully, as I hurry into the car and jab the button for the ground floor, the last sound I hear is Reece's unmistakable baritone, bellowing my name from the bedroom. His voice all but topples the walls between us, thundering straight to my belly and making me wrap both arms around myself.

As the doors shut, I lean against the elevator's back wall, seeking solace from the silence that encompasses me.

I'm doing the right thing.

I'm doing the right thing.

I'm doing the right thing.

And soon—*please God, soon*—the rest of my senses will catch up to the strength of that mantra.

Because right now, it feels freaking useless.

REECE

Useless. This is all fucking useless.

Even as I pulse yet another asshole bank robber into the waiting arms of the cops, I can't escape the ruthless claw of my feelings. Eight thwarted crimes in three days, and goddamnit, there's still nothing in my gut but half a bean-and-cheese burrito and a shit ton of unanswered rage.

Fury that seems to have only gotten worse since the moment I stood in the penthouse kitchen, watching the numbers over my private elevator doors descend—and never come back up again.

Ramping up the Dudley Do-Right gigs have only made the rage worse. It's like a field of electric towers in my brain right now, buzzing louder and louder and pushing the limits of my skull thanks to the screams of the civilians, the wail of the sirens, and the antics of the scumbag himself.

"Yeah!" As the officers scoop him off the floor, he jumps a few feet, a victorious grin on his face. "I was zapped by Bolt, y'all! I was zapped by Bolt!"

"Fuck," I mutter while whipping a double take at the asshole, who's juiced more by the cheering crowd. *What the hell?* And I'm unsure if my vexation is more from him or them. Why can't everyone calm the hell down and get back to work and their lives? On the other hand, why the fuck do I care?

My glower triggers his. "What the hell, man?" He nods, indicating my leathers—necessary attire despite the fact that it's nearly ninety outside today. "Come on. You're really him, right?"

"Him *who*?"

"You serious?" Harsh snort. "You really don't know?"

A chuff comes from the cop double-checking his cuffs. "He's probably been too busy lately to notice the news, asshole. You know, dealing with scumsuckers like you?" He tips a grin my direction. "Some of us are just more grateful than others for it."

I return his compliment with a tighter scowl. The move dances on the edge of asshole in its own right, but my bafflement doesn't know the difference. "The news about what?"

"You have a name now, buddy," the cop supplies.

"A *what*?"

"A name." He chuckles. "What? You don't like Bolt?"

"Bolt?" I pronounce the word so slowly, it almost becomes two syllables.

As two more officers come in and haul the criminal out, he's given the physical freedom for a shrug. "Beats 'superhero dude in tight leather,' yeah? Unless you're all about the look?"

"Sure." Now I soak it in sarcasm.

"That's what I thought too." He takes a step closer, going for a just-between-us-guys kind of thing, though giving his true outlook away by glancing over at his buddies with a shit-eating smirk. *Look at me. I'm chattin' it up with Bolt.*

Bolt.

Shit.

As nicknames go, it's not the worst. If I were a dog, it'd be a really badass name. Considering how I've chosen the mongrel therapy route this week, I should have seen this coming. *Dog discovers toy. Dog* really *likes toy. Dog loses toy. Dog deals by pissing electricity all over the city.*

Or something like that.

"Figured with all the power you're throwing around, the suit helps keep it in check. Something like that?"

"Yeah."

Speaking of moving on...

Though the cops still have the bank lobby locked down, the blare of camera lights through the tinted windows alerts me I've overstayed my welcome at this party. The cop, Officer A. Feliz according to his name badge, could've been a guy I'd hang with for a while, pounding beers and playing darts. The old Reece likely would've suggested such a thing. Hell, the new Reece likes the idea too. But the two Reeces don't get to share a universe. It was part of the deal I made with Karma. The bed I made and now must lie in.

Where I'm having issues with Karma is the bridge between figurative beds and real ones.

Like the one in which I'd finally felt alive for the first time in a year. Alive because of the goddess who'd slept in my arms. White-gold hair, cream silk skin, sated sighs. Who'd stayed the night. The whole night.

The first woman—the first *person*—who'd given me a gift more important than all the shiny objects I've possessed in my twenty-seven years of existence.

Hope.

I'd fought it that night. Damn, how I'd fought it. But after those hours of holding and smelling and breathing her, the sensation took root. The sliver of belief, however tiny, that maybe Karma would be merciful and give me one person who didn't feel like crawling out of their skin just because I was in the room. That maybe, just maybe, I didn't have to think about every day of my life going down just like this one.

Waking up alone. Putting some bad guys away, maybe saving a few thousand people.

Then going to sleep alone.

For a few amazing hours, I'd let myself think otherwise. Held the gift in my arms. Savored it. Treasured it. Been able to shove aside the fact that this nickname they've given is more ideal than anyone realizes.

Bolt.

Why the hell not? It's the way I've treated my own life for so long. Why shouldn't it be the way I'm treated now?

Why shouldn't it be the word I'm celebrated with as I crouch low, surrounded by cheers I barely hear, and sprint from everyone's view—and in a few minutes, from their minds too—as their lives go on again, secure because of the superhero they can forget as swiftly as a tabloid magazine cover?

Again.

CHAPTER FIVE

EMMA

"Seriously?"

I can barely huff it out before I'm approached by a swarthy ponytailed guy standing next to a black stretch Mercedes parked in front of my apartment building. He flashes me a crooked grin. "Well, good afternoon to you too."

I jab up my chin. "We agreed on this, Z. Yesterday was going to be *it* for this nonsense."

He adds a shrug. "It's not an imposition. I wasn't doing anything else."

"You're so full of shit."

The smile takes on a cute quirk. "Fine. You're right. Go ahead and gloat. You want to."

I resist the pull of his Armenian charm. "I swear by the planet you're named after *and* the insane god who created it—"

"Don't care about *that* god," Zalkon volleys. Yeah, a planet. Poor Z came along after his mom binged on *Star Trek* during mandatory pregnancy bedrest. "But the god who's making sure you get to and from work in this every day?" He jerks a thumb toward the Mercedes. "*Him*, I care about."

I'm tempted to yank out my phone and call said god-on-high. I have a direct line to his cloud. The all-powerful, all-knowing, overprotective Zeus in the penthouse has made damn sure I have the digits all but tattooed on my brain, thanks to his hourly texts for the last three days. Creepy? Under normal circumstances, yes—but what's been normal about Reece Richards's arrival in my life? Everything about this, about *him*, is a flash storm from fate, sizzling through my atmosphere and frying all my circuits. Yeah, including the man's texts.

Even the one vibrating the device in my palm right now—then quivering all the way up my arm, over my shoulder, and down my spine, gripping my whole torso in tendrils of heat I can no more ignore than my own breaths.

"Sorry," I mutter, turning from Z. "Just let me get this."

"Uh-huh."

I ignore his knowing jibe while swiping at the phone with the zeal of an Austen heroine opening a secret love note. I was responsible as hell getting myself out of the man's bed—*not* a decision my hormones let me forget during the solitary ride in the penthouse's private elevator—so I'm due the indulgence of at least knowing I'm still in the man's head. It's not like the situation's going to last. Nothing in the world of Reece Richards does, including models and actresses who spend the equivalent of my monthly salary on a single facial. Last year, the press didn't know what to do with themselves when he spent—gasp—a whole six months with some power blonde from France, and I'm nowhere near her league. I have to be real about that. I'm just a diversion during the man's quest for his next piece of sparkling arm candy.

But I refuse to feel badly about at least enjoying the ride.

The guy in the tower is thinking
of you from the velvet clouds.

Oh, yeah. He *is* good.

Too good.

I tilt my head, pondering the swoony wordage. This poetic shit is his version of outright chatty—and therefore, a huge tell. What's he hiding? And why does my radar instantly ping it in tones of melancholy?

"Get over yourself." I mutter the mandate at myself while tapping out a reply.

Good afternoon to you too.

The marine layer is thick over the city today, never achieving its normal noontime burn-off. That means, seventy stories up, he's texting from another world.

So how does the muck
look from the tower?

I think of adding a winking emoji but refrain. He'll get the humor without the emoji, though the reference didn't start with us as a laughing matter at all. Our first text exchange after *the night*—my private reference to all the so-good-but-so-wrong that went down in the penthouse—was definitely not Austen-novel material.

EMMALINA

I'm right here. No need to shout.

You're NOT right here.
Where the FUCK are you?

*I had to go. You know that too, even if
you don't want to admit it right now.*

I ordered you to stay in that bed.

But I never belonged there to begin with.

WHAT THE HELL?

Stop shouting.

We are not done.

*It was great, Reece. It was beyond
great. But you're you and I'm me.*

And that means what?

You live in a tower.

Irrelevant.

You have a private elevator.

Irrelevant.

You sign my paychecks!

Paychecks you risk your life to earn!

Excuse me?

*You're not taking the train to
or from work again, Emma.*

EXCUSE ME?

Who's shouting now?

*You don't get to be the boss outside
that penthouse, Mr. Richards.*

We'll see about that, Miss Crist.

And here I am, about to let him prove his point again. Zalkon—who's propped against the car's back bumper and waiting for me to climb in—will catch hell if I don't. Not to the tune of being strung up by his toenails or anything, but if I pull a disappearing act, Reece will undoubtedly let Z go. And he'd only be replaced by a new driver tomorrow—and by one who wouldn't be half as cool. Besides that, Z's banking the extra money from this gig with Reece to surprise his daughter with a birthday trip to Disneyland.

I nod to Z so he'll open the car door and do my best to snort instead of smirk as the god in the clouds finishes his reply to my query.

The muck isn't muck at all.
Not from up here.

I breathe a little easier. No more melancholy vibes, which were probably all in my imagination to begin with.

Unbelievably, my own mother's words echo in my head. *Oh, Emma. You and that oversensitive imagination.*

During my musing, Reece has had time to type a new note.

As a matter of fact, it looks
like a pillow-top bed.

His words make me squirm. Not noticeably. Just enough to remind my brain what happens to my body when it joins the idea of Reece Richards to the concept of a pillow-top bed. Of *any* bed. But one made of clouds? It already sounds wonderfully decadent. And potently dangerous.

Only thing missing is a beautiful
bunny with eyes like this sky.

I quit the squirming to make time for a sigh. Oh, yeah. *Dangerous.* This man. *This man* and the way he can get to a point—as if knowing exactly what it'll do to every tingling tissue between my legs...

But then there's the other point. The even more dangerous one. The one I can't help returning to, over and over.

I'm sure you can call other
pets to hop across that bed.

The three dots from his end instantly start dancing. My heart lurches to my throat, though I keep it from climbing all the way up the pipe by climbing into the car.

I'm strictly a rabbit
kind of guy these days.

Well, that takes care of that. I can feel my heartbeat all the way to my tongue now—the tongue that sneaks out, nervously wetting my lips, as I struggle to turn him down with words that are coy but real, witty but firm. Damn it, where's my inner Emma when I need her? Not the *me* Emma. The other one. The one Mother named me after. The one played by Gwyneth Paltrow, full of willowy charm and outfitted in flowy dresses.

I have to go to work now.

She's not in that damn text, that's for sure. Nowhere even near it.

But maybe that's a good thing.

Maybe I need to honor the other Emma a little bit more. The Emma who artfully presents a well-turned ankle to land a viscount to be the center of her worship. The Emma who wants so much more than the viscount, even if he *can* offer clouds like pillows—and a work commute with air-conditioning and leather seats.

I can't wait for you to get here, either.

And sends texts like that.
Which I can't help but tease him about. Just a little.

*So I can start contributing to
the Richards dynasty again?*

*So you can contribute to my sanity
again. When I know you're safe.*

Okay. Texts like *that* too.

Which, damn it, tangle my thoughts like the traffic Z guides the Mercedes through to get onto the 110 toward downtown.

Is it possible the other night *wasn't* just a quick fuck for him? Can it be Reece Richards felt the same electric connection I did? Is it even conceivable to think I'm not a temporary trinket for him? But if so, is that even what I want? I moved here to prove I could do this by myself. To prove I could face scary new stuff and be all right.

Ironic plot twist of the year.

"Scary new stuff" has never had a better definition than what I experienced with Reece Richards three nights ago. Than all the things he still makes me feel every damn day, even from way up in that spire.

Which circles me back to the same unnerving question.

Do I *really* want to know if he feels the same way?

There's only one answer to that.

I don't.

Because as fearless as the new Emma is, the old one is still afraid his answer will be no.

And even more afraid it'll be yes.

REECE

I stop typing, my fingers suspended over the keyboard.

I let a smile grab the corners of my lips.

She's here.

The bizarreness of this isn't lost on me—but no way am I fighting it. In a building filled with hundreds of others, I can feel her. The charge in every ion. The shift in every air current. The awakening through the whole building. Through every inch of me. Every drop of my blood. Every electron in my nerves. Every pore of my skin.

Every inch of my cock.

Damn. Nobody else has done this to me before. Only her. Only Emmalina Paisley Crist. Yeah, I know her middle name now too. Because yeah, I might've sneaked a fast glance at her employee file. And yeah, it might have been more than a "glance." And yeah, that might make me obsessed and consumed and probably a criminal, but I don't fucking care. She's a fever now. A fucking fire. A cliff to which she's pushed me all the way to the edge, now beckoning me to go all the way over—without safety gear. And hell, I can't wait. For the last three days, she's made it possible to wake up with a smile on my face again—and even to skip the ritual of the daily prayer I utter over morning coffee. The one in which I beg for the day to finally bring my death.

Yeah, that one.

I need to see her again. I'm tired of avoiding the admission, like some soaked cat sidestepping a rain puddle. Of letting *her* sit on the other side of the puddle, equally afraid.

Afraid.

I'm so damn tired of that word being a part of my daily vocabulary.

Fuck the fear.

You're better than that.

She's worth more than that.

It's the mantra in my head as I step off the Brocade's elevator at the second floor and make my way to the staff conference room. Those words repeat themselves in time to the steps I take down the hall, confirming the rightness of this move—an action I haven't taken in a long damn time for a woman.

Walking into the middle of her turf.

Of course, she doesn't know that yet—nobody down in the management conference room does—which, I realize at once, is kind of a cool thing. Even a full minute after I step into the room, I remain silent in the doorway, studying their tight huddle over what looks like a long rooming list.

Invisibility. It's kind of nice.

For now.

I study the bunch of them, pumped and energized, crediting the extra electricity in the air to their own power. But the best part? I get to gaze at Emma in the same unguarded state. She's facing away from me, leaning with one hand on the table, her hair a white-gold cloud thanks to some claw-clip thing. But enough of those entrancing tendrils fall loose that I conjure a fantasy of yanking them free, one by one, as I slide into her again and again, screwing her with carnal intensity...

As if the force of my vision is fierce enough to heat her thoughts—and who says it isn't—her head suddenly lifts. I'm mesmerized by how the motion elongates her neck, exposing an adorable mole in the middle of her nape, before she whips her head around.

At once, the world falls away.

And I'm lost in the endless blue skies of her eyes.

Two seconds of heaven before reality pushes back in. Fucking bastard.

The rest of the management team—I don't even know some of their names, and for the first time in my life, that's *not* cool—go restless and jittery, exchanging self-conscious glances. I stick to my act of glib and impervious, knowing I'm a double whammy of discomfort for them. The brooding boss man who never comes down from the tower and the freak who brings his special brand of weird to the air.

"Mr. Richards!" Neeta Jain pushes through the small throng, putting physical form to their nervousness with her rapid steps. "What a pleasant—"

I stop her with an upraised hand. "Pleasant isn't the first word on anyone's mind right now, Miss Jain." I sweep a knowing look around the room. "But maybe I can change that, at least a little."

"Pardon me?"

"This *is* the rescheduled time for the weekly management meeting? My calendar was pinged about the change."

The woman eyes the phone I hold up. "*Oh.* Of course you were. Yes, of course. Because you're the general manager."

"Of course." My jibe isn't lost on everyone. Chuckles ripple through the crowd behind her, but Neeta's smile is just as forced as before. "*Relax*," I finally admonish her. "I'm just going to sit all the way over here and listen in, if that's okay."

The majority of the faces shift from expressions of

amusement to happy surprise. The only abstaining votes on the referendum come from Neeta and Emma. While Neeta is still clearly confused, my gorgeous velvet girl looks like she's wrapped in sandpaper. Out of everyone in the room, she expected my appearance the least—and sees through it the fastest. Both recognitions only deepen my smirk. I like being the one to catch her off guard, but I also like being the one she can see right through—to an extent. No one on earth will ever know everything about me. Just the way I like it.

"Goodness." Neeta's murmur is full of warmth. "The gesture is certainly appreciated, Mr. Richards. And under normal circumstances, it *would* be okay..."

"But today isn't normal?" I ask.

"Define 'normal.'"

The crack is made in tandem by Wade and Fershan. Though Neeta flashes them a you-did-*not*-just-say-that-in-front-of-the-owner's-son glare, she goes on, prefacing with a light laugh. "*Ab*normal is what we do around here, Mr. Richards. Tonight, thanks to our friend Bolt, we all just have to do it a little faster."

"More than a little." Emma flicks a dismissive glance my way before jogging her head back toward the rooming list, now joined by a housekeeping shift sheet and guest-room floorplans.

Unbelievably, I roll with her little snub. Perhaps am even grateful for it. She'll fracture my attention, and right now I've got to focus on Neeta's fresh news and then alter my convenient excuse for coming down here. Thank fuck I've logged some experience with the suave-under-stress thing. Granted, that skill comes mostly from listening to supermodels whisper their plans for my cock while standing in the middle of red carpets, not nodding as an employee refers to my alter ego as her "incredible friend."

Grit your teeth. Calm your gaze. Pretend you care about what everyone else is talking about.

At least that last one's not a stretch.

"Bolt." I poke the tone into the realm of a question and tilt my head with equal curiosity. "Are you referring to a person or a laundry detergent?"

Everyone in the room bursts with shockingly sincere laughs. It's a bigger gift than any of them realize. I follow up by tossing a full smile down the length of the table. It slams into new waves of disquiet. As if a switch has been suddenly flipped, the apprehension in the air quadruples. But can I blame any of them, after the invisible amps I've tossed first?

"Bolt is a person." The second Neeta addresses my question, her face crunches. "At least I think so."

"Dude's definitely not laundry soap," Wade utters.

A petite redhead next to him bites her lower lip. "*Definitely* not."

"He's a badass," someone else declares.

"A god." The redhead sighs.

"Won't argue there," Neeta murmurs.

"The man is looking for a serious answer." Fershan stabs them with a glower.

"I *was* serious." The redhead throws back as much attitude.

Neeta quells them with a calming hand. Turns back to me. "They're calling him a superhero."

There are times for suave, and then there are times suave can screw itself—or whatever the hell it wants to do as I surge forward. "Excuse the hell out of me?"

"More accurate," Fershan puts in.

"And so much more *serious* than 'god,'" the redhead retorts.

"And none of it matters right now." Emma whirls, stabbing a frown at them both, instantly resetting me to suave mode. My composure is still a masquerade but the only logical choice. No way can I let my whole staff witness how fast this woman gives me wood when flaunting her finest case of peeved. God*damn*, she's resplendent. How the hell have I stayed away from her for three days?

Inwardly, I put Karma on notice. Tonight, no matter what it takes, this heart-halting dream of a female will be mine again.

With my gaze still glued on her, I nod slowly. "Yeah. I remember something about him on the news a few days ago. Looks like a motocross poser? Disappears once the cops get on scene?"

"Doesn't disappear." Wade steps forward while asserting it. "Just bolts so fast, it looks like he does. Get it?"

Though I render agreement with a jerk of a brow, the redhead—her name badge appropriately reading Scarlett Firenze—now decides to buddy up with Fershan for a shouted, "*Gotta bolt!* Whoop!"

Holy fuck.

Emma gives up her frown long enough to join the group in a cheer. Holy fuck, the sequel. Silver lining? The residual humor on her face turns into stunning glints in her eyes, blazing as she turns and explains, "Obvious morale boosts aside, Bolt's benefiting the city in more ways than he ever intended. Especially downtown, where he's been focusing his adventures lately."

I'm tempted to laugh. Instead, I arch a brow. "Adventures?"

Her giggle is like bright bells. "Ass kickings? Escapades? Bold acts of mind-boggling bravery?"

"You could really keep that up, couldn't you?"

"Yeah." Another little laugh, infusing the air with more warmth. "Probably." Then even more laughing, shooting white-hot flares through my nervous system. "But I won't." She nods again at the rooming list. "Because of him, occupancy for tonight just went from thirty-five percent to ninety-eight percent. We're hoping to call a full house by midnight."

"Holy fuck." I utter it aloud now, indulging a laugh of my own. Talk about things I couldn't have predicted.

Wade strides over. "Dude's been on fast-forward the last few days. Everything from putting down bank robbers to yanking kittens out of trees, from here to Ojai and back. The national news feeds have started carrying updates, and now the guy even has global followers."

I deepen my scowl. "Followers? What do you mean?"

Fershan holds up his phone. Sure enough, there I am. Out of focus, yes. Masked, yes. But the header on whatever social media platform it is—they all look eerily the same lately—proclaims me as "Your friend Bolt: Making vibrators obsolete." My gaze bugs wider at the number of followers. "Holy shit."

"You mean holy *ker-ching*." Wade smirks. "Because a whole bunch of those"—he stabs a finger at Fershan's phone—"are about to be a whole lot of those." He sweeps the same finger upward, indicating the nearly empty tower of guest rooms over our heads.

"A tour group." As Neeta explains the point further, she pulls off her blazer. Only now do I realize her normal shiny business blouse isn't beneath it. Instead, she's wearing a polo shirt with the Richards Resorts logo embroidered in the upper right corner. "They left Santa Barbara this afternoon bound for Anaheim but chose downtown LA instead."

"Yeah, baby." Wade pumps a fist. "A Bolt in leather is now hotter than the world's most famous mouse."

"*Anyhow.*" Emma stresses the point by peeling the light sweater away from her own shoulders, revealing a shirt that matches Neeta's. "With the last-minute booking, housekeeping didn't know to staff up for a fast turn, so the management meeting has been replaced by room-flip duty."

She beams a gloating grin while delivering the news. I say nothing, letting her have a moment of thinking she's done with dealing with me for the night. But only a moment. When it's over, I shuck my jacket and roll up my shirtsleeves. "Excellent. What floor do you need me on?"

As I expected, she thuds into silence. As I also foresaw, she's not the only one—though I can't blame the group for going slack-jawed. I throw my shoulders back, returning the questioning stares with one of conviction. This is different, shaking people up for good reasons—and not when they're about to piss their pants because I just yanked a robber out of their face or levitated their cat out of a tree. This feels pretty good. Actually, this feels *damn* good.

"Mr. Richards." Neeta spreads her arms. "That's so kind of you, but—"

"But what? You're shorthanded, right? Then let me help."

Everyone but Emma—who still pierces me with those twin irises of electric blue—exchanges skittish glances. With arms still open, Neeta approaches me like a trainer would a wild lion. "We were going to tackle the rooms in teams of two."

"And there're thirteen of you here." I lift my winning grin. In my other life, I called it *the look*, a deal-closer that scored me everything from sold-out concert tickets to top-shelf booze. Right now, it only turns the woman's patient smile into a forced grimace.

"Really, Mr. Richards. It's not necessary."

"Oh, for the love of..." Emma wheels around. "*I'll* partner with him." She mutters it like the kid taking her turn with the tagalong little brother.

"How big of you." I add a slight bow to my drawl.

"Emma." Neeta's tone is terse, her lips barely moving. "You don't have to—"

"She'll partner with me."

My growl isn't answered by anyone else. There's no more time anyway. The team gets down to business, quickly dividing up assignments for the rooms. The entire time that's happening, Emma stabs fresh glares my way. I return them with the Zen stare of a jujitsu master, having more fun than when I leveled everyone in the room with my surprise appearance.

And it's not the first time I plan on getting my way tonight.

CHAPTER SIX

EMMA

Damn it.

On about twenty different levels.

How many times have I resolved not to end up in exactly this situation, with exactly this man, over the last three days?

Okay, not the *exact* same. In the scenarios I've been banishing from my imagination more adamantly than chocolate mint ice cream during PMS, I haven't had a dusting mitt on one hand and a porta-vac in the other. A rhino-sized housekeeping cart hasn't been wedged between us in the back elevator.

And Reece hasn't looked half this good.

Cheese and rice, there has to be a law against the man getting even hotter when covered in dust, dander, and sweat from changing bed sheets, scrubbing showers, and replacing coffee packets. With his sleeves rolled up, dark stubble shadowing his jaw, and chunks of his thick hair tumbling over his glasses, he's like a dirtied-up version of a Rolex ad.

Oooooh. *There's* an idea.

On the other hand, I'm fairly sure I'm the first person on the planet who's ever seen him like this, and I'm not certain I want to share the privilege with everyone else. It feels...special. Intimate. Inaugural. Several times over the last hour, I've caught the man peeking in mirrors and windows, as if even he doesn't recognize himself. When *was* the last time he busted his ass for someone other than himself? Though technically, the effort *is* still about him. In one way or another, some of tonight's windfall for the Brocade will breeze back over to him—but it's still nice to see him actually acknowledge that fact.

"Sewing kit for your thoughts."

I leave my musings with a giggle, accepting his offer of the room amenity. His arms are folded over the top of the housekeeping cart, accentuating the breadth of his shoulders and the muscles in his forearms. Dear God, how I want to lean forward and explore those striations. With my tongue.

Which would make you different from all the girls in the country club clique...how? Which would prove your resolve that life can be about more than a man, a mansion, and the most perfect lawn on the block...how?

"Do I need to offer a pillow chocolate for your thoughts too?"

I smirk and reach for the foil-wrapped candy as the elevator dings at our new floor. "Now *that's* what I've been holding out for."

But at the speed of light, he snatches my chocolate prize out of reach and the entire cart off the elevator. For a second, I stand and gawk, wondering what trick I've just missed—though the Muzak version of Ed Sheeran's latest hasn't progressed more than a handful of notes.

"How...the hell..." I struggle for words that won't make me sound six kinds of crazy. Not that he's listening. I race to keep up with his long strides down the hall, concentrating on matching two of my steps for every one of his.

"Hop to it, Bunny." He moves with lithe grace even while towing the massive cart, making my throat go dry. It's one thing to flip through gossip magazine pictures of his globe-trotting exploits but another thing to witness the natural athleticism required for adventures like cycling the Dolomites, kayaking in Costa Rica, snorkeling in Tulum—and those are only the locales I can recall. "We're on a schedule," he says while waving a keycard to unlock our next room.

Room being an understatement.

We're now tackling our first suite on the rotation, and it's one of the biggest in the hotel. The view is nearly as incredible as the one from the penthouse—not a surprise, since we're just two floors lower. I gasp after pulling the drapes open and stop for a moment to simply stare. The city is a twinkling carpet tonight, cars forming moving threads in a tapestry of mostly amber, emerald, and cobalt. In the distance, the towers of Century City stand like diamond-studded obelisks.

"Wow." I can't help but murmur it, though I refrain from any China references now. There's a tiny win, at least.

"You mean that, don't you?"

I gasp again—this time from wondering how the man got from trashing empty bottles from the bar across the room to standing right behind me. Since this main part of the suite can patch into the hotel's house music, Ed Sheeran is still there to remind me not more than a few seconds have gone by.

"Of... Of course I do."

Maybe I can pretend my way back to normalcy. Hell, it's worked for the last hour. We've been a good team, turning rooms at impressive speed. But everything changed back in the elevator, with that single look he bore into me. With that stupid sewing kit he offered. With the chocolate he used as a follow-up. With his charming demand to see into my thoughts—as if he even needed to go through that motion. The way the man can always see into me already...as if he has upgraded x-ray vision... I mean, screw knowing my underwear color. Reece Richards can see the spectrum of my damn *thoughts*.

I should be worried about that, right? Even a little more than worried? Something like alarmed? *Scared?*

But all I can think about is how good it feels. To be *seen*...by someone as beautiful and intense and forceful and commanding as *him*...

"I mean, it *is* beautiful." After two more seconds of his expectant silence, I stammer, "Right?"

He pulls in a breath. I can all but hear the gears in his head working. "It's a city," he finally murmurs. "All cities are beautiful in their own ways, I guess. Lights. Architecture. Movement."

"Life." My exhortation has him do a double take. I know it as certainly as I know the lyrics of the song coming from the hidden speakers over our heads. "It's *life*." And it bears repeating, as I take a step closer to the glass. "A collection of lives. Every one of them is a different story, a different dream, a different goal...but all working together too. Meshing and mixing and reaching for something better than what they were the day before and twining with that same energy in others." I huff out a little laugh. "Oh, God. I just said all that out loud, didn't I?"

"Yeah." His reply, quiet as mine, is filled with a confident husk. I know this because he's stepped over, sliding closer behind me...and now nearly presses up against me. I sigh deeply, fighting not to lean back into his strength and size and heat. Instead, I focus on his movements, steady as Tulum seas, in the shifting reflection of the tinted glass. "And I could listen all night."

My laugh is nearly a snort. "You want some butter for that order of corn, mister?"

He shifts a little closer. "Only if bunnies like corn."

They do. Oh God, they do. Too much...

"And butter?" Melted to liquid, like the texture of my blood because of his nearness?

"Tell me more." His tone is rougher now. Lower. A voice for the bedroom...

Oh, no.

I can't start thinking this way.

We can't start thinking this way.

But all he's asked for are words.

Words are safe, right?

"It's also...energy." I must sound ridiculous by now, but he didn't flinch from all the quixotic shit I've already spouted, so why not? "A vibrancy, you know? A pace. A collective craziness, I guess. It's something..."

"Something what?" he prompts, filling in my self-interruption.

"Bigger." I go with the first thought in my head...my soul. "It's just...bigger." But what does "bigger" mean to a guy who's been around the world at least a dozen times? "To me, anyway."

I drag a breath in. The air is suddenly heavy, probably from the weight of my self-consciousness. I feel stripped and vulnerable. It's not comfortable, but stepping away isn't an option—especially as Reece moves even closer, nearly caging me against the glass with his tall, hard body.

Time for a tactics switch. Big-time.

Snark to the rescue. "Okay, buddy." I pivot, facing him

now and turning up a palm. "There are my thoughts. Now pony up the chocolate."

The man isn't deterred. His face is set in serious lines. His eyes are steel gray. "That's important to you, isn't it?" He clarifies. "Living...bigger. Having...more."

"No." I let him see my wince. "Not *having* more." I close my hand, pressing the new fist to the center of my chest. "*Being* more." At a loss for how to explain further, I face the glass again. "There just has to be...something more."

And now there isn't anything left to say. But why does it feel like I haven't uttered anything at all? The air is still too thick, and the new song filling it isn't any help. The Weeknd starts singing—I don't recognize which song, but does it matter when it's The Weeknd?—and my mind starts surrendering even more to the heat of the man pressing closer. I know it before even lifting my head to see him, a beautiful blur reflected by the window, towering over me with sensuous intent.

"There is." His assurance is a warm breath in my hair, a vibrant caress along my nape. "There *is* more, Velvet."

I swallow hard. Fight the shivers coursing down my spine, inching their way toward the front of my torso...into the curves of my shoulders and the tips of my breasts...

"Easy for *you* to say," I whisper. "You've already *had* more."

"Not yet." Aside from a frisson of tension in his shoulders, nothing else changes. He pushes in tighter. Forms his chest to the back of my head, frames his thighs to either side of my hips. And holy wow, what the backs of his fingers start doing to the lengths of my arms...

"Not yet?" I stammer. "What part of 'not yet' are you referring to? Swimming with the sea turtles in Tulum or skiing the Alps at Christmas? Or maybe..."

What the hell was I saying again? I care about that less than the title of the song playing around us, though the lyrics are magic in my senses. Words of being freed by a simple touch and never having to rush...

"You're my more, Emmalina."

It's pure heat against my neck.

Liquid fire through my body.

Awakened truth in my spirit.

A force I can no longer fight. *We* can no longer fight.

"Oh." It escapes on shaking breath as my head drops, unable to stay upright as this man slings a net of arousal across my whole body. I'm helpless in his snare, muscles going limp and nerves turning to ash, though I still try to fight the pull by slamming both hands against the glass and pushing back. No use, especially as I drag my stare up, only to have my vision filled by our reflection.

Our reflection.

One word now. One image now.

Bodies pressed. Breaths mingled. Energies joined. Desires awakened.

"Oh." I have no idea how I'm able to repeat it or if it even makes sense. "I...I see..."

"Do you?" His growl is a visceral vibration instead of a spoken reply, pressed into my neck as he slides his left hand along my arm. When he gets to the end, he meshes his fingers with mine against the window. Our clasp forms a heated cloud of condensation. "Do you really see?" He scrapes the corner of my jaw with the edges of his teeth. "Or should I show you?"

Yes. Show me. Please.

"No. Th-That's okay. I-I believe you." I push through the haze of lust, clinging to my last thread of pragmatism. "Reece.

We need to...get back to work..."

In my head, it sounds like badass management girl. On my lips, it's more like lusty French maid. The syllables break into breathy pieces as he sweeps his lips up and down my neck.

"Work? What is this strange 'work' you speak of?"

I push out a dry laugh. He doesn't. In the dark world beyond the glass, where our figures still tangle, he hunches over me like a forest beast examining its prey—before deciding the best way to kill it. I marvel at how tiny I look compared to him. How helpless. How stunned. Enthralled by my predator's power...

"Emma," the beast softly snarls. "Emma, *Emma*. How did I go so long without this? Without you?"

That isn't supposed to make it all right.

The goo of my kneecaps tells me otherwise.

I sag against him, startled when my bare backside scrapes the prominent bulge in his pants. How the hell has he hiked my skirt and dropped my panties before I've realized it? And *why* the hell didn't I heed Neeta's advice and not borrow some housekeeping uniform pants for this duty? And what the hell am I doing now, letting myself tremble and whine at the sight of his long fingers against my bare thigh...before he slides them toward my core...

"Oh!" My cry is answered by his growl—and the swipe of his fingers over the hot pearl between my legs.

"Yesssss." He hisses into my ear. "God*damn*. Yesssss."

"*No*. Reece, we—oh, *shit*." My head falls back as he pinches the most illicit part of me. "W-We can't. I-I'm your—"

"You're my more." He shifts his hand away, encouraging my right knee to settle onto the ottoman he's pulled over with his corresponding leg.

"Regardless, this isn't...and you're—"

"The man who's going to be inside you."

"No. *No.* This isn't right."

"Oh, this is *very* right."

"I *work* for you!"

"All right, then. You're fired."

"Damn it!"

"All right, then. You're hired again."

I'd slap him if his words weren't so damn true. *This is very right.* My mind resists every syllable, but every cell of my body and instinct of my spirit can't scramble fast enough to embrace it. To seize the gem of desire forged in the caves of fate from the moment we first set eyes on each other.

Fine. So it might be true. Doesn't mean I have to be happy about it.

I pulse my left hand, still locked against the glass by his. He pushes harder, forming his body over mine. I don't want to be happy about how good that feels either. With his chest molded over my back and his face tucked against my shoulder, it's impossible to keep animal tendencies from taking over.

Ravage me...please...

"I hate you," I grit out instead.

"I crave you." His stubble burns my neck.

I let my head plummet again. "I can't want this."

"No." The grate of his zipper cuts the air. "You don't want it." The heat of his groin flares across my ass. "You need it. Desperately. Completely. Like air. Like an emptiness in your being that's been expanding for days, throbbing and gnawing at your center. You need this in your head, your psyche... Like I do."

"Hell." It's a line of bitterness that really isn't, a punch I long to give him but won't—a resolve dwindling faster as he pushes down his pants and briefs, freeing the bold beauty of his erection. He tilts his hips in again, fitting his hot flesh between the swollen lips of my pussy, and I'm certain I've just uttered my own fate. A cock that feels this good can only belong to the devil. And here I am, willingly rocking my soaked center back and forth along that sinful stick. But if this is what hell's like, who needs heaven?

"Fuck." The strain in Reece's voice lends a sliver of vindication. His composure is balanced on just as thin a rail as mine. For a tiny moment, I let myself believe all his words are more than just pretty poetry to get my underwear open. Does it even matter if they aren't? The bastard has gotten his way. My panties are a puddle around my left ankle. My resistance is a few grains of sand washed away by his lusting flood. My senses are hurled like jetsam in the surge—flipped and tossed and drowned until I can't figure out where to come up for air. Every breath is full of his smoky, musky scent. Every heartbeat is synched to the hammering from his chest, pounding like tsunami waves against my spine. Every move I make is focused on making him swell bigger against my pussy, moan deeper into my ear, grab tighter onto my thighs.

"*Fuck.*" His echo is borne on a chest-deep groan as his body tightens and shakes. His lips are hot and brutal at my ear. "Fuck *me*, Velvet."

I release a shuddering sigh. "Is that a question or a command?"

He seizes my thighs harder, spreading fingers along my tender flesh and pulling my body harder against his. "You already know that answer," he growls into my neck, finishing it with a brutal bite that I answer with shaking moans and bursting gasps. This heat and need and lust are the most intense storm my body's ever been through—and he hasn't even entered me. How is this possible? How is he doing this to me, simply with the scrape of his mouth and the force in his fingertips? His touch is like lightning. His body is like thunder. He's a monsoon around me. A calling to my core...

"Emma. *Emma.*" His voice moves through me, vibrating along my skin and senses. "You..."

"No." I sigh, savoring how our muscles coil together. How our bodies form to each other. "No...*you.*"

His low, lusting breath flows with his long, slow slides. "You...drive me." He works a deep kiss into the bottom of my neck. "You illuminate me."

I shudder and smile as he works his mouth back up to my jaw. "It's my superpower."

I swear, just before his short chuckle, I feel a jolt take over his body. But his voice is smooth smoke when he drawls, "It probably is."

"You know what that means, don't you?" I wait one short beat, not giving him time for another comeback. "Now you have to show me yours."

There it is again. The silent but incessant jolt through his frame, covered by another laugh. It's sharper this time, probably because I waste no time in demonstrating exactly what "power" I need from him. Am beyond needing. Am beyond even thinking about. He's turned me inside out. Pulled me beyond my defenses. Taken me to the point of no return. I'm wanton and uncaring, riding my pouting sex along his engorged shaft, lost in a vortex of climbing need and growing fire and pulsing passion.

"Damn. *Fuck.* Emma—beauty—wait. *Wait.* I have to—"

"Hurry," I gasp as he slides his hand from my thigh and fumbles with something behind him.

"Christ." But it sounds more like "rice" because he's tearing a foil packet with his teeth. The next moment, the latex is a cool column between our bodies. As he slides the condom over his length, he dictates, "Say that again. Just like that."

"Hurry." I willingly oblige because one, I mean it, and two, I yearn to make him sound like that again. Like he can't take a breath until I speak again. Like he won't move without my begging gasps. "Please...just...hurry and— *Oh!*"

It's a moan of surprise and fulfillment, of pain and pleasure, of joy and sorrow. In his single lunge, I'm finally filled—but as he slides his cock out, retreating until his head teases at my tender lips again, I now know what it's like to be without him. Tears stab my eyes. Everything aches. He hasn't just taught me about the emptiness of my body. He's left me in a deeper darkness. An existence without his passion, his laughter, his energy...

His *more.*

"Reece." I don't care how pathetic it sounds. If he wants to hear me beg, that's damn well what I'll do. "Please. *Please.* I-I need—"

"I know," he husks. "I know."

A moan, deep and dark, pours out of me. He *doesn't* know. If he did, he'd give me more than just his tip, searing at the first few inches of my channel, teasing back into my weeping depths with painstaking seduction.

"But...but..."

"Close your eyes."

I do it because he could ask me to whistle *Mary Had a Little Lamb* right now and I would. I do it especially because his commanding growl is the sexiest thing to ever enter my body. Okay, the second sexiest.

"Both your hands. Flat on the glass." He pulls the ottoman over a little more, enabling me to reposition my body and comply. "Now both knees up on this."

A serrated snarl leaves him as I obey once more. The new alignment of our bodies seats him deeper, though the penetration isn't close to that first incredible lunge. I need him like that. I need him so far inside, it hurts. I need him to dominate every thought I have, electrocute every cell in my being, fry every circuit in my senses. With every new inch he takes over, my blood sizzles. My skin ignites. My pussy is white-hot from his branding. And still I crave more. I need more...

The lust spreads through me like a virus. I'm fevered with it. Delirious from it. I need relief but never want to be healed. It consumes me, driving every move I make. My limbs writhe and roll, thrusting my channel back over his stalk, a physical plea for his full invasion once more. He answers with sharp, shallow stabs, swirling me into enraged insanity. No. Not insanity. I'm indignant. Enraged. I didn't remotely want this. If we're discovered, he'll be banished to run an ice hotel in Mongolia and I'll never work in this city again. But now that he's turned my body into a raw frenzy, he refuses to give me the right antidote.

"Damn." He grits it as I pump faster. The timbre of his voice is a fireball to my sex, stretching the walls of my restraint, making me cry aloud.

"Please." My fingertips curl against the window. My shoulders snap back, molding against the perfect wall of his chest. He curls around me, draping me in his longing, firing the electrons of our passion even faster and hotter. His thighs are powerful and slick against my ass. He rakes his hands up my arms and slams them on the glass outside of mine. His cock conquers new depths of my body—a piston of such intensity, I wonder if I'm glowing from within. "Please!" I beg again. The piston needs to connect—*now*. The rod needs to strike—*now*.

"*Damn.*" His own echo is nearly a groan. "So hot," he snarls. "So tight. I need to be deeper."

"Do it." So finished with begging.

"I don't...know if I can hold it in for much—"

"Then don't." Really, *really* finished.

"It's...been a while for me."

I almost hurl back a glare of disbelief. "You trying to say you're out of practice? Because I call bullshit."

"I'm trying to say...dear *fuck*"—the oath escapes him as our bodies fit tighter—"that I don't want to hurt you..."

"Hurt me, Reece."

"Good Christ."

"*Hurt me*, Reece!"

"*Fuuuuck!*"

I exclaim the word with him—as his cock takes over everything left inside me.

For a moment, just one moment, we just are. We're locked. Tied by the connection of our bodies, the bond of our breaths, the electrons of the air swirling around us, through us, into us.

It's crazy—at least that's what I try to tell myself—but there's no other way to describe the marvel of the starscape bursting to life beyond my closed eyelids. The sexual race of my body is now the blazing force of my mind, shooting texture and color to my vision. Blue, gold, and silver streaks consume the valley of my passion, colliding so hard that I'm overwhelmed—

but when I open my eyes to escape the cataclysm, there's more impossibility for my mind to wrap around.

Are his fingers, still slammed to the glass beside mine, glowing? Is that same indigo hue igniting the crux where our bodies are joined? And why can I *see* every vein in his body as if they've turned into lightning?

"Reece? What the—"

But I can't get the question out. My scream slices the air as he thrusts fully once more.

Holy. Shit.

Every inch of my tunnel is invaded, every neuron of my body is detonated.

"It's okay, Velvet. It's okay."

Though his words are hoarse rasps, I believe every syllable. Though all of this is beyond surreal, I accept it. Maybe it's even easier that way. Remembering it as something like a wild dream will make it easier to forget.

Because once we leave this room, I *have* to forget.

Reece's breaths are rough in my ear. He bends one of his knees onto the ottoman, tilting his cock for even deeper plunges. "It's okay," he grates again. "Jesus God. It's *better* than okay."

The helpless underline of his tone is the release I need for a watery laugh. "I don't think it'll ever be okay again."

"Thank fuck."

"Yeah. Thank... *Ohhhh!*"

And now, even words are impossible. Nothing but a stunned choke falls from my lips as my pussy flares with pleasure, my eyes squeeze shut, and my senses are exploded beyond comprehension or recognition. I'm lost. So lost. And nothing's ever felt so damn good. The light ribbons are gone.

In their place is a solitary glow, a sun into which my senses melt. The heat funnels toward my pussy until the dam of my restraint is nothing but rubble.

And I'm drowning. Pulsing. Climbing. So close. *So close...*

Liquid light, all around me.

Molten completion, slamming through me.

My sex is pure lightning. My senses are raw resonance. My lips open on a soundless scream as the torch inside me brings wave after wave of perfect fire, sparking pleasure so good it's nearly unbearable.

"Reece. *Reece.*"

"Right here." His growl is my ark in the flood, my refuge from damnation. We're a pair of fallen angels, marking a path through the stars with the fire of our fucking. "I'm right here, Velvet."

"Wh-What's happening?" I hear my voice as if through a fog. I sound totally toasted, though the electricity in my pussy counteracts that theory. I'm not drunk. Even drunk doesn't feel this good.

"I don't know." His grate is filled with just as much wonder. His cock swells at my walls, foretelling his own approach to the cliff of climax.

"You don't *know*?" I'm incredulous. Maybe a tinge scared.

"I've never felt anything like this before."

I believe him but don't want to. Hasn't he felt *everything* before? But as he continues to fuck me, the answer is irrelevant. "Oh," I choke as new arousal drives my pussy toward a new mountain of awakening. "*Oh!*"

How is this possible? How am I this tightly strung, this stunningly turned-on, once again?

"It's okay." He meshes his fingers with mine, squeezing

until it hurts. I welcome his shackles, embracing the pain. It ensures me this is real. Achingly, blindingly real. "It's okay, beauty. Let it happen. Let it take you."

"Says the guy who doesn't *know* what's happening?"

I feel his smile against my cheek. "Then it's an adventure for both of us." He slides his grip along my body, sizzling heat following his fingertips all the way back to my waist. "An uncharted sea." His hold tightens. He controls our pace, ramming my body back over his with faster urgency. Then even faster. "Sail it with me, Emma."

"Yes." No other response makes sense.

"Come with me, Emma."

"I...I don't know if I..."

"Yes, you can."

"Reece—"

"Goddamnit, Emma. *Now!*"

"Yes!"

And I do. And *he* does.

We plummet together, descending into our own River Styx, where flames consume us—and then rocket us back to the stars. But now, we don't just zip between the cosmos. We *are* a star, made of light and heat and brilliance, flaring with such force, the supernova is inevitable.

"Christ," Reece snarls.

"Yes," I return the plea.

"I'm going to come." His voice wavers. Something about his moan snags at my senses. "I can't stop," he grates. "God help me."

What's going on? Why does he suddenly sound like he's confessing murder? But even those thoughts vanish as I burst once more, caring only about the convulsions of my walls around his gushing cock.

"Oh," I stammer. "Oh...*oh!*" And though my logic knows there's a layer of latex between our bodies, I swear I can feel every drop of him spill into me. A thousand filaments of energy spread through my sex, as if I've become one of those plasma balls at the geekboy stores at the mall. The sensation intensifies when that electricity branches out, filling Reece's fingers now spread against my hips, as he keeps pumping, rubbing out his scorching conclusion.

"Fuck." He finally breathes against the back of my neck. "*Fuck.*"

"We sure did."

My humor is met by Reece's thick silence, pricking a sixth sense in me. Why has the weight of the air doubled in less than half a minute?

Before the next thirty seconds are up, he curls around to swiftly kiss the edge of my jaw before muttering, "I'll be right back." While there's affection in his voice, its twinge of regret still lingers—but by the time I can turn around, he's already disappeared into the bathroom, closing the door with a *whump*.

Confusion hits. It's followed at once by curiosity. Enough to make me surge to my feet, yank my skirt down, and pad across the room. But once there, I hesitate in front of the closed bathroom door. Through the portal, I can hear his pronounced hiss. Then a slippery *fwick*, as he pulls off the condom. He whooshes out a breath. Whispers to himself, "Thank *fuck*."

My forehead bunches. What the hell?

"Errrmmm... Everything okay in there?"

A fast *thunk*—the used rubber hitting the waste can, I assume—before the door is flung back and the man himself fills the opening.

I don't disguise my sharp intake of breath. *By all that's holy*. Probably the *un*holy stuff too. I don't expect this new arrogance from him. Or its crazy effect on me. How can a male wearing his nerve like a second skin, though still covered by every stitch of his clothing, make me want to hump him again? I can't deny that truth as I take in his sultry smirk, half-lidded gaze, and tumbling hair. His arms are spread, elbows braced against the doorjambs. He crosses one ankle over the other, drawing my gaze downward—to the open V of his zipper and the gasp-worthy body part still bared in that gap.

"Right as rain in here." His gaze matches his tone, alluring and steady. His sultry scrutiny dips down my body. "How about out there, Bunny?"

I compel my own composure to stay even, though that means letting my blush run rampant. And no, the irony isn't lost on me. After what I just let him do to me, on the company's time—*his* company's time—my system shouldn't be granting me blush privileges right now. Yet there it is, acutely conscious of his bare crotch. And mine. The skirt might be down, but that stops none of his effect on everything beneath it. I'm wet all over again, my juices tickling as they slide toward my pussy. Reece's stalk, which has never gone fully flaccid, bobs half an inch the moment my arousal scents the air.

"Just...peachy."

He curls a smile, making me want to groan. *Holy shit.* The man's generous lips are as mesmerizing as his proud cock. "Peachy, hmmm? Glad to hear that." Just as swiftly, the mirth fades from his mouth...as fresh lust smokes his eyes. "You have no idea how glad."

"Oh, I have *some* idea." My effort at cute and coy is destroyed the moment he reaches over, dragging me close. In the same motion, he finds the top of the zipper at the back of my skirt. Before our bodies touch, he has the enclosure open. As our mouths tangle, the whole garment plummets to the floor. We're flesh-to-flesh once more, my soaked slit cushioning his stiff length, my hungry moan absorbing his harsh grunts. I'm dizzy with disbelief but high on gratitude. How is this even happening? How is my body, my spirit, my very core already so ravenous for him again? This isn't me. At least this never *has* been me. I'm the female with needs beyond my clit. The vanilla-town girl with the kaleidoscope-colored dreams. The one who can count past lovers on one hand and be fine—hell, be *proud*—of that fact.

"Yeah?" But his silken growl has me forgetting all concept of pride, especially as he sweeps me up, parking my ass on the marble vanity top. "Tell me about your ideas, beauty."

His mouth, elegant and entrancing, hovers an inch above mine. He doesn't leave the space empty for long. At once he sweeps down again, spearing his tongue past my lips, demanding a new and wicked dance. Though he leads the tango with smooth mastery, I'm struck once more by his urgent desire, which leads me to actually believe his earlier disclosure. *It's been a while for me...*

"Yours fascinate me more." The words quiver as he yanks me forward, nearly unseating me from the vanity as he wraps my legs around his waist.

"Uh-uh." His tone is as thunder-dark as his gaze. "Not as fascinating as you, Emmalina Crist." He dips in as if to kiss me again but hovers instead, raking those thunderheads across my face. "I want to know everything about you."

He speaks with such reverence, I don't know whether to be swept away or scared shitless. Then there's the option behind door number three. Total bewilderment.

I funnel all the confusion into a muttered question. "Why?"

He pulls back a little and looks at me with such perplexity of his own, I wonder if he's having second thoughts about this whole conversation—or whatever the hell this exchange is.

But he's still serious, even resolute, as he murmurs, "Why is there gravity, Velvet? Why does the sun come up every morning? Why do stars fall and mountains rise?" He pulls himself closer to me. "Some things are just inevitable." He slides his hips against mine. As he rocks, stroking my clit with the boldness of his cock, I swear his gaze flares with a million points of iridescent light. "Some things are just meant to be."

Well...hell.

Forget fighting the leap of my pulse. The sprint of my heart. The complete swoon of my better senses, turning my I-am-woman-hear-me-roar into I-am-bunny-let-me-melt.

"Meant...to...be." I push out the words between hoarse, heavy pants. "Like the fact that I need you to fuck me again?"

CHAPTER SEVEN

REECE

I grin so wide, it hurts.

Fuck. Everything hurts.

Every drop of power in my dick. Every molecule of air in my chest. Every crazy thought in my head.

It hurts, and I've never felt more amazing in my life.

I sure as hell haven't ever spouted such quixotic bullshit and truly meant it. I've never stared at a woman's face like this and sworn I'd never be tired of the sight. And my cock sure as hell has never demanded a repeat trip to paradise this fast after the first visit.

Most remarkably, my hands have never felt like this before.

Yeah...my hands.

They've never ached to hold a woman tighter. Never clenched into fists, fighting back the urge to cradle her face as I kiss her senseless and screw her into nirvana.

And they've never glowed brighter.

Ten garish reminders of the freak I really am.

Which is why I reach beneath us, gripping her ass as I lean in close, consuming her vision with nothing but me as I tell her through my teeth, "Close your eyes, beauty."

The center of Emma's brow pushes into a perfect little V.

"Why?"

My jaw clenches. "Emma—"

"You're so beautiful." She delves a hand into my hair. "Let me watch you this time."

"*Close your eyes, Emma.*"

I hate how it jolts her. Hate how it paints her face in nervousness, even though she complies. And I *hate* what it does to her body, tensing her before I can even drag the second condom from my pants.

I want to fascinate her again. Turn her into the mindless she-beast who let me take her in front of the window. Turn her into my partner to the stars.

So once again, I tiptoe into territory I've never traversed with a woman before.

Seduction. The real kind. As in, slow and sensual...and verbal.

"That's good." Simple, but an effective start. Also the truth, though I know everything I'm about to say is the truth. I'm just not sure how. This isn't my normal MO. I've always been a show-not-tell guy. A master in the art of stringing women along with expensive food, expensive booze, and the belief they'll be the one to get beneath the suave shell I show the rest of the world.

I don't want to be suave with her.

I just want to be real.

"Yeah. Very good," I say with more confidence. "You're gorgeous like this, Emma." I brush kisses across her eyelids. "No. Not even gorgeous." I swallow and hope she feels it. I hope she knows that texting this shit is one thing but speaking it is another. An experience that makes me feel like anything but a superhero right now. I'm so far out of my comfort zone,

I'm in the fucking desert—and she's the only oasis that can keep me alive. "You're...you're gravity." It spills out, lamer than I ever imagined but good because it's straight from my gut. My deepest instinct. "You're morning. And—"

I'm silenced—saved—by her grip around my neck and her mouth jutting up to mine. She shoots her tongue into my mouth. Rolls the gorgeous curves of her hips, drenching my throbbing head in her scorching juices. "And the woman who needs you inside her again," she grates. "*Now.*"

I growl hard. Kiss her harder. There's a charge in our contact now, making her taste sooty but sexy, which awakens an animal drive in my mind, my gut, my dick. She tastes like *me* and all the places I've already marked her from the inside out. And I want to find even more.

With that thought dominating my brain, I fumble the condom on. The second I've slammed it down to my balls, I grip Emma hard and position her for my full, fiery slam. No gradual build-up this time. Not when I'm a rod of rage, full of racing electrons and blazing come, manifested all too clearly by the neon-blue glow my fingers cast across her ass. I fixate on that sight, reflected back to me from the mirror, as I plunge deep and fast and hard into her wet, kneading heat.

Then faster.

Harder.

Driving to make her scream. Giving everything to bring her pleasure. Rejoicing in the view of my erection disappearing over and over again into her perfect sheath.

Succumbing to her magic.

Giving in to her spell.

Hailing her as my sorceress...as I give her every drop of my own superpower again.

EMMA

Two days after Reece Richards made sure I'd never think of that suite in the same way again, I return to my office from the water cooler, doing my best not to wince. Neeta has come in during my absence and secured herself in the chair on the other side. Privacy is no longer a luxury, so I'm forced to hide how every inch of my ass still feels as if I spent the day at Malibu lazing too long on my tummy, covering everything but my backside.

But that's the boring metaphor for everything that really happened.

For how Reece Richards gripped me so fiercely when fucking me, he left bruises that feel like burn marks.

For how he seared himself into my mind with the same ruthless force.

For how my body has turned pyromaniac on me, craving those flames again.

For how much it hurts to ache for him like this.

And for how much I really like it.

I frown at Neeta, but she's still furiously tapping text into her phone. She glances up as I place my water bottle, newly filled at the cooler, on the opposite end of the blotter from my computer. "If you add vodka to that, I'll steal a swig."

I chuckle, knowing damn well she's joking.

"I'm not joking."

"Okaaaayyy." My deeper frown counteracts the casual blurt. "Sorry, girl. What's going on?"

"You mean what's *not* going on," Neeta returns. "As in, what's happened to Bolt and his hot streak."

I resettle in my chair, jolted again by my personal hot

streak. "I've been...busy. Haven't even turned on the news. What's going on? Wasn't he just zapping every creep in town with thunderbolts and lightning?"

"Until a day and a half ago, yes." She pushes her sculpted brows together and slides a finger up her screen. "But now he's disappeared into his dynamo den or whatever." She rolls her eyes. "I guess cheese doodles and a *Lone Ranger* binge are more important than saving Los Angeles from rapists, thieves, and vandals."

I huff, progressing to the logical conclusion. "And let me guess. The tour group is now wondering why they bypassed Anaheim to stay here."

"Give the lady a prize." She rings an invisible bell.

With crazy-weird timing, a musical ding erupts from my computer. A window slides in from the left, topped by the name of the person hailing me via our in-house instant message system—set to a privacy level I've never even heard of much less been invited to share.

Reece Richards

Shit, shit, shit.

I grit my teeth to keep the words from spilling out, but a stressed sigh is inevitable.

Neeta charges. "What? Who is it?"

I shrug, praying I'm convincingly casual. "Rick from housekeeping." Thank God there's a supervisor in that department with an "R" name. If she glances at my monitor, she'll see that much before I close the pop-up. "He thinks the tour group is hoarding the comp shampoo bottles. And he might still be a little peeved about Ree—Mr. Richards and me forgetting to tuck the shams on the beds in the Sunset Suite during the team turnover."

My message box pings again.

Emmalina

Speaking of tucking a sham.

Emmalina

"Sorry." I flash an apologetic look at Neeta, not having to pretend this time. "I should get this."

EMMALINA

"Of course." Neeta waves an indifferent hand but shows no signs of ceasing her scrolling. Or moving from the chair. "Go ahead. I'm just hoping to find any random mentions of Boltalicious. Maybe he dropped off his hottie leathers for dry cleaning somewhere."

I concentrate on pulling in a fortifying breath but take my time about it. Acting like I'm thinking may actually lead to *doing* it. Besides, the action steadies my fingers on the keyboard.

> *You want pompoms with*
> *that megaphone, mister?*

A little line beneath my words, looking like a dwindling dynamite fuse on repeat, denotes he's typing a reply.

Nice segue.

Why?

Because balls ARE involved
with my intentions right now.

I had to go and bring up dynamite.
I pass off another long breath as efficient frustration.

Have fun with those, then. Don't dribble
both at once. You may hurt yourself.
I have to get back to work.

My lips twitch. Well, look who just got glib and sassy with the boss. I *am* woman, and my roar is full of sultry power. Maybe *I'll* go out and kick some bad guy ass.

You've been at work for four hours.

My fingers fly, taking advantage of the perfect comeback.

You only know that because you're
still the dictator of my commute.

Dictator Richards. Has a nice ring to it.

Have fun playing with that one too,
Your Excellency.

Four hours, Velvet. By law,
you have to take a break.

Hell.

How is his middle name not *Persistence?* And how does he crash my heart against my ribs by simply messaging that nickname?

I square my shoulders. I *have* to be stronger than this. Remind myself I'm likely not the first woman he's ever called that, no matter how special it feels or how many backflips my stomach insists on subjecting me to. Realize that a rich rogue with eyes like mercury, hair like satin, and the body of a god won't care about the moony-eyed manager he leaves behind once the fascination of the fuck is gone.

Not relevant. Salaried, remember?

I preen for a second before clicking send. "Ka. Pow."

While I wait for his dynamite fuse to reignite, Neeta looks up with an inquisitive smirk. "Is Rick being a douche again?"

I send a wry wink. "Nothing I can't handle."

Take a break, Emmalina.

I'm in the middle of something.

And it'll be waiting when you get back.

From visiting your spire?

You like my spire.

A new huff bursts out. He's right, so damn right, and I can't *let* him be. I really am in the middle of something. If the tour group is as pissed as Neeta alleges, my workload as Guest Satisfaction Manager is about to get heavier, and I can't even pretend taking a "break" with him will be "relaxing." Peace isn't an option when we're in the same room together, and the more I've pondered it, the more I realize what he said the other night is the only way to explain the wonderful war zone.

There's no explanation for it at all.

Unless stuff like the sun, stars, and gravity are worthy definitions. And they're not.

They can't be.

Which is why I must declare détente now.

I'm not going to the tower, Reece.

I send the reply before I can chicken out. And then literally sit on my hands while waiting for his response.

But his typing fuse never reignites.

I tap a toe on my plastic chair mat. The move is actually empowering, giving an excuse to admire the new fire-engine-red pumps on my feet. Okay, so they were the result of shopping therapy as a distraction from *him*, but they're still killer. But even their superpowers fade after a long minute of inactivity in the chat box.

I stop the toe tapping. And hold myself back from writing stupid scripts about why he's suddenly ghosted. I imagine him sitting there at his refined desk, in front of those penthouse windows, glorious even in his fury. Who knows what's prompted his silence? The man has a million other things to focus on besides getting peeved with the mousy manager currently serving as his fuck buddy side dish.

No longer.

It's for the best that he recognizes that too. That we *both* do.

Blasting aside the lead plate closing over my chest, I minimize the chatbox with an efficient click. "Any luck?" I query, converging my attention back to Neeta. "Mr. Lightning-in-Leather sighted anywhere at all?"

She jerks her head up, tossing her unbound hair across her slumped shoulders. "You mean other than a bad imposter on Melrose, using the lure to flash his junk?"

I groan but finish in a snicker. "So that's a giant no."

"Affirmative, kiddies." With the same wry emphasis, she stabs again at her phone screen. "So we'll probably have the group for just two nights instead of four. *Ugh.*" She turns the device over, slamming it to her lap while letting her head fall back. "That'll teach me to include a last-minute booking on the weekly forecast."

"But you can put a note on the report, right? Explain that the revenue loss was due to circumstances beyond our control?"

She stabs me with a new stare, now drier than her tone. "Last time I checked, a superhero no-show doesn't count as an Act-of-God excuse."

My encouraging smile twists into a grimace. "So who's going to tell Mr. Richards?"

"Says the new teacher's pet herself."

This time, I really need her to be kidding—but I see the unnerving truth sneaking through her sheepish smile. "Oh, come *on*. Seriously?"

Neeta rises, leaving her phone on the desktop so she can clasp both hands, practically petitioning me. "I'll bring you *ladoo* for the next month."

"Not fair." I've had a weakness for the coconut dessert balls since she shared some with me last week. The girl makes a mean *ladoo*.

"Then consider it a noble act. He likes you, Emma. And you're more comfortable with him and that strange aura of his than the rest of us."

I double down on the glower. Comfortable isn't how I'd describe the vibe between the man and me, but that justification is way different than everyone else's. They all act like he's a moving nuclear waste zone and they'll start glowing if they breathe around him. And me? I have to keep reminding myself the glow won't last forever.

"And you think that'll make him less ticked about the news?"

"What news?"

It's more dictate than question, issued from the doorway behind Neeta with the authority of an arriving king. The man to whom it belongs is such an image of sovereign glory, I'm shocked there isn't a crown atop his umber waves. That elegant suit. That regal stature. That all-encompassing gaze. *I own everything I see...*

I'm actually thankful for my next wave of astonishment. How did he get down from the tower so fast? And looking like he's been at some thousand-bucks-a-ticket gala or awards dinner, instead of giving me shit from his desktop in his dark office?

"Mr. Richards." Neeta really looks ready to actually curtsy, only I wonder how that'll work in her fitted navy pantsuit. I'm glad I chose a similar ensemble. If I'm not wearing a skirt, the man can't even think of invading his way up it—though the silver fire in his gaze leads me to believe he went there for a second. Maybe more than a second.

"Miss Jain." He nods with regal deference. "Have I interrupted?"

"No, no." Neeta's gaze zips back to me, flaring with meaning. "As a matter of fact, Miss Crist was just thinking of calling up to you."

"Is that so?" He jogs a brow, making me wonder if he might really be descended from nobility. The subtext in his eyebrows alone likely sent a few heretics to the guillotine in years past. "What a nice idea. I wouldn't have even had to shout about it."

As I glare, Neeta jolts. "Shout about it? Why?" Again, I wonder if she's about to nosedive for the floor. "Is everything all right? Is there something we can do for you?"

"Nothing I can't take care of myself."

His gaze, gorgeous and glistening, doesn't leave me.

Neeta's stare, pensive and penetrating, doesn't leave him.

"Okay," she finally says, very slowly—preparing the air for a pause as murky as his eyes.

At last, Reece fully enters the room and refreshes the expectancy in his gaze. "So...Miss Crist? There's something you wanted to discuss?"

Neeta's smile is brilliant, framed by her toffee-shaded lipstick. "Ah, yes. She did."

"I *didn't*." I burn a meaningful glare her way. "Nothing yet, at least." I gaze back to him. *Whoa.* Even pulling my focus for ten seconds instigates another first-look rush. "Besides, you seem to be having a busy night."

"*Have* had." He shrugs, rumpling his formalwear into even more delicious angles, before clarifying. "Dinner with an old friend. I was on my way up to the office but realized it might be a good idea to check up on things in the trenches."

"The trenches are fine." I insert it before Neeta can formulate anything more. "All systems just grand."

"Outstanding." He unleashes a smile that should be registered as a lethal weapon. Neeta practically simpers. He seems to notice but not notice, if that makes any sense, before stating, "So you won't mind if I glance at the latest guest satisfaction numbers?"

"Of course not."

"Outstanding." He accentuates every syllable, turning every one of them into aural caresses—so smoothly diabolical in his intent, my senses take a second to catch up. By the time they do, he's already pivoting to Neeta, arms casually folded. "But I'm sure *you* have other duties to attend, Miss Jain. Don't let me keep you."

If my gaze were daggers...

I'd never understood the idiom until this moment, having to pretend the man's suggestion means nothing more than business-as-usual when sensual intent flows like quicksilver from the back of his gaze. Even Neeta picks up on that blatant energy now. Her glances are curious, her shuffle slow, as she turns toward the door. "Of... Of course, Mr. Richards. I'll just be in my office should you need anything, but Emma's been right on top of the satisfaction scales."

His gaze thickens. The edges of his mouth become perfect parentheses for his shit-eating leer. "Satisfaction." He rubs a thumb along his lower lip. "Oh, I've no doubt about that...but really look forward to hearing about it from Miss Crist in greater detail. *Much* greater."

BOLT

PART 2

CHAPTER ONE

REECE

I'm not really a "meetings" guy.

I prefer to log most of my hours in the office during the late afternoons and nights, trusting that the leadership team of the Brocade, my family's high-end hotel in downtown Los Angeles, have been hired wisely for the jobs they know how to do well. If the numbers in everyone's reports add up to the results for which we're aiming, why have a meeting to micromanage the issue? I'd rather get to the good stuff: rewarding them for the jobs they've done well.

But right now, "micromanaging" has a nice ring to it.

A *damn nice* ring.

Almost as nice as the faint chimes in my ears as I wave goodbye to Neeta Jain, the manager of the hotel's night crew, adding a crisp nod to indicate she can shut the door on her way out...

Effectively locking me inside the room with the manager to whom the space belongs.

Emmalina Crist.

The woman who, just a few nights ago, had me silently comparing her to a velveteen bunny.

So now, am I caging myself in with the killer version of that bunny?

Holy fuck, I hope so. Especially after the night I've just had. *Dinner with a friend?* That's got to be the tritest gloss-over of the century, but no way in hell am I about to confess the truth to the woman for whom I've fallen like a chunk of hail out of a bulging rain storm. What Emma and I have is as new as a blown glass vase that hasn't even cooled yet. Informing her I went to dinner with my ex, in all of Angelique La Salle's most sultry blond glory, would be like lobbing gravel at the vase.

And trying to explain that I had no choice? That Angelique would've made life progressively worse if I hadn't sucked it up and gone to her? Screw the gravel and start with the river stones—which might as well have come from the River Styx in hell, since that's what a meal with the bitch had felt like. That's not such a departure from the truth, considering the woman betrayed me to a gang of scientific madmen and their electronic torture chamber.

So, "friend" might be stretching it. Juuussst a bit.

I'm ready to forget that now. To put Angelique—and even all those dark months—far behind me. To forget even my superhero style fuck you to the Consortium. As lousy as that'll be for business, it might even do the city some good. Maybe the criminals around here will slither back into their holes instead of attempting fuckery in the name of superstardom.

Fate has offered me something so much better to focus on. Beauty. *This* beauty. The woman willing to hand me her truth straight, even if that story includes her backed-in-a-corner glare as she secures herself behind the desk.

She points at her monitor, now swiveled sideways atop the desk, and then at the chair Neeta just occupied. "You'll be able to see all the reports from there. I'll stay back here."

"If that's the way you want it." I say it with confidence

because I mean it—and because she doesn't. She just doesn't know it yet. She still wants to deal with me from her corner. Still insists on putting *me* in a corner. The idea of me, at least. I'm still her safe little box of an explanation—*the billionaire bad boy and his little temporary toy*—and maybe that's not a bad thing. Maybe, ironically, the notoriety of the man I used to be is going to serve a greater purpose of all. Keeping her emotions at a safe distance.

Because I sure as hell don't know where *my* boundaries about this shit went.

Or if they ever existed to begin with.

Just like they're nonexistent now.

I soak up the beauty of her every move as she composes herself in her chair again. A long swallow makes its way down the side of her neck not covered by her cute side ponytail—just before a flush suffuses her in the opposite direction. I have to consciously put my self-control back on line not to lift a wicked grin. *Fuck.* Her face is so damn gorgeous when it turns that shade of pink. All too quickly, it reminds me of how other parts of her body blush so beautifully too...

"How far back would you like to see these reports?" Her voice is crisp and corporate, adorably serious about the reason I've pretended to come see her—which she's *got* to see as the pathetically thin excuse it really is. *Of course she does...*

My smile inches up a little more. Of *course* she does, and the little minx is just playing with me.

Unless she isn't.

My smirk fades.

Seriously? Does she really think the façade will snap me back to some hidden straight-and-narrow?

If that's the case...why deflate her? The executive

efficiency is ten kinds of turn-on, even causing me to reach and adjust the angle of my cock while she looks to her screen, whisking the little pointer around. "I've managed to get the guest-feedback sheets cataloged going back six months. My goal is to input everything for a year so we can detect trends and throw training toward areas in which we need the most improvement. That being said, I've already noticed a few interesting trends. What?"

She issues the question when finally looking up for my feedback, only to see I'm actively listening. My elbows are on the chair's armrests, and my hands are steepled in front of my chest.

That being said, I'm not going to dick around with pretty words. She deserves better. My truth. At least as much of it as I can give.

"You know I *do* care about those reports, right?"

Her smile blasts through me like an angel visiting hell. "Now I do. Thank you."

And I'm the demon lurking in the caves of that Hades. Why not? I've just been there for two goddamned hours, right? If the metaphor fits... "But you also know I didn't come down here to go over them right now."

She stops the cursor on the screen before slipping her hand away. She notices that *I* notice and clamps her opposite hand over it. "Haven't you had a long night already, Mr. Richards?" Her composure approaches electric aura status on its own as she zips a gaze over me. I can't quite read the source of the energy, either. Nervousness? Fury? Arousal? All three? I'm not sure I even want to know. The mystery is a bigger turn-on than her professional primness. "I mean, seeing how you're all decked out," she babbles, now twisting her hands together.

"Decked out?"

"Yes." She drops her hands while giving me another fast but lusty once-over. Dear fuck, what her attention does to every inch of me... "It's all...more than your usual, I mean," she goes on. "Your tie is so symmetrical, I bet you redid it a few times. That's different product in your hair. It's sleek but stiff, like you didn't want to have to worry about it. You're wearing stiffer shoes. My guess is, they hurt."

Blink. Again. "Yeah. They do."

She blinks as well, though her look is a knowing preen. "Like I said...long night."

For a moment, I don't say anything. It's not necessary when I can boomerang her attitude back, hitching my smirk along for the ride. "Why don't you let me be the judge of how *long* I want to go tonight, Miss Crist?"

Her breath snags. Her cheeks flush, hot and red, as she recognizes how my entendre has just turned the air between us into sensual smoke. I feel my forked tail flicking, my sharp horns growing.

She surges to her feet, bashing me with a tidal wave of the same energy, though one look in her eyes shows me there's an opposite motion in her mind and heart. I should be feeling a thousand kinds of shitty for knocking her on her figurative ass, but right now I've become too obsessed with her real-life backside.

And how sexy-as-fuck she looks, bending over to let me see it better.

And how adorable she is, a bold challenge stamped on her face, as she kicks off one shoe and then the other.

And how astounding she is, with the bottom half of her pinstriped pantsuit already unbuttoned, unzipped, and peeled off.

She glowers at me while draping the garment across her chair and propping one hand on her waist. "Is this what you mean by specifics?"

She marches around the desk, sending a vibe of determined sensuality that damn near turns my dick into an artisan pretzel. I grunt, the arousal growing from mild distraction to full-on attention, as she strides closer.

"Wasn't my original intent, but..."

"No?" She parks her hands on her hips.

"No." I gulp, fighting to string two logical thoughts together. "I missed you, Velvet. That was seriously it—until the last ninety seconds."

I force-feed the calm into it. Not an easy task. She's making this an impossible discussion to win, though I understand the intent beneath her accusation. There's been no opportunity to clarify things between us in the last couple of days, especially since I've made it a point to stay out of the fray and let the team do their jobs handling the huge tour group. So now, our interpretation of "teamwork" up in suite 6969—that irony isn't lost on me—has likely been hitting her with what-the-fuck-did-I-just-do-with-my-boss intensity.

In more ways than one.

Shit.

She shifts closer, making it possible for me to see the trimmed strip of hair beneath the panel at her crotch. She's not naked, but I crave her like she is. I'm harder than I've ever been with any woman before. Every seasoned seductress I've ever been with...was like eating water crackers compared to the hunger I feel for Emma Crist's nectar.

"So, what do you want now, then?"

I plant my feet more squarely and drape both arms along the chair's armrests. Six months of being locked down on a lab table doesn't make it easy for me to relax beneath anyone's control, but I sense she needs the surrender from me now. Maybe, if I'm lucky, I can even enjoy the fruits of my generosity.

"Hmmm. Why don't *you* supply the answer to that, Velvet?"

Her head tilts. The long gold braid points toward her cleavage. "In what way?"

I breathe in again, letting her gaze linger over the rising tent in my pants. "In any way you like."

She steps closer. I gorge my stare on her curvy, creamy glory and groan as my cock revels in the sight too. My erection is now as painful as it looks, but no way do I want to be anywhere else but right here, right now. My outburst coaxes Emma's stare down. A savoring smile kicks up one side of her lips. God*damn*. A little power looks a whole lot of *good* on this woman.

"Mr. Richards," she finally murmurs.

"Miss Crist."

She tosses her head, flipping her ponytail from the front to back of her shoulder—and twenty more switches of my lust at the same time. It's a playful move, signaling she enjoys the reins I've handed over. The heat in her eyes is the color of burning glass.

I twist my fingers tight around the chair's arms. I slide my hips forward. I clench my teeth. My psyche still isn't comfortable with the change in guard, but my cock and balls don't seem to notice one damn bit.

"All right, then." She comes in a little closer. "Perhaps we can just skip the bullshit."

I feel my stare constrict. "Skip...the..."

"Bullshit." Her echo, and its nod of punctuation, is succinct and sexy. "You know what I'm talking about. The mush. The pretties. The orchids on the appetizer plate. On second thought, why don't we just ditch the appetizer altogether?"

"Uhhhh..." I grunt as she parts her legs, straddling me. The sound becomes a new groan as she leans in to kiss me with heated, hungry sensuality, sliding her tongue along mine in savoring, lingering possession. Jesus *God*. This woman, and how she just *knows* how to kiss me...

When we break apart, both breathing heavier than before, she delves a hand into my hair and twists hard. "I want to be mad at you."

"Why?"

"Because I shouldn't want this so badly." She pushes in, eyes closing as she drops her forehead to mine. "I...shouldn't want *you* so badly."

"You mean the way I want you?" I press meaning into the verb despite my guttural grate. "The way I *need* you? Christ. Emma. *Emma.*" My growl trembles up from the farthest reaches of my being as I slide both hands beneath her blouse, savoring the contact with her warm, soft, pliant skin.

Emma emits a shuddering sigh. Breathes back in on hitching breaths. "I have to feel wrong about this."

"I know."

"But I can't feel anything but right."

"I know." I drag her tighter against me. "God*damn.* Emmalina..."

Her damp, warm triangle fits like a custom key against my crotch, unlocking rooms of arousal in my psyche. No. More than that. If I really am this city's superhero, she's my secret weakness. The crack in my shield. The stone to topple my tower. The enchantress driving me to my knees.

Yeah, this very second.

Yeah, to the point that I want to show her that completely... control be damned.

Yeah, as in I suddenly push the chair backward, making it possible to drop to my haunches before her.

Yeah, backing it up by grabbing her ass cheeks to steady her and force her sex against my nose. Her lower body is now in my power. Her armor cracks before my eyes.

Fuck. Yes.

Maybe this power swap isn't all one way after all.

"Oh!" She blurts it as I inhale her sexy essence. *Ambrosia.* She's musky honey and silken sweetness, making my mouth water all over the satin triangle. "Oh. Ahhhhh. *Ohhhhh.*"

Her sounds are a symphony of desire playing at crescendo level over her limbs and skin, making her muscles bunch beneath my hands. "Yes." I say it aloud, turning it into a commanding rasp along the seam of her panties. "*Yes*, little Velvet."

"Unnnnhh." She bucks her hips, making it easier to slide my tongue beneath the fabric. "Reece. *Reece.* Wh-What...are you—"

"Enjoying my meal." I savor the vibration of each syllable on her flesh as equally as her reactions. Beneath my questing mouth, she trembles and clenches, shivers and shakes, sighs and gasps. "You did tell me to have at it, beauty."

"This... This wasn't exactly what I..." She trails off, obviously forgetting her words and intention.

"Wasn't exactly what you what?" I don't refrain from the goad, even smirking when she snarls in retort. "What you had in mind when you told me to skip to the good stuff?" I reach in, pulling back the satin triangle, revealing the feast of her secret flesh. "Because Velvet, this *is* the good stuff."

"But...I..."

"Ssshhh. I'm going to enjoy this."

But she only lets me lick a couple of times before protesting, "This isn't...*ahhhh!*"

"Isn't what?" I grin, totally alpha dog about it, before daring to nibble along her labia. Her little yelp makes the gamble worth it.

She jerks, fighting my ironclad grip on her thigh. "This *isn't* the damn meal."

"Then what is it?"

"This is *you*, making *me*..." She huffs, becoming even more irresistible. "It's... It's—"

"Dessert?" I get in a couple more bites to her pussy. *Christ.* She's so succulent. So wet. So pink and lush and enticing. "I'm fine with that. Doesn't everyone like skipping to dessert?"

"But—"

"Ssshhh."

"But—"

"*Hush.*"

Technically, her throaty mewl isn't complete compliance— but it's a damn fine substitute. The sound splices the air *and* my bloodstream as I curl in my tongue, unsheathing her sweetest button from its protective hood. The second I touch down on the stiff bundle at her core, she cries out again. I give her more wicked suckles. Her knees give out. I'm ready with my supporting weight.

"Oh, my God..."

I don't bother demanding her silence now. I simply guide

her into place, directing one of her hands to the desktop and her opposite leg over my shoulder. "I've got you, Bunny," I vow against her pubic bone. "I promise." And before I can help myself, I'm widening my mouth across her mons and plunging my tongue back into her tangy fruit. *Yes.* Fuck. *Ambrosia isn't even the right word anymore.* "Lean in, baby. Let go. I've got you."

For one incredible second, she does. The rush of her weight, her *trust*, is nearly as good as plunging my dick deep into her channel, and my body tells me so by spurting precome into my briefs. I groan from the perfect torment, a sound she takes in all the wrong ways.

"But... But who's got *y-you*?"

Her voice quavers along with her clit, aroused but unsure, as if I've levitated her clear off the floor. She's sure as hell already done that to my senses—and the stiffening rod in my pants seems ready to jump on board with a similar plan. *Levitation for everyone. Fuck, yes.*

"Let me worry about that." I drive it into her wet folds as a command, giving her no option but obedience. Though a strained sound grits through her teeth, her muscles soften beneath my hold. She twists a hand into the back of my scalp and digs her heel into the center of my spine.

"Ohhhhh. Nooooo." Her moans are throaty but high as I greedily tongue her succulent slit, bottom to top and back again, dotting the movement with a determined stab into her tight hole. But not all the way in. Not yet. That moment's coming—and just thinking about it, I'm helpless to hold back my dick from leaking more. It's torture and rapture in the same erotic moment. Nearly unbelievable. Is this going to happen? Is this woman going to make me explode in my pants just from the honor of devouring her gorgeous cunt? She's the juiciest fruit I've ever opened. The sweetest dessert I've ever savored. The most breathtaking woman I've ever pleasured.

It doesn't even matter that I'm not inside her. In so many terrifying ways, she's already inside me.

"Try a new one, Velvet," I growl into her sexy seam. "Try giving me a gorgeous 'yesssss.'"

She obliges the humor in my tone with a warm tug at my hair but comes nowhere near complying with my suggestion. Which really wasn't a suggestion. I communicate that with a fast bite to the inside of her leg.

"Oh!"

"Don't you mean 'oh, *yes*'?"

"You have got to be kid— *Oh!*" Another bite, this time to the top edge of her clit, makes her jerk back by a couple of inches. I don't let her get farther than that. "Oh my hell," she rasps. "Oh my—oh *Reece...*"

It's not the first time in my life a woman has panted those words to me—so why does it feel like the first? Why am I zapped with awe I've never felt, surged with more power than I've ever celebrated? The logical grab is there in front of me, that my cock has been so direly neglected for a solid year it's now leading the parade for the rest of me, but that's the desperate—and inaccurate—way out. This singular desire, for this sole woman... It's more than drought-recovery dramatics.

But how much more?

I'm not the same man I was a year ago. Angelique's "friends" altered the color of my eyes. The length of my legs. The resiliency of my muscles. The chemistry of my blood. How much of me is *me* anymore—and is *that* the part falling so completely for this woman? Or are all these sensations courtesy of the new me, the phoenix from the ashes? If that's the case, what do I even know about him or what he's able to give a woman like Emmalina?

A woman who wants more. Who deserves more. Who deserves everything.

An everything neither part of me will be able to give her in the long run. Because eventually, if all goes according to plan, I'll be dead.

But right here, right now? Giving her ultimate pleasure? Working my lips to untwist the most mind-shattering climax she's ever known?

That I can do.

That, at least, hasn't been electroshocked out of my consciousness.

I summon it all back to my will. Use every erotic trick in my wheelhouse to bloom her, spread her, arouse her. I even slick my tongue across her with new flicks and strokes, emboldened by her mewls, moans, and prompts. The more responses she gives, the more engrossed I become. My world becomes the heady trembles of her thighs, the lush opera of her breaths, and the perfect vibrations of her cunt, enticing me to explore deeper...deeper...

As I do, it's making my cock harder. *Harder.*

"Holy. *Shit.*"

A stream of her honey fills my mouth. Yeah. *Fuck.* So damn good.

"Reece!"

She blurts the protest after trying to pull away, but I yank her even closer. With my hands cupped to her backside, I'm able to hide my glowing fingertips in the crack of her ass. Double win? The motion spreads her sex from behind, warming her pussy for the new invasion I'm about to launch.

As she keens a little higher, I moan a little deeper. Her thighs bunch and buck. Her ass squeezes and squirms.

"I-I thought you wanted to fuck me."

"Oh, I did," I growl. "And I *will*."

I feel the conflict take over her—possibly preparing for me to stand up, slam her to the desk, and ram into her. And yes, ramming *does* happen, courtesy of my tongue in her tightness, spearing her without pause or remorse or hesitance. Holy hell, she's delicious. I could fuck into her like this for another hour. Two. Three. All goddamned night.

And maybe I will...

She fists my hair. Her grip slips on the desk. Pens, papers, and a tumbler of water crash onto her chair as her gasp shudders the air.

I don't relent. Not for a second.

She needs this.

I can feel it in every inch of the plush walls clamping over my tongue, urging me farther inside her trembling, tight body.

I need this.

My cock, getting relentless friction from the trap of my pants, broadcasts the update with throbbing clarity. My balls second the motion, ignoring my efforts at readjustment. It's no longer a matter of *if* for those fuckers; it's a matter of *when*— though I'm pretty sure of the answer to that query already.

I'll blow when she does.

And fuck, how she does.

"Oh...gah!" Her voice is shaky and hoarse. Her body is tense and trembling. Her pussy is hot and soaked. "Oh, Reece. I'm...I'm..."

Her words dissolve as her body takes over, communicating

the rest. The second she throbs around me, drenching my tongue with the cream of her climax, my balls blast an inescapable fire up my cock. I explode too, horrified but a little giddy. I've come like a wild teenager—from the bliss of bringing *her* pleasure.

It feels good. So fucking good. And unsettling. And terrifying. So much so, I'm frozen in place for a long moment.

Fuck.

I just got off—literally—by putting someone else's needs before mine. This isn't a shred of anything I recognize, not even a drop in the ocean in which Lawson Richards taught me to survive a long damn time ago. On Dad's ship, only one motto mattered. *Every man for himself.* The patriarch himself values it so much, it's why I haven't been blackballed from the family altogether. Secretly, my douchebag rebellion pleased the bastard. I possessed the spine neither Chase nor Tyce had ever seemed to grow—which, before my spectacular fall, was probably why I took the behavior to such epic heights.

Or was it?

If my life hadn't wound down this exact path, I never would have arrived here at the most extraordinary epiphany of my existence. At a moment that is making more sense than all twenty-seven years before it. At the feet of the person who's brought me here.

The woman for whom I've fallen. Literally. Wholly.

The creature who crumples gently to the floor with me now, shuddering in the last throes of her climax, sagging into my arms with kitten-like surrender. I swear she starts to purr as I circle soft fingertips along the back of her neck, their soft glow illuminating the stray strands of her ponytail. With a resolved breath, I'm able to dial back the lightsabers of my fingers even more. Only my nailbeds pulse now in time to my heartbeat. I work on calming that pace, but it isn't easy with her face consuming my attention...and the satisfaction of knowing I alone brought that sated serenity to her incredible face.

After a few minutes of our peaceful silence, she releases a long, soft breath. "Mr. Richards?"

"Yes, Miss Crist?"

"We have to stop meeting like this."

"Couldn't agree more."

Her eyes flash open. Her pupils are huge and aqua—and alarmed. "Really?" A new flush takes over her face. She hastily clears her throat. "I mean, of course you agree." She sweeps a look over her nude lower half. "This *is* getting kind of ridiculous."

"Agreed once more." I feel shitty for leading her thoughts on, but only a little. Sometimes the endgame justifies the play. Only by throwing her off guard can I pry more edges from her armor, exposing her to see—and feel—the importance of what we've begun here. The undeniable significance of this connection. This electrofusion... "I'd even say it's gone beyond ridiculous."

"Well." She stiffens and attempts to straighten. "That's good, then—"

"Oh, I wouldn't call it good."

"Pardon me?"

I wrap an arm around her waist, preventing her from completing her frosty escape. I melt the rest of her iceberg with a thorough kiss, not letting go until she opens for the dominion of my tongue. By the time I pull back, she clearly craves more. Good. She doesn't get any quarter from my gaze, which I keep latched to her while spreading my other hand along the back of her head.

"Yeah," I utter, my breath ragged. "Beyond ridiculous. Which means you don't get to bring any reports or furniture dusters next time."

"Huh?" Her eyes flare. I'm torn between grinning at her and just kissing her again. "Wait. *Next* ti—"

"Which will *not* be two nights from now. As a matter of fact, I won't settle for *one* night."

Her brows crunch. "Reece, what are you—"

I kiss her into silence. It's quick and fast this time because my point isn't complete. "What am I?" I counter. "What I *am*, Emmalina, is fed up with this. With us and our treatment of this."

"This?"

"Yes."

"This...what?"

"This. *Us.*"

Her armor breaks away a little more. She quirks her lips upward, and her eyes shimmer like we're standing in full sun. "There's...an 'us'?"

Hearing her repeat the word drops a massive weight on my chest—with only one possible phrase to set myself free. "There is now."

Yeah. *Oh, yeah.* That *is* perfect. And so fucking right.

In my new lightness, I tenderly brush my lips across hers. "But that doesn't mean we have to define anything beyond now." The honey of her mouth is so damn tempting. "No projections or forecasts. No definitions or boxes. Nobody telling us what we are or aren't. Just this. Just the magic. Just the fusion. Just us, okay?"

She releases a high, soft sigh. "Okay."

"But that also means one more thing." I tug her hair harder, enforcing her attention. "I refuse to fuck you on another floor, footstool, or any other furniture not designed for being naked and horizontal."

She curves her lips again. *So goddamned gorgeous.* "Okay."

I tug again. Her amenability makes me want to push my luck. "So when you get off shift tomorrow morning, you're coming straight up to the penthouse."

Her grin grows. "Okay."

"And you're letting me make you breakfast."

Here's where her grin fades—though not enough to make me stressed. Not yet. "Breakfast." She cocks her head. "So is that before or after the naked and horizontal part?"

I kiss her again. I can't help it. Resisting her is like denying myself the privilege of breathing. There's tongue involved too. Lots of it. And hair pulling—hers *and* mine. And groping, twenty fingers' worth, as we feel and fondle and grab and possess, sealing the new bond between us in the most primal, perfect way possible.

CHAPTER TWO

EMMA

I emerge from my office, but I'm still in a fog. A giant, pink-tinted bank of the stuff—and for once, I don't fight. I'm like one of those cartoon girls with birds and stars swirling around my head—or in the anime version, with my pupils turned into bulging hearts. Maybe that's a good thing. If everyone's gawking at my eyes, they won't notice my knees have turned to taffy—another write-off, considering I don't need them anymore.

Knees aren't important when a girl can just float through life.

Okay, not *Life*, capital *L*. It's only *life* right now, all lowercase. It's not like Reece marched into my office and shut and locked the door with a ring in his hand.

Though the man did show how magical he can be on his knees...

And incredible. And passionate. And giving. And bold.

Stealing my breath. Demanding my surrender. Blowing my mind.

Yeah, even now. *Especially* now.

The comprehension has me gripping the frosted-glass countertop at the front desk for support. I actually glance down, confirming I'm still truly planted on terra firma, though the pastel cloud still lingers. The stratosphere into which

Reece Richards launched me with the power of one word.

"Us."

I run a finger along my lips after whispering it. I can feel the contact, meaning this must really be my life. Not a dream. Not a bizarre alternate world in which Reece Richards isn't a tabloid darling and a world-class rogue and hasn't just sneaked out of the executive offices in the back elevator with a dorky smirk on his lips and my Pentatonix tour sweatshirt tied around his waist—hiding the crotch he's just soaked while pleasuring me.

Holy *wow*, that pleasure. Right before he brought on the wizardry. The sincerity. The honesty.

The word that changed everything.

"Us." I dash it off again, almost in a song, while clicking into the guest-services log from one of the front-desk terminals. Fershan is also at the desk, though he's talking on the phone at the other end. Observing the lobby is busier than usual, probably due to the bored tour group members deciding to drink their night away in the bar, I stay put in case he needs any backup. Besides, a good song starts playing. A classic. My spirit as buoyant as the tune, I start quietly singing along with the anthem.

"I got me a Chrysler, it seats about twenty, so hurry up and bring your—"

"*Excusez-moi, mademoiselle?*"

I shut off my metaphorical microphone somewhere between "jukebox" and "money" before stammering, "Yes? I mean, good evening, ma'am. I'm so sorry. I was pulling something up, and then—"

"Singing?" The blonde, a stunning mix of classic Catherine Deneuve and Gwen Stefani, adds to the exotic factor with her French accent. I gawk a little longer as she lifts one side of her flawless crimson mouth in a droll smile. "What would the world be without songs, *n'est-ce pas*?"

"Valid point." My response is polite but guarded. Why is this creature, in her black cashmere dress and red-to-black ombré fingernails, making my skin prickle and my instincts edgy? Okay, besides the obvious—that she's worldly, sophisticated, and oozes more sexuality from one of those tapered fingers than I do in my whole body. This is the case for nearly half the women I meet up here, so that doesn't fly in this instance. There's something else about her. An aloofness but a watchfulness...

"How can I be of service to you this evening, *Madame*—"

"*Mademoiselle*"—she dips her head, smoothly deferential about the correction—"La Salle." A smooth arc of her hand produces a business card that wasn't there two seconds ago. The engraved header gives away her first name. *Angelique*.

Of course.

A name evoking the heavens for a woman who could tempt a dozen monks to sin. At the same time.

"International Commodities." I read the next line down. The only other text on the card is her phone number, prefaced by the international dialing code. There's no company name or her specific position in that organization—though for some reason, I'm anxious to find out. Or perhaps she makes me anxious, period. "Sounds...cosmopolitan."

"In a manner of speaking."

"What kind of commodities, if I may be so bold?"

"Collectibles." Her tone remains impassive. "Rare finds. Objects of wonder. Works of art." She moves at last, angling an elbow up to the counter, drawing out the last of it with curious vocal emphasis. *Worksss of arrrt.* All too clearly, I realize she isn't talking about Renaissance busts and oil paintings of virgins getting pounced by devils—though this makes me feel exactly like one of those maidens, gazing toward a heaven that doesn't care about the Lucifer about to rape her.

And did I seriously just go there?

This is what I get for skipping my protein bar and yogurt to let the boss feast on *me.* My brain's turned cannibal on itself, eating valuable logic links. But a logic deficit is still no reason to be rude.

"So how may I assist you, Mademoiselle La Salle?" Again, I take in her ensemble. The cashmere is luxurious and fits her toned curves flawlessly. She wears no accessories except for diamond drop earrings so brilliant they must be real. More bling flashes from her feet, adorned in a pair of peep-toe platforms with black insets. "Ground transportation, perhaps?" I dare a between-us-girls grin. "You haven't dressed up like this for the crowd in the bar. Who's the lucky guy you're going to meet?"

Her laugh is an elegant husk. "You mean...already *have* met."

"Ohhh." My voice rises knowingly. "That explains a great deal."

"*Comment ça?* A great deal of what?"

"Of everything." I nod toward her. "Here in LA, we call it your vibe...your energy. The French probably have a more melodic term."

"*Je ne sais quoi?*"

"Sounds about right." I'm able to smile and mean it, but when she responds with nothing but a silken silence, I'm once more the gawky nerd trying to chat it up with the prom queen.

"Well, then. It's clear that you're a woman who enjoyed her evening, at least."

"Hmmm." She leans a little closer, still looking like a cat contemplating a bowl of cream, until I even get the impression she's smelling me. "That depends on how you define enjoyable." Her gaze, wide and inquisitive as a Siamese, lifts to my blushing face. "Perhaps *you* have had some 'enjoyment' tonight as well, my friend?"

Heat floods my face. The woman's smile widens. I wave a dismissive hand. "I'm...working."

"Hmmm," she drawls again, one perfect brow arching. "Of course." She smoothly folds one hand atop the other and rests them on the counter, the move of a feline Bond girl in one of those scenes where you don't know if she's a good girl or a killer. "So I am just...imagining...that interesting scent of yours, then?"

I'm validated but weirded out in the same strange moment. She *is* sniffing. "I only wear light body spray to work. Maybe that's strange in your circles, but it's common courtesy in mine."

"Ah. Of course." She backs away, dipping her head. "*Désolée.* I meant no intrusion. It is only that..."

"What?" I'm more irritated than interested now. The only creature fascinated by a cat's string is the cat—except her teaser has a chunk of psychological Godiva tied to the end. I only hope the chocolate isn't laced with arsenic.

"*C'est rien.*" She quirks another half smile. Zero sincerity backs the look. "It is nothing."

I return the look, probably with more gusto than I should. Hanging with the high-end circles of the OC, where every pretentious person irked me, I honed that skill to perfection.

Kill 'em with kindness—and if kindness isn't possible, fake it. "So how *did* you need our services tonight, mademoiselle?"

"Ah." She dashes a finger up, and I almost expect to see a reminder string tied to it. Instead, she opens her graphic-print Balenciaga and produces a pair of items much nicer than string. The cufflinks are simple but luxurious, squares of silver inset with black diamonds. They're the kind of thing a man would never buy for himself but would wear with pride if given from a special woman.

"Ah." I repeat it with meaning—and more than a little relief. Deneuve has a weak spot after all. "These are stunning."

"*Merci.*"

"And the man for whom they're intended?" I go there, but with care in my voice.

"Equally as stunning."

Just like that, my relief disappears—though I don't return to unnerved either. I'm confused. Maybe a little weirded out. Her words don't match the vibe from her eyes. *Je ne sais quoi* has gone *au revoir*.

"Unfortunately, we were caught up in a...discussion. He left them behind in the car."

"Well." I try to focus on my monitor, clicking to the in-house guest registry instead of gawking at her mysterious expression. No luck. She's riveting, but not in a fun way. Not a trace of a smile touches her lips, though her longing is a palpable force on the air. "That must have been an epic discussion."

"They usually are with him."

It's none of your business, Emma. Mademoiselle La Salle and I have already skated on the edge of too much information with each other.

"And his last name?" There. Cordial but impartial, likely

what she's been after this whole time anyway. "So I can call up to his room for you," I clarify. "Or, if you prefer, I can just store them in the hotel's safe and leave a message in his room."

Another win for professionalism—until the woman picks *that* moment to break the surface of her cream, erupting in a light laugh. "Room? Oh, he is not a *guest* in this hotel, *mon amie.*"

My face tightens into a scowl and a vise closes over my chest. "He...what?" I manage to ask, despite my instincts suddenly clicking and knowing what her response will be. And dreading it.

"*Non.*" The worldly smile slides into place. "He *owns* this hotel. You know him, *oui*? Monsieur Richards?"

I'm rocketed out of my fog, only to descend into another. A darker mist. No more cotton-candy clouds. Sherlockian gray and Jack the Ripper black are the new colors of my vision, shrouding my movements.

Somehow, I manage to make an excuse—more truth than *she* needs to know—that I'm suddenly not feeling well. I hand her off to Fershan and stumble away. *Far* away. A black corner. An empty office. Somewhere with space for my shock to choke out, the *shit-shit-shits* to fade, and the nausea to pass.

Or maybe not.

"Em? Dearie?"

Neeta finds me in the copy room, butt parked atop the shredder, head between my legs over an empty trashcan. Returning to my office is nowhere near an option, not after what I just did in there with Reece.

After what he did before *that* with Angelique La Salle.

Us.

His perfect spell of a word.

Did he use it with her too? Before or after she got him out of those cufflinks? Taking off the cufflinks meant she'd gotten him out of his shirt. I've never even seen the man without his shirt. But there I was just an hour ago, two offices away, letting him "us" me into visions of pink castles, swirly stars, and omelets cooked in his decadent designer kitchen.

The comprehension brings back the fog. And the sick.

"*Dearie.*" Neeta crouches next to me. Her voice is husky with concern. "What is it?"

"I don't know." Not a lie. Have I known Reece Richards at all? Were *naïve* and *desperate* plastered that clearly across my forehead this whole time? "It just hit me." I'm more sickened when realizing *his* lie from earlier in the week now provides my perfect alibi. "Maybe I never got rid of the other bug that bit me."

Neeta's features tighten. She shakes her head. "And both times, you had to spend time with Reece Richards."

I push out a long huff. "He's not a Zika mosquito, woman."

"But he's just as strange." She shakes her head. "Gorgeous but strange."

"I refuse to validate this conversation." That's the truth too—though it's also a convenient cut to the real issue at hand. "I... I think I just need to go home."

I need to be anywhere but here.

In an environment *he* can't control. A place where I can think.

More to the point—where I don't have to think at all.

"Of course." She starts, glancing at the clock. "But it's nearly eleven. Will you be all right on the train? Maybe I can spare Fersh or Wade to drive you..."

"The hell you can." I inwardly applaud myself for always

insisting Z drop me around the corner from the lobby. I also know he's already waiting in the same spot, which is perfect. My route to the train station is the opposite direction. But I don't care anymore. Or feel the need to answer to his "employer" about anything.

⚡

It's oddly comforting to ride the train again, especially at this time of night. Rush hour is long over, giving me space to breathe along with the comfort of anonymity. The roar of the cars on the tracks is perfect too—a fitting sparring partner for the rage of my senses, the tumult of my heart.

The Purple Line ends at Union Station, and I walk to the platform for the Gold Line with my head down and arms tucked in. It's a warm evening, with summer tickling the early June air, but I can't stop shivering. As much as I hate being cold, I welcome the chill. I don't want to be warm right now. Don't want to even think of the last time I was warm, just an hour ago.

A lifetime ago.

A heartbreak ago.

I'd been giggling at the sight of Reece's ass wrapped in my sweatshirt, along with his sheepish smirk. He'd asked how I'd like my eggs. I'd responded, "Hot and firm—like your fine backside, Mr. Richards."

He'd grinned like a loon and told me I'd earned champagne with breakfast too.

I wonder how Angelique likes her eggs. I wonder if she earns herself champagne too.

The train arrives. I stumble onto it as the tears hit again.

By the time I stop, I'm honking gobs of snot into a tissue—and realizing I've bawled my way through three stops. Going the wrong damn direction on the line.

After groaning in three different octaves, I glare up at the salsa ad mounted over the door. It features three parrots in mariachi outfits, complete with little ornate vests and sombreros. I can see the humiliation pouring out of their little birdy eyes. "Been that kind of a night for you guys too, eh?"

I hurry off at the next stop. The train pulls away, leaving me alone on the platform to wait for the line going the correct direction. Not entirely alone, if I count the family of opossums scuttling in the shadows next to the tracks.

A gust of night wind howls through the station. The chill in my bones seeps deeper, prompting me to head for the shelter of the empty exit stairway. It could be fifteen or twenty minutes before I see another train, and I miss my sweatshirt for more practical reasons now.

"Think warm." My mutter is low, rough, and miserable. "Think Palm Springs. Think hot bubble bath. Think Malibu in July."

Yeah. Malibu. My go-to for long afternoons with my beach chair, a book, and a can of Cactus Cooler. The drink is one of my guilty indulgences, a holdover of childhood memories before we moved to the land of green tea and vitamin water. Bright orange drink. Glittering blue ocean. Brilliant cyan sky. So bright, it hurt to look at the horizon. So bright and silver...

Like Reece's eyes.

No.

I refocus, thinking more about Malibu. The powerful rush of the waves countered by their gentle fizzle on the shore. Might and mist...

Like Reece's voice.

"*No*, damn it."

It's barely more than a grunt, but it echoes through the stairwell like a shout. In reply, the air just gives me more ghostly wind...

And then a quiet laugh.

And another one.

Arms still crossed, I whirl around and peer across the station. Still nothing but the opossums.

I whip back toward the stairway.

And come face-to-face with three leering gazes.

Men.

Okay, boys—though they swagger and stare and salivate like men, taking me in like a pack of hungry wolves surrounding a rabbit. I attempt a polite nod while backing away. All three of them step with me. One of them moves farther, sliding around to my other side.

"Good evening, gentlemen." I try to give them the benefit of a doubt. Who am I kidding? It's for my benefit too. I can't allow my fear to buy into the intentions I sense behind their eyes. It's true, right? What they say about predators being able to smell fear? With that thought in mind, I tuck a hand into my purse. "My hand is on my mace, so let's ensure I don't have to use it, all right?"

I'm so busy being calm, I never take a moment to tack on vigilant—demonstrated when my purse disappears off my arm. The whole thing is tossed across the stairwell except for the mace can, which flies twenty feet as the middle creep moves in, slamming me against the wall. He's also the largest, with sizable muscles under his track pants and plaid shirt.

"We'll show you how to use shit, all right." He slides a

greasy kiss to my cheek while the third guy scoots in, breaking open the fastening of my pants. My heart clutches and my breath halts as he uses the tip of a knife to slice the fabric open the rest of the way. "And if you're quiet and pretty, we won't have to show you how Freddie likes using his blade in other ways, either."

"She *is* pretty," the first one croons. "I like her, man."

"Bitch is gonna be good," says Freddie, twirling his knife. "I can tell. Called us gentlemen and everything. Hey, we should even use condoms."

Shit-shit-shit-shit.

Help-help-help-help!

The pleas pound my spirit in time to the frantic air that's cycling between my lungs and nostrils. The asshole handles the knife with enough fearless finesse that I know he's used it on human flesh before. That he won't hesitate to do the same right now. Wasting my strength begging for mercy isn't viable either. The guy's stare is jacked with enough insanity and arousal, I'm sure he'd enjoy my pleas—and my pain. He backs up the theory by barely flinching when his tall friend kicks him in the shin.

"Fuckface." The big one grunts. "We used our last ones on that little thing with the pink hair in Santa Monica last night."

"Ohhh yeah. Sorry, man. I was baked."

"Like you are right now?"

"Hmmm. Maybe."

"*Pffft.* That settles it." The first guy drops the front of his pants. "I get to go first. Freddie takes forever when he's high, and I'm not waiting this time."

"Yeah?" Freddie retorts. "And what did you have to lose? I nailed her good and hard. Lubed her for you, dickhead. Wasn't like we had to worry about Boltalicious poppin' outta the woodwork."

The comment primes my tears, making me acknowledge the thread of weird hope to which I've been clinging—that someone, anyone, will come along with both the guts and the force to prevent this from happening. But the Lone Ranger is just a comic book character, and *Boltalicious* is on his mysterious do-gooding break—meaning this *is* going to happen.

I squeeze my eyes shut, hoping it'll happen with me still in one piece at the end.

Too late.

Physically, I'm still whole. Mentally, I've already started to detach. *Survive*. The goal stamps on my mind, my beacon in the darkness of what these monsters prepare to do.

Tall Boy laughs, cinching my hands even tighter. He moves to the side, which angles his armpit over my face. I struggle not to breathe, an impossibility given the new force of my tears. Stenches assault my senses, each of the odors at least three days old. Grease, motor oil, sweat, pot—and those are the elements I *can* identify. A few others are nasty mysteries, for which I'd likely be grateful if I could feel anything except terror. "Ha. Good one, cuz," he says. "Boltalicious. That shitpile's as ragged as a wad of chewing gum anyhow."

"Pretty on the outside, gooey on the inside?" The creep still playing with his penis drawls it.

"If *I* ever got to mix it up with the guy? Shit yeah. I'd expose that hustler for what he really is. Penny pranks, special effects, and low-budget magic tricks."

He pauses, but only for a second. Encouraged by his friends' snickers, the asshole clearly has more to say.

Until he doesn't.

The air is blasted, sucked, and moved around us with such violence, all four of us are toppled to the concrete floor like a rug has been yanked from under us.

Whomp. The guy who was just pinning me is slammed back up against the wall. His arms and legs splay out, pinned in place by giant invisible thumbtacks. That's the only way I can describe it. The asshole squirms, fighting bonds that aren't there, incredulous shock claiming his face just before a wet splotch appears at the front of his jeans.

The force of nature that put him there steps out of the shadows surrounding the tracks.

A badass in black leather. Hybrid ninja boots. Maserati mask. Lips curled in fury.

"Abracadabra, motherfuckers."

REECE

Thank fuck this isn't one of those gigs requiring me to get it right on the first try. Because right now, I'm a superhero with completely screwed alignment. As in, enraged-to-the-point-of-impaired screwed.

After three failed attempts that resulted in two of the three jerkwads bonking around the station like pinballs at the mercy of a maniac, I finally succeed at my original intent—knocking them together hard enough to land them in the same unconscious heap. That being done, and after vowing to send a check to LA Metro as penance for crashing them into five lights, two vending machines, and several support pillars, I wait for the calm to settle in. I force deep breaths in. Back out. Concentrate on loosening my fists. No use. Fuck me.

I raise my head, getting a glimpse of myself in one of the chrome tube railings, and am stunned I'm not the color of glowing broccoli. On paper, my reaction makes sense—but the daggers chopping up my gut aren't garden-variety fear. This shit is terror, stark and sick, spawned the moment I got back to the penthouse and obeyed a gut instinct to check the security cams in the executive office hallways. Watching Emma all but crawl out of the copier room while leaning into a clearly concerned Neeta pricked my first alarm. The shit clanged to five alarms once I clicked to the front-desk feed—in time to watch Angelique making nicey-nice with Fershan Bennett.

Angelique. Goddamnit.

The bitch from hell who dared to enter my turf. That refined smile on her lips...and my cufflinks in her hand.

Those fucking cufflinks.

Yeah, the ones I haven't been able to even look at for a year, so deep and Pavlovian is their hold on my memory. On my fear...

Fear not rising to half of what struck when I comprehended the scope of Angelique's game—resulting in Emma leaving her shift and fleeing the Brocade.

Running from me.

In the middle of the damn night. In the heart of downtown LA. Into the very situation I've been paying Zalkon to help avoid. But this isn't his fault. This is my shit to own. My mess to fix after thinking a neutral meeting with Angelique wouldn't end up with the woman trying to keep me on her hook, no matter how dirty her tactics.

Like showing up at the front desk of my own damn hotel and smearing that dirt on the one person who never deserved it.

Garbage I'll have to clear from my life another day.

Right now, I've got other nonrecyclables to worry about.

Fortunately, two of those chunks are down for the next few minutes. Now to deal with the Grand Poobah trash daddy.

"What the *hell*?" the blow stick yells. I let him dangle, getting a firsthand taste of my "penny pranks" with his ass still flattened to the wall. Indulging a sadistic streak, I focus another electric pulse south of his waistline. He screeches as I push the energy harder, crushing his balls like a device in a BDSM dungeon, turning his erection into a raisin. "Wh-What are you doing?" he gasps. "Come *on*, man. Th-That's my *junk*, dude!"

"Couldn't have said it any better myself, *dude*." I twist my wrist the other way, giving his nads a new spin on the Blue Balls Tilt-A-Whirl. "Stop whining. You'll be back to normal in two or three weeks."

"Two or three *weeks*?"

I shrug. "Give or take. Though, keep sticking that shit into places it's not welcome, and I'll be back up your ass, turning it into permanent pieces for the county scrap heap." Finally, I yank back the magnetic field, letting him crumple to the floor and tuck into full fetal. "We copasetic on that?" When all I receive is a hurried nod, I take a step closer. "Sorry. Speak a little louder. We 'hustlers' have shitty hearing."

"Yeah," he finally grits. "We're copasetic."

I nod, though I'm hardly relaxed. Now the difficult part of the night. Turning to Emmalina—and communicating Reece's message using *Bolt's* persona.

As soon as I face her, I'm shocked but not shocked. Yeah, this is going to be hell to pull off—but for reasons I hadn't foreseen even from miles away.

As always, her beauty temporarily sucks out my breath. Even now, with her hair a brilliant tangle, her cheeks streaked with makeup, and the front of her pants slashed open, she mesmerizes me in ways I can't describe. Flips exclusive buttons. Wakes primitive urges of possessiveness. I want to haul her close. Inhale her until I breathe nothing else. Kiss her senseless and then ban her from ever taking the goddamn train again.

Not a possibility anymore—but not because of the façade I have to keep up. Because of all the shields *she's* had to drop and her estrangement from the creature she's bared. A woman who gapes at me, eyes as wide as always, but in fear instead of wonder. Who trembles in a rush of night wind but recognizes her chill extends far beneath her skin's surface. Who opens her mouth, trying to form words, but only croaks helplessly—and clearly hates herself for it.

Lost, and visually pleading with me for answers, she closes the distance between us with three faltering steps. As she grabs onto me, red-rimmed stare not leaving me, she rasps two words that stab to the center of my gut.

"You're...real."

I nod, wondering why I suddenly feel like the mirage to her desert traveler. But I'm not the one who vanishes. Her eyes roll to the back of her head, and she goes unconscious in my arms.

With a soft, sublime smile on her face.

CHAPTER THREE

EMMA

I'm smiling.

I know it before I even open my eyes.

It's puzzling, because I know I'm not even in my own bed—*am I even in a bed?*—though right now, none of the "important" details seem to matter. I feel like I'm waking up from novocaine. Something should hurt, but I don't give a damn. I may not give a damn again. Everything's soft and quiet and smells so freaking good.

I roll over. Whimper a little. *Okay, ugh.* The earlier question? About what should hurt? The answer is *everything*. Have I been hit by a truck?

I amend that assessment the second my eyes are open.

If it was a truck, it knocked me to a damn beautiful spot. At first sight, I wonder if I'm back in the penthouse at the Brocade. The view is just as sweeping, with the beginnings of dawn sifting through the maze of city lights below. But geographically, everything is wrong. The ocean's a little closer. The neighborhood's a little nicer. There are a couple of broad greenbelts nearby. I'm sure one of them is the LA Country Club's golf course.

The bedroom I'm in is no less breathtaking. Though the color palette is California mission tones, brown and sand

and gold, there's nothing traditional about the furniture. Everything is elegant but practically space-age, looking crafted especially for its place in the room. I've never been in a bed this huge, which seems like a king and a half, with several pillows as long as I am tall. There's a control panel in the nightstand with more buttons than a starship from one of Wade and Fershan's games. Though each of the buttons is accompanied by an icon, I'm hesitant to push anything with my novocaine brain still in full effect.

"Where the hell..."

I let the query fade. It's not the proper question. Another horse belongs in front of this cart.

What the hell happened to me?

Suddenly, my memory kicks in—but only in crazy flashes. *Really* crazy flashes...

Reece, waving from the elevator. Adoration in his eyes. My sweatshirt around his waist...

Blasted into nothing by Angelique La Salle. Her siren's smirk. Those cufflinks in her hand...

Blasted apart again, the only choice my heart would allow. Running. Refusing to confront my own stupidity. My blind trust in an idiot's fairy tale...

Really blasted then, by the creeps in the train station. Their hands on my body. Their knife in my clothes. Their threats in my ear...

Then the biggest explosion of all.

Him.

Flinging them through the air. Pinning them to the wall. Black leather. Grim fury. Effortless power. Supercharged. Supersonic.

A superhero. Saving me.

Saving me?

"Holy shit."

I sit straight up. Mess up the covers with a bunch of swipes and kicks. I need to confirm they're real. That *I'm* still real. That being real won't smash away the memories.

Memories? Or a dream?

"Holy *shit.*" I whisper it this time, along with the gentler strokes I give to the million-thread-count sheets. I keep roaming with my hand, up and over the plain white T-shirt into which I've somehow been changed. It fits me like an oversize gunnysack, but it's as soft as these damn sheets and smells as clean as cedar. Most importantly, it beats the hell out of the *eau de gangbanger* in which my work clothes are likely drenched by now.

But for all that, I'm still left with no clues about who it really belongs to. *What the hell is going on?*

I'm saved from confusing contemplations about that by a harsh vibration from the nightstand. My phone, inside my purse, is easy enough to grab. I smile in gratitude at the caller's picture and eagerly swipe at the screen.

"Neeta."

"Emma!" The punch of her voice makes me lean away for a second. "*Baap re!* You are okay!"

"I...I think so."

"Where are you?" Her demand is pitched with panic. Before I can come up with a decent answer, instinct steering me away from the obvious, she rushes on. "We saw you. On the news. It was everywhere!"

"On the...news?" I shake my head, trying to free it from the fuzz. "What was? Why? How?"

"The security camera feed from the Soto metro station."

She takes a huge breath. Her tone softens. "You were attacked, Emma. Do you remember?"

"Yeah," I say too quickly. I rub my forehead with the opposite speed. There's so much to process. *Too* much, even before the most daunting thought of them all thunders back into my gray matter. "Yeah. I remember it all."

Tangible stillness. Then her reverent murmur. "Even the last part?"

"Even the last part."

"So...Bolt is real?"

"Yeah."

And I think I'm in his apartment right now.

Fortunately, Neeta's occupied with her own high gasp. "By all the gods. *Emma.*"

I wince. Her fervor slams me, too huge to take in. I'm motion sick, and the only thing turning is the earth on its axis. Maybe if I beg hard enough, God will do me a solid and halt it for a few minutes. "Can... Can I call you back in a little while?" The Almighty will likely want my full attention on the stop-the-globe request.

"Of course. *Wait.*" There's shuffling from her end. Her breaths are hollow, as if she's cupped a hand over her phone. "Are you still with him now?"

"No." Not a lie. I still have no idea what this place is or how I got here. Hell, I don't know if I'm a guest or a hostage—though when I hear a door open somewhere nearby, I sense that answer is near. With heartbeats attacking my throat, I mutter, "Call you back soon," and disconnect the line.

I scramble out of the bed, following the noise despite my uneasiness. Gingerly, I walk toward the sounds.

"Whoa."

I definitely didn't expect...*this*.

First, there's a built-to-fit architectural island constructed out of custom-hewn rocks and curved insets of dark wood. It's formed by crescent-shaped bookshelves that arch over a curved, see-through fireplace. On either side of the fireplace, narrow steps lead to a sunken reading area with plush couches. A second bookshelf brackets the other side of the area.

In short, my idea of heaven on earth.

Sealing the deal? My own angel comes with the package.

He stands in the doorway off to my left, leading to what looks like a bathroom as oversized as the bed. Steam billows around the lean muscles of his towel-wrapped hips, as if he's really just emerged from heaven and the clouds don't want to let go. Can they be blamed? He's glorious, from the bold cut of his abdominal V to the rippled plateaus of his proud shoulders.

And every damp, defined striation in between...

No. *No*.

I don't want this. I don't want him. I *can't* want him.

Because he's not my angel.

Because somehow, in some strange twist of fate, I've ended up here with him—wherever *here* is—and now must deal with looking at him like this. Knowing the shirt he pulled off to *get* like this had cufflinks with it. *Those* cufflinks...

We were caught up in a...discussion...

"You're awake," Reece states.

I push one foot back. Another. "Yeah." Finally, I'm able to step away. "In a lot more ways than one."

"Velvet—"

"Do. Not." The point is worth halting for. I stand my ground, stabbing one finger at him. "You don't get to 'Velvet' me anymore. Or 'Bunny' or 'Baby' or 'Foo Foo' or whatever the hell else you've cooked into that Kool-Aid." I let the finger fall. "I'm not drinking it anymore, Mr. Richards."

"I'm not asking you to drink." He should be given points for not budging from the doorway. "I should have never even asked you to take a sip."

I pivot from him. I know I should let him have that as the last word, accepting accountability for layering more meaning on our fling than he ever should have, but my legs are locked in place. My heart is intractable, clinging to its need for logic. So stupid. There's no logic here. Not with a player like him, who enjoys the big boys' version of chess. Shifting real-life people as his pieces. Playing with their hearts.

No. Not my heart. *You don't get that part, damn it.* "Is that why you had him bring me here?" I peer around again. I don't want to—resisting the interior-design lusties all over again—but I can't help it. "And where *is* here?"

A humorless chuff. "You think I live at the Brocade twenty-four-seven?"

I don't answer. Of course that's what I think, especially now. In the space at the hotel, it's simple to slot him into one role. Arrogant, breath-robbing boss man. Here, he's more reachable. More real. He does stuff like read, sleep...take showers.

"And who, exactly, did I have bring you here?"

"You know who." I stab him with a glare as vicious as my tone. "That...person. Or whatever he is. Bolt. You know him somehow, don't you? So you contacted him after I passed out. Or maybe you had him knock me out somehow..." Which is a disturbing thought, so I don't finish it.

"Why would you think I know him?"

I ignore the subtle scalpel in his tone too. I don't want

to be nicked by whatever has sharpened it. Apprehension? Tension? Do I care?

I shouldn't. I can't.

"Don't you know *all* the special people, Mr. Richards?" I finish it off with pure snark before descending the stairs to the sunken reading heaven. I shouldn't be doing this, purposely closing the gap to such incredible temptation, but I refuse to keep talking to him anywhere near the bed. "People like Angelique La Salle?"

Perfect words for reinforcing my resolve. The man may be only be in a towel now, but less than twenty-four hours ago he was in the back seat of that woman's car—letting her take off his cufflinks. And the logical things that came after that.

Reece doesn't follow me down the stairs. He remains on the higher level, arms folded, feet braced, once more in misplaced pharaoh mode. And I have *got* to stop equating his smooth-talking, perfect player ass to every brand of royalty there is. He's *not* king or pharaoh or czar material. He's barely duke material, and that's only because dukes are notorious pussy chasers already.

"You think Angelique La Salle is *special* to me?"

I match his stance before pushing out a confused huff. The question isn't rhetorical, but it sure as hell isn't compassionate. He wants—demands—an answer.

"You going to tell me she's not?"

He hauls in a long breath. While letting it out, he steps down to my level, though little else changes. He's still in his Ruler of the Universe stance. His gaze is the color of armor in the rain.

"She used to be...a good friend," he finally murmurs. "She was in town. I met her so I could return some things to her."

"Like a pair of cufflinks?"

His next inhalation is sharper. "Yes. Among other things."

I glower carefully. "Good friends." I tell myself not to finish it...but what other choice is there? Bleed out slowly or just rip the damn bandage off? "How good?"

"We were...involved. About a year and a half ago."

I back up by a step. Swallow hard. It's the blood I asked for, just not the pain I expected. "Involved." And as long as I'm hemorrhaging... "Like lovers?"

His posture tightens. The sight of it is both exquisite and excruciating. The man isn't built like a tank, but the creator spared no detail on his defined, beautiful body. His muscles are carefully carved, utterly decadent.

"No," he states at last. "Not like lovers."

"So you didn't fuck her?"

"Oh, I fucked her a lot. But she was *not* my lover." His gaze is now as intense as lightning. "She let you believe something differently, didn't she? When she came to the hotel. When she tried to bring back those goddamned cufflinks."

"But how did..." I shake my head, answering my own question. "The security cams. The same way you knew I'd left the hotel, right?"

"Yeah." He draws out the word, making room for a strange subtext in his tone. I'd usually call it tension, but not the same kind I've seen in him before. This stress is different. It doesn't make him scary anymore. It makes him vulnerable. "Something like that."

"Something like that?" Damn it, I want to ignore that tenderness. To pretend that side of him isn't speaking out at the wrong, wrong, *wrong* damn time. "How?"

His nostrils flare. His mouth compresses into a solid line.

"What did Angelique say to you?" he finally counters, nearly in a growl. "You two talked. She was at the front desk for a while."

I turn from him again, for a couple of different reasons. One, it's hard to remember my own name with him in that towel, let alone what his va-va-voom ex-girlfriend said to me last night. And number two I go ahead and voice out loud. "Why should I answer your question when you won't acknowledge mine?"

"Because your answer is going to help me keep you safe."

"Safe?" I practically laugh out the word. It's either that or I'll start bawling—and hell if I'll let him see *that*. "That's a funny term to me right now, buddy."

"I am aware of that, Emma."

"Are you?" I whirl back around. *Now* it's time to get delirious. And pissed. And outraged. And scared. "Are you really *aware*, Mr. Richards, of my 'safety' when it comes to your crafty ex?"

His hands coil. His jaw squares. He jerks his head, raining drops from his hair over the taut slabs of his chest and the chiseled dessert tray of his abs—but dessert isn't an option as he slowly steps closer, brandishing hard eyes and flaring nostrils.

"Crafty?" He growls the word but punctuates with a harsh chuff. "Crafty. Well, there's a piece of funny."

"Excuse the hell out of me?"

He breathes in again through his nostrils and exhales with vicious force. "I think you don't know *shit* about 'crafty,' Emmalina—and that frightens me most of all." He leans over, skewing the towel sideways, exposing the strain of his extended hip—not that I get more than a glance as his ire blatantly grows. "'Crafty' is a word for your shoe-eating dog, your scrapbooking neighbor, or the grandma who makes Christmas wreaths out of used soda cans. It's *not* the word for my lunatic bitch of an ex-girlfriend." He closes the gap between us and opens one of those fists to grab my shoulder. "Do I make myself fucking clear?"

My breath wads at the back of my throat. Forget considering his vulnerable side. What he reveals now isn't even a run-of-the-mill soft side. This is him, genuinely spooked by the idea of Angelique even talking to me last night.

Angelique. His "lunatic bitch of an ex."

A claim that should mean something—more than what it means now. But every time it seems like the man rips a mask off for me, another is swept into its place and glued on. I know he's telling me the truth—just not all of it.

Not the biggest part of it.

"Reece? What the hell?" I let him hear every note of my desperate confusion. Let him feel the force of my searching stare. But if I make a dent in his ire, it's impossible to tell. His features remain the texture of solid, inscrutable granite.

"I *said*," he finally growls, "do I make myself *clear*?"

I huff out a sigh. "Yes." I wrench my arm away—or try to. "Now let me go." When he's as responsive as a ninja gripping a katana, I resort to yelling. "*Reece.*"

When he jerks his stare up, his eyes are glazed.

"Let me go, or tell me what the hell is going on. Do I make *that* fucking clear?"

REECE

My hand slips from her shoulder.

Let me go...

A breath slowly flows from her body.

Or tell me what the hell is going on...

With equal sadness, she takes a step back. Then another.

Only in that moment, in the dip of her head and the stiffness of her shoulders, am I bulldozed by an awful recognition.

Warning her away from Angelique, I've done nothing to protect her—and everything to alienate her.

She's just as serious as I've been. Letting her go...means *letting her go.*

No. *No, damn it.* Not an option.

Which means I have to consider unveiling what's behind door number two.

"Emmalina."

She stops, one foot angled on the corner of a stair. She waits, hands at her sides with fingernails jabbing into her palms. I watch her wrists shake from the effort—and know I'm the cause of her pain. And hate myself for it. But that's just the beginning. I'm on a roll now. I hate myself for that, plus every dumbass, douchebag move I've ever pulled in my short but notorious life. From all the antics of my youth to sticking my dick in the crazy of Angelique to landing myself right here, right now—where I finally wonder how the hell I'm going to break this to the most amazing woman I've ever met.

There's no instruction manual for this.

Isn't there supposed to *be* an instruction manual somewhere? *Congratulations! You're a superhero! Quick and easy FAQs, including how to talk to your doctor, your dry cleaner, and your girlfriend.*

And during my dumbass sulk, she's moved on, turned away, and cleared the stairs.

"Emmalina."

This time, she doesn't stop. She leans over the bed to scoop up her phone, derailing every thought in my mind again with a peek of her ass, perfectly cupped by her pale-pink panties...

Christ. There needs to be a chapter in the manual about dealing with panties too.

"Please. *Shit.* Emma. Damn it!"

She stops and straightens but doesn't turn back. "Reece... I..." The nightstand light throws golden light across the side of her face and the cloud of her hair, transforming her into a vision of innocence and illicitness in one breath-stealing second. "Look, I want to..." She sets down her phone and pushes out a soft *tsk*, as if admonishing *herself* for this tension between us. "I just want to say thank you, all right? Whatever this is, or *was*, between us...it was really awesome, but—"

"Goddamnit." I stomp up the stairs. "No way. We're not a 'was.' We're *not*—"

"Reece." She grabs one of my hands with both of hers and lifts a wistful smile. "We're not even a 'we,' and that's okay. It's not good or bad or wrong or right. It just *is*. You have a lot going on. I mean, you're...*you*...and—"

"Fuck." I yank my hand back and drag it through my hair. Punch out a wry laugh. "No, Emma. I'm not me. I mean, I'm not him. That guy you think I am. That prick—"

"You're not a prick."

"Not anymore."

"Not ever." She pushes forward, lifting her hands to bracket my jaw. Her gaze pulls me in, the aqua light mesmerizing every neuron in my body. "It took you a little while to free the good man hiding underneath that other one, but he's there. *I* see him, I believe in him, and he's beautiful. Now you just have to believe too."

I jerk my head in vicious defiance. "You have no damn idea what you're talking about."

The woman actually hurls back a growl. Her boldness is so breathtaking, I'm reduced to a stunned stare as she pushes on. "Oh yeah? Who came down from the tower, rolled up his sleeves, and helped us turn the rooms for the tour group during that crunch?"

"And snagged a nice fringe benefit from the deal?" I jab a knowing smirk.

"Okay, then. Who's the guy who keeps insisting on paying Zalkon every day just to haul my backside to and from work?"

"You mean when you'll keep your backside *at* work?"

"I think my backside gets an excuse note after last night."

"I think it deserves a number of notes on *any* night."

She whacks my shoulder. "You're ignoring the point."

"Which was what again?" Not that I've forgotten. More like I hope *she's* forgotten—since I'm beginning to. *Fast.* Discussing any part of this woman's anatomy, much less the hot temptation of her backside, derails my senses, consumes my will, blazes every drop of my blood. For the first time in my life, I really know the meaning of *obsession*—in the best and worst ways.

"That I'm not going to let you get away with the 'just a dick' excuse?" Despite her sassy tone, her hands haven't moved off my shoulders. I watch them now, as she starts exploring my collarbones with her fingertips. It feels so fucking good. I clench back a savoring moan.

Just a dick. Oh, Velvet. If you knew exactly how much I could validate that...

To turn her explorations into my seduction. To chisel her point down to craving *my* point. To make her forget everything except the one thing I *can* do better than anyone else.

Which will do what?

Delay the inevitable, *that's* what.

Tell her—or let her go.

"You're still not convinced, are you?"

Her prod makes me chuckle. "That I'm a dick?"

"Ugggghhh." She smacks me again. Though I attempt another laugh, she refuses to join in. "Fine. As long as we're talking about my lame move from last night, who was the 'dick' who tracked me down to the train station and then came and got me—after I passed out in another guy's arms?"

I almost laugh again. It's the way I roll when fate opens a door so hard, the wood knocks me between the eyes. But I'm not spinning so hard that I don't see the gaping break she's handed over.

It's time to jump through.

No matter how black the abyss on the other side.

"Yeah...uh...about that *other guy*..."

EMMA

Weird.

It was the word Neeta, Wade, and Fershan frantically whispered that first night I'd met Reece. The description I'd been irked about, much less couldn't understand. The label that's lingered at the back of my mind this whole week, mostly because it still hasn't made any damn sense when it comes to the Reece Richards I've come to know...pretty damn intimately.

Until now.

Now, he's weird. Not even that. His vibe is something I'm really not getting. This is more than his usual mystery, or even the unnamable energy that's like threads of solid steel between us.

He's...distant.

No. That's not it, either. He's not distant, but I sense he wants to be. That he's fighting his pull to me. What the hell *is* he? Enigmatic? Cryptic?

Scary?

The descriptor fits better than the others, but I don't want it to. Yet something about how he takes both my hands and guides me to sit on the bed sears my senses with nothing *but* scared.

The apprehension worsens when he releases me to take a measured step back. He breathes in, as if preparing to peel back his lips and reveal gleaming fangs.

I sit up straighter. "Okaaayyy," I finally utter. "Reece? What is it?" I manage to grab one of his hands again. "That other guy?" Then tighten my hold around his stiff fingers. "What are you..." A frown sets in. "You mean Bolt?" Another slice of fear, though he reaches for the nightstand drawer as if he's just searching for a tissue. "What happened with him? Shit. What did he do?" I shove furious air through my nostrils. "Did he hurt *you*? Because, I swear to God, if he tried to—"

I freeze as he turns, trailing something from the drawer between two of his long fingers.

Not a tissue. A mask.

A sleek, black, Maserati mask.

"What...the..."

He lets the molded leather fall to my lap. I look at it like he's dropped a killer spider.

"I...don't understand. Where did you—" My breaths come faster and faster. "Did he give this to you? Like a souvenir?"

He laughs. Not hard, but enough to make me want to smack him again. No. Punch him. He needs to be telling me I'm right—that the leather in my lap is just a gift from his buddy or a memento found on the train platform.

Because if I'm not right, that means...

Oh shit, oh shit, oh shit.

"He didn't give me the mask, Emmalina."

...that every knowing note in his tone is right...

"Then why was it in your nightstand?"

...that every ounce of dread in mine is too...

"Because it's mine."

...that the unreal is suddenly very real.

I lurch to my feet and force them to move in a frantic figure eight, countering my exploding mind and churning stomach. My fist twists against the molded leather game-changer he's just laid on me. My other hand opens and closes in time to my wild-woman pace. "But not because it's *yours* yours, right?"

When he issues nothing but silence, I freeze in place. Gape at him with new urgency. Mentally, I drop the towel from his body and redress him in black leather. My imagination secures the mask across the chiseled planes of his face.

All too easily, the result blooms in my mind. All too clearly, I can see him in that god-in-leather finery. Filling it with his regal posture. Turning it into visual poetry with his stride, his grace.

Dominating the very air he's in.

Controlling it. Using it.

Like his weapon.

The guy's weird, Emma.

He's not the person you think, Emma.

"Shit." I sink back to the bed. "*Shit.*"

"Emma—"

"It *is* yours." I lift my head, staring, as if seeing him for the first time. "Because you're...him."

He averts his gaze. Twists his lips into a ruthless grimace. "I'm just me, Emma. And I'm just trying, for the first time, to do something with my life besides being paparazzi food. What everyone else chooses to call it, or how they want to glorify it..." He shrugs—*shrugs!*—turning the errant drops on his shoulders into planes of muscled luster. "That's not up to me."

I let that statement steep in a long damn silence. At last, I murmur, "Which is why you've kept it a secret."

"Among other reasons, yes."

"But you finally did tell me."

I lift the mask, still dangling from my palm, back toward him. I'm not sure what I'm trying to tell him with the act, but he gazes at the leather with the same intensity I do, knowing the gesture stands for something. Not my total understanding—that may not ever come—but perhaps my gratitude. Exposing himself like this... It's taken trust that turns his body into a block of tension and his energy into a strained matrix.

He drops the leather piece back on the nightstand before lowering himself down next to me, curling one of his hands with mine. "Because it was tell you or lose you."

I turn, taking in his face more intently. Most specifically, the truth now speaking to me from his eyes. "But you're still not sure I won't run away flailing."

I don't expect his sardonic snort. "I'm just a guy playing the odds, beauty."

I turn my hand in, twining my fingers with his. Comprehension slams hard. The recognition that, despite the informational warhead he dropped a minute ago, *this* moment blows me away more. The rogue savior of our city, the idol who's fascinated the land of the jaded, is sitting next to me wrapped in nothing but a big towel and a lot of uncertainty. A superhero who keeps his mask in the nightstand has clearly placed his heart in my hands.

Is this really my life?

Am I really lifting his hand and gently turning it over to trace a finger along the pulse beneath his wrist? Am I really watching a tremor take him, rolling through him like a bank of summer thunder, turning his blood vessels into a web of lightning? Are his fingers actually glowing blue and gold against mine, their light corresponding to the heavy breaths pumping his sculpted chest?

"Tell me." My whisper is weighted by demand as much as curiosity. I join a second finger to my first, flowing my touch up his arm...watching the amazing light of his bloodstream beneath his skin.

Beneath my touch, Reece's limbs jerk and shudder. He grips me, digging into my hips, all but pleading with me to keep exploring him like that. "Tell you what?" he grates. "You can have anything, Velvet. *Everything.*"

I lift a hand to the thick artery pumping down the side of his neck. As it lights up like a hose holding radioactive acid, I stroke a little harder. The glint intensifies. "Is this why you always ordered me to close my eyes?"

He swallows deeply. "Yeah."

I lift my head, confronting the gorgeous glow from his pupils too. "It's beautiful."

"*You're* beautiful." He pulls my fingers to his lips. His kiss carries a tiny shock, inciting a gasp. He does it again, sending a similar zap to the tender layers between my legs.

I angle my body more toward his. He releases my fingers and settles his incredible lips over mine. I thread my touch through his hair as we kiss for long tender moments. Static flows in the wake of my fingers, transferring white-hot energy back into my hand and up my arm.

"Wow." I let out a delighted laugh.

"No shit." His commiserating grin is mesmerizing.

"Dork." I say it as a tease but turn sober enough to add, "As if all this is new for *you*?"

He kisses me again. New energy arcs between us, making us both gasp and quiver. "Every moment."

"Bullshit."

"*No* shit." He dares me to doubt him with a harder, deeper kiss. Well over a minute later, when my tongue has gotten reacquainted with every hungry, electrifying inch of his, he lets me up for air once more—and I openly gawk.

"So...you *weren't* kidding the other night? About it being a while?" I watch the slow, steady shake of his head. "Because of...what happened to make you this way?" Refusing to accept his thick silence as an answer, I tug at his hair. As silken as the strands are, I stay focused. "You said I could ask anything, Reece. That you'd give it to me."

His brow furrows. I can all but hear him cursing himself, but that won't get him a bye on my purpose. *I need to know*.

"This shit...it's part of me now," he finally utters. "It's in my blood, my sweat, my nervous system..."

"And you didn't know what that would do to someone if you were intimate with them."

I release a long breath as the understanding sinks in. He answers by jerking another nod. "To be honest, my head wasn't even there anyway. My life was ass-backward and upside down, and all I cared about was righting it again."

"Then why did you end up here?"

"In LA?"

"Yeah."

"I don't understand."

"Richards Resorts International is headquartered in New York. You're as far away from that as the contiguous states will allow."

"And?"

"Well, if you're trying to get your shit together, why did your dad banish you out here?" I tilt my head. "You have to know that's what everyone is saying, right? That the family sent you out here for some heavy shit that went down in Europe. Parties? Women? Drugs?"

He chuffs. "Yeah. That's all still pretty funny."

I right myself. "So it *didn't* happen like that?"

His stare turns droll. "Hell if *I* know, Velvet."

"You were too strung-out to remember?"

"I was too *not there* to remember."

I blink hard. Then again. "But there were pictures of you..."

"Cut, pasted, and altered, and then strategically released to the media," he supplies.

"*What?*" I gape. "For how long?"

"Nearly six months."

"*Why?*"

"So nobody would figure out where I really was." He cuts me short from the logical follow-up to that with a look I can only describe as shellshock. He juts his jaw, inhaling deep once more. "It was six months of fucking hell, and that's the only 'everything' you get about it."

For a long second, I swallow hard. I believe every word he's said—and by doing so, I have to wrap my mind around what he's already survived. The pain and misunderstanding he *continues* to live with. As I slowly absorb it all into my conscience, my heart squeezes. My throat constricts. Air is my new enemy, hurting with every intake, as I slide my hand to the back of his neck. I wrap my other arm around his waist, rejoicing as he pulls me even tighter.

And just like that, it's back. The sizzling, encompassing force field of his, binding our energies like lightning in storm clouds but with a thousand times more magic. I give into it with a jagged sigh, tucking my lips against his neck. I press kisses from his ear to his jaw and back again. His breaths rumble into my hair, sparking more fierce need between us. My pulse sprints to match his. My hand races up and down his spine. I marvel at his corded strength bunching beneath my touch like power cables wrapped in satin. Tanned, taut, muscle-laced satin. I yearn to dissolve into him, to tangle myself with him. The admission pushes another shaky breath through me, echoed by a similar sound in his chest.

Between those rough breaths, I finally compose words. "Wow." Okay, one word. Saying it all yet saying nothing. How do I tell him he's fried the neurons of my mind? Blown apart every imagining of my soul? Given my heart one of the greatest gifts it could ever receive? How do I tell him *all* that, without making it about Bolt?

Because he'll never believe me. I even wonder if I'll believe myself.

Because without the hell he endured to become this man in my arms, he likely wouldn't *be* the man in my arms.

And I've fallen helplessly, hopelessly in love with the man

in my arms.

The man who envelops me tighter in his hold, wreathing my torso in greater sparks of awareness and awakening, before whispering, "Wow is a damn good start."

"A start." I trail my mouth down to his shoulder. I breathe him in, all fresh sandalwood soap with a hint of his natural smoke and cedar, while sliding my tongue over every hard, hewn, heroic muscle of his shoulder. "But...*just* a start, right?"

"Only if you'll have me for more." He issues it in a soft snarl, which quickly becomes a fierce choke. The sound bites the air as I do the same to the bottom of his neck. "*Fuck*, Emma. Say you'll have me. Say you'll stay with me. Please."

He digs a hand deeper into my waist, bunching fingers into my shirt. *His* shirt. I revel in the awareness. I'm in *his* bed, wearing *his* shirt. And now, I'm twisting to straddle his lap before planting my knees in his sheets. I'm surrounded by him—his scent, his fabrics, his bed, his energy—razing me from scalp to soles, inciting one consuming need in return.

To surround *him* with *me.*

"I'll have you, Reece Richards." I brace my thumb and forefinger against his jaw, securing him with possessive intent. "I'll have you. I want you."

I love you.

For a second, I'm terrified I've let it escape aloud. The way his whole frame stills—stopping as if I've shot him in the chest—has me dropping my hand.

"And you'll stay?"

I smile, stroking his beautiful, noble face. Suddenly, all the royal comparisons are so perfect. So *right*. "Yes. I'll stay."

His features take on a breathtaking new hardness. His gaze beams with a force *nobody* would question twice. A message confirmed by every thrumming, throbbing, cell of my body, just before he lunges in until our lips collide.

Wow. *Wow.*

He's untamed shrapnel in my mouth, everywhere at once, setting me afire with every sweep of his tongue. In response, I give a shaky, needy moan. I'm already collateral damage, gutted from his assault, gorging on his passion...

Ripping off his towel.

Looking down at him—all of him—with savoring hunger.

Rejoicing in every magnificent muscle I see. And caress. And spark into electrified glory as his blood heats and pulses and funnels to the most fascinating bolt in his body...

I wrap both hands around his cock and stroke him from glowing balls to the bold beacon of his head, wanting him worse than I ever have before.

This is going to be good. So *damn* good.

CHAPTER FOUR

REECE

"Emma. *Fuck.*" Both words are barely breaths, breaking past my locked teeth as her talented fingers coax more heat to the surface of my cock. *Surface?* Who am I kidding? Every inch of me, from the core of throbbing magma to the veins pounding at my stretched skin, is a new slave to her mastery, a new convert to her religion.

And what does my new goddess give me in return? A stare brimming with just as much adoration, worship, amazement, devotion. Blowing me away. Spinning my senses. That's before she even speaks again.

"Reece. It's beautiful." She drops her head, brushing the glowing drop off my tip with her lips. "*You're* so beautiful."

I smile. At least I think I do. It's hard to know what's real right now. "You mean that, don't you?" My astonishment is authentic. "You don't think I'm a freak? That this is fifteen kinds of weird?"

"Of course it's weird." She licks her lips, spreading the sheen of my precome across their delectable curves like space-age lip gloss. "But it's wonderful. And incredible."

"And freaky?"

"Oh, that's the best part."

I join my gruff laugh to her sighing giggle as she resumes

touching me. Squeezing me. Gazing at me. Fuck, yes. That's the best part. Getting to see her eyes, wide as Caribbean seas, drenching my body with their heat and light and lust. Seeing that even though I could lead Santa's fucking sleigh with my cock, she still can't stop touching it and then kissing it once more.

"*Fuck.*" My hips convulse as she sucks off more drops from my strained head. "Velvet...baby...that's..."

"Freaky." She laughs it out while kissing her way up my torso. Her lips, still heated by the drops she just took in, close over one of my nipples. "Guess it's a good thing I'm into freaks." Then the other.

"*Damn* good thing." I cup the back of her neck, directing her to do it again. She flattens her tongue, forming a hot wet trail between my pecs as I use my other hand to push at the T-shirt covering her. Though she's turned white cotton into a fashion statement I'll never tire of, naked is how I need her right now. Her tits are what I crave, smashed against my chest, smeared in the same fiery river blazing the plain over my heart.

I finally strip the shirt away from her. With a starving growl, I yank her down to me. In a crazy torrent, we kiss. Bite. Devour. Spar. Fighting to expel our passion while feeding the monster with every passing second. It's frenzied, fiery, passionate, and frightening—and I never want it to be any other way.

Hell. It was the word I just used to tell her what made me this way.

A hell I'll endure again, a thousand times over, if she's the prize waiting at the end.

"Ohhhh...*wow,*" she exclaims against my lips as her breasts pillow against my chest. I lift a smile in return, nipping at the soft nectar of her mouth.

"One way of putting it." I scrape her chin with my teeth before jerking at her hair, forcing her head all the way back. *Jesus*. The sight of her like this, like my velvet Valkyrie in captivity, swells my mind with amazement and my cock with fresh heat. All of this just keeps getting better, especially as I scratch two fingers down the exposed column of her neck. Her skin is so creamy and smooth...and ready for my mark. Needing to be branded.

I lift my head, growling as she gasps, scoring her skin with my rough kiss. Between our bodies, my cock jerks again, growing by the second. More arousal spurts from my head, soaking the barrier of her panties. I curl my head tighter to look down there. The sight of the spot I've made, turning the satin from light pink to dark, unhinges something even more feral in me. Something that needs that underwear out of my way. *Now.*

I twist a couple of fingers into the sweet pink lace and jerk hard—only to have the material battle my grip. *Damn it.*

I lift her and flip her all the way over. Pushing back for leverage, I'm treated to the world's best aerial view. The landscape of her body is a silken dream, topped by the succulent berries of her erect nipples. All I need to see now is the bare peach between her thighs.

A satisfaction I need this second.

"Close your eyes, Emma. Only for a second, beauty," I add as she sends an *are you serious* glower. I make good on the promise, pulling up on the lace at her hip so it's nearly a taut pink rope—and now, a perfect target for the blue laser my forefinger becomes.

Inside a second, I sear the material away. Emma's gaze

pops open as the smoking satin falls from her body. I take a deep breath, forcing the heat to subside, though it's damn awesome not to worry about hiding my ten lightsabers anymore.

"Holy...wow."

I wiggle my fingers slowly...before lowering their tips to the graceful ridges of her pubic bones. "Wow," I echo, spreading my touch outward, coaxing her thighs to spread the same direction. "You enjoy that word, don't you?"

"In this case, it fits." As my thumbs meet, toying with the top of her pouting slit, her hips writhe. "It fits *you*."

I work my thumbs downward and spread the rest of my fingers along her pulsing lips, reveling in how they eagerly kiss at the air. "Fitting *you* is my goal, Miss Crist."

"Oh," she mewls. The sound deepens and darkens as I work my thumbs in more, spreading her wet depths. Soon, I'm pushing into her as well, a tender but steady finger fuck. My other fingers spread out, keeping her thighs apart. I brace my elbows against her knees—which start to shake, becoming erotic turn-ons in their own right. Holy hell. Because of her, I'm now a knees guy.

Fuck.

Because of her, I'm now an everything guy.

"Reece."

"Emma."

"*Reece!*"

I replace my fingertips with my hips and gulp hard at how good her inner thighs feel against me. At how good *all* of her feels against me.

"Open wider for me, beauty." I lean over, kissing her in long, passionate pulls as she complies. "Yeah. Like that." My own breath stutters. "Do you know how many times I've

imagined being with you like this? Completely bare like this?"
I skate my touch back up over her puckered breasts. Watching
her nipples light up beneath my touch is a turn-on beyond the
dreams I've just referenced. "No holding anything back. No
more hiding."

Emma clutches my hand and guides it to the side of her
face. "Never again." Her tawny lashes lift. Her stare is pure
blue conviction, engulfing mine. "No more hiding."

I curve my fingers in, catching the edge of her hairline,
outlining her features with an ethereal glow. *My* glow. "Fuck."
I gulp hard, struggling to put what I feel into words but finally
accept that uselessness. I can only stare, gutted and grateful,
for what she's done for me in this moment. Her elegant profile
illuminated like this turns my garishness into a gift, my curse
into inspiration.

Because of her, I'm no longer a victim. I'm a survivor.

I'm stronger.

And maybe, someday, I can even think of calling myself a
hero.

Right now, it only matters that she sees me as one.

With her eyes glimmering and her lips parted, she
releases my hand and slides her touch up my arm. Once she
gets to my shoulder, she doesn't stop. Tremors radiate across
my back as she skates her hand down, skimming past my waist,
before molding a palm across my ass. Before I can process how
fucking amazing *that* feels, she grips my other cheek too.

Pulling me closer to her softness. Urging me deeper into
her beauty.

I fall onto my elbows. Our faces are inches apart, and
our breaths weave into each other likes mists meeting in
sacred canyons. She's just as perfect a sight, with her eyes like

sapphire smoke and her skin a glistening sheen of arousal. I inhale as she exhales. Her breath smells like sex... The essence she's already kissed off my cock. The desire I have yet to sate.

The lust with which she grips my ass, seating me tighter between her legs.

"Light me up, Reece." Her voice is a shimmering, demanding plea. "*Do it*. Light me up. From the inside."

"Emma." I shake now too, fighting for restraint. There are more words to be said here. Words that must be said. Shit about being careful and grabbing condoms and...

"It's all right." She rocks beneath me, lithe and lusty, taunting my dick with the soft, soaked layers of her pussy. "I'm on the pill. I didn't tell you before because—" She interrupts herself, coloring a little. "Well, because..."

I kiss her nose in reassurance. "It's all right, beauty. I get it."

"And now you've got *me*." She lifts her legs, crossing them at the small of my back. "And I need *you*. Please. All of you. Every freaky, weird, magnificent, glowing inch of— *Oh!*"

As hot as I am, she's hotter.

As taut as I am, she's tighter.

As bright as I am, she's so much brighter. Illuminated. Ablaze. A sensual, incredible angel, looking like a goddamned page out of a comic book herself. Her hair fans against my sheets as if she's flying. Her face, surrounded by my neon fingers, is alight with strength, sensuality, surrender, joy. Her body, spread for me, is a collection of muscle and might and power—especially in the center of the gem where we're joined. As we rock, completely in sync with each other, the light of that juncture pulses and intensifies.

"Ohhhh!" She screams it again as I shove at her legs.

"Ohhhh!" Once more as I stretch her deeper.

"Ohhhh!" Even louder as I slam into the tight, dripping oval welcoming my cock. She's perfect. *So fucking perfect.*

I stop only for a second to grab at the pillows and bunch them behind her head. "No more closed eyes, Emmalina." I angle her head down, ensuring she focuses toward the sight of her body sucking me in, over and over and over. "Watch," I dictate. "*Watch me.*"

"Yes." Her breath-filled obedience is like rocket fuel to my swollen dick. "*Yes.*"

My balls constrict.

The fusion of our bodies is raw radiance.

"Do you like the freak fucking you?"

The beast inside me growls into my words, feeling so damn good to be let out.

"Don't see any freaks around here, Mr. Richards." She puts a coy spin on the smirk. "You sure you got the right address for that claim?"

"Oh, I'm sure."

"Better check again." Her eyelids go heavy, emphasizing the tease of her pouting lips. "Or knock a little harder."

My grin splits wider.

My cock swells against her walls.

"You are *really* asking for it, Miss Crist."

"Damn right I am, freak."

I'm not sure what drives me more blissfully insane—the sexy sarcasm in her tease or the come-on in her eyes. In the end, it doesn't matter. In the end, I'm ramming her tight, perfect cunt with all the force I can flex into my hips, all the power I can surge into my cock...all the passion I can summon to my spirit.

All the pleasure, heat, and fire I can give her—bursting into the high, aching joy of her climax.

"Reece!"

"*Emma.*"

"Need...you...with me!"

"On my way, beauty."

Not a lie.

Because I am. Because I do.

My cock isn't just the color of a laser beam anymore. It *feels* like a laser beam. I'm consumed by a cataclysm as I push through a cosmos of blinding heat and fury, bursting like a goddamn star and pouring liquid life into ultimate darkness. And defeating that darkness with the brilliance of this epic explosion, a fuck that's like nothing I've ever experienced or known, until there's nothing left of the light anymore either...

But everything left of the ashes.

And the freak is rising from them like the most bizarre phoenix in the history of ashes. A guy I'm not sure I recognize. A man who might actually be ready for this superhero gig. Like he just might have something worthy to add to the narrative.

Not that I'm ready to go spreading that shit around.

I mean, it's just a thought. At the end of the day, I'm a man more used to VIP ropes than police tape. I'm happier finding discrepancies on spreadsheets than tracking down bad guys in sewers. I thought it might be the right thing to do, after all the douchebag moments to which I've subjected the world, to pay back Karma—and, yeah, the Consortium—by going out in a blaze of glory instead of headlines of scandal. Who thought a few do-the-right-thing moments might actually *feel* right too.

Not that I was ever really taught anything about "right." In boarding school, "conduct" and "character" were ideologies to make fun of between chasing tail and sneaking booze, not part of the life lessons I ever learned from Lawson Richards.

Maybe that's why I question how good everything feels now. *How right.*

It's her. Emmalina. I'm obsessed with her beauty, slammed by her passion, floored by her purpose, consumed by her simple but sublime wonder. And I know, even if the world never does, that with this, with her, I got shit right at least once in my life.

I know it with the certainty still flooding me, hours later, when I drag my eyes open and still find her in my bed. I know it as I reach over to brush her hair from her face and feel a smile breach my lips in tandem with the one curling hers. I know it with every thump of the heartbeat that greets her as she burrows against me.

"Mmm." She inflects it with kittenish gusto. "You're warm."

"And you don't even have to plug me in."

"Oh, there's another one for the he's-a-keeper column." Her teeth snag her bottom lip. "*Not* that you're a *keeper* keeper. I mean, not like that. I mean"—she gulps—"*shit.* Can I have a do-over?"

"Not on your fucking life." I jam a firm kiss to her forehead. "I like being your keeper." I slide my lips down the bridge of her nose. "Just say you'll be mine too."

"I...I want to..."

"You already promised you'd stay," I growl.

She narrows her eyes. "You meant for tonight, and so did I. Now that we're talking about more..."

"What?" I don't mean to bark it but that's what comes out.

She nibbles the inside of her bottom lip. "I'm not opposed

to more either. But Reece..."

"Yeah?" *Stay open. Stay calm.* But that's easier said than done. I'm the one used to doling out this kind of anxiety. Suffering it is *no* fucking fun.

She flattens a hand over my sternum again and gazes right into my eyes. "I need to know everything." A careful swallow. "About Angelique."

I roll to my back and suck in a long breath. She shifts too, rolling to lie on her side next to me...her stare palpably intense. "What about her?"

"She's the one, isn't she?" Her query is soft and knowing. "The one you trusted. Who led you into the hell that changed everything."

I snort out a laugh. She looks like I just hurled in the bed. I'm sure as hell tempted to, especially when replying. "I wasn't exactly white milk, apple pie, and innocence about the whole thing, okay? I met the woman in Paris, in a club where condoms and blow were offered on the menu next to appetizers, and the private rooms were more crowded than the dance floor. We did the circuit there together for a week, and I was enthralled because she knew more people than I did."

I'm not comfortable, but I keep going. She deserves the truth, and in this case, the truth doesn't come in a scrapbook surrounded by hearts and flowers.

"When she told me the scene in Barcelona was more interesting than Paris, I jumped at the chance to follow her there. She played me perfectly, knowing the exact bait to dangle. I wanted the goodies none of my friends had seen yet. The experience none of them could buy through the normal channels."

Emma curls her hand into a fist, forms her other hand over

it, and then parks her chin on the stack. "You wanted more."

Three simple words, meaning so much. Meaning too much.

"Maybe." It's more like *probably*, but it feels wrong to lay the filter of my depraved life over the earnest honesty of hers. To her, "more" has been a synonym for expanding her world. To the man I was, it was a chance to get off on new thrills and expand my empire of illicitness.

Pathetic, stupid man. Grasping small, insignificant dreams.

I had the capacity to do so much more. To be so much more.

Thank fuck she's there again, her tender voice hauling me out of my moroseness. "So what happened then?"

"We'd been in Barcelona a few nights. I was getting bored with the scene, but Angelique kept me on her string—and finally told me about a private rave on the outskirts of the city. A real Bohemian bash in some secret warehouse with designer drugs and royal family cousins and shit."

"Only it wasn't a party."

At first, I give her only thick silence. I use the pause to turn my stare back up at the ceiling while reaching to the back of her head and combing my fingers through her strands, using the movement as subliminal Zen. "You know that urban legend about the businessman who sleeps with the hooker, gets drugged, and wakes up missing a kidney? It was sort of like that, but if there was sex first I missed it, and the 'hooker' was a bunch of big guys in lab coats telling me they'd formed a global conglomeration called the Consortium."

"The *what*?" She stiffens. "What the hell does that even mean?"

"Wasn't sure. And I didn't care, since I'd just been checked into a joint that sure as hell wasn't the Ritz. Slowly but surely, they let me in on the joke—but it wasn't a joke. I'd been recruited as a subject in their groundbreaking research in the field of human DNA improvement through electronic enhancement."

She jerks upright and stares as if I'm about to reveal the big joke of the story, but with her lungs pumping frantically, she knows I'm not. She hears my truth. And crazily, *crucially*, she believes it. "Oh, my God," she rasps.

I shrug again. It looks caustic, but I know she sees that truth too—that it's the sarcastic shield to lessen the stain of the memories. "God wasn't around much," I mutter. "Plenty of his son-of-a-bitch friends, though. What's that fun expression? Devil's in the details?"

With that, even fixating on the ceiling won't help. I push away the covers, roll to the side of the bed, and plant my feet on the floor to make the room stop spinning—and keep the cockroaches of memory from invading my mind. "Those bastards were *very* detailed."

I let my eyes slide shut and my head drop down. In my mind, I escape to visions of mountains and meadows and peace... My refuge when the lab and the walls and the pain threatened to drown out everything I was.

Not working. Not anymore.

What works now...is her.

Emma's fingers, soft as wind, brushing my hunched shoulders. Her body, like a waterfall, draping across my back. Her kisses, healing as herbs, following my jawline. She coaxes my body back, though my mind clings to the fear. The vow I made to myself over and over again during those months before one of the guards got careless with my shackles one night, giving me the sole chance to escape that hell.

But along with that memory, I also recall the mantra. The vow I swore I'd never forget—or betray.

Never. Trust. Again.

A year. I've honored the crap out of every syllable of that oath through every second of every day for the last goddamned year. Haven't even been tempted to abandon it.

Until now.

Until, bathing in the perfection of her touch and the light of her comfort, I'm torn to let it all go. To let her all the way in. I've already given her the truth of my existence, and she's already returned it with the gifts of her adoration, her acceptance, her passion. But there's more. So much more. So much still bricked-up and blocked—those parts of me that were young and arrogant and stupid. Maybe they don't even exist anymore. *I* haven't even looked behind the wall in a year. Maybe they were fried by the lightning and are now shriveled husks in the heart that once pledged to keep them alive, hoping some extraordinary someone would come along to heal them one day.

Someone like her.

"You're not there anymore, Reece. You're right here, and you're perfectly safe with me."

"Thanks." I want to add more but can't. The vow has been embedded deep into my psyche.

Never. Trust. Again.

"Hey." Her fresh tone, inching toward a little playfulness, makes my head perk up. "You got any wheels around here? Other than Z's?"

I bark loudly, this time in laughter. Before she can deliver much of her confused scowl, I sweep off the bed, scoop up the T-shirt, and toss it at her. I fish into the dresser for a pair of my drawstring shorts, usually reserved for home gym workouts, and add the Pentatonix sweatshirt I borrowed from her last night. "Those'll fit you for now. Come on."

A few minutes later, we've descended to a garage below my building's public space, gazing over a row of gleaming BMWs in different shades of gray and blue. As Emma takes it all in with a wide gawk, I grin like a kid showing off his Lego collection. "Welcome to the nursery."

She swings her gaze around the garage and takes it all in. In this light, her eyes perfectly match the Long Beach blue of the M2 right behind her. "Excuse me?"

"One advantage of being in LA over New York, besides destiny's slam-dunk win this last week"—I clarify this with a wicked stare over her body—"has been indulging my little Bimmer addiction."

She giggles. "*Little?*"

"I blame my buyer. Shannon keeps finding me deals I can't pass up. She calls the machines her 'sweet babies.'"

"Ergo, the *nursery*."

"Bingo." I rub my hands together with eager joy. "So, which one do you want to play with?" I waggle my brows as she brightens the whole garage with her laughter. "How about the one that matches your eyes? She's cute—and fast."

She shakes her head and points to one of the M4 convertibles behind me. "I like going topless. The sun's about to set. Let's head for the beach."

I impale her with a mock frown. "Excuse me. I didn't hear a word you said after 'topless.'"

She snickers again. "Dork."

"*Your* dork."

A grin lights up her face as she gets into the passenger seat. "If you insist."

While waiting for the M4's roof to retract, I dip over the center console and yank her into an adamant but chaste kiss. Annnnd that lasts for about two seconds before I sneak in some tongue. Just a little. Okay, maybe a lot. I can't get enough of this woman's taste. I don't think I ever will. "I insist."

Our hands stay entwined the whole trip to the coast.

Her idea was a damn good one. As we park at Pacific Palisades, the sun is just a gold disk on the horizon, still casting brilliant rays across the waves. The sand holds the heat of the day, and it surrounds our feet with grainy warmth as we make our way to the berm. We've stayed hand in hand. It still feels fucking amazing.

We walk to the edge of the berm and sit, butts in the softer sand and feet edging the firm moisture where the tide starts to tease. I release a satisfied sigh as Emma tilts her head onto my shoulder. Her sigh blends with the seagull caws and the rhythm of the waves. It's resonant with trust.

For right now, *this* space feels pretty okay.

More than okay.

"Reece?"

"Yeah?"

"Tell me if I'm overstepping...but since it *was* what sparked all the drama last night..."

I turn in, pressing lips to her forehead to indicate I'm able to fill in her implication. "I have no idea why Angelique's in LA, Velvet." I see a sailboat on the water, tacking south toward Marina Del Rey, and pray for the calm of its glide to permeate my tension. "She called out of the blue the day before last and insisted on seeing me, saying she had important shit to discuss with me. I agreed only because I knew she wouldn't relent about it. I looked forward to it less than a root canal."

Her head lifts, and the curiosity in her eyes turns them the shade of the water at the horizon's edge. Brilliant and blue and piercing. "Important shit like what?"

I expel a heavy breath. "I don't know. We never got that far."

She's still—too still—before murmuring, "How far *did* you get?"

"Up to the part where I tried giving the cufflinks back." I finally glance over, letting her see the pain I can't convey in my tone. "She gave them to me the night before—" A growled grunt. "Well, before everything changed." Then a rough chuckle. "They actually meant a lot to me at the time. When you have more money than everyone you date, there's an expectation *you'll* be buying the presents, you know? I was floored that someone had thought to get *me* something."

"Only to find out she wanted something from you after all."

"You could say that."

It's dry and bitter, but it's my truth. But even as she brings some comfort with the press of our foreheads, I can't set aside what I must say after that. *The fucked-up follow-up.* It's almost a hashtag. If only it weren't so goddamned necessary.

"And Emma..." I pull back a few inches, just to make sure she's really listening. "It's probably what she still wants from me."

The Pacific waves crash harder, ushering in the tide. A couple of seagulls fight for a corner of a trashed sandwich. Salt and smoke rush on wind, changing midway from the balm of afternoon to the chill of night.

The woman next to me has gone eerily still again. "What do you mean?"

"Exactly what I'm saying." I press a hand to the side of her neck. "Angelique picked me up from the Brocade last night, presumably to go to dinner—but I got in the car and she instructed the driver to take us 'back to the house.' Not a restaurant. Not even another hotel. *The house.* Why would a woman passing through town be staying at a house?"

Emma frowns. "Maybe it belongs to a friend?"

"I assumed that too, but my gut told me differently. The blanks have been damn easy to fill in since then. It took my legal team about ten minutes to learn the Consortium's already filed for business licensing in the state. The address they used is a mansion on two acres out in Rancho Palos Verdes. I haven't dug any deeper than that, but I'm willing to bet the second owner on that place is Angelique La Salle."

She pulls away from my grasp. Pushing to her feet, she shakes out her head, turning her hair into white-gold streamers on the wind. "So what does all that mean?"

I scrub my face with both hands. Her crossed arms and hunched shoulders convey volumes of meaning. I've dropped so many damn bombs in the last few hours, and I'm about to pound her with one more—but like the others, this can't be helped.

"It means the Consortium is likely expanding their search for recruits into the States, targeting Los Angeles first."

Her shoulders visibly tighten. She drops her head, dipping it toward me without glancing all the way back. "Because of Bolt?"

"Probably," I mutter. "That and a city full of people who

already envision themselves as somebody like him."

"So what are we going to do?"

I reach for her and gently pull her back down. I coax her into my lap, where I can fill her mouth with a long, lingering, I'm-gonna-melt-the-polish-off-your-toenails kiss, which leaves us panting against each other's mouths.

Finally, I rasp, "Thank you."

"For what?" She's genuinely curious.

"For asking what *we're* going to do."

Her eyes go butter soft. She reaches her fingertips to my jaw and tenderly scrapes at my stubble. "I'm in this with you, Reece Richards." At the finish, she kicks up a corner of her mouth, emphasizing the adorable glory of her dimples. I stare for several seconds, feeling as giddy as a horny thirteen-year-old again. I swear to God, I'm a twenty-four-hour hormone factory, and *she's* the glorious, delirious reason. "Until you kick me off the boat, I'm in this thing through any storm that bitch wants to bring."

Yep. Hormones. And feeling. And passion. And obsession. And the flood of desire that orders me to kiss her again, twice as long and doubly as deep. But her hands, one pulling in my hair and the other gripping my shoulder, compel me to touch her as well. Along her face. Down the curves of her breasts, her waist, her thighs, and then inward, teasing at the warm triangle between them.

She groans softly into my mouth. I growl determinedly back into hers. She tastes like sea salt and arousal. Smells like wind and sweat. *My* sweat. I want to drench her in it all over again. I need to feel her washed in me, confirming the truth Angelique stole from me.

I'm still human. I'm still me. I'm still passion and fire and need and feeling...

And love.

Holy shit. *Holy. Shit.*

I love her.

I love her.

I should tell her.

But then what?

What if all my suspicions about the Consortium are true? Was that what Angelique wanted to meet with me about last night? To join their recruitment team here? And if I'd said no—translation, *hell fucking no, you deranged bitch*—what then? Would I have been dragged off to another secret rave somewhere? Is that still the fate that awaits me? After all this time, fighting some of the dirtiest criminal scum LA has thrown at me, am I still doomed to die on a gurney in a lab, fried by the lightning of my own blood?

If those bastards capture me again, it's a certainty. No guard will let the shackles slip on me this time.

And where will that leave the woman I've fallen ass over elbows for?

Pining pointlessly for me, that's where. Wasting her life—a life meant for so much more—in fruitless madness waiting for me to escape a life of being the Consortium's number one lab rat.

I won't do it to her. I can't.

But I know what I *can* do to her...

"Shit!" She exclaims it on a laugh as I reach up one leg of my shorts, which look a hell of a lot better on her than me, and swiftly find the trembling pearl of her desire. "Reece...*damn*." She quivers as I push back her intimate hood and pinch the hot ridge of her clit. "Wh-What...are you..."

"*We*," I correct her with a serrated growl. "You mean what are *we* going to do?" As I massage her clit, I lie back and swing her over to straddle me. Yeah, right here, in the middle of the beach. In the spell of the twilight. In the grip of everything I can only communicate to her in this way. Commanding her body, to prove how thoroughly she's conquered my heart.

"Oh. Kay." She bites her bottom lip to finish it, enticing me to kiss that stung cushion as I pull her down, molding her against me. "So...what are *we* going to do?"

I release a rickety breath and lift my gaze to meet the blue silk of hers. "Keep the sweatshirt pulled down," I instruct quietly. "Because I'm going to open my shorts and let my cock out. Then it's going to slide up inside you, and we're going to fuck like we can't get enough of each other."

"*Huh?*"

I slide a seductive smirk and caress her with heavy-lidded seduction. "You telling me you've had enough of me, Bunny? Because your pussy says otherwise."

She bites her lip harder. "Th-That's not it, and you know it."

"Then pull down the sweatshirt."

"Here?"

"Here."

"Now?"

The only answer I give is the grate of my zipper—and the surge of my dick. I owe her more of a churn than this. Romantic words and slow, wet kisses. Erotic imagery and flowery poetry. Sonnets and songs and soliloquies about how she makes more than my blood glow—only now my blood *does* glow, so before I become the main attraction for the whole beach, I need to get my hands hidden beneath her clothes and my cock buried inside her sweet, silken body.

Fuck. Her body.

Her legs, tensing against mine as we begin to rock. Her cunt, such a tight, torrid channel around my swelling length. Even her back, with lithe muscles flexing against my grip as we thrust and writhe and climb together toward the ultimate, erotic burst.

But most of all, right now, her eyes.

Entrancing me like summer smoke. Drowning me like ocean depths. And with her fearless, dauntless desire, keeping me locked to her face as we surge together toward completion, giving me another gift I don't deserve but will greedily, thoroughly seize.

And completely, shamelessly, need.

Her glow—emanating from the best power source I've ever known or seen.

Her heart—my ultimate treasure.

The prize I can one day, somehow, be worthy of asking for in full.

Right now, I can only tell her that with the force of my own gaze and all the passion in my body—and hope it's enough.

Dear God, let it be enough.

CHAPTER FIVE

EMMA

"The dude's getting laid."

"Has to be."

"Regularly."

"Definitely."

"Legit."

I stop where I'm at, in the doorway of the Brocade's break room, interrupting myself from my badass humming of "Believer"—I'm positive I'm going to make a billion dollars once Imagine Dragons hears this and demands I go on tour with them—to pay more attention to Wade and Fershan's back-and-forth.

"I mean, come *on*." Wade stabs chopsticks into his ramen and twirls the noodles in emphasis. "The Hagakure ramen bar today and Sandwich Heaven last Friday? Fresh flowers on all the tables in here?"

Fershan cocks a brow. "*Flowers* are what you notice? We both got instant cash bonuses for positive guest satisfaction."

"Which were whose idea to begin with?" I use the line while sliding between them to grab an edamame pod from the bowl they're sharing.

Fershan chuckles. "I officially bow to the queen of good ideas."

"Bows not necessary." I swipe a few more of the pods. "Just more of these, please." I moan while sucking out another of the tender green beans from their warm casing. "Damn. So good."

"Fine," Wade says. "Props to Em for the bonuses. But the rest of these bennies?" He swirls an empty chopstick in the air before stabbing it toward the hotel's main tower. "I'm sticking to my theory. Methinks, my friends, the weird one in yon gilded tower has been dipping his golden wick with blissful frequency."

"Ew." It's a fast way to disguise my furious blush, which I hide further by turning for the ramen bar. Though I could make a meal out of the edamame alone, I force myself to mull over the sauce choices while regaining my composure. Reece's little "gifts" for the team, sprinkled with care throughout the last two weeks, have meant more to me than jewelry, candy, or stuffed animals. As for the flowers? He's made sure they're part of my world every day—even here in the basement break room.

My hero. Sweeping me off my feet...in all the ways that matter.

"Forsooth." Fershan snickers while adding on to his friend's theory. "Methinks I doth agree with you. Our prince must be wooing a lady fair and extending his happiness to his people."

Wade groans. "Wooing? What the hell is that, man? *Wooing?*"

I toss a scowl over my shoulder. "A lot better than 'dipping his golden wick,' that's what."

"Whoa."

"Wade, the man's 'wick' is none of our—"

"No. I mean *whoa.*"

The stab of shock in Wade's voice is a compulsion, causing me to pivot around as he snatches the remote to the break room's TV. As he scrolls the volume up, a heart-halting image consumes the screen. A muscled figure in black leather is leaping through the air like rockets are powering him.

Holy *wow*.

"Our dude's up and at it again," Wade exclaims. "Literally."

Fershan rises, dropping his chopsticks in favor of hoisting a hearty geek fist. "Oh, snap it up!" His eyes go wide. "Wait. Is that the power plant out at El Segundo?"

"Duh." Wade snorts.

"By the gods. What is he doing *there*?"

"Kicking ass, power-pulsing dickheads, and saving the city." Wade's tone implies the second *duh*.

"In*deed*." Fershan skirts the table, intensifying the whoop-whoop fist. "Bolt, my man!"

Actually... I slip into a chair at the table behind theirs, smirking like a loon, as they both spin into fanboy mode. *He's* my *man*.

But in instances like this, I don't mind sharing. Not one bit. The only thing I *do* mind is throwing my own mask on. And, in many ways, I don a whole outfit to go with it. The guise is invisible but in place as blatantly as Reece's leathers and eye cover—a façade that allows me to *oooohh* and *ahhhh* along with everyone else but hold back the rest of what I feel when watching him jump, spin, battle, and bash with the body I've come to know, desire, and cherish.

And love.

Oh God, how I love him.

And oh God, are there moments when it sucks harder to mask that fact. Like right now.

"Fucking bad*ass*," Wade exclaims.

"He's rocking it!" Fershan adds.

"You should see him with a finger vibe and some lube." My barely audible utterance is absorbed by the guys' excitement.

"He's rocking this shit."

"Rocking it out *loud*."

I smirk a little wider—and squirm a little more. My boyfriend's rocking this shit. Out loud. That means he'll have *a lot* of extra voltage to fry off tonight...

Lucky, lucky, *lucky* me.

But first, there's getting to watch him—how did Wade phrase it?—kick ass, power-pulse some bad guys, and save the city.

There's just one thing missing about that theory. Big-time.

I notice it at the same moment Wade and Fershan do.

"Where are...all the dickheads?" Fershan leans forward, asking it first.

Wade stands up. "He doesn't have any dickheads."

Fershan rises too. "Just a dick...girl?"

As I push to my feet, my heart plummets the opposite direction. It thuds in my stomach, exploding like a bad cold fusion science project, spreading shards of terror throughout my body. "N-Not a girl."

"Huh?"

I hardly hear Wade's comeback.

"Em? Are you all right?"

Or Fershan's anxious probe.

"Not. A. Girl." I seethe the words this time through my gritted teeth. "A bitch." I compel my feet to move, stumbling in front of them both. "A bitch he needs to kill."

I've never spoken such words before. But I've never been

captive to such ruthless terror, which is worsening as the scene on the TV plays out even more. Only it's not a "scene." It's the truth, happening beyond my control and despite my horror.

The news station, only able to carry an aerial feed, shows Reece in full Bolt mode, dashing across ducts and roofs at the huge power plant across town, next to the ocean. Sure enough, it looks like he's chasing absolutely nothing, until the cameras pan to show another figure sprinting—with cascading blond hair, the legs of a stripper, and the boobs of a porn star. The whole damn world now knows this, thanks to Angelique's leather corset, matching mini skirt, and bloodred hip boots. Any shred of doubt I've had about her identity is erased by the sight of her upper back, where a red and black tattoo of angel's wings spreads from shoulder blade to shoulder blade.

Frankly, I don't care if the woman is sporting a tramp stamp and a genie girl outfit. She's throwing down one-on-one with the man I love on behalf of the criminals who kidnapped him, held him prisoner, and hijacked his bloodstream in the name of their higher science. They took his *life*—only to return now, ready to end it.

I don't know how else to interpret what I see Angelique doing to him.

For every energy pulse Reece throws, she has a comeback in the form of a giant shield, somehow connected to the force of the station itself, deflecting and then reflecting the punches. In strategic places, she stops to throw her weight on massive levers, unleashing smaller versions of what seem like electromagnetic pulses. As lights flicker, steam billows, and alarms blare, Reece crumples to the ground like a dog hit with a silent whistle. As soon as the pulse finishes, he gets back up, though he is visibly weakened by the smackdown.

My heart shoots to my throat. My mouth erupts with a terrified moan. I grab the edge of the table, the only thing preventing my knees from crumpling. But what good will that do? What good can *I* do at all? I can't be there next to him, as my soul yearns. I can't run to him, help him, be there for him. I can't even yell at him to get up, as Wade and Fershan can. What if I lose my shit and spill his name? I can only watch, clutched by the same mortification as the rest of the city, as a female dressed like a Santa Monica hooker and moving like a million-dollar action star keeps driving their superhero to his knees.

After the fourth electromagnetic pulse, Reece can no longer struggle to his feet. He unfurls from the fetal position and rolls to his back, dusty and defeated. I stagger closer to the TV, unable to stop the tears from rolling down my cheeks and the air from pounding in my lungs, despite my attention being fixed on someone else's chest... On any sign of life from the man I love, still sprawled on the ground in a hailstorm of power station sparks, fighting to accept he has, at last, been defeated.

I sense it even as I watch him from this distance, through this impartial lens. Hell, maybe the news cameras make me see it better, sense it deeper. It's as if I'm soaring in there next to him. I almost know what he's thinking just by watching him...

He's giving up.

"No," I rasp.

Preparing himself for the inevitable.

"No!"

Defeat is written in the rigid set of his head. The fists formed at the ends of both arms. The pallor of his skin, noticeable even from the altitude at which the helicopter hovers.

"*No!*"

Any moment now, Angelique will appear at his side, gloating like a triumphant Deneuve, missing only her Balenciaga tote and her fancy French cigarette. Doubtful she'll be toting a glass of water for her new captive either.

Unless...

The glass of water finds a way to the party anyway.

Unless...

The miracle for which I've just given up hope is delivered by the angels themselves, in the form of mist that turns to rain. Inside a minute, the concrete slab under Reece becomes a solid wet sheen.

And then one of the loose power lines flies over, touches down, and ignites the slab with blinding ribbons of electricity.

Shooting the man I love straight into the dark sky.

Shit, shit, shit, shit.

"Fuccckkkker!" Wade shouts.

"*Booooyaaaahhh!*" Fershan yelps.

"Reece!" It detonates from me in the same instant. I'm beyond caring. I can only spin and race to where I dropped my purse, diving into the thing for my cell. Once it's in my grip, I can't get to the speed-dial list fast enough. Tears blur my vision, and I cuss as I tap on the wrong window. Calling the dry cleaners for a rush job right now is the last thing on my mind. Summoning Zalkon for the same thing? As Reece would say—Bingo.

Reece.

His name is the only thing I allow into my mind. The only thrum of importance. The only thought that matters. And yeah, that includes how my two coworkers follow every inch of my movements like kittens after a laser, finally finding their opening in the forever it seems to take Z to pick up my call.

"The hell?" Wade blurts.

"Krishna's balls," Fershan gasps.

"Not now," I snap at them both.

"But—"

"But—"

"Not. *Now.*" I leave the room with the phone locked to my ear. The second Z picks up, a smartass one-liner prepped to fling through the line, I interrupt him too. "Reece needs us. Don't bother with getting me at the front of the hotel. I'll meet you at the employee entrance. *Hurry!*"

REECE

"Wh-What the hell?" I mutter. "*Where* the hell—"

"Ssshhh."

In the chaos I used to call my senses, this woman's voice is the only thing of worthy clarity. It cuts through the raging voltage in my blood, the flooded capacitors of my muscles, the torched circuits of my brain. "Emma?"

"*Sssshhh.*"

"Fuck." I fight to push up. "C-Can't stop, Velvet. Not now. Angelique—"

"Is gone." She says it simply, but there's a terrified wobble beneath it. Her fear isn't ribbons. It's gigantic ropes, holding her back. No. Holding her *in*. She's keeping her shit together. For me? Why?

I stow that question in favor of the easier one to answer.

"Dead?" I'm not proud of how much hope I punch into the word. Angelique told me enough about her life that I believed, and still do, in some kind of good tucked deeply inside her. More than that, I'm an asshole, not a murderer. But with so much of my system fried, my filters have gotten tossed into the fire too.

"No." Her voice trembles. "M-Maybe. We don't know." I barely hear the last of it as a huge truck rumbles by. I gather enough of my senses to realize I'm lying in two inches of mud in a shallow ditch halfway between the power station and the road.

"Holy shit," I mutter.

"No kidding." The interjection belongs to Zalkon, hovering a few feet away. His tie is loose, mud spatters his black suit, and freaked-the-hell-out is written all over his swarthy face.

"There was an electrical burst." Dots of mist outline Emma's profile as she eyes the power station, now crawling with police, firemen, and energy company reps. "A live power line came down on the wet cement, and—"

"I remember. At least I think I do..." It's hard to think straight. My brain is a ball of pain. The careening lights of the emergency crews are red and blue lances on my throbbing gray matter.

"The impact threw you all the way over the fence," she supplies.

"Fuck." Yeah. Okay. Now I *do* remember.

Her fingertips shake against my skin as she smooths a chunk of hair back from my forehead. "Do you remember anything else? What happened before that?"

"Yeah." It's dark, and my head still whirls with dizziness, but I fumble a hand up and grasp hers. "I got a ping on my police scanner and couldn't ignore it. They said there was a break-in at the plant. Some person was packing serious heat, looking like they were going to fuck with the city's power grid."

Emma stiffens. "And it was her."

"Yeah."

"Knowing exactly how she could fuck with *you* in that environment."

"Yeah." I feel like a bigger asshole when she shivers, right before her composure breaks on a messy sob. Desperately, I pull her down, absorbing the flood of her grief with my shoulder. "Hey. *Hey*, beauty, it's okay."

She twists a hand into my hair and detonates a new sob against my neck. "It's not okay!"

"Emma?" Z steps back over.

I shoot him a thank-you-but-stay-away look, soothing my protective caveman but screwing my reformed douchebag. I have no right to be holding her like this. Fuck, I hardly *can* hold her like this. My arms feel like noodles. My brain's still filled with excruciating fuzz.

While I know the drain on my system is temporary, the implications in my life aren't. Never has a moment been more symbolic of that truth than now. She should be at home tonight with a man like—well, like Z. A good guy in a nice suit, with a steady job and ready humor. Someone who will always be there for her, not a drained sap in a ditch, offering her nothing but agony, tears, and mud.

"I'm fine." Her protest is watery but determined. She pushes up, squaring her shoulders. "*I'm fine.* But I swear to God, if Angelique La Salle ever *thinks* she can come near you again—"

I cut into her rant with a hard squeeze to her forearm. "Then I'll be more prepared than I was tonight."

"Who's Angelique La Salle?"

"Bet your hot ass you'll be prepared." Emma rocks her head with more swagger than a rapper, stabbing her free hand into the air. "You'll be prepared with me at your side, ready to show her bad pleather and hip waders with heels only work on desperate johns in Santa Monica."

Z goes silent. Clearly, he's not sure whether to laugh, growl, or high-five my girl. I'm in the same boat—technically, mired in the same ditch—only with one more available option, which I readily grasp.

I kiss her.

Then again.

Then a third time, letting our lips linger longer, taste deeper, twine tighter. I groan hard, drinking in her strength like a damn vampire, especially as the force of her passion works its way into the electrons of my blood, the power cells of my spirit, the fiber of my muscles.

And in that moment, I know.

I'll never be able to live without her.

Which is why I *must* live without her.

Never has a decision felt more right—or more shitty—in my life. It hits my heart like a sea change and moves mountain ranges in my mind. It feels catastrophic and cataclysmic but destined...and determined. When I figure out why, I bark out a soft laugh.

I've just made a life-changing choice that doesn't involve a shred of my own needs.

Meaning that maybe the woman was right about me all along. Have I truly been a good person hiding behind a douchebag façade? Was I so afraid about embracing the real hero inside that I pretended to be one on the outside? Bringing all these bad guys to justice... Was it my way of trying to bring myself to the same reckoning?

The reckoning...of now.

"Reece?" My reaction hasn't been lost on Emma. No surprise there—though I feel the energy slowly returning, along with the need to beat myself up, as her anxiety clearly skyrockets. As she touches my face, she furtively utters, "What is it?"

"You mean," Z cuts in, his jaw struggling to form words, "other than the fact that h-he's..."

"Ready to fire on torpedo bay one?" I laugh again, waving my glow stick digits as if to zap him. "Guess the boss *is* a fun guy now, huh?"

An easy grin replaces Z's bewilderment. "Just tell me where the Death Star is, and we'll blast off, sir."

I roll to my feet. The strength is regenerating faster now, zooming through me like a squadron of fighters zooming at their own Death Star, enabling me to sprint toward the Mercedes. "Good idea," I return to the guy. "But now that you know the classified shit, I'll have to kill you."

Z, keeping pace with me until now, halts in the sludge with a loud *slup*. "Errr—"

"Kidding."

"Thank fuck," he mutters.

"Thank God," Emma rasps at the same time. In the second I take to frown down at her, standing in the space between the car's door and back seat, she darts a nervous glance up through her lashes. "Because I *might* have been a little stressed when the news outlets broadcasted your showdown with Angelique..."

"And?" I prompt.

"And...I might have told Wade and Fershan about you too."

Zalkon, standing next to the driver's door, snickers. "Which, in those guys' minds, really did turn you into the coolest boss on the planet."

Emma giggles. "No argument here."

I lean down, kissing the playful tilt on her lips. "Even if I decide they have to be killed too?"

"Oh, no." She blinks wide doll eyes. "Not *that*, Mr. Richards."

"Well..." My stare dips down the length of her body. "Maybe I can accept your penance for it."

Her gaze flares. "My *penance*?"

"Mmmhmmm." I nod with lascivious languor. "I'll take it out of you...in flesh."

"Oh. In *that* case." She topples backward onto the seat, yanking me into the car after her. I barely drag the door closed before Z has the motor gunned and the car in motion, lurching my lips onto hers through the sheer magic of Newton's first law.

I keep letting my mouth fall over hers. I bite her and dominate her and sweep into her, roaring my tongue into the dark, hot cavity of her, plunging in a simulation of what my cock's about to do to her pussy. She groans her acknowledgment, reaches her hands for my neck, and lets me continue to fill and possess her mouth.

"Z." I raise my voice at the guy but don't look away from her. "Put up the barrier."

Emma's mouth twitches. She lifts a leg, thunking one of her pumps against the sliding door between us and the front seat. She giggles again as her shoe falls off, clunking to the car's floor. "Looks like he already did."

"Good man."

She shrugs, a good excuse for bringing her hands to the front of her button-up blouse. "He works for the coolest boss on the planet. Of course he's a good man."

I watch her fingers, mesmerized with every new inch of alabaster skin she exposes, especially as the lace of her bra comes into view. But the recognition hits, hard and violent, that this *will* be the last time I'm with her like this. Gazing at her open and exposed like this. A spell only begun with her physical perfection...

But what an amazing place to start.

"I'm not a good man, Emma."

At this moment, despite all the internal resolve for gallantry through which I've just put myself, I mean it. I *want* to mean it. Need to embrace everything about me that's wicked and wanton and nasty, symbolized in the low growl I unfurl while pushing my hands up her legs. I grip her black pantyhose, ready to rip the things off—only to learn the hose are actually thigh-high stockings secured to her legs with a sexy-as-fuck garter belt. At the center is a tiny triangle of black satin that, in some crazy alternate universe, can be called underwear.

My breath snags. I snap my stare back toward her face. Her smile of impish seduction already awaits. "Well, what do you know?" She swings her other leg out, raising it over my shoulder. "*I'm* not good either, Mr. Richards."

Before I can help it, a laugh erupts from the depths of my belly—and the core of my soul. *This woman.* This incredible, unforgettable creature. The lightning in my blood might be responsible for how I met her, but the storm she's left in my heart will never, ever subside—a secret confession that takes hold of my mind while I shove the panties away from her gorgeous cleft.

"My sweet, shiny surprise." I slide a finger in, trailing through her trembling folds from top to bottom.

"Thought you'd like it." She rests her head back against the car's door while lifting her chin with sensual invitation. "I got them online. It was a little weird putting them on in the bathroom at work, but they made me think of you the rest of the day."

I stroke her again, zeroing in on her clit. "I'm glad you did."

Her hips buck. Her lips fall open. "Maybe I should get a few more."

And maybe I need to change the subject. Fast.

A good man would.

But I'm not a good man.

Definitely not.

At least not right now.

And right now is all that matters. All that *can* matter.

I push out her leg a little more, absorbing the heady sight of her pussy, wet and waiting and spread and slick. A tight groan leaves my lips as I whip at the fastenings of my leathers with primal urgency. Then a new growl, thick and harsh, as my dick surges out, hard and ready.

Emma's gaze, already lowered to my crotch, heats like a pair of blue flames. "Oh, I'm *definitely* getting a few more."

I position myself at her dark slit, working my rigid bulb between her waiting folds. "You should probably hold off on that promise."

Her brow knits. "Why?"

I push in by another fraction, lubing her tight opening with my burning precome. "Until after."

"After...?"

"After I fuck your cunt raw."

Her whole frame shakes. Her lungs, pumping heavily, push her breasts into her waiting hands. She claws aside the edges of her bra from the middle out, baring herself in a wild rending, a la the most famous superhero move on earth—with a twist that's uniquely, erotically hers.

Sassy, gorgeous siren.

Sexy, incredible superheroine.

Mine. Mine. Mine.

If only for this last, ill-gotten collection of moments... *mine*.

The sight of her naked tits plucked by her own greedy hands drives my sanity past the edge of control. I surge forward, stretching her pussy with one push of my full erection. I fuck her so full and hard and deep, she sighs and shudders and screams with the force of me.

"You want more, Velvet?"

"Yes. *Yes*."

Gladly, I give it to her. Over and over and over again.

"More?"

"Yes! More of your cock. Please, Reece!"

"You want this cock to make you come?"

"*Fuck*." She whips her head from left to right and back again, consumed by erotic ecstasy.

"I asked you a question, Emmalina."

"Y-Yes," she manages. "Damn it, yes. I want your cock to make me come!"

"Then do it." I roll into her, scraping her exposed nub with the pressure of my abdomen. "*Do it*," I order through locked teeth, even as I feel her thrumming around my dick, milking me with the force of her release.

Pulling the orgasm out of me too. Taking it all from me. Taking all that *is* me.

Until more astounding words form on my lips.

"I love you, Emmalina Crist."

A song bleeds over from Z's playlist in the front seat. The guy's into every icon of classic rock, meaning David Bowie's voice doesn't come as a surprise—nor does the song. Perhaps it's the rightness I feel about this moment. The recognition that this *is* the choice, at last, of a superhero—no matter how fucking hard it's going to be, especially after just slapping my heart on my fucking sleeve.

Especially as the song ramps up more. Bowie sings, in his Bowie way, about nothing but everything mattering. About forever and ever existing in one day.

"I love you too, Reece Richards."

Her admission doesn't shock me—but it doesn't make me feel great. Not as great as I'd expected. Her voice is a sparse rasp on the words...as if they make her more sad than joyous. As if she agrees with the bittersweet ache of Bowie's croon, blending its dystopian feel with the rumble of the wheels on the freeway. I pull my body from hers as the song talks of guns and kisses, of a king and a queen...and of becoming heroes...

She turns so I'm embracing her from behind. I already hate feeling this detached from her but bitch-slap myself for the mush. Do I want to know that she's close or safe? What would have happened if she'd been anywhere close to me in El Segundo? What would Angelique have done to take Emma out of the picture—out of *my* picture—in a remote location like that?

I refuse to focus on the answer to that. I'll accept tonight as the easier way to learn that lesson—and I'll do it with gratitude.

Our silence continues as downtown's distinctive landscape looms closer. The circle-shaped tops of the US

Bank and 777 towers. The proud obelisks of the Aon Center and Union Bank Plaza. The purple dome of the arena at LA Live and the City Hall building used in hundreds of films and TV shows.

And tucked between them all, the stylized gold tower of the Brocade.

The moment the hotel slides into view, the woman in my arms releases a weighted breath. Again, she doesn't sound happy. More like...resigned.

And sorrowed.

"You're getting out there, aren't you?" The same conflict crowds her soft challenge. "At the Brocade." She presses a hand to my chest, as if the move will give her a temperature reading on my heart. As if *that* will work—or tell her that what my heart wants right now isn't what I can give it.

"Emma—"

"Just answer me, damn it." Her voice thickens as if tears are about to break through, though her eyes are dry as desert skies. "You're going to get out, ride up to that penthouse, and shut out the world, me included, like you have for the last goddamned year, all because of your idiotic fear—"

"Idiotic?" I push away. I stuff my cock back into my leathers and refasten them. If she wants fear, I'll give it to her. "You were watching tonight, right?" I charge. "You said you were."

"If I said I watched, I watched." The syntax is defensive, but her tone goes far beyond. She's clearly pissed. Good. Maybe pissed is where I need her to be so she'll clear the love out of her ears and listen.

"So you saw what Angelique tried to do to me?" I snarl. "What would have happened if you'd been there with me?

What would have happened if we were just out on a date together instead? What's *going* to happen if she ever finds out I've split the sidewalk falling this hard in love?"

Her lips quirk, despite her obvious effort to control the knee-jerk at my metaphor. "You think I don't know how to handle the sidewalk, even *with* Angelique on it?"

I steel my jaw. "I think you don't understand the Consortium. They're not some fringe band of radicals with a weird scientific hair up their ass, Emma. They're cold, they're methodical, and they're ruthless—and I'm the loose thread in their ugly orange sweater. They're determined to sew me back into the thing or cut the thread loose, including any other threads that are now attached to it. It's a no-win game, and I've been just fine with letting them come after me for that win—"

"Until now," she supplies dismally.

"Yeah." I finally unclench my teeth enough to talk again. "Until now." I slide my grip back into her hair. I crush her brilliant strands with the intensity of my fist, gulping while imagining *her* sprawled on a sidewalk, killed in the name of the Consortium's crazy quest. "It's not going to happen," I vow. "It's *not* going to happen."

She lifts her head to fervently search my face. "So what are you going to do?"

"I'm taking myself out of it. *And* you. Fuck. *Especially* you."

I enforce it by yanking her up and kissing her hard. God*damn*, she still tastes so good. And feels even better. She compels my mouth back to hers with an aching whimper, her fingers twining in my hair. She pulls to the point of pain, accelerating my blood from the heady rush. I can't refuse the stab of her tongue any more than I can turn down air. We make out like that, hot and horny as teenagers at the beach, Bowie still crooning as Z exits the freeway and winds through the noisy avenues of downtown.

When we part, taking in huge gulps of air, that sad sound flows from her again. She launches at me, clutching hard, begging in a whisper against my neck.

"Don't." She claws ruthless half-moons into my nape with her nails. "*Don't*, Reece...*please.*"

I wrap my arms around her. Inhale her, all rain and honey and grief, and force out my answer. "I have to."

"You never *have* to hide."

I duck my head against her hair and shake it slowly. "Right now, hiding is beating them."

"Hiding is *losing* to them! Damn it, if—"

She chokes into silence as soon as my fist rams the car's window. The reinforced pane, now exploded into a thousand interlocked shards, resembles stained glass with its reflections of the city's lights.

And there's the pretty way of looking at it.

And maybe that's for the best, considering the hard truth that fills the air in the car.

A couple of minutes later, Z rolls the car to a stop beneath the lonely awning of my private entrance to the hotel. I suck in a huge breath. Shove it back out, trying to reconsider her words. *Is* there another way, or do I have to be *that* brand of douchebag too? Yeah, the one who just screwed his girl with the full intention of leaving her afterward. The one who told her he loved her somewhere in that mess.

The one who's now going to leave this car yearning to touch her once more in some small way but instead ordering myself to get out with barely a glance backward. Taking one more breath. Fighting through one more second, which will be like the other disgusting seconds, torturous minutes, agonizing hours, and miserable days of the lonely weeks and years to come.

"Send me a bill for the window, Z."

"Of course, Mr. Richards."

"I love you, Emmalina."

"Fuck you, Mr. Richards."

CHAPTER SIX

EMMA

Damn him.

Damn him, anyway.

I've only heard of this kind of sorrow before. To be honest, I thought it didn't exist. What kind of heartbreak dives so deep into a person they can't even shed tears because of it? Anything a person spends life on is worth spending grief on too, right? And that means tears, right?

But as Z drives me home, my senses are a desert.

When I wake up the next morning, they're just as barren and lifeless. I look inward, only to find all the rooms of myself charred and dark. Seared beyond recognition.

The kind of damage only possible from an electrical fire.

Damn him.

I climb into the shower, douse myself beneath the spray, and wait for the water to flush out the feelings. But even here, in the safest space for my emotions, my soul clings to the sorrow.

Do I *like* being this numb? This huge hypocrite, hiding behind a mental wall right after yelling at Reece for doing the same damn thing? Okay, *duh*. Of course not. But my frustration about that is the beginning of my answer. I'm feeling *something*, meaning I'm not totally emotionally cauterized. It's just one box that my heart refuses to open: the compartment bearing his name.

Reece Richards.

Who just a month ago was nothing to me but an enigmatic concept in a high, distant tower.

Who has now ordered me to revert him to that same status in my heart.

"Screw you, Richards."

My voice falters on the last of it, raising my hopes that the fissure of my composure is finally cracking open wide enough for the tears, but there's still nothing behind it but an arid wasteland. A parched horizon, broken only by snakes that taunt with hisses of heartache and scorpions threatening with fury-driven pincers.

So just make him part of it too.

Toss him in. Let him burn. Make him wither.

"You'd really like that, wouldn't you?"

I bite it out while climbing out of the shower and heading to check my phone—as if in the last five minutes the bastard will have suddenly come to his senses and figured out what I already know. What I've *always* known. That I'd rather be sewn into his ugly orange sweater, even by one measly thread, than to own an entire wardrobe of beautiful coats.

The affirmation makes me stop. As in, completely. I'm frozen halfway through sliding on my pants, my gaze locked on my awkward position in the mirror, as realization stabs me like a knitting needle.

I need his sweater. Even if it's only in my mind, I need every last loop of that obnoxious orange thread to hold, to cherish, to remember.

But giving in to the tears means tossing out the sweater. Never.

Never.

"Never."

The mantra spills from between my gritted teeth as I slam my bare leg into my pants and fasten the button of the high waist with angry twists. I welcome even more of the fury while getting into the cropped jacket and striped boat-neck shirt that complete the outfit before combing out my hair, yanking it into a side ponytail, and turning the strands into a long braid. After some basic foundation, blush, and lip gloss, I decide the "work look" for today must be declared complete. No way am I capable of the precision or concentration an eye ensemble will take.

To be honest, I barely know if I'm qualified to be going into the hotel tonight.

But what's my alternative? Sitting around the apartment, checking my phone every three minutes and getting only notifications about pizza coupons and penis enhancements? Going to the gym, where I can *also* check my phone every three minutes, with the same damn interruptions? Or perhaps getting something accomplished—and getting paid for it, at that?

Ding, ding, ding. Door number three it is.

Yeah, even walking wounds can do the world some good, especially when they're distracted by something other than their own pain—which, the gods of tourism be praised, come in the form of sixty rooms booked at the last minute for a group of Australians unable to get onto their temporarily disabled cruise ship. Diving into the room-preparation fray forces me to slap a Band-Aid on the wound—until around two a.m., when I finally stumble into the break room for some coffee and find Wade and Fershan already claiming a couple of spots, scrolling through their phones and trading the latest updates from their feeds.

If they're getting the same notifications I get, I do *not* want to know about it.

"How the hell did I not know the suburban soccer mom meme chick is really a romance writer?" Wade mutters.

"For truth?" Fershan returns.

"You mean 'for real'?"

"No. *You* mean for real."

"Huh?"

Fershan huffs. "Is the suburban soccer mom meme a romance writer or are you just turning me on?"

"*Dude.*"

"What?"

Wade's turn for the huff. "If I'm turning you on, we'd probably better talk."

"Why?"

"Oh, my God. Never mind."

"So she's not a romance writer?"

"And who's on first?"

My crack makes them sit up and spin around so fast, they bonk heads. While their enthusiasm doesn't surprise me, the collision makes me grimace. Or maybe the expression is an advance payment to fate for the "chat" I'm anticipating with them now.

"Emma! Uh...hey!"

Wade's so awkwardly cheerful, I find it hard to stay casual. Nevertheless, as I head for the fancy coffee bar—another new feature of the break room, installed just yesterday—I manage to return with breezy sincerity, "Hey yourself."

While I wait for his response, I let my gaze bulge at

the luxurious setup. *Wow.* There are separate machines for tea infusions, specialty lattes, and flavored hot cocoas, with themed biscotti, chocolates, and cookies in another rack. It's a Tiffany store in caffeine form—and easily ushers in another could-this-finally-be-the-tears moment. Though it's just another false alarm from my tear ducts, my heart hangs on to its bittersweet ping.

The guy in the tower really does still care.

"You big dork," I whisper, hiding the chastisement as the latte maker shrieks with steam. "All I want is the ugly sweater, damn it."

I'm saved from any more thoughts about tangerine-colored togs by the workmates suddenly flanking me—though they're not smooth enough to hide their furtive trade of glances before I turn in place and lean against the counter. My heart twinges again, but this time in the form of some feels for these two, who have likely been on the fanboy versions of pins and needles—gamepads and styluses?—since the last time the three of us were in here.

And then, the circumstances in which I dashed *out* of here.

And the bomb of information I dropped on them before I did.

The same bomb with which they've just played a glaring round of hot potato, each daring the other to grab the spud and face me with it.

Their discomfort almost makes me wince again. Instead, at least knowing I can save the two of them from any more burned fingers, I lower my cup, rush in a deep breath, and state, "All right, boys. Let's go ahead and kill the elephant in the room right now."

Wade has the grace to let out a good-natured chuckle. "Oh

now, come on. There's *no* elephant..."

"Not a single one." Fershan nods like a bobblehead with a rocket booster. "No pachyderms in sight!"

"Not even one named Bolt?"

They both stutter into silence.

Until, a few seconds later, Wade mutters, "Errrmm...what about him?"

I send back a serene smile. "Neither of you are idiots, Wade—nor would I ever insult you by treating you as such. You heard what you heard..."

"Which neither of us have told a soul about." Fershan looks ready to fall to his knees and pledge it on a sword dipped in his mother's blood—or something damn similar. "We swear!"

"Which isn't necessary." I clap his shoulder to emphasize my point. "If anybody clearly gets the rules about all this, it's you two. I know you'd never betray Reece like that."

Wade's wild ginger brows shoot up. "*Reece*?"

I pick up my latte again, sipping it with serenity I couldn't be farther from feeling. "Did I say 'Reece?' I must have meant... *cease*. Or...something along those lines."

I'm counting on the two of them to take the hint and back off a little. They're not dumb guys or even the craziest fanboys—except, it seems, when it comes to *this* particular subject. *Lucky me.* Their reaction rapidly ramps up into a combination of fervor and terror, complete with bulging eyes, thundering carotids, and breathing patterns that make me look around for brown paper bags.

Once more, Wade is able to compose himself first, though he locks his hands behind his head like he's become the crazed systems tech in charge of Fershan's rocket booster. "Okay, so..." He pauses his tiger-in-a-cage pacing to latch his gaze directly back on me. "Reece Richards really *is* Bolt? Is *that* what you're saying?"

Another full inhalation. Another self-reprimand, to keep my composure in check—since their excitement feels like they've dipped a pair of swords into liquid fire and are now juggling them over my head. "Now, Mr. Tavish," I admonish. "You know I can neither confirm nor deny that—but would certainly not give you a lot of shit if that's the theory you choose to stick by."

Fershan plummets back into his chair. "By the gods."

"By the holy fucking firmament of gods." Though Wade stays on his feet, he's now got his hands balled up in his hair, yanking and stretching it out like the crazy rocket tech with a foot stuck in a light socket. "Our boss is a superhero." His gawk zeroes back on me. "And our friend is bonking him."

I swing my gaze away—and don't protest when the rest of me wants to follow suit, finding my way into an empty chair of my own. "Yeah, well...about that..."

"Aw, crap."

It's impossible to prevent his dismal blurt from reaching all the way inside and then twisting every chamber of my heart. My spirit. My nerves. My lungs. I should be used to this by now, but I'm not. I can't breathe—and now I can't even focus on their fun frenzy as a distraction. If only Wade could've been shallow and selfish about the exclamation—but no. His voice is weighted with the opposite. Deep concern infused with discerning insight—now followed by him walking over, lowering into the seat next to me, and then lifting one of my hands.

"You want to talk about it?"

I sigh again. Damn it, why is he being so sweet? "Sorry,"

I whisper, slowly shaking my head. *Sorry because I know you really want to know. And that if you can, you even want to help— but that if you do, you're in a lot of immediate danger from some scary-as-hell bad guys.*

And I'm sorry because processing all of that was not what I wanted to do.

Because now I understand every damn reason Reece did it.

Because now I understand the agony he endured in doing it.

Because now I have no choice but to let that desolation take over. That desperation to become reality. And the tears, at last, to fall.

REECE

I'm still breathing hard as I collapse at my desk in the Brocade's penthouse. The snarls bursting from my parted lips are ferocious but fulfilled. They match my smile, a continuation of the celebration from helping put away the fifteen-person credit-card-skimming-ring who decided tonight's Dodger game would be a great place to cheat thousands out of their hard-earned money. Less than a half hour ago, I'd helped the cops escort the gang into booking at Central, where even now, they're all being processed for arraignment.

Fifteen jerks arrested. Every collar clean, clear, and by the book. The kind that remind a guy that maybe the system *does* work. That maybe his freak show fingers *are* good for something worthwhile after all.

Until the freak boy leans back in his chair. And takes a look at the different security cam feeds from around the hotel tonight.

And locks his gaze on the feed from the employee cafeteria.

Where a beauty with a long blond braid is hunched over, her slender shoulders clenched as she sobs, being comforted by the two gamer guys from the reservations bay.

Who take turns looking up at the camera—as if knowing said freak boy can see every second of this. And hoping he feels like trash about it.

I ditch my smile in favor of growling the F-word.

Because I don't feel like trash.

I feel ten times worse.

I shove back to my feet, trying to ignore how the analogy follows my steps across the room. I feel like the monster from a dystopian movie, covered in rotted things and smelling like ass, as I trudge back and forth in front of the security monitors.

"*Shit.*" I hiss it out while reaching a finger up to the image of my woman bawling her eyes out on the shoulders of her friends. Wade and Fershan still take turns glaring up at the camera, their expressions doing the talking for them. Loud and fucking clear.

You're an ass.

If this girl was mine, I'd be treating her much better than this.

They don't get it.

They don't get even half of it.

If they did, they'd know how brutally this crap is killing *me* too. That getting out of the limo three nights ago, I might as well have crawled back into this place on the bloody stumps of the knees I'd just sliced from under myself. That every damn second of every damn day after that, there's been no relief from the pain, except during the hours when I get to go out and make the city—*her* city—a better place to be by putting criminals away.

And yeah, they don't get that the most heroic act of my whole fucking existence was the decision to separate her life from mine. That I knew, and still know, that as soon as the Consortium has a chance to yank their tails out from between their legs, they'll be sneaking back through the junkyard like the dogs they are, ready to sniff at my trash pile again.

And this time, maybe they'll be armed with matches and kerosene.

So as much as I admire those two kids for "standing up" to their boss, especially since they now know what *he* does on his midnight break times, I still refuse to cede the joust to their lances. They don't know the entire story here. They still don't know that two people have been existing in this hell. They still don't know that I completely get where *she's* coming from. That all too clearly, I can imagine *myself* in the back seat of that limo, watching as Emma handed *me* some lame-ass line about "saving me" from her "dangerous" existence. That I would've been just as pissed and devastated.

No. That I would have been worse. I would have demanded to climb to the summit of her trash heap. To be her helper instead of her handicap. To—

I slam to a complete stop.

Thump a hand, flat and frozen, to the center of my chest.

I stand there for a solid minute, focused on nothing but the crashes of my heartbeat against my ribs—which reconfirm everything my traitor of a brain has just smacked into me like the clueless bitch I am.

But then, I'm not even able to stand.

I back up by two steps, letting my ass fall to the front edge of my desk. Curling my hand, still in the center of my chest, to grip at my leather jerkin like the shit's about to turn to sackcloth and I'm about to declare myself dead to the world.

But that's just my brain talking again—the same gray matter that screams at me for being the world's hugest jackass about this, and follows up *that* little rant by ordering me to dig out the business card I've stashed in my on-desk caddy "just for giggles."

That's *not* my brain talking again.

That's my fucked-up pride. Probably joined by his cute little friend, my stubborn ego—both of whom have become so used to playing in their exclusive sandbox that they kicked out the cute, smart, funny, perfect girl who'd been making the place a hell of a lot better.

A place they could actually tolerate living in.

It's time for those assholes to get out of my way.

I prove it to them by fishing out the card and quickly punching the number on it into my phone. The "rings" are unlike any sound I've ever heard—unless a Tauntaun and a busy signal decided to have phone sex—until, fortunately, the noise stops in the middle of the third ring.

"Speak."

I feel my forehead hunch from bewilderment. The voice is a one-eighty from what I expect. It's beach-bum casual wrapped up with bold command. At once, I get an image in my head of the lead baddy from *Point Break*—Patrick Swayze's version, not the poor sap from the reboot.

"Mr. Foley?" I murmur.

"You've got him," the guy replies. "Who's this?"

"My name is Reece Richards." I pause there, waiting through the three to four seconds it's going to take him to place my name, then another two or three for him to process his version of a coolest-guy-on-the-planet response. It's a chore, especially because I'm in a tangible hurry now, making me wish I *had* gone ahead and made up a name just to get this conversation going.

"Okay," he finally answers. "What can I do for you, man?"

I pull in a long breath—but only a hoarse catch of air emerges. "Do you have time to meet in person? This is probably going to take a while."

"How so?"

"This isn't like any of the stories you've read about me before."

His snort is short but gruff. "I've never read *any* stories about you, dude."

"You don't stand in line at the grocery store? Glance at the billion gossip rags there?"

"I don't go to the grocery store. Most of my food is picked from my own garden, and I use custom organics for my body, hair, and housecleaning."

And that was more than too much information. "Fine. Cool. But I'm still going to require a signed NDA."

"Is your money green?"

"Excuse the hell out of me?"

"You heard me. Is your money green?"

"Is your surfboard dope?"

"Ha!" The laugh is short but genuine, giving me hope he's connected to the real world in at least a few ways that count. "Okay, man. Don't stress. Whatever this is, I'll help you handle it." And weirdly, though I haven't shared a syllable of what "this" is, I believe him. "When do you want me to start?"

"How about now?"

Because the sooner he starts, the sooner I can make things right with Emma again. And have her by my side again.

And when that's a sealed deal?

I swear to God, I'll never let her go again.

CHAPTER SEVEN

E M M A

Three more days slug by.

Seventy-two more hours in which I'm given a handful of moments, tiny and perfect, in which I start to think everything will be normal again—just before it all returns in a crash of pain and regret and breath-robbing grief. The memories. The aching. The loss, in places so far and awful inside me, no food will stay down, thought will stay planted, or feeling will take root. The limbo of this damn darkness. The pain still so deep, I even start to hope for tears again, even if Wade and Fershan are likely still drying off from my last sob-fest.

Because despite what I'd thought, crying over Reece Richards didn't wash a drop of him away from my heart. If anything, it all just deepened the tank of my sorrow.

On that "cheerful" thought, I pack up the last of my snacks and water bottle for work, tuck them into my shoulder satchel, and set off from the apartment to catch the three p.m. train downtown.

While walking down the two flights of stairs to the courtyard, I think about the new day-shift slots that have just opened at the Brocade. Maybe taking one of them, just for a little while, might be a great idea. I'll miss the gang on the night shift, but maybe this is the step I need to escape the Reece-themed slap I endure every night at work. Neeta was actually the one who mentioned the new shifts, sensing my struggles and perhaps even guessing Reece is at the root of the problem.

But it's not like the man has been hovering lately. The exact opposite, in fact. Recluse Tower Reece has definitely become a thing again. And yes, I've been noticing. And yes, I've heard about all the Bolt sightings in the last week, triple their normal numbers. The whole city couldn't be more ecstatic.

Goody for the city.

Yaaaay, La-La Land.

On that morose thought, I plunk to the bottom of the stairs. Once there, I stop and give those ruminations an open huff. "And here she is, folks. The most depressed girl in the world's safest city. Give it up for...Emmalina Crisssssttt."

As I finish my fake crowd noises, I scowl. Damn. I just used my own full name on myself.

The way Reece does.

The way Reece used to.

"Well, at least you *look* runway ready, baby." I reward myself for the pep talk with a soft laugh directed toward the bow-front kitten heels upon which I splurged as my heartbreak shoes. They've been sitting in the box for two days, but their Kelly-green color meant I had to wait for the ideal blouse to come back from the dry cleaners. Tonight, the whole ensemble has come together. I may not feel totally rockin'-red-carpet again, but at least I look it.

"Did I miss the punch line?"

So much for considering steps on a red carpet—or *any* steps at all—as I swing a glower toward the source of the quip. The line is as friendly as a greeting from one of my neighbors— if any of them had a Catherine Deneuve accent and smelled like Baccarat perfume mixed with clove cigarettes. But the scent isn't what lodges my heart in my throat. I'm not even struck senseless by the fear Reece warned me to be so nutballs about—which is disconcerting but not entirely disturbing.

Because I like what I feel in fear's place.

I let the rage settle in, raw and invigorating, while glaring at the bitch from head to toe. When I'm done with the once-over, I let out another laugh. Louder this time. And so much longer.

"Angelique La Salle." I rock back on one foot. "The woman with the name of a princess and the wardrobe of a skank. Should I congratulate you on being well-rounded or just a puppet ho?"

The woman adopts a similar pose, her lips hitching like a droll doll. For a flash of a second, I catch something else on her face too. It's the dread Reece kept warning *me* about—and it almost makes me feel sorry for the woman. For half a second.

Then I'm right back to hating the woman.

I only have to remember her sending Reece to his knees at the power station, adding humiliation to her initial betrayal. Deepening the sorrow that convinced him to never believe in the word *trust* again.

In so many ways, this bitch has already killed the man I love.

"Puppet ho." She issues the echo with a mirthful half smile. "That is...*très créatif*, I will grant you that." Her head tilts. "Hmmm. I see it now, a little bit, I think."

"See what?"

"The quality you have...that captivates Reece."

"Captiv*ated* Reece. Past tense. I haven't seen the man in five days." I'm thankful I'm able to fling it and mean it.

Thankful to the tune of considering calling in sick tonight and replacing the work hours with copious wine consumption and a trash-TV binge.

Shit. Surreal second number two. Have I just understood a little of what made Reece cut things off with me last week?

The...Consortium...is...cold...methodical...ruthless...

For five days, I've been stewing about him being a pussy, choosing to hide from them with the grander excuse of protecting me. But right now, I'm damn relieved *I'm* able to shield *him.*

"Haven't 'seen' him, or haven't *seen* him?"

"Okaaaaayy." I'm still grateful she's getting only my gut-level truth—meaning my genuine confusion. "You have hidden cameras in the bushes, right?" I peer into the bougainvillea, using the moment to disguise my next emotion. Pure triumph. *I don't know where Reece is—but neither do they.*

"Are you able to answer the question?" As she takes a few steps forward, she reaches into hidden pockets in both her boots—releasing matching switchblades from the hidden compartments. She triggers the blades simultaneously, *thwacking* the steel on the air. The knives gleam in the afternoon sun as she advances with steadier purpose.

For two seconds, I indulge the folly of being concerned.

And then use my lunch pouch to knock one of them free and my water bottle to rid her of the other. Yeah, just like that, watching her scramble to scoop them up, pressing my lips to keep from laughing. I try to remember Reece's warnings about the bitch, but my rage really has taken over, blinding me to common sense. The only thing I can think about is giving this Twinkie an LA-style version of karmic payback.

As she crouches lower for the second knife, I land a kitten

heel in the center of her spine and dig in to knock her forward. She rolls over, but I've got kitten heel number two at the ready, and I jam it deep enough into her windpipe to ensure she gets the message.

"You ready for my answer now, darling? I haven't seen Reece in almost a week, nor do I plan on seeing him again. But if I *did*, I'd be advising him to run like hell from a woman who doesn't have the sense to trash a pair of boots like that after the whole city saw her on every news feed in town trying to take down their most beloved local hero and a chunk of LA's power supply."

I finally release my foot. Angelique lurches to her feet and grabs at her throat, choking out stuff in guttural French while running for the street and disappearing around the curve in the road. I'm pretty sure she called me either a raving bitch or a bowl of soup, though I'd bank on the former. I'm also pretty sure there's a car waiting for her around that bend and I should chase her to take notes or other superspy stuff like that, but I wouldn't bet on my knees carrying me another step, let alone into a Bond girl chase scene. On top of that, every drop of adrenaline in my body now migrates to both ends of it. My head becomes a tornado. My feet quiver like I've strapped them to shake weights. The guts in between are a directionless mess.

Miracle of miracles, I'm able to climb the stairs to my unit without tripping. Aligning my apartment key with the little hole in the door? Not even a miracle's going to help now.

"Emmalina."

I whirl—to behold a walking, talking, six-foot-three miracle.

No. A blade of lightning. A force of nature. The heir with the hair. The billionaire bad boy. The sexy asshole in the sparkling tower.

My Bolt.

My man.

"Oh." The syllable is all I can produce, my voice high and hurting but joyous and jubilant, as I fly into his arms without restraint or regret.

He lets out an, "Oof!" before laughing as I circle both legs around his waist, letting him take the keys and work my apartment lock open.

We move inside.

And I'm home. Really home.

Right where I need to be—after five damn days of hell.

Five days. A hundred and twenty hours. Anyone else would say they're blips in the span of time, but I call everyone else freaking crazy.

"Oh...wow." As I gasp it out, he drenches me in one of his lush laughs. I dive again for him, kissing him like crazy.

As my tears finally fall.

As I flood him with them, unashamed about turning the front of his dark-blue T-shirt into a piece of cobalt pop art.

As he returns the passion, trailing kisses through my hair.

He feels *so good.* His embrace is perfect, powerful, complete. I can feel his heartbeat mating with mine in our triumphant homecoming.

No.

This isn't a reunion. It can't be.

Nothing is different. Nothing has been fixed. As a matter of fact...

"What the *hell*?" I shove away from him and race around the room, slamming the blinds shut. "Oh my God, Reece, you can't be here. Angelique—"

"I know."

"Huh?"

"I know. She was here."

"You..."

"I've been tracking her."

"You've been *what*?" I turn, grabbing him by both forearms. "How?"

He drags in a tight breath. Releases it with matching determination. "I got a guy."

I clutch him harder. That doesn't help me tamp my giggle. "You...got a guy? Seriously?"

Even the edges of *his* lips twitch. Holy shit, the man is hot in sneaky ninja mode but even hotter when in reluctant humor mode. "Let's just say I was ready for the help. And finally hauled my head far enough out of my ass to ask for it."

Deeper frown. "Needed help?" I have to admit, the concept is crazy. I've watched this man command entire boardrooms, pin hoodlums to walls, and clean huge hotel suites until they sparkle like TV commercials. Is there really something in this world he needs help with? "Why?"

He takes another deep breath. In the doing, he brings a meaning across his features that I can't describe, except in terms of what it does to my senses. I feel dunked in something thick, warm, and mesmerizing. Hypnotizing. Galvanizing.

Just like the first time he ever looked at me with such open need.

"I realized I'd made a huge fucking mistake," he finally grates. "And that in order to fix it properly, I'd need some professional help."

Oh, God. Here comes the fresh giggle. "I take it you *don't* mean a shrink."

"Don't push it," he grumbles, sliding in closer so his hands brace my hips. "Though if that's also what this is going to take, then sign me up for the shrink too."

I give up the mirth for more confusion. "What *what* is going to take?"

He leans in more. His gaze intensifies, holding mine in its magic like silver angel's wings. "Keeping you in my life, Velvet. But so help me fucking God, keeping you safe too."

"Oh." For a long collection of seconds, it's all I can say—as shining, incredible happiness is all I can feel. "Oh. Okay."

He wraps his hands around to my back. Presses in with delicious possessiveness. "So yeah, I got down off my high horse and asked for some help. And this guy I found—"

"Right." I laugh again. Can't be helped. It's a shock I'm not doing the Charleston along the ceiling out of sheer joy. "This guy. *Your* guy."

"He's been helping me track Angelique everywhere she goes. We determined she hadn't left the country or even the city. In fact, she's stayed close. Too damn close."

Okay, forget the Charleston. "Well...shit," I utter, newly somber.

"Yeah," Reece utters. "But it's been a good thing wrapped in a bad. Tracking her has been much easier."

"And what exactly has the wicked witch of skank been up to, besides going *Swim Fan* on *my* ass?"

He chuffs at the obscure pop culture reference, solidifying another reason why he's my soulmate wrapped in a hard, gorgeous candy shell. "She's mostly been back and forth from the mansion that the Consortium's surely using as their hub out here—which was why I fired up the M4 and followed as soon as we pinged her coming this direction." His grasp tightens. "I got here just as she pulled the knives on you."

"Way to jump in on the hairiest part of the movie, dude."

"Which was why I *didn't* jump in." His nostrils go wide, and his mouth becomes a tense line. "It was sheer hell to watch her do that to you."

"Wasn't too peachy from where I was at either."

"But you were...incredible." His features transform once again. His face ignites with something like awe, and his generous mouth spreads in a wide smile. "No. Not incredible. Magnificent." He pushes into my personal space, cupping the back of my neck, and takes my mouth in a tender kiss. "You became *my* Bolt, Emmalina Crist."

I moan in soft delight when he repeats the kiss with more demand, suckling his way into my mouth. Every cell in my body blazes to new life. I can tell he's on the exact same page when his blue and gold fingertips flare in my peripheral, but I push back, ordering my hormones to stand down.

"I'm proud that *you're* proud, Mr. Richards, but we're still back at the same place we were before." I sigh heavily. "Maybe even worse since I now understand how the Consortium really doesn't know the meaning of the word boundaries."

He dips a terse nod. "I know." As he pulls away and starts methodically pacing the room, I take just a second to admire the view. The tailored black slacks he wears with the T-shirt fit his ass as perfectly as any pair of jeans ever, perhaps even better.

"This won't be the last time Angelique decides to make a house call," he goes on. "I guarantee the Consortium will pick up *some* vibe that you and I are still in contact, no matter how quiet we try to keep it."

"And being apart completely is *off* the table."

"On more levels than the obvious." He flashes a wink over his shoulder.

A long pause goes by, thickening with our combined tension. Not so jokingly, I mutter, "Maybe there's a remote island in the South Pacific somewhere. A cute hotel where everyone pays in puka shells and smiles? I could wear a muumuu to work every day..."

"Uh-uh. Wrong direction." He turns and folds his arms, openly admiring me with that electric, mesmeric gaze. "You need to find a place where work attire is just the shells and the smile."

I help out with the smile part, at least. That entices him back across the room, and we kiss softly before I snuggle against his chest. "Puka shells aren't much of an effective disguise for a superhero's secret girlfriend."

"Good point." His growl resonates in my ear. "Fuck it all."

I snicker softly. "We'll figure this out, gorgeous."

"*I'll* figure this out, beautiful." He presses his lips into the top of my head. "I got you into this crazy mess, Emmalina."

"I *like* the crazy mess—as long as I'm in it with you, okay?"

"Okay." He lowers his head, fitting his forehead to mine. "But I just need a few more days to make sure we can do that in full. Can you give me that?"

I sigh again. Heavier and longer. "Yeah. Of course."

"And...can you do that while moving to the penthouse at the Brocade?" When I stiffen, he rushes on, "Just for a few days, Velvet. Just until I don't have to worry about that bitch lurking at the Persian chicken place around the corner, dripping pickled beets into her boots while waiting to pounce on you again."

I lean back a little. Flatten my hands against his chest

before finally dipping a quiet nod. "Fine. You win, Mr. Richards." Twisting peeved lips. "Just don't get used to it." Then even harder. "And wait a second. How the hell do you know about the Persian chicken place around the corner?"

He has the grace to blush. And damn it if he isn't more delectable in blush mode than ninja mode and reluctant humor mode combined. "I got a guy?"

I lift both hands, only to bring them back down against his pecs in punishing slaps. The next second, I soothe the blows by laying kisses over the same two spots. Beneath my lips, his muscles bunch and tauten, making me dizzy with the temptation to slide my mouth right over and nibble his stiff nipples right through his shirt. But I know exactly where that will lead. He'll want to feast on my nipples in return. Then he'll want to feast on *other* parts of me. Then I'll want more parts of *him* on me, besides his incredible mouth. Then we'll both be naked on the floor, setting aside the possibility that his lunatic ex might still be prowling the neighborhood, with or without pickled beets in her boots.

"Fine." With groaning effort, I straighten and gaze into his eyes. *Only* his eyes. "But one day soon, all your superspy hero dude secrets will be mine too."

He chuckles, but swiftly turns the sound into a new kiss, brutal but worshipful, that melts my bones and sears my blood, leaving nothing but my soft smile to cling to as any vestige of control I still have over my senses. As I tilt my head, letting him have the full resplendence of that soft, needy expression, he angles his face over mine, ensuring that our stares stay connected.

"Until then, can you promise to simply trust me?"

I pull on his shirt, dragging him closer for a lingering kiss to seal the deal. "Always. *Always.*"

⚡

But three days later, "always" is getting a little harder to keep believing.

Those are my exact words in a text message to Reece, sneaked in during a trip to the ladies' room that I can hopefully stretch out for another minute without suspicion. I've purposely picked the facilities farthest from the ballroom at the Pelican Hill Resort, hoping Mother, Father, and Lydia decide to forget where I am. If I'm lucky, maybe I can pass the next hour here in my cozy stall, smelling the "tropical flowers" being automatically spritzed into the air and trading messages with the man who's turned sexting into an art.

The same way he's turned over every inch of my heart.

I love him. I can't stop telling him. Because he's the only one who ever gets to know.

Ahhh, the fantasy life of a superhero's girlfriend.

I text something close to that, giggling softly at his reply.

Well. I specialize in fantasies, Miss Crist.

You're just hard up, Mr. Richards.

For you, Miss Crist.

Oh yeah? And when was the last time you were in the penis-crushing hell of Orange County?

More recently than you think.

Now this sounds interesting...

I'm settling in for a juicy story when the bathroom door creaks open.

"Emmalina? Are you in *this* bathroom?"

I grit my teeth, fighting the temptation to scream at Mother's summons—a wasted endeavor even if I did indulge. Screaming doesn't help when it comes to my family. They love me, in their shrouded way. *Deeply* shrouded.

"Right here." I force civility to the response. It's not her fault that I can't seem to jump on the Newport-Beach-is-nirvana boat. I've given up on even finding the dock. "I'm almost done."

"Oh, good." She makes primping sounds from the bathroom's vanity area. "Dinner will be served in a while, and then they'll start the awards ceremony—but you're missing all the fun stuff."

"Of course."

My forced pleasantry might pass acting muster with anyone but Laurel Crist. In two seconds, her maternal lasers pierce right through my sham.

"Honestly, Emma." She rises as I emerge, folding arms over her St. John crinkle silk picot gown. She's wearing matching heels and gemstone earrings, all meant to highlight the eyes that nearly match mine in color. "You're in the hospitality industry. You need to be more...hospitable."

"I *am* hospitable—to my guests." I smile, squeezing out a little charm—especially when pondering how my primped, perfect mother would react if knowing how *charming* I've just been with Reece freaking Richards. But that's not a truth she gets to know. Not a secret the world will ever discover.

"Can you just say you'll try, darling?"

I take a Zen breath, gritting to continue the smile. "Yes, ma'am."

"And put on some darker lipstick. You look washed out."

I deflect that one the best way I know how. "*You* look super pretty tonight."

"Really?" She skips a look backward. "You think so? Does this cut make my hips look—"

"You look stunning." Though I mean it, I can see she doesn't believe me. She eyes herself in the full-length mirror, her stare critical.

"Your father told me to wear navy." She *tsks* and shakes her head. "He thinks I look jaundiced in this. But he thinks I look jaundiced in everything."

I reach and grab her hand. "Well, he's wrong."

"You say the nicest things, honey." She pats the side of my face. "But you still need a darker shade of lipstick. Maybe your sister will have something you can borrow."

We reenter cocktail reception hell. I hide out in my typical place, at Lydia's side, letting my tennis star sister bask in the smooches, air kisses, and half hugs from people here to see her. Actually, the affection stuff isn't so bad. It's the conversation between all of it, centering around the same twelve subjects, that makes me wonder if a person can truly slit their wrists with a butter knife.

At times, I do try to engage—only to be greeted with the same glassy-eyed expressions in response to any of the tidbits I get hounded to share.

"Ohhhh. You're living in *downtown* LA? Why?"

"But there are so many adventures right here. I mean, have you *seen* the new yogurt place?"

"Why do you work the night shift? Aren't you good enough for the day one?"

"What movie stars have you met? Or do they get handled by the normal hotel workers?"

"You take the train to work? Well, what's wrong with your driving?"

What's wrong with you?

My teeth lock, freezing my smile in place. My hands clench behind my back. My head starts to pound, and I fight an insane craving to jump out the window.

What's wrong with you?

I should be used to the refrain by now, right? Then why does it seem more relentless now? Why does it weigh on every breath I take and move I make, closing in like the inside of a grand, pretty box? *But why would you want more than this? Isn't the box enough? Why do you want to be more, when you have this?*

I find my place setting and sit down to watch the frozen butter rosettes start to melt, wondering when they'll stop looking like flowers—and feel weirdly sad for when they do. People don't like butter as much when it doesn't look like a rose. But doesn't it taste the same?

Yep. It's official. I really *am* in hell.

Except suddenly, hell comes to a complete stop.

An all-consuming hush—interrupted by waves of fervid whispers. Then astonished gasps. Then high outcries. Even a few elated little old lady *yeep*s.

Lydia appears at my side. Her face reflects the same

stunned curiosity as everyone else's. "Holy *shit*, Em."

"Holy shit what?" I scrutinize her. "'Dia? Are you—what the hell?"

"Stand *up*." She titters a little, urging me to my feet. Doesn't take much effort. She's been playing tennis for nearly twelve years and her arms are like Mack Truck pistons. "Stand *up*, girl. Ohmigod, what's he doing here?"

"He who?"

"I'm going to pass out. This is epic."

"*What* is?"

Epic. Well, that's one way of saying it. Breathtaking could be another. Beautiful too. But no matter how many descriptors I add to the mix, they don't come close to the twist of my stomach, the leap of my pulse, the race of my blood, and the lightning in my heart as a flawless figure in black leather strides across the room like he owns it. Who knows? Maybe he does—but that's the last thing dominating my mind and caressing my libido. Like every other woman in the room, my breaths are shallow and my pulse is triple its norm as he swaggers arrogantly on those custom ninja boots, his electric eyes gleaming behind that sleek Maserati mask.

Holy shit.

Holy shit.

He's here.

BOLT

PART 3

CHAPTER ONE

EMMA

I'm seeing this—and still not believing it.

He's here.

In the flesh.

In public.

In every inch of his mighty, magnificent, leather-clad, muscled-out splendor.

Striding through the ballroom of the Pelican Hill Resort like he owns the damn place—yet for all I know, he does.

Because I know what everyone else in the room doesn't.

Underneath all that sigh-inducing black glory is Reece Richards, the man with whom I've fallen hopelessly in love. The hero who's not just saved me but swept me off my feet. The soulmate who has seen so much of me. The lover who has electrified every inch of me.

The superhero with whom I've fallen in love—in secret. But now, the man I can't help gawking at—in the open. He's. Here. Out in just as glaring a way at a five-star resort that, at least on the surface, isn't a hotbed for any hoodlums.

What the hell is he doing here?

I get my answer the second Reece locks his lightning gaze on me. Dipping his head with new determination, he marches directly through the crowd. *At me.* Somehow, I stay on my feet, barely subduing the giddy grin on my face as a roomful of female tongues drags in his wake.

At last, he stops.

For at least a minute, we're silent.

Stares tangling. Energies renewing. Our bond reaffirmed.

Dear hell, I want to jump him. Worse than ever before. Will he ever stop stirring this feeling through every fiber and nerve and pore in my body? Do I want him to?

He gives me the answer to those questions as soon as he scoops up my hand. His gloves are barely a shield for our heat, our need, our attraction.

Deep breath. Deep breath.

The mantra is no use. My blood heats, all but dictating me to slam him to the wall and nail him right here. The silver sparks in his eyes reveal the exact same battle.

He clears his throat. And then again. Executes a low bow with more grace than any movie prince before brushing my knuckles with his lips and zapping every one of my fingers with instant, incredible electricity. He sneaks a tiny bite to one, and my heart turns over in my chest. Three times.

"Hi there, beauty."

Audible swoons spread through the crowd like lightning through a storm cloud. Damn good comparison, considering what he's doing to my nervous system.

"Hi there, gorgeous."

The murmur has barely left my lips when my parents appear. Mother's St. John dress is perfectly smooth. Father, from whom I got my light-blond hair, deep dimples, and round face, steps forward. He grabs Reece's hand and pumps it wildly, not letting go until the event photographer snaps at least ten shots.

"Mr. Bolt." Father's not going to lose his chance of milking the marketing op of a lifetime. "What an honor to have you at our humble event, sir." Of course, the "humble" event is a regional tennis league awards dinner with movers and shakers who paid a thousand bucks apiece just to walk in the door, but semantics are trivial at the moment. "Are you a tennis fan?"

Reece nods. "I've dabbled. Though I'm more of a high-intensity thrill seeker."

Father gives the line a heartier laugh than it needs. "Of *course* you are! Ha-ha! Yes, yes."

Mother deftly slips into the exchange, clasping her hands demurely at her waist. "We must admit, this is quite a surprise. A pleasant one, of course."

"I know," Reece interjects, saving her from having to bumble through any more "charming" disclaimers. "And thank you for not throwing me out right away. I'll be glad to pay for a ticket."

"Oh, dear heavens." Mother gasps. "We wouldn't *dream* of asking you to—I mean, you can even sit at the head table with us, if you'd like..."

Reece raises a hand. "Oh, I won't be staying for dinner."

"Ah." She smiles but can't hide the disappointment in her eyes. Clearly, this is the best thing to happen to the tennis awards gala since three years ago, when an honoree's brother, a Disney Channel star, attended to support his sibling. "So, what *has* brought you here?" She circles her head around, mouth dropping in mock horror. "Nobody here has been naughty tonight, have they?"

As laughter drifts through the crowd, Reece assures her, "You're all off the hook." But then his scrutiny lands on me. "Well, everyone except her."

More stunned murmurs spread through the room. "Emmalina?" Mother stutters, as if being told the coffee bar has run out of soy milk. "Really?"

"*Really.*" Reece looks as if he wants to chuck the soy milk at her.

"Why?"

"Because I'm in love with her."

My heart melts.

My limbs become puddles.

As my mother gawks.

As my father glows.

And my boyfriend? He just keeps on smirking. Then robbing me of breath as his grin beams even wider—the moment he sweeps his free hand to the back of his head, fingers twisting at the clasp of his mask.

"I'm in love with her," he announces again. This time his face is exposed. "And I want the whole damn world to know it."

The air leaves the room.

No. Really.

"Well, hot dog," Father finally utters.

"Holy hell," Mother gasps.

"Oh, *sister*!" Lydia's exclamation is like a permission slip of reaction for the rest of the throng. Cell phone cameras are brandished and shouts are volleyed as walls of humanity press in on us from every side. I grab Reece harder, hoping my gape somehow communicates the thousand questions in my heart. In return, he palms my cheek with a gloved hand, his touch as tender as his kiss.

"It'll be all right, Velvet."

I twist a wry look. "Says who, hot stuff?"

He answers that by raising a hand into the air. At once,

the room returns to silence, meaning my astounded gasp is an audible stab in the air. Even without the mask, the man brandishes special strength.

"Mr. and Mrs. Crist." My boyfriend, looking a dozen kinds of sexy, with his thick, messy hair and leather-clad strength, pivots back toward my parents. "I'm here tonight because your daughter is worth this. She's *my* superhero, and that's a truth the whole world needs to know." He draws a breath to follow that up but stops himself, shaking his head, before looking out across the crowd. "You people see me doing all the flashy stuff, and you think I'm the noble one, the bold one, the badass against the bad guys." He ticks one side of his mouth up. "But what I do is the easy game. Real heroes aren't made of roundhouse kicks or fancy fingertips that make lightshows or dudes who lob electric snowballs from time to time."

He turns and brings himself nearly toe-to-toe with me. Holy God, how he takes my breath away. My vision is consumed with the silver strength of his eyes, the conviction in his jaw, the loving lift of his lips.

"Heroes are people who choose more for their lives and those of others and are brave and bold and real about seeking those dreams." He declares it in a raised voice, but it's one of the most intimate things he's ever said to me... One of his most meaningful gifts. "They don't accept anything less than living their truth and encouraging that bold, brutal honesty in others—like this amazing woman has done for me."

At that, the room erupts again—in a wild burst of applause. I think.

There's not much I'm conscious of as tears blur my vision and joy rushes my heart, propelling me forward. Reece's mighty arms crush me closer, until our chests are pressed and our lips are meshed. "I love you," I tell him once we can stand to pull apart again. All three syllables are drenched in the desire and amazement of my mind, my soul, my spirit.

"And I love you, Velvet." He dips in again, taking my mouth more gently.

"I know. *Wow*, do I know."

He grins while pulling me out of the ballroom, thanking Father for letting him "steal me away" as the dinner service begins. Before we go, I promise Lydia I'll return in time, with Reece in tow, to see her awards, but know I won't miss the meal one bit. What girl in their right mind has time for food when a hero in leather has just unmasked himself for her, in more ways than one, in front of two hundred people?

Once we find our way onto a walking path overlooking the ocean, Reece stops and spins me around, smashing me against him once more. Before I can say a word, his lips have descended, plunged, devoured, and dominated, tilting my balance and stealing my breath. Once I get my equilibrium back, I pull away a little, though maintain my hold with both hands deep in his hair. Doesn't look like the man minds one damn bit. He's full of seduction and adoration, windblown and sexy as hell.

And now someone's sucked the air out of *me*.

"So," he murmurs.

"So?" I tilt a coy grin.

"We *wow* worthy yet?"

I rear back to smack his shoulder but decide on a better torture—smashing my mouth back to his, parting his lips with my tongue, and not stopping until his crotch is hard and incessant against mine. When we're breathing hard and all but mauling each other on the path, I whisper against his lips,

"*Wow*."

"Good." He dips closer, cradling my hips in his powerful hold. Wind gusts over the bluff, carrying the sound of crashing waves and the electricity of the burgeoning night. "Because I want to give you a lifetime of wows, Emmalina."

Heart stopping, yet again.

And restarting at twice its speed, snagging my breath. "I want you in my life too."

His smile fades. He leans down, pressing his forehead to mine. "Even now?"

I grab both sides of his face and dig in my fingers, letting him know I understand the scope of the question. This is it. He's gone public—the superhero version of a handwritten invitation to all the globe's bad guys, especially the Consortium. He has no idea how easy he's just made my answer, given from every crevice of the heart he's filled.

"Yes, Mr. Richards. *Especially* now."

"Thank fuck." His exhale is a sexy growl as he gathers me close for another mind-bending kiss. As my thoughts fly and my blood heats, I release an eager sigh into his mouth—but attempt to compose my features once he lets me go. It's hard to chastise him when he looks this damn good, but I'm fixed on giving it my best shot.

"What took you so damn long?"

He snorts. "Three days?"

"Forever."

A wry nod. "Yeah. You're right. Forever." He nuzzles into my hair. "Fuck, I missed you."

"That's not an explanation."

"Right again, woman of mine." *Holy hell. Those words.* It's a struggle not to launch myself onto him once more, but I gulp hard, waiting for the follow-up brewing behind his stare. "I needed to take a beat. To recalibrate."

I laugh, biting my lip. "*That's* what you're calling this?"

He chuffs. "Why not?"

"Good point."

He takes another breath. "Before I came back to you, I just needed...to be sure."

"About what?"

"About all of it. The way I've been approaching this... superpower." His brow furrows. "The way I've been approaching life."

I let a hand slide down to the middle of his chest. "You mean the life you were ready to chuck."

"Well, yes."

"Which was why you started going after criminals like a honey badger."

He's silent for a moment, caressing the curve of my waist, his fingers finally meeting at the small of my back. "I felt as freakish as a wild animal, so why not?"

I slowly shake my head. "But you made a very human decision. To make things better."

"Atonement," he volleys. "Hoping I'd tip the cosmic favor back my way a little bit—but that was before you came along and changed everything."

I attempt a laugh, but it's stolen the moment his gaze, as silver as the stars yet as tender as the moonlight, pierces into me. "Hey." I lightly bat at his sternum. "You walked into *my* office, remember?"

He pulls me even closer, refitting our bodies together. "And from the moment I did, life wasn't the same." The wind, smelling of sea salt and night flowers, blows a chunk of his hair at the edge of his eyes. "Life was something I *wanted* again. And after you filled my heart, something I needed."

I circle my arms around his neck. "Reece." My whisper is paltry in the shadow of what he's given me, the enormity of the life he's made *me* need too. "God...Reece..."

"What is it, Velvet?"

"You're...my more."

"And you're my life." He utters it while sliding his lips within half a breath of mine, until I can feel the thunder of his heart and every electron in his bloodstream. But all too fast, his expression sobers. "This is kind of crazy. Emma...I'm..."

"What?" I prod when he chooses a harsh grunt instead of finishing his sentence.

Finally he utters, "I'm in really new territory here."

I slide out a gentle grin. "You mean being an outted superhero?"

He chuckles before tilting up my head and capturing my lips beneath his. "I mean being in *love*."

My heart skips at least three beats. I lean on tiptoe to kiss him in return. "That was a damn good answer."

"That's just the truth."

"And that's okay, mister." I form a hand around the strong cliff of his jaw. "This is new territory for me too."

"We'll figure it all out." We touch foreheads once more. "Let those fuckers come. We'll be ready."

I smile—from all the jubilant depths of my heart. "We sure as hell will be."

He regards me with new concentration. "It's not going to be easy, Velvet. This is real life. We don't live in a comic book, where we get to skip through the tough stuff with a few boxes of *ka-pows* and *zaps* and then magically end up on the last page with the key to the city in our hand."

"I know." I pull on the back of his neck, taking his mouth in a long, adoring kiss. "But we'll be together."

He kisses me back. "Thank fuck."

I swallow hard before our lips meet again, a multitude of colors exploding in the sky. A synchronized laser show flashes up to join the fireworks.

It's beautiful. Electric. Chaotic. A little bit of insanity. A *lot* of intensity.

Just like our love.

Our indelible, unmistakable bond.

Weirdly, the thoughts incite a light, loving laugh as I duck my forehead against his chest. I'm close enough to hear the strong, beautiful cadence of his heartbeat layered with his quiet rumble of confusion at my action.

"I'd offer a sewing kit for your thoughts," he murmurs, "but the best I could do was this lousy fireworks show over the ocean."

I chuckle and lift my head. Dazzling colors reflect across his lowered face and in his incredible eyes—red, blue, amber, and violet each take their turn at transforming the features that God obviously put His best work into.

"I was just thinking that you're so beautiful, I wish I really could draw you into a comic book."

"Oh?" His brows jump. "Now *that* would be something."

"Right? Except..."

"What?"

I bite my lower lip. "The fangirls would insist that you're shirtless."

"Hmmm. Well, that would mean giving the fan*boys* what they want too."

Soft giggle. "For *me* to be shirtless?"

He leans in, letting his stare drop to my cleavage. "That's a damn good start."

I bask in the tingles of his adoration, even angling back a little to let him get a good long view, before prompting, "And what about *you*, fanboy? What's on your 'I insist' list?"

He pulls me tight against him once more and continues his possession with long, sensuous strokes along my back. He glides his mouth against my neck, nipping and sucking until shivers tumble through me like the sparks still raining through the sky. "That's a question best answered by showing and not telling." As if the husk in his voice needs more proof, the bulge between his thighs swells against the joining of mine. "But we're standing here overlooking the front nine, without even a bush to dive into..."

I back off a little, but only to slide my hands down, meshing all ten fingers of mine with his. "But isn't that what sand traps are for?"

"Excuse the hell out of me?" The incredulity in his voice is overruled by the tilt of his lips, the silver fire in his eyes... and the dull glow at the ends of his fingers, which rushes my backward pace onto the grass of the dark, empty fairway.

"Trust me?" I giggle it out, knowing damn well he won't refuse. He just asked me to trust him for three days—that might as well have been forever—while he pulled strings and made machinations for the astounding step he's just taken in the name of our love. And I'm grateful, believe me, I am—but right now, before letting the rest of the world in on our supersized fairy tale, I want to give him one more chapter that will be ours alone to savor.

He just needs to know how much I'm truly his. In every

way possible.

When we get to the sand trap, I guide him to the curve of the steep slope. We're shielded from the lights of the clubhouse, with only the rising moon and the winking stars as our light. And oh yeah...his fingers. And the magical, spectral glow emanating from the back of his gaze as he leans in to take my mouth in a consuming, kneading, deep, drowning kiss.

At once, I'm spread open for him. Letting him claim my tongue and my breath, my oxygen and my equilibrium, as he delves farther into the source of my high, needy moans. And yes, I give even those to him—letting him have every sound I make, every breath I take...

His. *His.*

Even now, after what he's declared to my mother, my father, my sister, and at least a hundred social media feeds, the truth is almost too much to believe. The world's most notorious playboy is now the man of my soul and the keeper of my spirit. My heart bursts painfully in gratitude for every step we've both taken, separately and together, to get here.

Pain I'd gladly endure all over again.

For a *together* that's meant to last for the ages.

Our perfect fit. Our electric love.

A union that needs its physical manifestation, right here and now.

As if Reece has heard every syllable of my soul—and I wouldn't be surprised if his superpowers include *that* talent now—he moans against my mouth, his breath audibly accelerating. We break our hands apart so we can fully cling to each other, like a pair of trees wrapped around each other for the rest of time. He doesn't stop kissing me, even as his hands cup my ass and sear through my clothes. Not even as I dive both hands into his hair and twist his thick strands so tight, his moans become grunts. Not even as our hunger for each other makes us tumble into the sand, rolling into the valley created by the carefully raked knoll and the scoop of earth into which it's nestled.

Somehow we settle with him on his back against the grassy alcove, his leathers making moist *shoosh*es against the damp stuff as he reaches up again for me—only to growl as I lean up, enticingly out of his reach. I sit astride him but scoot down his body by erotic increments, taking extra time to work my crotch in little circles atop the swollen hill beneath his fly.

The fly I start working on as soon as I reach his thighs.

"*God.*" The fierce eruption from between his teeth extends into a hiss as I unbuckle the top strap, work the zipper down, and gently graze the crown of his erection with one fingernail. Immediately, his cock spurts a couple of silky drops, an entrancing contrast against his burnished skin and black pants. I run my tongue along my lips. *Holy shit*, he looks delicious.

"*Fuck.*" It's not even a growl anymore. He rasps it while letting his head drop back and his arms go slack. "Emma. *Velvet.* What are you..."

"Sssshhh." But the exhortation isn't necessary. He's nothing but gargled chokes as soon as I part the zipper more, releasing his huge length into my waiting hand. My strokes spread more of his precome down his stalk, which pulses with a faint blue glow in time to the primal heaves of his chest. "I just want to make sure your trip down to the OC wasn't for nothing, Mr. Hottie Bolt Man."

A gruff chuckle vibrates through him. "Mr...Hottie... Oh, that's good. Real good. But—" He cuts in on his own sarcasm with a groan I can feel down to the thighs I'm still straddling. "But holy fuck, *that's* even better." He bucks into my grip as I close my fist around his swollen rod, working my thumb against the bottom of his crown.

"Better is good," I tell him, massaging the ball of my thumb against his ultrasensitive spot. "But tonight, I'm going for *best.*"

CHAPTER TWO

REECE

"B-Best?"

I let my tone do most of the talking for me—mostly because I'm unable to even think about structuring the rest of the words, much less string them together. Not with her hand on me like that. With her thumb pressing against me... right *there*. With the mesmerizing little tune she hums while working the zipper of my leathers all the way down until she's bared my balls to every star in the sky and ground squirrel on this golf course.

Still, I can think the words. Sort of.

What the hell does *best* mean?

And why the hell is she still humming as if she's just stirring soup, when she's heating my goddamned cock like the prized mutton she's about to toss into the stew?

Or maybe not.

She's not going to wait for the stew.

She's going to devour me raw.

And oh *God*, how she does.

She all but impales her wet, tight mouth over me. Onto me. Taking me inside her orifice as far as she can get me, before she inhales deeply and slides herself even farther down my screaming, ecstatic dick—which I force her to accept even more with the violent demand of my surging hips.

"Damn," I growl. "*Damn!*" It's twice as ferocious due to how she trails her fingers down, skimming my balls with pressure and rhythm born from instinct completely tuned to mine. Desire utterly aligned with mine. A heart completely knowing mine. How did I ever think just fucking my way through women would be all right for the rest of my life? None of that was *right*. None of that was this. None of that was Emma.

None of that was love.

My senses go pyrotechnic again as Emma reaches beneath my jerkin with her other hand, scratching at the ridges of my abdomen before trailing lower, through my pubic hair, working her magical touch back toward the base of my length. She braces me there for one excruciating, indelible moment—just before taking my erection into the darkest recesses of her mouth.

As the magma in my balls dances for her other hand, the head of my cock knocks at the back of her throat. The feeling makes me jerk again, aligning my senses with every single star over our heads. My cock has become her air. More of my precome slides down her throat. And soon it'll mix with her vital fluids...and work its heat to the most sensitive core of her body...

And I'll become more than her air.

I'll become her reason for breathing.

"Emma." My croak blends with her eager moan. My quick-fire breaths are the backbeat for her full breaths, whisking in and out of her nose. "*Emma*. Fuck. Baby..."

I try pulling at her shoulders, needing more of her—needing the connection for which we've both worked so hard—but all I get is a protesting moan as she works her pretty mouth up and down my stalk. She sucks at me like a kid who's never tasted a candy stick before.

Like a woman who wants me to get off in her mouth.

Holy. Hell.

My dick craves exactly the same thing, though it's now got my heart and soul to contend with. The parts of me that need to watch as I give her that load. The senses that need to experience her own completion at the exact same time it hits her.

Only there's not much time left.

"*Emma.*"

This time, I back up the order with my physical strength. I'm not gentle either—not after beholding the force of the aqua fire in her gaze and knowing that right now a John Denver fuck isn't what she wants.

It's time for something more like Nine Inch Nails.

And *there's* my ideal segue.

"I want to feel you from the inside."

My vocal abrasion isn't nearly as cool as Reznor's, but her eyes flare as if it is, and that's all that counts. With a slow, knowing slide, letting a thin line of saliva trail in her wake, she drags her mouth free from my cock and works her body back up, not stopping until the apex of her thighs is positioned over my jolting erection.

She wipes her lips clean with one sensuous slide of a finger while hitching her skirt higher with the other. "Then feel me," she rasps, her gaze hooded with lust as she rocks her panty-covered pussy over my aching cockhead. "And take me."

"Damn..." I grit it while shoving aside that thin satin barrier. "*Goddamn.*"

"Unnnh!" Her little cry is accompanied by a massive

shudder that rolls through her body as I push into her wet, clenching tunnel. She releases another moan, louder and longer, as soon as I grip her bare hips and grind her harder on me.

"Fuck yourself on me." I husk it out with every ounce of the ruthless prick in me, satisfaction churning stronger when her lips part in raw desire. "Drive your cunt on me like an animal."

"Yes." She's more breath than volume, finishing the sound by grabbing the side of my face and ramming her mouth over mine. As she fucks her tongue into my mouth, she rides me like a possessed she-beast, illustrating the effects of my juices through every drop of her heated blood. "Yes," she repeats against my mouth. "Say it again. Order me again."

Whatever my horny little harpy desires...

"Do it." I seize her with force that'll likely leave marks but bank on the fact that she likely won't mind. "Rut yourself on my cock. Harder. *Harder.*"

A crazed harlequin smile dances over her lips, right before she smashes them again on mine. When she's done invading me, she pulls up just enough to keep her blue fire eyes burning me alive and her hot, sweet breath fanning across my face.

"My lightning," she rasps, fucking me even faster.

"My storm," I breathe, meaning the fuck out of it. She's my hurricane. My cyclone. My blizzard. My force of nature.

"My miracle," she whispers.

"My angel."

"My..."

Her throat clutches.

Her body stills.

Her pussy, shoved all the way down on me, clenches tight.

But only for a couple of seconds.

Two exquisite heartbeats—before every inch of her cunt is claimed by merciless, ferocious tremors. Only then, as she comes with violent force, does she gasp out words again, pushing them between the breaths that heave her stunning breasts against her bodice and make the main veins of her life force throb wildly against her neck.

"My...everything."

And with the gift of her confession, she gives me my climax too.

I'm rocked to my core. Strained to my limit. Burned and consumed and drained, my searing seed claimed by her gripping, tremoring body, until there seems nothing more for my cock to give—but then there is, and I'm coming for what feels like forever. And I pray that's exactly the case. That the universe has finally declared my debt to Karma paid in full and my reward for all the good deeds is now an eternity of this wicked fire...the burning bond only possible with this mesmerizing creature. My own Emmalina.

Mine.

Mine.

Dear God, just let forever start now.

Please...

But all too soon, a cool wind rushes up from the ocean. And all too quickly, a burst of applause from the ballroom reminds us that anonymity isn't on our side tonight. As if we need any more reminders, there's at least three tire screeches from the clubhouse's main driveway, followed by what sounds like heated arguments.

"...a private event. Invited guests only..."

"...don't understand. We're with channel seven..."

"...we're with CNN..."

"...World News Now..."

"World News Now?" Emma jerks a little, making me groan. Having her sweaty, exhausted body draped over mine, her tight channel keeping our bodies locked, isn't a heaven I'll give up without protest. "Are they freaking kidding?"

"Probably not," I grumble against the curve of her neck while circling my arms around her waist. "They have crews all over the place waiting to pounce on breaking news."

She quirks the edge of her mouth. "Well, this is probably the best action their OC crew has had in years."

"Oh, come on." There are few things that make me happier than some post-fuck teasing with the goddess of my dreams, especially when she's into the let's-not-move-until-we-have-to thing as much as me. "I'm sure they've had other dazzling events to hop on."

"Other than the *Housewives*?" She snorts.

"Well of course other than the *Housewives*."

"Yeah?" she retorts. "Name one."

I give it a few seconds of sincere thought. A few seconds more. "Okay, hold on," I protest as soon as she begins to snicker. "You're not giving me enough time."

"Take alllll the time you need." She tosses her head, cascading the glistening waterfall of her hair across one elegant shoulder. "I'm still going to win."

"Bummer for the World News guys."

Her adorable shrug pops the ball of her shoulder up through her blond tangles. "Sucks to be them."

I school my features into a thoughtful stare. "Unless..."

"What?" She doesn't mask the suspicion across hers.

"We give the poor bastards some more scoops to hop on."

I waggle my brows. "Maybe come down for more visits. Find some more sand traps to christen..."

She drops her forehead to my chest. "Oh, gawd," she groans into the leather.

"Something wrong, Bunny?" I go for feigned candor.

"I've created a monster."

Deep chuckle. "Yeah, but you had a hell of a lot of fun doing it."

With her head still bowed, she echoes my laugh. "And there you go again, reading my damn mind."

⚡

So maybe we sealed our own doom with the sand trap pillow talk.

Or maybe, as she so eloquently phrased it, she *did* create a monster.

Because here I am, on my second trip to the OC this week—which officially doubles the number of trips I've logged to the OC over the last twenty-eight years—pulling up to the Balboa Bay Resort while silently ordering the dragon in my pants to go take a goddamned nap.

That's what I get for taking the long way down here, purposely going for the route that took me past Pelican Hill. But that was fifteen minutes ago. I'm now in the land where a yacht-filled harbor fills one side and a Ferrari dealership and "Car Spa" fills the other. Here in civility land, only pinkies can be erect.

As if sensing I need help with the messaging, a flood of laughter spills into the air the second I get out of my i8 and toss the keys to the valet. *A lot* of laughter. High-pitched. And wild.

And female.

Damn. The hormones pouring out of that restaurant could turn the Newport Bay waters pink. As I kick off my loafers, walk out onto the resort's small private beach, and take in the sparkling sapphire of the water, I'm glad that's not the case.

At once, gazing out over the canal where gulls cavort around upscale yachts and sailboats, my serenity is recalibrated. And no, the word's not just a placeholder. "Serenity" is an accurate tag on the current Bolt mood, still cruising along on the high of getting to acknowledge the woman I love to the entire world. And yeah, I realize the past six days have been a strange honeymoon phase of sorts, since everyone from LA's mayor to the president of France has sent messages, presents, and mushy support of a "superpowered love" to Emma and me, but I'm going to ride the feel-good train for as long as it wants to chug along...

Even if I have to endure another burst of feminine screams, gaining even more volume as a waiter opens one of the restaurant's beach-facing doors. Just as fast, he closes it. Thank fuck.

I blink rapidly, wondering if I'm the only one to notice the uproar from inside, until movement catches my periphery. A hotel bellhop has come out to sit on the low wall fronting the beach, catching some rays and a few puffs on his vape during a break.

"You're not losing your mind, man," the guy confirms. "It's really that crazy in there."

I twist my lips. "I thought it was a baby shower." One that Emma felt strongly about attending, for a friend from high school.

"So did we. But somehow, it took a turn for the wild side."

"Clearly," I remark. "But why?"

"Dunno. But the waiters tell me they're now all talking lingerie, multiple Os, and battery life expectancy on sex toys."

"So...the mother-to-be is also the naughty bride-to-be?" Explains the whole otherworldly theme a little better. On the other hand, it's not that crazy an idea. Judging by the laughter, the kid will be surrounded by a lot of love from day one.

"Nah." The guy takes another drag on his vape. "It's not her. Guess there's someone else at the party they're all fascinated with. Apparently, the chick who inspired Bolt to come out last weekend." He loosens his tie. "Okay, not *out*, out. But—well, you know what I mean."

I settle on the wall myself, a few feet away. "Sure."

The kid grunts and then tightens his frown. "Did you hear about all that?"

I school my features. "About what?"

"Bolt. And what he did." A hissing grunt pops from his twisting lips. "Dude just ripped off his mask. In front of all those people. Just like that, you know?"

"Ohhhh, yeah." I nod with feigned contemplation. "I did hear about that."

"*Hunnhh.*" A new pull on the vape. "Just seems whack, if you ask me."

Because you've never been in love, kid. Completely, totally, down-for-the-ride love.

I simply ask, "How so?"

"Well, that woman's into him, right? Just as much as he's into her? If that's the case, why does the whole world have to know about it? Why can't he keep putting down bad guy fuckers but go home to her every night? Why do they have to go broadcasting it and shit? That's like painting a target on both their asses."

I blow out an audible huff of my own. Can he tell I really want to smack him? I'm just not sure if it's a smack up the side of his head or a more solid smack to his chiseled boy-toy cheek. On the one hand, even in the midst of his vape cloud, the kid's got a point. My love for Emmalina Crist will still be the same, even if we were sequestered with each other in the middle of Iceland. But on the flip side of the coin...

"Do you play video games?"

The kid stops, holding back from taking his next drag. "Huh?"

"Simple question," I volley. "Do you play video games?"

"*Pffftt*." His side-eye is full of are-you-kidding-me angst. "Doesn't everyone?"

"So what's your all-time favorite?"

"*Pffftt*. Easy. *Bioshock*. Wait...no...*Gears of War*. No...it's gotta be *Call of Duty*. Shit, that's hard."

"All right, well—whichever one it is, let's just say you played that thing for years, and one day you found out you'd just finished with the highest score of anyone in the world. Could you keep quiet about it? Would you *not* want to tell the whole world about your victory and your pride in it?"

The guy tilts his head. Squints out over the water, obviously weighing my analogy. "Well played, weird stranger on the beach. Well played."

I acknowledge his compliment with a subtle chuckle before dipping my head as well. "That all being said, you really think that guy would have a problem?" I ask. "With getting recognized and all?"

Harsh snort. I almost think I've earned myself another

pffftt, but then the kid drawls, "Oh fuck, yeah."

"Yeah?"

"Have you *seen* that guy? That Richie Rich guy?" Again, the outer reaches of a *pffftt*, but not quite. "He's like those guys on the romance novels, you know. Jaw that could cut diamonds. The dreamy Prince Charming locks. Then all the protein shake commercial shit in the other departments."

I duck my head all the way, disguising my bark of laughter as a cough. "Well, *that's* what a guy wants to hear. Protein shake commercial. Suh-weet."

"Well, you know what I mean."

He re-crosses his ankles and eyes a decent-sized yacht as it skims by, two couples drinking wine with droll ease on the back deck. They're picture perfect, carelessly beautiful, and likely not an ounce grateful for the beautiful life they've been given—and I fight the urge to throw up in my mouth, recognizing how much I used to be just like them.

"Yeah," I mutter, changing out the inner vomit in favor of a jutted jaw. "I know what you mean."

"Seriously. If *you* were a chick, wouldn't you want to mount that muscle?"

Thank fuck for the buzzing in my jeans.

More accurately, for the vibrating phone in my back pocket, with an incoming text from a sender identified only by a blushing cartoon rabbit. I smile at the little vixen bunny from *Bambi* before sliding a finger to open the entire message.

> *Stop talking to the bellman and come*
> *rescue me from this madness. Now.*

I lift my head, peering toward the restaurant, but nothing's changed from before. I see a lot of high heels and hear a lot of noise—but despite the chaos, I can feel the force of my woman's stare, like an arrow across the sand, piercing into me. Not that it stops me from having a little fun with her.

> *Madness? But it sounds like*
> *you're all having so much fun.*

I swear my phone feels hotter, burning with the force of her seethe.

This is not fun.

I quirk the edges of my mouth.

> *Oh, come on. Are you just*
> *being a party pooper, Bunny?*

Fuck you and all the poop.
Just get your ass in here.

The potency of her glare is no longer an arrow. It's a whole spear.

And I, sucker for the woman's passion in *any* form, rub at the center of my chest, hoping to preserve the perfect pain for just a few more seconds.

Christ.

And maybe you'll start wearing a vial of her blood around your neck. Or have your cock tattooed with her initials. Or start timing your period with hers.

Yeah, it's true. Emmalina Crist has turned me into a

whipped, twisted, hearts-in-my-eyeballs sap. Worse, I don't want to change one fucking shred of it.

The bellhop, grunting dismally as the yacht motors out of sight, flicks his regard back to me. "You okay, man?"

"Hmmm?" I'm distracted by the trio of emojis she's just tacked on to her desperate decree. The smiling turd is self-explanatory, but the long-nosed demon and the purple alien have me stumped—and entertained. Will there ever be a moment when she's not challenging me? Delighting me? Do I ever want there to be? "Oh, yeah," I finally tell the kid. "Couldn't be better. But I do have to go."

I rise, jamming my phone back into my pocket. He nudges his chin out, clearly snapping two and two together. "Summoned by the old lady?"

Fast smirk. "Something like that."

He swings his head toward the restaurant. "She in there? Ordering you to spring her from the fray?"

I shrug. "More like...she's keeping me on schedule."

"For what?"

"I have to work tonight."

"On a Saturday night? Bummer. I'm off in two hours and headed to Huntington to hang. Was gonna invite you along."

"Appreciate that, man—but the bad guy fuckers really like playing on Saturday nights."

As I turn and make my way toward the den of craziness where my damsel is being held hostage, I give in to a few seconds' worth of the cockiest grin I've ever cracked—courtesy of the guy now thickening the air more with his shock than his vape cloud.

CHAPTER THREE

EMMA

I can't breathe.

I know, I know—melodrama like this is usually more Lydia's forte than mine, but my big sister isn't the one being pelted with more asteroids of pure crazy by the second.

Okay, so a few points scored for the metaphor, which sticks nicely to Renata's party theme that's based on the *Lunar Chronicles* series we all loved so much in high school. But I'm logging negatives again the next second, fielding my pregnant friend's tearful glower. None of my apologetic winces seem to penetrate Ren's frustration, either—not that I blame her. Today is supposed to be about her and the bambina in her tummy, not the bizarre, Bolt-themed turn the party has taken over the last half hour. Why am I not surprised that said weirdness coincided with someone talking the restaurant staff into opening their bar an hour early too?

Why am I *also* not surprised that Mother's suddenly become the coolest kid in the room, all but holding court on her side of the gathering? Watching her and the posse, all giggling with wine and martini glasses in hand, breaks my heart. How is this right, when their guest of honor sits there sipping on Perrier and prenatal vegetable juice? And how can they be any sort of comfortable shooting questions at me like these?

"So, Emma. *Do* spill. Has that man ever electro-levitated *you?*"

"Well, that could make certain things interesting, if you know what I mean."

"Does he sleep or just recharge?"

"Does he ever keep his mask on when you two...well, you *know*...the whoopee..."

"Better question! Better question! Does he ever let *you* wear the mask?"

"Who cares what they wear. Just tell us how it all *is*..."

I jerk to my feet so fast, my glass of Perrier sloshes. After chugging a bunch of it and hiccupping past the bubbles, I blurt, "Ladies, my *mother* is in the room." *And "whoopee?" Really?*

"Oh, it's all right, honey." Mother raises her fresh glass of Lafond Pinot, her smile effortless and dazzling. "You're among friends. And this kind of stuff isn't anything I haven't talked about with Lydia before."

"Oh, for the love of—" My sister, also in the "dry fish club" tonight because she's prepping for a huge tennis tournament, plunges her forehead to her fingertips. "*Once*, Mother. We talked about a few things *once* because I was training so hard I skipped a month on my cycle and was worried, and—" She cuts in on herself, blushing as bright as the natural strawberry highlights in her hair. "Oh, my God. I'm as horrid as the rest of you crazy bitches."

As she mouths *I'm sorry* at Renata, Mother leads the charge on her group's collective shriek of laughter.

"To the crazy bitches!" someone else yells.

"To the crazy bitches!" comes a collective echo.

"Oh my freaking God," Lydia mutters.

I text feverishly to Reece.

Where the hell are you?

And then wait, damn near pacing. He's disappeared from the beach outside, so I keep looking at my screen, waiting for his reply to appear, telling me he's out in the resort lobby, and—

And I've forgotten that it's Reece Richards I'm dealing with here.

That my noble, unstoppable superhero of a lover, whose side gig is facing down criminals in dark and dangerous places, will be completely undaunted about walking into a room full of half-drunk socialites.

And does.

And lifts a gorgeous grin as all those women notice him.

Then scream.

"Wooooo!" Madison does the beer stein lift again, this time on her feet. "Greased liiiightniiing!"

"We're riders on the stooorrrm." Mother joins her, a little steadier on her heels.

"Oh, my God." Even Renata rises, taking a few extra seconds for obvious reasons. "My baby's been Bolted. This is epic!"

Reece has the poise to look bewildered without surrendering the smile in his eyes. "Good afternoon, ladies. Everyone having fun?"

The group's scream makes the light fixtures sway. I wouldn't believe it if it weren't happening before my eyes, and I'm glad Lydia makes her way over to corroborate the sight. "Well," she murmurs for my ears alone, "at least you're off Ren's shit pile now."

⚡

An hour later, off the shit pile and onto the freeway, I'm in the passenger's seat of Reece's BMW i8 but still battling to enjoy the ride—a dilemma due in no small part to the laughter filling the car. *His* laughter—at the account I've just given, fuming through every word, of the interrogation I endured before his grand entrance at the restaurant.

"Are you even hearing what I'm saying?" I demand past gritted teeth and folded arms as we pass the border into LA County. The industrial sprawl of Norwalk, Santa Fe Springs, and Commerce whizzes by outside. I ignore it all, along with the gawks at the car from other drivers in the Saturday afternoon traffic—which is, shockingly, moving faster than thirty miles per hour right now.

"Every word." Reece adds to the assurance by stretching his right hand over my left knee—which does nothing to improve my ire. Now I have to fight the allure of his fingers, their long elegance melting my blood even if they aren't in glow stick mode. "They asked if I sleep or recharge. Then came the kinky mask questions—though not before the theories about the bedroom applications of electro-levitation." He slips me a sultry side-eye. "Which I'm kind of mad *I* didn't think of first..."

"Oh, my God."

"What?" He turns his hand over, jogging it in open question, as I yank my leg away. "I'm a *guy*, Bunny. And frankly, the idea of being able to manipulate your sweet body any damn way I want to..."

The fresh glow of his fingers amply fills in the conclusion of that.

And, damn it, is also the final snip at the tightrope of my

outrage.

I tumble into a giggle, still pissed as hell but unable to control the humor from taking over. His laughter gains warmth and is joined by a cocky wink—along with the suggestive slink he gives his fingers again, traveling up the inside of my thigh...

"All right, mister." I lift his hand, kissing the center of his palm. "Don't push your luck. Focus on the road."

He shrugs, emphasizing the hewn cliff of his shoulder beneath his navy Henley. "Never stopped, my sweet Velvet."

"Yeah, yeah. And flattery will get you everywhere."

I thoroughly expect a comeback with another reference to levitated sex, but he gets in a new broadside by gentling his expression and sobering his tone. "Look. I know all this attention is a little jarring..."

"A *little*?"

"But things will even out. I promise. As soon as the world moves on to its next best canoodling couple, we'll just be the old fart and his hot mama on the block. Hell, the bellhop at the hotel didn't recognize me."

"Babe, the bellhop didn't know where his own feet were." More mirth spills out as I shake my head. "Some people are celebrating the state's pot legalization more than others."

"Huh." His forehead creases, adding to the rugged beauty of his profile. "I thought the smoke in his vape smelled a little interesting."

"Oh, dear." I kiss his knuckles this time. "Maybe you *are* the old fart on the block." A new sigh. "Trouble is, you're the only superhero on it too."

"Which also won't be such a big deal in a little while."

I puff up my cheeks and then let the air blow out, allowing the sight of the LA skyline to work its comforting sorcery on my senses. The bold monoliths of the skyscrapers, jutting like sentinels in protection of the lower buildings, have always been symbols of strength to me. If normal men and women could conceive and construct those gleaming structures, my normal life courage has never seemed so hard to stir—even now.

"A little while," I repeat, admitting that just hearing the words makes their possibility seem real. Guess there *is* something to be said for the power of affirmations. "A little while. Okay, fine. As long as this isn't forever...we'll muddle through."

Reece pulls my hand over to his side of the car. He brushes his lips across my fingertips, those expressive edges caressing just enough of my skin to make my skin tingle...and certain parts of me clench. And then drip...

"Yeah," he rasps, traveling his light kisses up past my wrist. "We'll muddle. Somehow."

I pull in a breath, given no choice about the matter. And the fact that it sounds like a duck dancing on sandpaper? Also not my choice—or control. "Yeah, well, as long as you don't mention levitation again..."

A rumble rolls out of his chest. "Well, fuck."

"Not at the moment." I add a giggle for good measure. "Nor for the next few hours, I'm afraid."

"The *fuck*?" The thunder has siphoned into his voice.

"I'm filling in for Neeta tonight, remember? Her sister's having a bridal shower."

He frees my hand to secure both of his on the wheel, guiding the car smoothly through the tight off-ramp at Grand Avenue. "Feel like giving a brother a hand here, big heavenly guy?" he grumbles as we pass the backside of the Cathedral of Our Lady of the Angels. "All these showers are raining on my fiy-ah."

I dissolve into laughter as we zip past the Music Center and its famous plaza, the steel sails of Disney Hall, and the white concrete veil fronting the Broad Museum before closing in on downtown proper. It's not lost on me that the cocky, one-liner-flinging Reece Richards is the side of the man most of the world has experienced, while the hotel we get nearer to is like a castle of the true king he's become—and the man *I* know. While I wouldn't give up my fierce, loyal lover for the retail value of every car in LA, it's fun to get peeks of the naughty bastard who once charmed so much of society with his daring irreverence.

Reece keeps me in stiches by continuing his theme, warbling Adele with off-key bravado. As we pause at a few stoplights, we endure a number of *what the hell* stares—and a carload of gaping USC kids who whip out their phones and record video. Before I can order Reece to refrain, he starts serenading them as well.

"Sing it, Bolt man!" one of them calls out.

And he does. Louder. Even more off-key. Even more dorky.

Even more breathtakingly beautiful than ever before.

"Reece!" I yell but melt into mirth again as the kids in crimson and gold whoop and cheer. He adds arm motions too, getting louder about setting fire to the rain and burning and crying and screaming names—in short, all the subjects that make up the best musical melodrama.

"Oh, hell." I shake my head, simply accepting that I won't be able to check my YouTube feed for weeks—especially as half the kids lean out of their Countryman to join my crazy boyfriend on a last, rousing round of the song's ham-worthy chorus.

And thankfully, the light turns green.

But as Reece hooks a right onto Wilshire, the Trojans get in a bunch of farewell hollers I'm not sure I'll ever forget.

"You're the bomb, Bolt baby!"

"Drop that fire like rain, dude!"

And my favorite:

"Emma Crist is the luckiest wench alive!"

As he presses the button to power the windows back up, I lean all the way over the center console, targeting the plane of his jaw with my heartfelt kiss. With my lips still pressed to his skin, I whisper, "And damn, does Emma Crist know it."

With the timing usually reserved for movies, we stop at another light. Inside that thirty-second pause, the man manages to twist his head, capture my lips against his in a heart-halting kiss, and lodge my hand firmly atop the hard rise in his jeans. Before I can even think about what's going on, I close my fingers around him, a nearly instinctual move. He groans, deepening the kiss and sucking in my tongue—

Until a honk from behind us gouges the air.

I lurch backward into my seat, taking my trembling fingers with me, as he sets the i8 into motion with a flustered stomp on the gas. Somehow, we manage to keep our paws to ourselves for the next two and a half blocks, even while Reece waves his key card at the private portico and the gates glide back as if sloths are controlling the tempo.

The second the entrance is clear, Reece punches the gas again and directs the car into the third of his three private spots. The first holds his Long Beach blue M4; the second, his space gray Gran Coupe.

But after setting the vehicle in park and turning off the engine, he falls into an odd stillness. If *he* were a car, I'd think he was idling in the checkered square part of a raceway, anticipating the very second the countdown bar turns green so he can open up the throttle and smoke the tires.

"Hey," I finally say, after he keeps it up for the better part of a minute. "You okay?" Though I must admit, the rugged energy he radiates is doing crazy things to my system. His aura of bottled danger, emphasized by the firm set of his lips and the razor's edge of his jaw, makes my heart skip every third beat, my lungs pumping hard to keep up. And I don't dare acknowledge how those staccato pulses start to affect my intimate places, plumped to greater awareness from the second I pivot in my seat and tuck one leg beneath me. "Reece?"

At last, he works the tip of his tongue between his lips. But doesn't return my scrutiny. Instead, with his hands still on the wheel and his gaze fixed straight at the wall, he quietly asks, "Do you need to change for your shift?"

I look down. Technically, I'm fine in the cobalt sheath dress and tapestry-textured ankle boots that I wore to Renata's shower, but since the hotel night shift on a weekend is usually more chaotic, especially with the summer weather kicking in a few weeks early, I'll be ready to jump faster in a pantsuit and flats.

"Y-Yeah." I stop, stunned to hear myself stammering. What the hell? Am I *nervous*? And why?

The answer comes in the two seconds it takes to look back up at him. Five minutes ago he was daring to butcher an Adele song in front of local rowdies. Now he's as opposite of rowdy as they come. He's more like the enigma I first met last month. Back in his shell—if that's what it can be called.

His dark shell.

His scary shell.

And damn it...it's kind of a turn-on.

But there's no time for letting him turn me to mush right now. I promised Neeta I'd be there for her, meaning—

"I should have just enough time to get into a new suit and freshen up." I express it as much for my benefit as his, if only for affirmation that his new, sexually charged strangeness hasn't stripped me of the ability to speak clearly. As soon as I know that for sure, and he recognizes my statement with a brief but tight nod, I plunge on. "Reece, what the hell? What's going on?" I twist my hands against my bent thigh. "Did I say something? Do something?"

He jerks his sights over as if I've just pinched him awake from a dream. "What?" He reaches out and cups a hand around my nape. "Jesus, Emma. *No.*"

"So how come you look ready to belt out more angst, without the screaming groupies this time?"

At least that grabs at the corners of his lips, producing a pair of entrancing dimples as willing companions. "You," he utters. "This. Us. It just...makes me happy. Happier than I've been in a long damn time." A sheepish shrug. "Perhaps ever."

Take one flustered girlfriend.

Add one part beautiful boyfriend confession.

Stir for less than three seconds for heart-halting swoon.

"*Reece.*" Now *I'm* the one with the angsty tears.

"So like the selfish prick I am, I don't want to give you up tonight."

He tacks on another shrug, though it's a gruffer action. This time he's some kind of a baller, bluffing his way through a shoulder displacement. His face returns to that pained tenacity too—and though it brings a lot more arousal to the girl parts, my caretaking side takes over, spurring me to kiss along the ridge of his brow.

"I'll be right here, mister. In the same building."

"Hmmmph." He pulls away and rolls out of the car, adding as he arrives at my side to pull my door open, "Not exactly my idea of 'right here,' Velvet."

Though I let him help me out, I straighten with a rigid spine—and a matching expression. "I *like* my job, Reece. It's important for me to help people. To feel like I'm making their lives a little easier. Like—"

"You matter." He busses the tip of my nose. "And you *do*, Emmalina. Not just to me." With a small tug, he lifts my face. "And for the record, I *never* want you to stop helping *anyone*. Not your friends, not the guests..." Tiny gold sparks dance against the silver of his eyes. "And definitely *not* the three cats you're all but boarding off the back door of your office."

I tug my teeth on my bottom lip. "Well, shit."

He chuckles. "Busted you, woman."

I curl four fingers into the V of his Henley. "But they take care of the mice in the gardens!"

"Which we have staff members to do as well."

"I named them Rey, Finn, and Poe!"

He opens his mouth but is speechless. I pump my free hand, victorious. The Galactic Resistance for the win.

Without another word, he scoops one hand into mine. Then pivots and starts a Poe Dameron-worthy stomp toward the penthouse's express elevator, not seeming to care that I'm all but sprinting to keep up with him. I don't mind the effort, knowing whatever's going through his mind must be squeezed into the next twenty minutes so I can be back down in the lobby to take over for Neeta. The ticking clock only feeds my excitement as we rush into the elevator and the doors slam shut, readying the car for its bullet ride to the seventieth floor.

But before the car even starts its launch, Reece swings me around until my back hits the wall. I have the chance for half a breath before his body follows, a slam of sinew and force along with the domination of his mouth and tongue. He rakes his hands under my dress, filling the car with the brutal bursts of him ripping the side seams to get his hands on my thighs. As soon as he's yanked my legs around his waist, parking my softening center against the erect ridge of his, the air is thick with our primal moans and lusty pants.

We go at each other like that for at least twenty floors, kissing and sucking and grinding and grabbing, until the physical need for air has us parted but not broken. My stare is consumed with the resplendence of him, sweaty and lusty. My body is a mass of violent shivers from the feel of his sex, bulging and demanding. My senses soar as the elevator does, getting dizzier and brighter and wilder, as if I've been swept up into a perfect erotic dream. Funny thing is, that just might be the case. In the universe according to Reece Richards, absolutely anything and everything is possible.

And right now, I wouldn't want it any other way.

Even as he plunges his hands into the mess of my hair and pulls hard enough to jerk my face back, making me feel utterly exposed and vulnerable to his ruthless stare. He presses closer...

And then just hovers there.

And watches me. Takes over me...

And yeah, he gets scary again.

Just a little. Just enough. Right to the edge that spikes my anxiety *and* my arousal. Where once again, I'm not quite sure what he's up to...

"Fuck," he finally rasps. "*Fuck me*, Emmalina Crist. You take my goddamned breath away."

I wet my lips. Swallow hard. And somehow manage, in a tone that won't give him instant diabetes, "That's a damn good thing, Reece Andrew, because you take away more than my breath."

Finally, *finally*, he swoops his mouth down, though his possession is carnal and thorough instead of a boldface demand. Despite the speed of our climb, he takes his damn time about this kiss, lapping at every crevice of my mouth in time to the sexy, savoring rolls of his hips. He doesn't stop even when the elevator does, reaching out to lock the open doors as I quiver against him, desperate mewls clawing my throat. *Holy God.* He's going to dry hump me into a climax right here and now, and there's nothing I can do to stop him. Nothing I *want* to do to stop him.

Yes.

Yessssss.

"No." The protest is a whisper as he pulls away just before my most shattering shudders. I grip at the elevator's railing to stay upright, my legs a pair of useless ribbons after he all but unwrapped my darkest desire.

Except that his gaze tells me differently.

Those eyes of his, transformed to the color of sharpened scissors, already bearing promises that he's only begun to tear me open.

Holy shit.

At this rate, I'm really, *really* going to be late for my shift. Already, I start floundering for what I'm going to say to Neeta.

"Velvet."

"H-Huh?"

"You'll be on time for work. I promise."

Damn him. Bless him. *No*, definitely damn him. Will there be a time when I'm not stunned with his ability to scan every syllable of my thoughts? "Oh. Okay." Or a time I'll be able to reply like something other than a turned-on clod?

He threads his fingers through mine, restoring a modicum of balance to our exchange by revealing his neon-blue fingertips, and tugs me out of the elevator. As I follow him—miracle of miracles, my legs really do work—I plant a frown on my lips.

"You wrecked my dress."

Dark smirk. "And Christ, was it fun."

"Just helping me get to my shift in time?" I quip.

"Helping you is what I'm all about, Velvet."

I jerk my brows. "Tell that to my girl parts."

"Oh, I still have a few things to say to your girl parts."

I step back, turning my expression into a glower worthy of Mary Freaking Poppins. "Not before my shift, you don't."

He barely flinches. Instead, adopts a stance with his feet firmly braced and his fingers curled in halfway toward completed fists. "Get your gorgeous ass into the bedroom. Change into your clothes for the shift. Then meet me in the kitchen."

"The kitch—"

But before I can get it all out, he's about-faced and gone, his steps strangely ominous against the hallway tiles.

And again, I'm a little scared.

And a whole hell of a lot aroused.

⚡

Ten minutes later, feeling a little more composed thanks to the clean lines of Ann Klein charcoal and gray pinstripes plus a pair of take-no-prisoners flats, I stride into the kitchen and break into an instant grin.

Reece is, as he promised, waiting.

With only the overhead can lights on.

And his shirt off.

I give myself a reward for the fast-change job by taking a long moment to drink in his glory. And I do mean *glory*. The man's body is crafted so exquisitely, it's like the angels dropped him into the wrong time frame. He should be commanding a chariot. Wielding a saber. Riding bareback across a windswept moor. He's too perfect to be concealed by three-piece suits or even skin-hugging leathers.

And he's mine.

All mine.

A fact I barely refrain from screaming about now as I approach him with slow, purposeful steps. "Well. There *are* nice perks to your bossy side."

He lifts one side of his mouth. Yeah, the mouth that belongs on some wicked clan laird in nothing but a kilt. "Oh, this isn't bossy, beautiful," he murmurs as I rub a hand down the valley between his pecs. "This is part of the plan."

"The...plan." I lilt it with slight curiosity, hoping to garner more hints about all this from his expression. No dice. He still stares at me like I'm prey. A hapless lass wandering into his sinful lair. "Well, I do like the plan so far..." Though I narrow my eyes while glancing at the counter and the tray of round, red designer ice cubes resting there. The balls have special meaning to us, as the man learned early on how sensitive my nipples are to extreme temperatures. If those red plastic spheres could talk... "Though you know we can't exactly play like *that* right now, R—"

He cuts me short by claiming my lips with a short but sharp bite of his. "I said you'd be on time," he softly reprimands. "And I meant it." That part is a hot blast against my neck as he whips me around to face the counter. "Only tonight, you're going to take me to work with you." He spreads an even steamier breath along the bottom of my back while pulling my shirt out of my slacks.

"All...all right."

He grazes a hand up my spine with undeniable pressure, commanding me to flatten my torso atop the counter. Only then do I swivel my head and see a cocktail tumbler on the other side of the counter. There's nothing inside the glass but three of the round ice cubes. But they're not red anymore. They're purple.

Because red plastic containing an infusion of blue electricity makes purple.

"Holy...*shit*!"

But my second syllable emerges more as a helpless gasp, as Reece unzips my pants and whips them down to my knees. He doesn't skip my panties either—meaning the cool wind from the air conditioner blows at once across my naked ass and pussy.

His breath hitches along with mine.

I wish I could be heartened by that again, but this time, I'm not. I shiver as he rubs both his palms across the planes of my backside, angling his pulsing fingers inward until he's scraping the sensitive lips of my sex with his buzzing tips.

"Oh...God," I manage to stammer as telltale sizzles fill the air between my thighs.

"That's it, Velvet," Reece coaxes in a husk that revs me as thoroughly as his touch. "Fuck, yes. That's it. You're dripping for me." He circles one middle finger in a little deeper, making me scream and squirm. Damn it, how the man knows how to touch me...and tease me...and tantalize me... "Say it, Emmalina," he dictates in a low snarl. "Tell me exactly what I'm doing to you."

"I— *Mmmm*"—he fingers me with more force, temporarily taking my ability to think, let alone speak—"I'm...I'm wet," I finally spill. "My pussy is soaked for you. Oh. *Ohhhh!*"

"And do you want me inside you?"

"Fuck." I slam the counter. *Down for the count.* "Reece!"

"Answer me." With his other hand, he spreads my backside a little wider. I know what he's planning now, his filthy intentions blatantly clear.

"Oh...*shit.*"

"That wasn't an answer, Emmalina."

"Yes, damn it. *Yes*, I want you inside me." At the last minute, I add a pleading moan. Maybe if I beg prettily enough, he'll oblige with his beautiful cock instead of his clever little solution to our separation tonight.

I'm not going to get that lucky.

It's obvious as soon as he stretches over and scoots the glass closer. I watch the container pass, with its pulsing purple orbs reflecting off the countertop in time to the flashing light inside his long, determined fingers.

"And I *will* be inside you, beautiful. All night long."

His voice is like melted butter on my skin...with a chaser of flaming tequila. I want more, but in the end, I know there will be hell to pay.

Especially as he parts my pussy lips a little more.

Removes the tingling pressure of his fingertips.

Replaces them with the throbbing invasion of the first ball.

It's...incredible.

Unbelievable.

Impossible.

He expects me to get through the next eight hours with *this* happening deep inside me? With these pulses, constant and incessant, a never-ending reminder of the parts of me that are made most perfectly for him? Basically taking his sensual invasion but unable to do a damn thing about it?

"Oh, *no*." I jolt and push back, then writhe and slide. Anything to get away from the ruthless hold he has on my lower back, keeping me in place as he presses the second ball against my trembling nether lips. "No, no, no, *no*."

"Yes." He's murmuring like I simply don't want to try a bite of his brussels sprouts. Right now, I'd even succumb to *that* if it meant not having to go down to the damn lobby in this condition. "*Yes*, Velvet. God*damn*, you look so good like this. Your cunt... Dear *Christ*. You're so gorgeous and pink and wet." He nudges the ball in deeper. "I'm going to be in agony all night, wishing my cock could be doing this to you instead."

"Then just *make* it your cock," I snarl. "Damn it, Reece. I'm not going to be able to— *Ohhhh!*"

And I'm pummeling the counter as he adds the third ball.

And I'm moaning like a banshee as he gives it all a final push, ensuring it's firmly seated.

And I'm already an exhausted puddle, as he draws my slacks and underwear back up.

Sealing the torment inside me. Locking me down and

loading me up with his electricity as his special "bullets."

Yippee ki-yay, lightning chucker.

I'm still flat against the counter, longing to throw him off but unable to, as he slides from behind and molds his body on top of mine. His breath is labored and lusty in my ear. His stubble is a masculine abrasion against my neck—sending new vibrations through my body. Freaking great. Now all my limbs are colored the same shade of horny-and-helpless as my pussy.

He rustles his mouth along the shell of my ear while running a reassuring hand along the top of my arm. "You're my strong, incredible woman. You can do this, Velvet."

I flick his hand away, beyond mad. Which—no shit—just spikes my libido higher. "Do *what*? Reece, I can barely *move*."

He kisses the flat of my cheek. "You'll adjust."

"Says the guy not getting a nonstop vibe job from the inside out?"

"Says the guy who'll deal with *this* all night long."

Well, damn it. The ridge of flesh he uses as his underscore is the texture of an industrial flame thrower and all but sears both layers of our clothes with matching intent. "Fine," I bite out as he steps back, yanking me upright at the same time. "Point made, Mr. Richards."

And yes, it's a concession to my complete dearth of ideas for resistance—meaning I'm going to have to learn how to live with this. How to concentrate harder on shit like taking fuller breaths. On even taking *steps*.

To my relief, it's all actually an aid toward minimizing the misery from the balls—leading to my next firm decision. I can't allow myself any downtime during tonight's shift. Downtime means thinking time, and thinking time means I'll refocus on every teasing vibration the man has just ensured I'll spend the next eight hours enduring.

That I *will* endure.

Yeah, even willingly.

Because of him.

For him.

And yeah...even *with* him.

The bright side? Absolutely nothing I'll face tonight will be as rough as this.

Or so I think...before walking through the executive offices and emerging out to the Brocade's front desk.

To find a dozen frustrated guests waiting to be checked in.

And an army of at least fifty tabloid photographers hovering right behind *them*.

Well...hell.

I repeat it in a mutter beneath my breath but refrain from adding anything else to that litany. So much for thinking downtime was going to be an issue tonight.

CHAPTER FOUR

REECE

Three hours.

As fucking rough as it's been to stick to my self-imposed time cushion for checking in on her, I'm proud of myself for the fortitude. But now that the timer on my watch conveys there's only a few minutes of the ordeal left, I realize how necessary the stricture was. Just the concept of restarting the executive-office and front-desk surveillance cameras has my skin prickling, my fingers twitching, and my cock leading the way back to the penthouse office like a dog straining at its leash.

Okay, yeah, I could've easily filled the hours by doing something useful. There's a mountain of work on my desk. Folders full of emails to return on my laptop. And oh yeah, a city full of crazies and creeps having some Saturday night "fun" in the City of Angels. But every one of those options entails conscious and careful thought, and thinking means inviting Emma back into my head—especially in the case of the leathers, when the small head's invited in on the ride too. I love the crap out of putting bad guys away—but all the electrons in my blood enjoy throwing a superhero after-party in my balls.

And tonight, *different* balls are foremost on my mind.

"Christ," I grit out, having to fall into a chair as soon as I round the corner into the penthouse office. Normally my hard-ons are easier to tame once I cross the threshold of this room, lined by filing cases on one side and video cam feeds on the other, and assume hotel leader mode. But tonight, I'm twisting my balls with an open grimace to keep everything in check down there.

Though the task is about to get a lot fucking harder.

One more minute.

Yeah. Harder.

Because no matter what's happening seventy floors down, I know my woman is handling it with her level head, her quick intelligence, her ready smile, and her joy for service—despite the dastardly chaos I've wrought to her pussy. She'll be her gorgeous, refined self on the outside, while inside, I've ensured her wildest cave-girl self is beating at the walls, begging to be free.

Now, I just want to see it for myself.

To witness even the tiniest breaks in her control...and know I've put them there.

The pumps of her breaths. The gloss of her eyes. Maybe even a few pissy looks at the cams, their intent for my eyes alone.

Acknowledging my invisible control.

Giving me the consummate power.

Feeding the addiction of my domination.

One more minute.

I squeeze my balls again. "*Fuck.*" My sack must have bruises by now. So who does that really put in control here?

Forty seconds.

I lurch up from the chair, wobbling like I'm drunk, fighting that damn dog between my legs again.

Thirty.

Fuck it. The dog can have his day a little early.

I jab the monitor buttons two at a time, jiggling a knee in order to stay in one place as they warm up. As the screens warm up, I rake both hands along the sides of my head. Why are these fuckers taking so long?

"Shit."

My exclamation extends for at least twenty seconds as I bounce my gape from monitor to monitor in search of her. I'm relieved the quest doesn't take longer considering the sea of humanity filling every camera feed. The first three, featuring the images from the three devices placed at the left, right, and center of the front desk, would be the most captivating if she were anywhere near that area. Those feeds definitely feature the most movement, due to the throng of photographers restlessly milling about in spite of the three LAPD Five-Os keeping them corralled at the south end of the lobby. At the other end, where the hotel's bar is located, a full crowd takes advantage of the fact that last call is still an hour away—with the media presence a good augury for upcoming excitement.

My scrutiny shifts to the next five monitors. The first gives a clear shot of the hallway outside the executive offices, while the next four are feeds from inside that sanctum.

Where Emma looks determined to wear out the carpet before the sun rises.

She sits—though hardly rests—as Wade moves into the frame, clearly explaining something to her. Something that's definitely not making her night. She pinches the bridge of her nose, staying that way even after Wade finishes, his own expression tight.

Only then, after watching her without mercy, do I spot it. *There.* The wiggle in her knee, small but violent, as if a current of hot electricity is powering it. As she presses her legs together, the other knee takes up the same cadence—making it all too easy to tell that the balls I energized three hours ago are still pulsing at maximum power.

Goddamnit.

I should be high on virile victory. Soaring on my semi-sadistic rockets. But I'm not jacked by even a frisson of satisfaction. Not a damn drop of fascination either. I'm a wicked bastard only on an even playing field. There's nothing fun in teasing a cat unless it gets to grab the yarn at the end—and there's nothing fun about taunting *this* pussy if the press have been turning her into a back-office hermit for the majority of the night.

Unwittingly, my woman provides her own version of backup proof for that, as she turns around with a face drenched in frustration, fury, and a hell of a lot of pent-up lust.

By now, I'm damn sure my features are coated in the same lovely mixture.

Especially after I turn and examine the camera feeds from the Brocade's front porte cochere.

"Jesus Christ."

Now I'm just pissed the hell off. There are just as many reporters and photographers strolling around out there. Judging by the angles of their hands and the thin white haze across the shot, that's the smoking crowd. Not that I'm ready to stand here and decipher the whole thing.

Time's up on this crazy circus. *Past* up.

The thought is on its way to becoming my full resolve by the time I'm done punching in the four digits for the office phone closest to Emmalina. But the second it rings, I watch her start as if electrocuted. Damn if that doesn't do something significant to how the balls caress her channel, because she squirms her hips with such suggestive little rolls, I'm tempted to hang up and call again just for the pleasure of watching. God*damn* what this woman does to me, even when she's being adorably uncomfortable.

"Mr. Richards."

So much for my hands cooperating with my libido.

Or for her being "adorable" about anything anymore.

Now she's just downright full of vexation and impatience. In all the most gorgeous ways.

"Miss Crist." It's impossible to subdue the husky admiration from my voice, clearly cluing her into the fact that I can see her now—an intrusion that ticks her off as much as what the media mob has pulled off.

"Nice to have you back." She remarks it coolly, knowing her direct glare at the camera is doing the heavy lifting for her ire. "Did you have fun saving the world tonight?"

Well, shit.

Leaving her out of the loop on my real "fun" for the evening—pacing, peeking in on the Dodger game, pacing, logging in two hours of weights, pacing, deciding an episode of *Project Grizzly* was better than the game—seems like a damn good idea at the moment. "Looks like you've been having more fun."

She whips a new glower up at the camera. "Don't go there, mister. I'm not even half a step ready for the light side of this. *Any* of this."

"I'm on your side, Emma," I attempt to soothe. Her caustic laugh doesn't deter me. "Talk to me. What's going on? Have those assholes been here all night?"

She nods. "Apparently, we're now officially *numero uno*

on every magazine's 'must have' list—ever since a certain video went viral earlier tonight."

I gulp hard, racking my brain through all the years when I was the poster boy for the Bacchanal billionaire's club. God, I really did behave like an ass, though I always drew a strict line at recording sexcapades. I was a sinner, but I wasn't stupid. But that doesn't mean some resourceful woman didn't secretly make one and has been waiting for the right moment to go public...

"A video? Of what?"

I'm stunned to see the bow of her mouth into a blithe ribbon. "Of a certain superhero destroying an Adele song while cruising down Grand Avenue with his girlfriend."

"Holy shit."

"Took the words right out of my mouth, buddy."

"I'd laugh if I weren't so sure you'd kill me for it."

"Oh, I'm already going to kill you, but those reporters have nothing to do with it."

I swipe the phone downward, careful not to let her hear my audible effort to hold in the mirth now. And the relief. *Shit tons* of relief.

And arousal.

A hot, heavy new wave of it as she pivots back toward the wall, ensuring no eyes can see her but mine via the camera over her head...before she frees the top two buttons of her blouse until her bra is exposed. And then yanks that aside so her nipple is exposed. And starts pulling at the already erect nub beneath, joining the sight of it with her angry, sultry eyes, until the inches between my mouth and the receiver can't hide my tortured groan from her ears.

"God*damn*."

She jogs her chin and continues looking into the camera, but now at an angle that thoroughly reminds me of how she looks when I'm between her thighs, fucking her senseless. "You're very right, Mr. Richards. I've been damned for the last three hours, and you're the god who's done it to me."

. I gulp again, stumbling backward. When my ass hits the edge of my desk, my bulging cock screams at my strained zipper. "*Fuck.*"

She keeps plucking at her breast, turning my imagination inside out. The camera feed is black and white, meaning I'm forced to imagine how deep a shade of red that gorgeous tip has become. "You know what all this makes me now, right?" she says between a couple of dense breaths.

"Wh..." I clear my throat, searching for a tone other than a croak. "Wh-What?"

She makes me wait for the reply. Through two, then three more twists at her beautiful erection. "The demon who's going to demand my revenge."

EMMA

"I'll be right down."

The line to the penthouse clicks dead with such a crash, I almost laugh.

Almost.

There are still a whole bunch of barriers left in the way of that glee. Like the way I've just screwed myself royally by making my point to Reece so well, my nipples are now twin points of hot anguish. Like the fact that they *wouldn't* be if he hadn't come up with this damn bright idea in the first place. Like the fact that I've invented more creative profanities for .

ANGEL PAYNE

the man in the last three hours than in the last three *weeks*. I've never had a more challenging or unforgettable night at work.

And that I've kind of liked it.

Not that he'll ever get *that* willing confession out of me.

Especially because it would've been more fun to focus on controlling the need between my legs than the reporters swarming the hotel like ants on honey. And, knowing *I'm* their honey, having to do that mostly by proxy—with the exception of the initial moment they took me all by surprise and got off the first round of pictures while I stood at the front desk like a *frozen* drop of honey.

Since then, I've been holed up here in the offices, the ringleader trying to run the circus from outside the tent. Thank God for Wade and Fershan, who have been pulling double duty between the reservations bay and the command center my office has become. Not only have they kept me apprised of the media invasion of the lobby and the status of guests' reactions from the smaller guest hallway cams, but they've tried to keep tabs on the police scanners across the city too. While they've reported no definitive Bolt sightings, that only means Reece has been handling minor shit in order to beat feet before the cops arrive on the scene. For that, my superhero earns himself a few free points of my gratitude. The concept of having to worry about *his* ass in significant danger is a stress *my* ass doesn't need right now.

Especially because every inch of that body part now clenches, struggling to handle the new influx of lust to everything south of my waist, as the penthouse's private elevator dings to a stop—and Reece emerges at full, furious stride.

Dear freaking God.

He hasn't changed from his earlier outfit, and his anger-puffed chest stretches his blue Henley to eye-popping magnificence. I curl my fingers against my palms, battling the instant craving to run to him and grip him by those impressive pecs—and then to keep going, exploring every defined ridge of his taut abdomen...

And I don't dare let my fantasies drag any lower.

Not with what my pussy has already been aching to do to that part of him for three damn hours now.

Not with what it *really* wants to do as he pins me with a look that glints like handcuffs, barely moving his lips to order, "Stay. Right. Here."

Not with how all my tissues vibrate so hard, I sag against the wall in full compliance—watching helplessly as he wrenches open the door leading out to the lobby.

I wait, really unable to do much else, until his thunder of a bellow shakes the building.

"What the *fuck* are you idiots doing in my hotel?"

I tremble harder. Then grate to myself, "Holy crap."

Fire in the rain, indeed.

At least enough to finally spark my ass into gear. I sprint across the office, along with Wade and Fershan, to peek around the doorway behind the front desk...

At my boyfriend, now in the center of a flashbulb lightning storm, his hands at his hips and his legs positioned wide.

And rage crackling the air all around him.

Literally.

"By the gods," Fershan blurts.

"Holy *crap*." I deem it worth a repeat.

"Effing awesome," Wade exclaims—at full and confident volume because not a damn person in the place is going to hear him over the riot to which the press has now dedicated themselves, becoming a textbook case of mob mentality. I find it hard to remember I'm watching human beings, as they scramble over and atop each other like monkeys trying to ring a bell for peanuts.

"Reece!" one of them yells. "Reecy baby! Over here. Smile like ya mean it, man!"

"Now sing like ya mean it, too. Come on, dude. Just a few bars for the fans."

"Especially because you'll look so damn good doing it. What're you wearing, man? D&G? Massimo? Varvatos?"

"Target off-the-rack." I snort softly at Wade's and Fershan's incredulous gawks. "What? It was an impulse buy during my monthly run. You know...for the essentials?"

"Doritos and Gatorade?" Wade offers.

"Tampons, vitamins, workout water, and cat food."

Fershan hurls a glare at his friend. "You had to go there?"

Before Wade can get in a zinger in response, the air gets a lot more tense. The reporters have amped up their assault on Reece.

"Where's Emma?"

"Bring out Emma!"

"She was out here earlier. She looks great. You've got great taste, Richards. Always have."

"Yeah. We want Emma too. Call Emma out! Will you sing to *her* if she comes out?"

"Holy *shit*." My repeat is twice as strident as the first. What the hell is he up to? And if he even *thinks* of rewarding these goons after they've hindered our work and clogged our lobby for the better part of the night...

My ruminations—and most of the din from the reporters—

are cracked down by one snap of Reece's fingers. The friction of his action turns his hands into miniature cherry bombs, the force of his fury turning the fireworks nearly silver. As soon as he's commanded their attention, his stance stiffens. His jaw hardens. His nostrils flare.

"Ladies and gentlemen, I'll only say this once," he finally intones. "Emma is *working* tonight, so she won't be joining us in any capacity. Further, you're hindering her from accomplishing that job successfully—and doing it while trespassing on private property." He lifts a sizzling finger, stopping the one reporter who dares to draw in a breath, poised with a protest. "And Pete, I *know* the laws about privately held public space, which is why I'm sure my friends with the LAPD haven't hurled you all out on your asses by now." Slowly, he uncurls his other four fingers. Turns his hand over until his palm is up, and there are jolts of blue and white light dueling across the taut surface. "But at the moment, ask me if I care about the law."

Pete the would-be protester is joined by another guy with a man-bun and hipster glasses accented in the same purple finish as his camera. "That's not the way it works anymore, Richards. You're not the darling boy breaking the rules now, and that means—"

"That I don't need all of *you* to sway public sentiment to my side?" Reece counters.

Purple Glasses fumes. "Yeah, but that also means you owe us a few. *More* than a few. So just stand there and smile pretty and call your bird to come join you, and we won't—"

"What?" Reece leans a step closer to the hipster. "You won't *what*, asshole? File a complaint with hotel management? I can predict how far *that'll* go right now. Or maybe you just won't have me arrested? Was that the gist?" With his glare still fixed on the guy, he lifts both his arms and swings them toward the cops, who've actually stepped off to the side with visible relief upon Reece's arrival. Not anymore—especially as sparks start to dance atop Reece's other hand. "Fine. Do what you must, officers. Arrest me."

The policemen shift from foot to foot.

The hipster's lips twist from side to side.

Reece's stare slides between them, steady as a lead beam in a hurricane.

And for a long moment, nobody does anything else. Even the hotel guests in the bar *and* the bartenders have gone utterly still.

"Bearer of pure brass," Fershan murmurs.

"Uh-uh," Wade instantly defers. "Bolt of pure badass."

I smile softly, knowing they'll be dickering about it all night—but also confident none of their permutations will change the assignation that already exists in my heart.

My hero.

As if the truth of it needs more proof, Reece slides his hands down from their cuff-ready pose while their pyrotechnics keep going in and around his hands—which he curls into full fists. With those fires now encased with nowhere to go, blue and silver charges jump up and away from his hands and climb his arms like electric roots around dual tree limbs. Incredible, beautiful, muscled tree limbs.

"I'll only say *this* part once, as well," he announces to the throng. "Our security cams on this area are up and running. My staff is taking careful note of who's here and what publications you sell your 'scoops' and images to. If you're still here in ten minutes, those publications will be omitted from any notification about, or invitation to, the forthcoming *official* interviews with Emmalina Crist and myself."

A few hours ago, I'd compared him to an array of historical hunks. Now, I feel like the corset-wearing counterpart to one of them, light-headed and short-breathed, swallowing down huge chunks of emotion at my modern-day Galahad as he defends everything I hold dear. My dignity. My privacy. My ability to do the job I've worked so hard to get and keep.

"Goddamnit, Reece Andrew. How I love you."

I don't even care that Wade and Fershan are privy to my heart's confession. But I do push back from the doorway and dash back through the offices before they hear what I mutter after that.

"And holy shit, how I want you."

Right now.

Right here, if that's the way he's going to demand it.

But I'm not sure I'm going to give him time to consider that.

Because as he launches back through the door from the lobby, with the sound of a hundred shuffling footsteps muting his own wide stomps, I'm already waiting to leap on him. To wrap myself around him. To mash my lips onto him and ram my tongue between his. To let all the juices in my core loosen those damn balls in my pussy, which roll and rub and pulse at me with a force I've been battling all night.

Not anymore.

Especially not as he returns my kiss with just as much hot hunger and stabbing ardor.

Not as he secures my legs against his waist with his elbows and locks my crotch on his broad bulge by cupping his hands around my ass.

Not as he maintains the hold while carrying me into the

private elevator to begin our ascent.

CHAPTER FIVE

REECE

Seventy floors.

Nearly a thousand feet.

A single minute.

The hottest strip-down I've ever had with a woman.

Buttons ping and bounce everywhere as she rips off her shirt. My growled profanity counters them as she strips away mine. Our breaths, hot and rough and guttural, get heavier as she unsnaps her bra and hurls it away. My feral groan fills the compartment as her breasts tumble free, her nipples stabbing into my chest.

"*Emma*. Christ. *Yes.*"

"Shut up." She barely gets it out before biting into me with a new kiss, descending so hard that our teeth knock and our tongues are a clumsy tangle—a mess never sorted out because she yanks back as fast as she's plummeted and now seizes both sides of my face. "Shut the hell up and get these pants off me."

I smirk. "Yes, ma'am."

"Shut *up.*" Her command is barely more than breath as we plunge into another round of tugs and jerks at snaps and zippers, her hands working my fly as eagerly as I fumble with hers, until our legs are bare and puddles of fabric constrict our ankles. I kick my pants free before she does, so I bend to help with hers—but instantly recognize that dire mistake. As soon as her first leg is free, she's able to step a little wider—exposing my senses to the perfect, heady scent of the pussy that's been clenching for me since the start of her shift.

She smells like honey.

She smells like *ready*.

She smells better than any damn dessert I've ever eaten, in every fine restaurant around the globe.

"*Emma.*" I move in, pinning her thighs to the elevator's wall as I literally salivate, anticipating her taste. "Christ. You're like ambrosia..."

The goddamned doors slide open. The *ding* that follows is worse than a time's-up bell from a bad game show. *Too late. You forgot to buy a vowel.*

Except that now, I'm running the game show.

And I know exactly what vowel to nail down next.

I lift her again, my hands at her ass and my face at her neck, with one pant leg dangling from her ankle. Both of her flat shoes are still in the elevator, and I don't fucking care. Every muscle in my body and neuron of my mind is consumed with getting her back into a position where I can lick and suck and sample every delicious drop drenching her impossibly sweet cunt.

"Reece! Ohhhhh..."

And *there's* the vowel I need, flowing from her as I make it as far as the entry to the penthouse living room before setting her down once more—and instantly dropping to my knees before her.

Inhaling her into my deepest being again.

Closing my eyes as the near-Godiva goodness invades me again.

"God." It's a shallow groan, mostly because my lungs refuse to function for speech. Every breath right now is for one purpose alone. Getting my lips closer to her sexy-as-fuck honeypot. "*God*, Emma. Let me in, beautiful. Spread for me. *Now*."

Thank God she's in no place to be feisty, at least for the moment. The second I park my hands to the wall on either side of her hips, she reaches and braces her hands on my forearms, securing her balance. The slide of her hair on the wall, likely coinciding with the backward jolt of her head, adds an erotic sibilance to the air as I lap at her nectar for the first time.

"Ohhhh!"

The magical vowel again.

As her juices burst on my tongue.

As her scent invades my whole system.

As she makes my cock jut straight to attention, even spilling telltale white drops on the floor between my knees.

She's the most perfect thing I've ever tasted. The headiest delicacy I've ever known. The newest obsession of my rampaging lust.

I have to have more.

I widen my lips, openly sucking at her. And suddenly, excruciatingly, knowing why.

As the first of my altered ice balls slides out of her pussy and into my eager mouth.

Fuck. Me.

If licking her outer folds was heaven, this is the outer limits of paradise. Her tangy arousal enhanced by the electricity still shivering the orb is the best damn piece of candy I've ever sampled. It's sensual and silken and sweet...

It's all her.

And holy fuck, there are two more.

With a savoring growl, I toss the clean ball over my shoulder.

With an even more eager moan, I dip my head in for more.

"*Reece.* Ahhhhh!"

Technically, it's still a vowel. And officially, I'm enjoying the hell out of this game show—though soon I'm sure the network will reclassify us as after-hours adult fare. Just fucking fine by me, because never in my life have I enjoyed devouring a woman more. Feeling her inner walls shift and move as I do. Savoring the little river of sexuality that drenches my mouth between each undulation. Listening to the changing cadences of her sighs and cries and moans, telling me exactly how good those balls feel for her...and how close she's coming to giving up number two.

"Oh...*God.* Reece. It's there." She moves a hand into my hair, twisting the strands from my scalp and ramming her pussy against my lips. "Take it. *Take it!*"

Her new verbosity only increases my enjoyment of the second candy—though I don't linger as long on it because her body is undulating like a seductress as the third ball begins to descend her channel. Sure enough, nearly from the moment I press my lips to her again, the last bulb is waiting for me to pull. To triumph. To take.

As I do, she unfurls an ecstatic scream—a sound so addicting, I can't even think of giving it up. Not yet. Not *fucking* yet.

So I don't take time to lick her candy coating off the ball. Instead, with the ball poised in one of my hands, I hook her thigh over my shoulder with the other—to keep her locked in place as I roll the pulsing orb right back over her sex. Across her labia. Through the glistening, trembling folds surrounding her gorgeous, intimate entrance. Then, with ultimate purpose, I spread back her soaked hood and brush the ball over her most sensitive button...

"Shit! Ohhhh, *fuck!*"

No more vowels.

They aren't needed.

The grand prize has been unveiled.

And she's shivering against my fingers. Bucking around my ears. Clenching and clutching and climaxing and climbing, higher and hotter and fiercer, toward a paradise even better than this one. The nirvana of another release already building through every inch of her. I can read its approach in the need on her face. Feel the tension forming in all her muscles. Feel the anticipation in every air molecule around us. She's commandeered all that energy from me, and god*damn*, it feels amazing. For once, to not be the glaring isotope in the room. For once, not worrying about hiding myself. Instead, completely losing myself...

To her.

For her.

All of it. Everything I am. Every move I make. Every breath I release and touch I give. Hers. *Hers.*

"Reece! Oh, God. *Reece!*"

"Here, Velvet." I grate against the inside of her lifted thigh. "I'm right here."

"I know." Her reply isn't much more than a couple of sounds from between her teeth, mashed to seem like words. She makes up for it the next second, screaming through her enunciation. "Goddamnit, I *know.* That's the problem!"

And now I understand. And break into a savoring grin

about it. And continue to relish the moment while kissing my way to the valley between her thigh and pussy and then up and over the silk of her stomach. With a growl, I tongue the indent of her navel before licking wet swirls up to the space between her breasts, giving both the attention of the vibrating ball still in my possession. As her nipples turn red and stiff for me, she crosses an invisible line between needy lover and writhing she-demon. No part of me confirms that clearer than my cock, now smashed between our bodies and enduring the friction of her every demanding thrust.

"This what you want, Emmalina?" I push back at her, making sure she feels every inch of the state she's gotten me into. Not that I wasn't here before. Now, it's an unstoppable pain. A pounding need. A feral, jungle obsession...

"Mmmmm." Her face is awash in soft arousal and dire need, limned in the cobalt glow from the swollen veins throughout my dick. "Yesssss," she's finally able to add as she lifts her hands, clutches my shoulders, and uses the leverage to mold her body closer to mine. She's so stunning, I can't help but stare at her and then string her...just for a few seconds longer...

"This?" I scrape the word along her forehead, adding small, wicked bites along her eyebrows. "The cock swelling for you? Hurting for you?"

A high cry trembles off her lips. Faintly, she nods. "Hurting," she murmurs. "Make it stop...hurting."

"Yeah, baby. I will." I duck my head, trailing my teeth and tongue down her hairline. "You hurt too?"

A new nod, just as dreamy and languid, clashing with the talons her fingers have turned into against my shoulders. As she digs in deeper, I hiss against her ear—and shove my cock tighter along her belly. Holy fuck, I need to be inside her. At least five minutes ago.

No.

Three goddamned hours ago.

"I hurt too. Christ, Emma. All fucking night I've been like this. I wasn't even able to go out on patrol. I was like a caged animal up here, practically scaling the walls..." The ball falls from my fingers as I glide my hands down to her hips and start to guide her body in the tempo I plan on pounding her at. *Soon. So damn soon.* "Thinking about just that small part of me, living and throbbing inside of you..."

"But not anymore." There's a sob in her voice as I rear my face back and align her body forward. Lifting her to straddle me...and soon to ride me... "Not anymore," she repeats from gritted teeth. "And I'm empty. So damn—"

Her scream takes the place of her plea.

As I lunge all the way inside her with one thrust.

"Christ," I growl.

"Yes!" Emma shouts it again and again, drawing out every part of the syllable in time to my movements. The *Y* trembles out as I pause with my cockhead at her sleek pussy lips. The *E* she extends during my long, forceful stroke up the silken fist of her passage. She draws out the *S* once I hit home deep inside, adding to our mutual pleasure by circling my hips until my crown has said hello to the most intimate parts of her shivering core.

Over and over again, I take her like that—until the power surge in my sack starts to crackle and sizzle, threatening to blow me apart if I don't give the electrons somewhere to go. My ass is clenched. My thighs are burning. My balls are matching lightning storms, wild with need, charged with light, on fire with demand. The only force keeping me rooted to reality is the lock of our stares, where turquoise light engulfs me, keeping me safe but urging me on. Where the smaller pinpoints of cyan are like lighthouses guiding me through the squall of a lust I've never dealt with before. A need I've never known. A longing that terrifies me...but inexorably lures me. A pull I'll never be able to resist.

A bond I'll never give up.

The woman who composes more and more of my purpose with every new lunge, every fresh flame, every hoarse breath. She knows it too, thank fuck. I can see it in every soft, adoring inch of her face as I brace my forefinger beneath her jaw and tuck my thumb against her bottom lip. *Fuck*, how I adore her like this. Locked for me and accepting every drop of my power as a man, not a goddamned *super*man. But ironically, because of it, turning me into that hero all over again. Larger than life for her. A man of steel because of her.

"Good?" I growl it, letting her know I want the response from her lips as well as her eyes.

She swallows hard before whispering, "Yeah. Good."

"Your cunt is happy?"

"Yeah," she rasps. "Oh, yeah. Happy."

"Full now?"

"Yes. *Yes*. So full."

"And now your pussy wants to come?"

"Yes. Oh God, yes, please!"

"Words." I push my thumb in, using her tongue to wet it, and then rub the pad along the gorgeous blush of her bottom lip. "Say the words, Velvet."

"I...I want to come."

"Again. All the words this time. Every filthy one. And

you'll look at me this time."

Her lashes flutter. Her chest heaves, a bellows of passion and nerves and lust. Holy fuck, her nipples are perfect arrowheads against my chest.

"I...I... My pussy needs to come. *God*, Reece, please. All over your cock!"

"*Damn.*" I reward her for the bravery with a smoldering, tongue-filled kiss while returning my hand to her hip, joining the other to start ramming her sweet body even harder over my raging, burgeoning erection. With our gazes meshed again, I set the pace of our bodies to a brutal rhythm. Our fucking flesh sounds like whip cracks against the walls. The echoes are an erotic backbeat to the driving, decadent pulse of our mounting, soaring completion.

"Oh, *Reece!*"

"Hang on, baby."

"I...I can't..."

"Hang. *On.*"

"Shit. *Shit!*"

White fire bursts in my balls. Silver specks dance in my vision. "Tell me. *Now*, Emmalina. Tell. Me!"

"I'm...coming." Her mouth falls open. She flares her aqua eyes. Her entire face is a sunbeam of wonder and desire and devotion and ignition...

Sending me all the way over too.

I'm a torch of lust. A missile of purpose. A burning staff of damn divinity, sworn to worship her and her alone. Powered higher and hotter only by serving her...fulfilling her...fucking into deeper and darker parts of her...

Giving more and more to her.

My cock. My climax. My seed. My essence.

My soul.

My heart.

My being.

My world.

The only thing that matters or exists, for a long and perfect time, as I empty into her hard and long enough to finally slow our pace into a rolling reverie—though as I gentle my thrusts, my heart still attempts to punch out the center of my chest to be closer to hers. Not that I blame the thing one damn bit. Even the inches between our torsos feel like a canyon of separation, inciting me to lean in close again, expelling my heavy breaths along the back of her neck.

As we go completely still, we're also totally silent, soaking up the perfection of still being one. Shamelessly, I inhale the scent and the sensuality, all sugar and silk and satisfied sex, that form the pheromones of this woman, still driving me utterly crazy even in my satiation with her body. There's no riddle to it either. With every other woman, my curiosity usually ended at sex. With Emmalina Crist, that's just the beginning of my need. I don't even waste time being shocked by the fact. It just is. It always will be.

She makes me crave more.

She makes me want to *be* so much more.

Before my mind can sprint off into *that* enormity, I haul in a long breath and force words back to my lips.

"Damn."

Okay...one word.

"Emma. *Damn.*"

And now two. *Yeah, folks. We're really winning here.*

It's beyond funny, if I really think about it—because never before have I had more things to say to her. No. That's not right either. Not *to* her. *With* her. Talking *to* her implies that she's an entity separate from me, outside of anything and everything that I've become or ever will be. And frankly, that's just not the case. Not by a mile. Not by an inch. Not by a single breath.

With her is the only way I can ever be now.

The way I *want* to be.

Which is why, as I pull out and her knees start to buckle, I don't even think before pulling her up into a princess hold, securing her even closer by tilting my head so my cheek touches her hair. When she responds by tucking her face against my sternum, I don't hold back on my deep rumble of pleasure. Realizing my legs aren't going to last long for support, I walk briskly into the living room, lowering us both onto the thick pile rug in front of the glass-enclosed fireplace. Turning on the flames feels strange for July, but it's also just past three a.m., and the warmth will ensure neither of us has to cover up.

And damn do I enjoy this woman when she isn't covered up.

I settle in next to her, leaning my head on a braced elbow, following the firelight after it reflects through the window and dances along her body. Golden patterns on creamy curves. Amber beams glistening on lingering beads of sweat. Flickers that turn the cranberries of her nipples into bronze candies and the V of her thighs into a fascinating valley of mystery. She's an entirely new creature to discover. And to touch. And to stroke.

And to drink in with my eyes like a man newly arrived at the damn oasis.

Especially as I flow my fingers all the way up to her face. And once there, explore her with even greater care. She's more than a creature here. She's a diamond with a thousand facets, from the tiny indents that frame her mouth, to the graceful sweeps of her tawny brows, to the high, sculpted planes of her cheeks...and more. So much more.

There's always more with her.

And that's my conclusion even before meeting her gaze again.

Which, to my bafflement, is narrowed and shadowed.

Before I can think of how to address that, my mind whirling with what went wrong between our departure from the elevator and our arrival on this rug, she opens her mouth first—and blurts, "Hey."

I blink. Then again. "Uhhhh...hey?"

"Are you all right?"

Bewilderment gets upgraded to astonishment. "Are *you*?"

She inhales with quiet purpose. As she lets out the breath, she sweeps her stare toward the fire. The tightness at the corners of her eyes gives away the contemplation she's throwing into my question—which I'd be really stressing about but for the slight wisp of a smile that now teases her lips. "It's been...quite a night."

"And you just scored diplomat of the year." I don't layer it with too much sarcasm, largely because I mean it. Placing a hand across her stomach, I rub in at her flesh to emphasize. "Velvet...if I'd known the media was going to vulture in on things like that..."

"I know." She forms one of her hands atop mine. "I *know*, Reece. You wouldn't have added to my 'stress' by getting creative with the sex toys." She spurts out a little giggle. "But dear freaking mother of *oh my God*, what sex toys."

For the life of me, I can't connect the dots to why she's still laughing. "You mean the edge job I forced on you and left you to deal with for three goddamned hours while I—"

Her slap—and it's a slap, even if she's dishing it in affection instead of fury—stops me cold. "Hold up there, Squidward. Nobody *forced* anything on anyone, okay? In case you weren't paying attention—and I'm pretty damn sure you *were*—I was soaking wet by the time you got all three of those things into me."

I feel my forehead crunch. "Valid point."

"You're damn right, valid point. And hang on to your pineapple under the sea, because here comes another one. I have a brain and vocal cords, and I'm not afraid to use them. The second you start in on something I'm *not* okay with, you'll know about it."

No more creases at my temples. Instead, I take that tension and apply it to the edges of my lips. "I believe you." And incredibly, I mean it—an expression I don't think I've sincerely given to a woman before. Loneliness makes people promise things they don't mean—and their equally lonely lovers simply believe those lies, perpetuating the cycle.

"Of course you believe me." Her saucy smirk, coupled with the dance of her fingertips up my arm, becomes something softer as soon as she spreads her hold around my bicep. "You'll always get nothing but the truth from me, Reece. This—whatever it is between us, bonding us—it's too damn special to mess up with anything less."

Now, the fire isn't the only heat source in the room. As warmth suffuses my chest, I bend down to take her lips in a loving, lingering kiss. "*This* is called love, and once more, you are completely right."

She delves her other hand into my hair, keeping me hovering as the shadows in her gaze give way to Caribbean hues. "Oh, I like that 'love' part."

I tilt my head, regarding her with newly wicked intent. "Even when it involves Bolt-style Ben Wa balls?"

"Mmmmm." She squeezes my arm and writhes her gorgeous limbs, making the deep pile of the rug caress her in enticing new ways. "*Especially* when it involves that." Then tugs on my hair, yanking me down for a wet, thorough kiss that peels me apart from the inside out. "I didn't forget you all night. It was freaking awesome."

I chuff out a laugh. "You really *are* the woman God made for me."

"And you're the hero who's fulfilled all my dreams." She looks ready to kiss me again, but a new laugh chops across her lips instead. "And the knight who swept in and slayed the dragon for me tonight too. About a hundred of them."

I groan and roll my eyes. "Why didn't you call me about all that?"

She winces. "I thought you were out on patrol."

"You don't think I would've left the LAPD on its own for one night?"

"Which you did anyway?" she asserts.

"Hard to slay the bad guys when Clint Eastwood between the legs wants to be at home."

She busts out in a full laugh as I dip my head toward my Outlaw Josie Wales in his half-erect glory. *Christ.* Less than fifteen minutes after being balls-deep inside her, the cowboy wants to jangle spurs again?

"Well, I'm glad Clint decided to take it easy, no matter *what* the reason," she states.

New frown. "But you like me in my leathers."

She trails her hand across my deltoid and pecs. "You spent

some time working out, didn't you?"

"And you're avoiding my question, aren't you?"

The shadows spread back across her gaze. They're more dense than before, the shade of thunderclouds against her Caribbean skies. "I *love* you in your leathers," she mutters with a sigh. "But I don't love the idea of you running around in alleys, storm drains, and flop houses, facing down people who now know exactly who you are and where you work."

I huff. "You mean people who can barely emerge from their sludge in the middle of the night, much less dare to show their face in an arena as glaring and public as our lobby?" With my knuckles, I caress the side of her face. "Those scumsuckers don't concern me, Velvet. I'm more worried about when the Consortium will start feeling bold again, but it's way too early for that shit."

But I have plans for when that timing *does* come into play—and have kept my new friend, Sawyer Foley, on retainer for that exact occasion. Briefly I consider telling her that but clamp the information down since she hasn't let go of a single furrow in her brow since I mentioned *scumsuckers*. Another revelation for another day, not a confession to be made in the middle of the night, after what she's been through in the last few hours.

After a pause in which she adds an anxious twist of lips to her tight expression, she utters, "I just don't see why you can't help the PD out with other duties."

It's my turn for the corrugated brow. "I'm not exactly the phone-answering, form-completing type, Emma."

She bats at my chest. "I meant like from a PR angle. Public appearances and cultural events. Talking to civic groups, school kids. Just say no to drugs..." Her eyes sparkle. "And dark alleys. And storm drains."

"You forgot flop houses."

"Those too."

She's so cute about the quip, I lay a fast kiss on her lips again. That does the trick. Her body softens beneath me, her anxiety seeming to melt away as I heat up my assault. She opens her mouth wider when I push in with more purpose, and Josie Wales decides to go for the showdown with a stiff rifle barrel at the ready. He's encouraged even more by the movie now playing in my mind—a reel consumed by the thought of rolling over, sliding my thighs between hers, and using my knees to spread her before surging forward and again fucking all the way into her...

Except the next second, all I'm humping is the empty rug. And looking up, glare blazing, at her delectable backside. And shaking my head, senses spinning, as she strolls across the room with the house phone in her hand.

"Fershan. Hey. It's me." She glances at me from over her shoulder, flashing a smile with which I'm more than familiar. The sorry-baby-but-I'm-going-back-to-work-now smile. I love *all* her smiles, but this one is absolutely at the rock bottom of that list. "Sorry I went MIA," she continues to her coworker. "Yeah, I *know* you know where I am, but break time is over, so I'm on my way back dow—"

Her face changes. Fast. A collection of shadows overcomes her features, and I start to wonder if the going-back-to-work smile will be truly usurped in my standings. I wouldn't call the look "dark." More like...dismal. And hurt. And sad.

"Oh," she mutters. "You do? Well, what about the weekly reports and the P and R printouts?" She turns completely away from me, slumping her shoulders and kicking at the floor with the tip of a toe. "You're sure? I don't mind. And with Neeta out too, what if you guys are hit with a rush?" Two more jabs of her toe at the floor. "Yeah, I *know* you're capable, Fersh. And I do thank you for being concerned, but—" A heavy sigh leaves her. "Right. Okay. I get it. I'll...uh...talk to you tomorrow then, I guess. Take it easy." In a hurry, like a kid eager to get on the playground roundabout while it's already going, she calls, "Buzz my cell if you need anything!"

Yeah, it's official. As she ends the call with a soft tap at the phone and sets the receiver down with even wearier resignation, her whole stance droops with blatant dejection.

Fuck.

I'm damn near drowning in the craving to jump up and go to her, but a stronger instinct bellows at me to stand down. This isn't like marching into the lobby and slaying the media horde for her. Unlike then, my shining armor is no good here. This is about shit that can't be solved just by lopping off a monster's head for her. All right, technically speaking, I *could* go and do that—but only at the risk of her retrieving those vibrating balls and ramming them somewhere inside *me* in return.

Because this is a woman who has already defeated so many of her own dragons.

Because this is *my* woman, who has claimed her very life's identity by figuring shit out on her own.

Because even right now, in her defeat, she'd be doubly beaten if I took the action that every fiber in my being burns for. As thoroughly as I hate this truth, I know it as fact. I'd earn nothing but her horror by getting dressed, hauling ass downstairs, and telling "Fersh" and the gang—who think they're being kind—to take *their* asses home so she can do all their jobs at once, with one hand tied around her back, looking goddess perfect as she does.

But that's what *I* crave right now.

Not what *she* needs.

So as thoroughly as it eviscerates me, I don't budge. I barely breathe. In the space of several terminable minutes, I only move one part of my body—my free hand, twisting into a glowing fist—as I keep watching her. Waiting for her. Allowing her to process. And struggle. And hurt. And deal.

This sucks.

But I'm not leaving.

At last, she sucks in a halting breath and turns around but not toward me. She speaks at nearly a whisper into a silence only possible in the hours between deep night and early morning, with the firelight turning her nude form into a vision of gilded beauty—and palpable sadness.

I push to my feet but don't move beyond that. Doing so would shatter the air around her, and I'm pretty positive that's what's holding her up right now.

"Emmalina?" Again, battling the craving to go to her. "Everything okay?"

She wobbles her head, courageously attempting a nod while blinking back obvious moisture in her eyes. "Fershan says everything's calmed down since the press left. That there's really nothing I'm needed for now."

As she tries to shake it off, hauling in a long breath, I ball my other hand, blue light throbbing at a furious cadence between my knuckles. "You know that's not true." The words are calm only because I lock my back teeth to get them out. "They're just trying to help."

"Which is all *I* want to do!" But as fast as her frustration erupts, she kills it off. When she shakes her head and flicks up a hand, dismissing me with a flimsy attempt at anger, I already see she's made up her mind about how this is going to conclude.

Meaning there are much deeper conclusions beyond it.

Convictions betrayed by the shaky rasp of her voice as she wraps both arms around herself and shuffles toward the bedroom. "Guess they have it all handled, then. And there's even a few more hours for you to go make the world right too. Nobody has to worry about me anymore. Yaaaay, team."

Fuck.

I step forward. I can't take this anymore. I need to *move*. To help her. Fuck...*somehow*... "Emma—"

"I'm tired, Reece. Good night."

She shuts the bedroom door with a click that hits the air like a pistol shot, and I again battle the yearning to grab my clothes—my scariest leathers this time—and march down to those offices to tell her "team," in no uncertain terms, exactly what kind of hell they've just sent her to.

But goddamnit, who would that help?

Not her. Not the one-of-a-kind woman—gifted to me by some mind-boggling turn of karma—who really only wants to do one thing in this world.

Serve it.

Make a difference in it.

"A difference." I utter the words, in my naked solitude, as if it's the first time I've ever heard them. Though that's not the case, I'm positive it's the first time I've ever *understood* them.

How they can galvanize a person.

How they're now moving me.

How I'm in action again, moving through the suite with purpose and passion that damn near frighten me. In the ignorance of my youth and then the selfishness of my early manhood, I scoffed at people with this kind of fervor. Dismissed them as zealots who never knew how stupid they looked, thinking their solitary actions could possibly transform the world.

As I sprint back toward the elevator landing to retrieve my pants, I envision those stupid versions of myself shedding like useless snakeskin.

As I stab my legs back into my slacks, I start a to-do list in my head.

As I make my way to my office, I swear not to be daunted by that list.

It's doable. Insane for a timeline of just a few hours, but doable.

But more importantly, it's vital. And exceptional.

And difference making.

All right, so I can't always save her.

But this time, maybe I can do something better.

CHAPTER SIX

EMMA

"Gah!"

My groan reverberates through my head, instantly shooting my thoughts backward. What did I do last night? And did it involve enough drinking to make me forget how I got home?

"Whoa."

I mean that one even more. Because I'm not at home. Though technically, the Brocade's penthouse should qualify as home by now. But as I straighten up in the huge king bed, prying my eyes open by increments in the room drenched in blinding California sun, the gloom of my mindset from last night is corroborated by the stark walls and high-end modern art around me.

Saying nothing about me.

Actually, saying nothing about Reece either.

My eyes fully open, I gaze at it all in more depth—wondering why none of it has made me clutch a bowling ball of melancholy in my stomach before. While I'm not a Rams cheerleader, I've always taken pride at focusing on the bright angle of any situation in life, including this one. Perhaps *especially* this one, considering Reece's insistence on keeping me close is founded in the fact that I was charged on my own front sidewalk by his nutbitch of an ex-girlfriend.

Besides, coming here with him has never really felt like leaving home.

Until now.

And yeah...especially now.

A glance at the other side of the bed tells me that Reece was never here. Did he sleep in the other bedroom? Or, more realistically, took a cue from my spiteful playbook and went out to pay the bitterness forward by knocking some bad guy skulls together? And can I even give him shit for it?

My belly gives up that answer. The bowling ball starts churning, using my intestines for torque. I wince but accept the pain, hoping it makes up for my morose dredge of an exit after what had to be the most earth-shattering sex of our relationship—and definitely of my entire life. Yeah, even after Fershan gave me a hall pass on completing the shift, which would have—and should have—been my green light to jump on my superhero stud again. Reece had obviously, and gloriously, been up for the encore...

The bowling ball, with my guts now added, shoves at the bottom of my boobs. The pressure incites a groan I let out at full force into the pillows as I collapse back into their silky depths.

"It's official," I tack on in a miserable mutter. "Emma Crist, you suck."

As I lay there, wondering whether my self-pity wallow has gotten deep enough for a quest to the kitchen for a pint of something that'll coat the bowling ball in lots of chocolate and cream, the bedroom door is suddenly swung open with a flourish worthy of a Broadway musical. Or a slasher movie.

I jolt up, not sure which would make me scream louder—

only to release my breath in a stunned whoosh as my beyond-beautiful boyfriend fills the doorway. His gaze is so brilliant, it makes him look a little crazy. His grin is even brighter, almost out-dazzling the sunshine. His arms, with biceps bulging out of a black and purple Judah & the Lion T-shirt, are spread wide due to carrying a tray with a decadent breakfast spread on it, complete with a little red rose tucked into a cut crystal vase.

"Well, there she is."

"Uhhhh..." I manage to stammer as he strides in, humming a tune I don't recognize. That's likely because it's off-key, but even after the viral video craziness of yesterday, I realize the man and his warbling are better for my mood than all the rose-embellished breakfast trays on earth.

Though damn, does that food smell good...

"Time for fuel, beautiful. We have a big afternoon ahead."

"After..." I don't get a chance to finish. As Reece scoots the tray onto the bed near my feet, I realize the breakfast spread is actually a *lunch* array, with finger sandwiches, homemade potato chips, veggies and hummus, a chopped green salad, and huge cookies sprouting thumb-sized chocolate chips. "What the hell time is it?" And nearly as important, what the hell is with his wardrobe? I blink in wonderment, realizing I never knew he owned even one rock band tee, let alone a kick-ass one. My amazement doubles as my gaze travels down and turns into a gawk at his ripped jeans and loose-laced black Chucks.

Chucks.

The man owns jeans and Chucks?

"Nearly noon," Reece supplies, but stuffs a carrot stick into my mouth before I can get out a gasp of horror. "And you're not going to give me a syllable of lip about letting you sleep in, woman. After the paces you got put through last night"—he hitches up one side of his gorgeous, full mouth—"both the crappy *and* the carnal, you needed the rest." As he loads up a plate with at least two of everything for me, including the cookies, he adds, "And now you need to recharge. Big-time. So you *will* empty this plate, with one happy watchdog sitting right here to make sure." As he slides the plate next to me, his gaze swirls with lusty smoke while dropping to my bare breasts. "Don't worry if you drop crumbs or anything. I'll be happy to...tidy them up for you..."

Slowly—very slowly—my bowling ball starts to shrink. I even think I feel a smile approaching my lips as I finish the carrot stick and reach for a sandwich square. The hint of gourmet cheese on French bread hits my nose, and my taste buds instantly thank him for bringing an entire plate of those. "Hmmm. Do you have time for...crumb duty?" I tease. "Wasn't there something you said about a big afternoon?" As I lean over for another sandwich, I purposely push my shoulders together to create some significant cleavage for his ogling pleasure. I'm *so* bad but *so* enjoying it. "Or maybe your idea of 'big' perfectly matches *mine* right now."

And should have been nearly nine hours ago, when he was a naked, half-erect Adonis in front of me...

"Oh, *baby*." With one move, he whips the plate to a spot several feet away on the mattress. With his second, he nosedives his face into my cleavage, lapping at my skin with desire-filled strokes. "There's *always* time for crumb duty." But a couple of minutes later, after he's ensured nothing's spilled on my chest except his kisses, bites, and sucks, he pushes away with a gritted groan. "But right now, fuck *me*, there's only time for that."

In the bright light, I echo his dark sound. Falling back against the headboard, I jab him with a disbelieving glare—moaning again when it doesn't stir his resolve. "I thought fucking you *was* the general idea, hotshot."

The line is good for a definite spark of reaction. He's beyond gorgeous as his nostrils flare, lips part, and nipples stand out against his T-shirt, especially as he rolls his shoulders and sets his arms back. If we were in the weight room, I'd swear he was prepping to get in some reps with a well-loaded dumbbell.

But it turns out *I'm* the dumbbell.

The shrieking, flailing dumbbell—as he ducks his shoulder into my middle, wraps one arm around my thighs, and rises from the bed with *me* over his damn shoulder.

"For that line, missie, you're getting dunked in the shower *before* the water heats up."

"Whaaat? Reece! What the *hell*?"

I'm not sure whether it's my goosebump-covered nudity or my strangled goose screams that ultimately do the trick, but the big sap gives me a mixed collection of tender and torrid kisses while we wait for the shower to heat up. I return his sexy "mercy" by attempting to grind my nakedness up and down his sinewy frame, my lust only aided by his bad boy rock god look. There may even have been a few filthy suggestions in his ear about pretending I'm his shameless groupie, ready to take his wad in my mouth for an autograph. In the end, he's still intractable about indulging any action with me beyond sucking face beneath the pelting spray.

Whatever he has planned, this better be damn good.

When I reemerge in the bedroom with a towel around my body and another around my hair, the man has loaded my plate with more food and laid out clothes for me on the bed. Like him, my attire for the day is jeans and a T-shirt—only mine is a basic red crew neck with the Richards Resorts logo silkscreened over the upper left corner.

And now...so is his.

I push my brows together and crank my head on my neck, not hiding my curiosity as he walks back into the room, plate in hand, sucking hummus off his thumb. He can't be blamed. Chef Bruno's homemade hummus is the best in the land.

"Okay..." I draw out the end of the word. "I guess the big afternoon doesn't include a Judah & the Lion concert."

"Dope idea," he returns, biting into a cookie. "But no. They're not in town until next month." He winks, his eyes alive with happy silver glints. "Today is for even better fun."

"That I don't get to know about?"

"Not yet."

"Why?"

"Because you're still naked."

"Huh?"

"If I tell you and you're still naked, you'll start crying. And even if you're crying in happiness, I'll want to kiss away your tears. And if I kiss away your tears, and you're still only dressed in that towel..."

"Got it. *Got it.*" I chuckle and hold up my hands, which loosens my towel and turns it into a puddle at my feet. Its plop on the floor is muffled by the stringent groan from my boyfriend's chest. I have to swallow down another laugh as he openly ogles, hummus on his lips, need in his eyes, and a rock star-sized bulge in his fly.

Before he pivots and stomps out of the room, he yells, "Great. You got it. Now get your sweet ass dressed before I *give you* something we both don't have time for, woman!"

⚡

"Gah."

The word isn't usually one of my key vocabulary go-tos, but this occasion—an astounding logistical feat of a surprise by my incredible boyfriend—more than warrants its second occurrence in the same day.

Though "surprise" doesn't serve this moment by even a fraction.

As we turn down a humble street in the southeast corner of LA, Reece is still telling me about where we're headed: the home of a Hotel Brocade employee I don't know because of our opposite shifts but whom I now can't wait to meet.

"So everyone just calls him Cal?" I eagerly ask. "But I'll only have just met him."

Reece wraps a hand around my fidgeting fingers. "And you'll only weird him out more if you go by the name on his paycheck. *Relax*, Bunny. It's going to be great."

"Okay," I mutter. "*Okay*." But after a second of gazing out at the passing cottages and tiny homes, I prompt, "Just tell it all to me again. I don't want to forget."

The man doesn't reply at once. Instead, he sweeps my fingers up to his lips and presses a couple of fervent kisses into them. "You take my breath away, Emmalina Crist."

And just like that, impossible as it seems, I melt by a few more degrees. "And you're not answering my question, Reece Richards."

"You're just amazing. You need to know that every day—but today especially."

I snort. Hard. "Says the man who made this all come together with a few hours of texts and God knows how many phoned-in favors?"

As anticipated, *that* gets the man to circle back around to the subject. With one hand still on mine and his other effortlessly steering the large utility truck he introduced as "the epic ride" back at the hotel, he states, "As you know, Cal's been working full-time in the engineering department for about three months."

"And he's only twenty-one." I shake my head in bewilderment while confirming the additional facts he's already revealed to me. At twenty-one, my "engineering" knowledge consisted of replacing light bulbs and scoping out coffee houses for outlets in which to power up my laptop for homework. "Employment" was a seasonal part-time thing at one of the souvenir kiosks in Downtown Disney.

"Well, he was nineteen when that bad flu season killed his mother," Reece goes on. "Things were rough for a while—"

"Rougher than *now*?"

"Topic for another discussion." His jaw tenses, filling in enough of that answer for me to know he means it.

"But he got through." Again, I reiterate the basics of what he's already disclosed. "And when he was old enough, he petitioned the court for custody of his sisters. They're both seven now, right?"

"Right. And both thriving because Cal won't accept anything less. They're earning straight As in public school, just like he did. The kid did well and was offered several full-board college scholarships, but he had to turn them all down. Between making payments on the medical bills, keeping the twins clothed and fed, and maintaining all the utility bills on the house, the kid has to work full-time at the Brocade just to make ends meet."

"Wow."

"Yeah. Wow."

There's so much more I want to know about Cal and his story, but at the moment, Reece pulls the truck to a stop in front of a house that's tidy but sparse, with a waist-high chain link fence bordering a small but well-kept lawn. The home itself appears clean but in need of repair. The front step is missing, and the window screens are torn.

My heart swells and then bursts to see the small group of people waiting just outside that little fence, all proudly wearing T-shirts that match ours. Among them are Neeta, Wade, and Fershan, as well as some familiar faces from the housekeeping and catering departments. As soon as Reece swings me down from the truck and gallantly pecks my cheek, everyone surrounds me with hugs, smiles, and high-fives. Now, my heart's beyond the bursting point. It's a flood of emotion, gratitude, joy, and excitement.

That's before the day gets even better.

A pair of high, joyous shrieks hits the air—as a matching set of pigtailed beauties bound out of the house, across the porch, and down the front walk. Both of them even know to leap extra far to accommodate for the missing step, which makes my heart wrench. How long has that step been in disrepair? Worse, how long have these two cuties, with their pink and purple dresses, their crooked smiles, and their wiggly, infectious energy, lived in conditions like this?

I look at Reece, despite knowing he won't be able to supply the answer. He gave me as much information as he could during the brief trip from downtown to here.

With that explanation still echoing in my head, and now the two adorable munchkins hugging my legs, I suck in a huge breath to face a challenge twice as huge as the press mob from last night.

Blinking back a million tears.

Like the grins from these two upturned faces are going to make that one drop easier.

"Hi," the first one chirps, her cheeks as rosy as her pink pinafore dress.

"Hi," her sister in purple adds.

"Well, hello there," I answer, spreading my arms to pat both their backs. I tell myself they're just kids, but the jut of their shoulder blades makes me wish we'd brought food too. As much as their refrigerator can hold. "Now, who do we have here? Princess Sparkle Bottom and Princess Unicorn Breath?"

The twins erupt into laughter. "Nooooo!" they yell in unison, having to release my legs in order to let out some excess energy with excited squirms.

"I'm Tosca," says the imp in pink.

"And I'm Jina," says her sister, brandishing her auburn pigtails like little whips.

"Is that so?" I throw my widened gaze at both of them. "Well, those are great names. Made for warriors instead of princesses, I'd say."

Tosca pops her mouth wide. "You think so? Really?"

"*Pssshhh.*" Jina drops her hair in order to brandish her hands as fists. "I already *am* a warrior. Cal says so. I can kick his ass in five moves or less."

Unbelievably, Tosca gapes wider. "Ummmm! You cussed, sister."

Jina glares. "So?"

"*So*...I'm telling Cal."

"Telling me what?" The interjection comes from a handsome guy now emerging from behind the gate—and earning *my* instant gawk, despite my efforts at concealment. But my astonishment can't be helped. If I passed Cal on the street, I'd peg him not a day younger than twenty-six or twenty-seven. There's a balance, perhaps a confidence, that a man's movements gain once they hit the halfway point to thirty—a weight I've always just attributed to the passing of chronological years. Now, I see it has everything to do with emotional burdens instead. This kid is too damn young to heft this huge a load.

And today, thanks to the force of nature that *my* man is, we're going to help lighten that weight.

In one small way, by just one small increment, we're going to help change the world.

Though Cal nods toward Reece and me, he gives the first priority of his attention to his little sisters. "Tell me what?" he prompts once more to Tosca—who turns as bright as her dress and vehemently shakes her head.

"Nuffin'." It emerges as a nervous slur.

"You mean *nothing*?" Cal corrects.

"No*thing*." Now she's just pissed, throwing a glower at her preening sister. "Except that Jina cussed!"

"Well, then." Cal folds his arms, looking for all the world like a young movie star with his broad chest outlined beneath his dark T-shirt. "You know what happens now. Ten seconds with the soap bar for you, J. And T, instead of policing her, you can scoot yourself into the bedroom and finish cleaning out that closet. You were supposed to be done an hour ago."

Two little faces scrunch up in fury. But nearly in unison, both girls grumble, "Yes, sir," and go back to the house with doomsday stomps.

As I watch them, I shake my head in obvious awe. "Wow. *Cal.*" I snap my focus back to him, knowing I should be helping the rest of the Richards gang in unloading all the materials Reece has gathered for repairing and improving the house today. "Are you *sure* you're only twenty-one?"

He laughs softly. "There are times when I wonder, like when Jina's got me glued to the floor under her Wonder Woman sword. Those are the times I wonder if God's decided to just fast-forward me into my forties."

I feel my lips quirk. "And Tosca's method?" Because even after three minutes with those girls, I can tell the warrior term applies to them both.

"Lightsaber. She's a Rey girl."

I pump a fist. "And a soul sistah."

Though he joins me in another chuckle, gravity settles back over his posture almost immediately. "I...don't know what to say about all this, Miss Crist. Honestly, I'm a little overwhelmed. I'm just so used to handling everything on my own, so this is kind of weird..."

I grab him by one of his forearms, which are still settled protectively across his body. "I know." I pause for a swallow as he blinks, exposing the tragedy that's forced him to go from his teens to his forties at the speed of light. "Probably not in all the same ways that you do, but I *know*."

After another couple of blinks, he's cloaked his pain once again. But the vulnerability it exposed is still a presence on his chiseled face. "Yeah," he murmurs. "I can see that you do."

It's a brief conversation, ending with a sentence that's

less than ten words from the reserved guy, but even from that collection of syllables, I extract a strange yet stunning kind of energy...

Energy that turns into thoughts. Thoughts that blossom into inspiration.

Inspiration that formulates into a dream.

A dream that, six hours later, I'm all but bursting to tell Reece.

Yeah, even though I'm exhausted and dirty and splattered from head to toe with plaster and paint, every pore of my being is still overflowing with anticipation and excitement, a special verve I only seem to be sharing with two other people on this block right now. Still, I'm not sure either of them is up for listening to my grand plan at the moment. They *are* only seven.

But damn if they aren't worth quadruple their weight in gold for the entertainment value—a dose of double girl power, wielding lightsaber and sword, as the rest of us watch from our weary sprawls across the new furniture we've brought to complete Cal's new front porch décor.

"Get the dragon, Diana!" Tosca screams, circling her blinking plastic lightsaber in the air. "He's got the magical crystal in his claw!"

"And if he delivers it all the way to General X, it could be used to blow up the entire planet of Flixsa!" Jina yells back.

"It's no use." The first girl stops with melodramatic flair. "We won't get there fast enough. We need Transformatron to take us."

"Yes! Transformatron! He has the laser blaster rockets given to him by Starman. He can surely help us!"

"Who wants to tell Hollywood they're missing the next blockbuster genre mash-up idea?" Wade murmurs.

"On my list," Neeta mumbles back. "As soon as I can move again."

"I'll never be able to move again," Cal adds—punctuating it by joining our collective gasp as a third figure races in from the side of the house, all ten fingers spread out and glowing.

"Did someone call for Transformatron?" Reece's boom is all but drowned by the girls' combined squeals, which conquer even higher octaves as he swoops in, shirtless chest rippling as he extends both arms, letting them latch on like monkeys hanging from his tree limbs.

At once, everyone's gasps turn into groans.

"Transformatron's a showy bastard." The mutter comes from Harrison, Neeta's day-shift counterpart on the front-desk team.

"I'm still getting another slice of pizza." Wade adds a loud *oof* while struggling to his feet and shuffling back inside the house. His remark almost makes me sorry for the capper I've got to add to it.

"Well, *I'm* not tired anymore."

Like I said, *almost* sorry.

As I pay for my cheek beneath a bombardment of wadded pizza napkins, Reece reappears from his lap around the small house with two giggling aerialists in tow. Nope. I am definitely *not* one speck exhausted anymore—and now start to wonder if the grand vision in my head is going to be asking one favor too many from the universe. I mean, *look* at the man. He's got the chest of Triton, the legs of Apollo, the penis of Eros—and a heart that's all Bolt. I can't even comprehend all the phone calls he had to make and favors he had to call in to make this day happen for Cal and his sisters, but seeing those girls light up when beholding just a few painted butterflies and new bedding in their room...and the look on Cal's face after we set up the new swing set in the backyard and then turned on the new bells-and-whistles computer and monitor set, placed in a stylish corner hutch and seating combo thing that will be perfect for the girls' homework sessions...

No major construction, taking us only an afternoon.

But imagine the good we can do if given more time and resources...

A resolve that reinvigorates my mind at just the right moment. Because here comes my glorious man again, this time with the kids at his heels instead of on his arms.

I leave the porch, giving high-fives to the returning warriors when they announce the "dragon" has been defeated, tamed, and turned back into a reptile who only wants good for the universe. As I continue my own quest, walking toward Reece with my heart thudding in my throat and my love brimming in my eyes, I'm actually a little thankful when he yanks his T-shirt out of his back pocket and tugs it back on. This conversation is going to be nerve-racking enough without his gleaming abs to waylay me.

"Congratulations, Transformatron," I quip, unable to resist smoothing a hand down one of his biceps. "You helped save the galaxy."

His cocky grin does *not* help my nervous pulse. "That's what I do."

"Obviously." As if my rebuttal needs backup, I sweep my gaze back toward the house. And its repaired front stairs. And the shiny screens in the windows. And even the new camera mounted over the front door, connected to the app that'll display visitors on Cal's phone screen.

I turn back, discovering Reece's stare hasn't departed

from me. His eyes are the shade of graphite, which fits with the flinty new angles of his face. I blink, wondering if this is the same guy who smirked at me like a flirty guitar god just two seconds back. Not that I'm complaining. This mien is better for what I have to say. And then the huge thing I have to ask.

Deep breath. Stay calm.

"So," I finally murmur.

"So," he replies just as softly.

"I'm...not sure I've really thanked you for this yet, mister. Not officially."

A chuff escapes him. "Yes, you have, Bunny." He steps closer, brushes a strand of hair off my face, and leaves his long fingers cupped at the curve of my cheek. "In about a thousand different ways."

I get down a huge gulp. One more. Floodwaters, meet matchsticks. The waterworks are on, my heart is overflowing, and there's not a thing I can do to hold back the tears now.

"Damn it, Emma."

I sniff hard, hoping that'll help. "Sorry. *Sorry.* They're all happy tears, okay? You...you're just too good to me. My superhero in so many ways."

He slides his eyes shut. "I know. And I never want to *stop* being that."

Shit, shit, shit. He's so earnest and serious, making me feel even weirder about all this. But if the fast-and-direct approach works for yanking off bandages, maybe I'll get lucky in this case too.

"I have something I need to tell you."

My rickety laugh blends with his, the same way we just issued the same sentence at once. As the mirth fades from his lips, his grip intensifies against my head. "You first," he utters.

"Yeah, I'm going to be a wuss about this."

"Not wussier than me." I lift my hand, fitting it atop his. "*You* first."

"*Emma.* Fuck."

"*Reece.* Fuuuuck."

But my tease doesn't ease his disquiet. He jacks his head back, looking to the remnants of the sunset in the twilight sky. I drop my head and concentrate on my paint-spattered shoes in the cool grass.

"I'm giving up Bolt."

"I'm quitting my job."

This time, I couldn't be more thrilled we walked on each other's sentences. Or more ecstatic about the content value of his. Fighting to keep my grin somewhere in the realm of happy instead of leaping up in pure elation, I stammer, "You...what?"

He clearly doesn't know how to interpret my expression. His face contorts with an intense emotion before he resets all the angles with solid command, even nodding with G.I. Joe gravity as he does. "I'm doing it, Emma. I'm putting away the leathers. And the missions. And the scumbags and the assholes. I'm sure as hell not going back into hiding, but I'm not going to give everyone a bigger target to aim at by the day."

I tighten my hold around his arm. Gulp against even more tears as I whisper, "Reece..."

"You're not upset, are you? Not too much?"

"*Gah.*" And unbelievably, there's number three. A record, for sure—in a record-making, extraordinary day. "You incredible, clueless man." With my hand already in his hair, I yank him down for a kiss that's damn near punishing. "I couldn't be happier, okay?" I stay close, needing to feel every vibrant, pulsing inch of his life and vitality. "No more worrying about some bastard distracting you while another puts a bullet in your face. No more worrying you might have been jumped or shivved or—"

His bark of a laugh cuts into my diatribe. "*Shivved?*"

I tweak on his hair again. "You know what I mean. And does it matter anymore?"

"Not one damn bit." His gaze turns the color of mist, and he leans down to take my mouth in a softer kiss. "Besides, I may have some new semantics for you to worry about soon."

"Huh?" I let go of his hair and relock him with my gaze. "Mister, you *did* just hear my little announcement too, right?" But before I'm finished, I already see the affirmation of that— in every inch of the new smirk spreading across his lips. "Well, shit. Don't tell me..."

"That I was already anticipating your resignation letter after our little adventure today?"

"*Little?*"

"New semantics." A shrug of broad shoulders. An even cockier grin. "So I won't tell you that I wasn't just anticipating it. I was hoping for it."

"Excuse the hell out of—" I drop my hands and push hard against the grip he's now secured around my waist. No dice. I'm stuck here. "You were *hoping* for me to resign from your night crew team?"

He soothes me with a firm press of lips to my forehead. In return, I fume. I don't want to be soothed. Most of all, I can't handle the idea of him "anticipating" all my moves like that. It should seem creepy to me—but the thing is, it doesn't. And that's even weirder, right? It just makes me feel...exactly like I do now. Protected. Valuable. Purposeful. Like what I'm doing actually matters to someone. Liking what I'm doing matters the most to an incredible man like *him*.

"All right. Truth," he murmurs against my temple. "If you didn't resign, I probably would have asked you to anyway."

I splutter again—just not with the force of Transformatron's girlfriend. "Why?"

"Because I need you to work on something else."

I lean back as far as he'll allow. Travel my gaze downward. "Mr. Richards, even with your python of a sex drive, there are only so many hours in the day we can—"

"Not on *that*," he chuckles out.

"Then...what?"

"A new arm of the Richards organization that I feel strongly about. And won't entrust to anyone but you."

I frown. "A new arm...how?"

"Richards Reaches Out." He jogs his head an inch higher. Squares his shoulders to match the determined set of his face. "Something completely crazy for us because it's going to be a nonprofit facet of the brand."

"Nonprofit?" I abandon the frown for an *are you batshit* stare. "Like Papa Dearest is going to go along with *that*?"

He shrugs again. Damn it, he needs to stop doing that, because every lift of his linebacker-worthy lines does crazy things to my concentration. "Spoke to him this morning. Dad doesn't just approve of this idea. He's volunteered to help you get the whole train chugging and rolling along." In response to my bugged-out eyes, he qualifies, "Look. My father may be a self-absorbed dick from time to time, but he also knows a strong nonprofit can do amazing things for public perception— and in this case, as a viable resource for bringing along future leaders for the company." He swoops his sights back toward the gang on the porch. "Leaders like Cal."

"Who might need more than just a cosmetics touch-up on their house for a day." At the encouragement of his proud, intense stare, I go on. "Who may need financial assistance with daycare so they can get themselves through college. Or even a car for commuting. Or introductions to people for job interviews." And I'm just getting started, because as he keeps nodding, I just keep sharing. So many possibilities and ideas, which have all been darting through my head like balloons in a hurricane, are now gathered and pushed in one epic, shiny bouquet of thought. "Life coach and mentorship match-ups. Internship opportunities. Partnerships with organizations like Working Wardrobes and Young Professionals of America... *hey*." I emphasize the protest with a whap on his chest and stare up at his jawline as he releases a chest-deep chuckle. "What's so funny?"

He shakes his head, gazing down at me with thick, meaningful intent. "Not funny, Velvet. Just *happy*. That crazy, amazing thing you do to my heart every time you're near." He cups both sides of my jaw now, cradling my face in his perfect protection...and adoration. "And god*damn*, I'm so grateful."

Sigh.

Just. Freaking. Sigh.

But I'm able to emit half of one before he claims my mouth beneath his again, twisting yet soft, thorough yet seeking, claiming me yet freeing me.

Knowing me.

Bonded to me.

Ignited with me.

Bolted with me.

And dear God, I never want it to be any different.

"All right, all right," I say with a mocking gripe when he

finally releases me to give me air again. "I quit, I quit."

"Good." He smashes my mouth with harder significance now before pulling away. "Because you're now officially hired." The most magnificent smile I've seen on his face reaches all the way up to his eyes, perhaps even into the follicles of his thick, luscious hair, now blowing in the balmy breeze of a classic LA evening. "Welcome to Richards Reaches Out, Miss Crist."

"Why thank you, Mr. Richards."

"Anything you need to ask about the place? Like where's the coffee maker? Copy machine? And when do we start changing the world?"

"Oh, I already know the answer to that one, mister." I reach up, wrapping my arms around his neck and then arching my brows, already promising him the hottest kiss of our day. "We already have."

Continue the Bolt Saga with Part 4

Ignite

Available July 31, 2018
Keep reading for an excerpt!

EXCERPT FROM *IGNITE*

PART 4 IN THE BOLT SAGA

CHAPTER ONE

E M M A

Funny how life changes when the world knows you're sleeping with a superhero.

Funnier still how the differences are most glaring in the tiniest details. Like finally finding one's way to the ladies' room after a five-hour flight and a twenty-minute gate taxi only to have one's three-by-six-foot sanctum pierced by an urgent whisper from the next stall over.

"Hey."

At first, I clear my throat and ignore her. The chick's probably just on the phone with someone and isn't aware of my presence next door.

"Hey. *You*. Emma Crist."

"Uhhhh..." I repeat the throat clearance with a little more emphasis. Believe me, I'm painfully used to being recognized in public these days, but it's usually not when I'm pausing for a second of relief in the airport bathroom. "Yes? Can I help you?" In any case, professional mode is best. She's probably just asking for toilet paper or a tampon.

"So tell me what he's like."

I watch my eyes bug in the reflection from the stainless-steel door. "He...who?"

"Come *on*. You *know* who."

"I...uh..."

"Reece Richards." She adds a conspiratorial giggle. "You know. *Bolt*. What's he like, girlfriend?"

"I beg your pardon?" My confusion is authentic on several levels. I'm really in the weeds about what to do. I'm done with my business but afraid to budge. If I make a move, will she flush just as fast and corner me against the sinks? If I don't, how long will she hold me hostage on the pot in order to win her answer?

"I bet he can fuck like a machine. Right?"

"Pardon *me*?"

"Probably doesn't even need a recharge—even if that cover story you're floating is true, about the thunder and lightning being a big ol' magic trick and all."

"Well." Forget professional. Maybe I just need to show my whole hand now. A full house of irked, peeved, and get-lost-lady. "Reece has already made his official statements on the matter."

Statements that were meant to buy us some time. Badly needed time. A moment's breath to figure out our new reality, which feels no more real now than it did back in July. The night he'd taken off his mask in that room, in front of my family and a hundred other Newport Beach socialites, and changed my life forever. A change I thought I was ready for—but quickly learned I wasn't. Since then, despite the changes and compromises we've both made, life still feels like a gigantic roller coaster, with no return back to the loading platform in sight.

Which means I need to learn to hold on tighter or seriously invest in some barf bags.

"Come on. Just tell me." Annnnd, Stall One is still damned and determined to girl-talk her way into a confession from me. "He's better than the little battery bunny, isn't he? But does he come with a...*drum*?"

The threads of suspicion in my gut form into a bigger ball. This chica's pushing the metaphors hard. Just like a good gossip reporter would...

"I..."

The trill of my cell can't be better timed. With a whoosh of relief, I grab for the thing. "Sorry. Have to get this."

"Oh, God. Is it *him*?"

Of course it's him. Not that I'm going to tell *her* that.

Using the nickname we openly borrowed from the world's most notable superhero creator provides a perfect way to do that.

"Mr. Lee." Like the real Mr. Lee, my man has a tendency of showing up in the most unexpected places at the oddest times, earning him instant street cred for the designation.

Reece Andrew Richards has a different view on the matter and makes that clear with a dark, dangerous, arousing-as-hell growl.

"How can I be of service to you this afternoon?"

Reece repeats the sound but with more sensual undertones. "That all depends."

"Yes. Go ahead. Of course I'm here." Attempting to keep up the calm, cool, and professional thing is *not* easy when the man has the power to flip my stomach like a pancake simply with the force of his voice.

"On whether you plan on fully apologizing for using that

little zinger."

I clear my throat again, using the sound to cover what it takes to clean stuff up and get back to my feet. "We fully understand your frustration with the situation, Mr. Lee. Richards Resorts wants to make things right. I'm still at the airport, but I'll be back at my desk in about an hour and will be happy to—"

"No."

One word, full of carnal command, turns the pancake to mush—along with my knees. I fight to stay upright with a fortifying breath through my nose. "So sorry. Could you repeat, please? I didn't quite get that."

Reece's grunting laugh fills the line. "Oh, you'll get it, my little Velvet Bunny. Just not back at the office." He adds a subtle hum because he knows, no matter where I am or what I'm doing, how hot the sound makes me—and exactly where. "It's Friday. You're taking the rest of the day off."

I unlatch the stall door and march to the mirrors and sinks—where my flushed cheeks and aroused eyes are waiting to gloat at me in full. *Damn him. How I've missed him.* "I'll have to double-check that request with upper management."

"*Upper management* is waiting for you at the curb, woman." His tone drops into the rugged valley between seduction and fornication. "Which means get rid of whoever's gawking at you and get your sweet ass out to the VIP pick-up curb."

"Well, I have checked bags—"

"Which Z is already handling," he supplies. "So you have no more excuses. Get out here. Into my arms. *Now.*"

"Wait. What? Into your—" I'm cut off from the rest of my gasp as my new bestie from stall one strides out in all her glossy-lipped, sprayed-on-jeans glory. I can read every thought in her head just by glancing at her knowing smirk. She's on to me. More accurately, she's on to "Mr. Lee's" true identity. "I'm certain that can be arranged, sir. Your satisfaction is always our first priority."

Stall Girl yips out a laugh that echoes in the oddly uncrowded bathroom. The moment couldn't be better timed. Reece's verbal foreplay is causing blood to collect in parts of my body where it shouldn't, and a full-on sprint out to Mr. Snarly and Seductive has started beckoning like the swoony romance-movie cliché it is. Maintaining my cool for the strange woman is really a blessing in disguise, especially because everyone wants—and expects—the whole passionate reunion thing between Reece and me now, with "EmRee's" magic three-month mark just hurdled.

EmRee.

Seriously. That's what they call us in all the papers and tabloids that seem to matter to people like Stall One Girl, who follows me out of the restroom and down the concourse.

EmRee.

It's so stupid, it's cute.

And still a little surreal. And definitely a lot of crazy.

But maybe that last part *does* fit. Because damn, am I crazy about this man—a truth never blazed so boldly into me than the moment I step out of the terminal and into the heat of an LA Indian summer day, only to be riveted by the one sight hotter than the heatwaves rising from the asphalt. Yet oddly, even in the charcoal suit precision-fit to the millimeter for his powerful torso, Reece stands as if he doesn't know the meaning of the word sweat. He's polished and tall and suave and perfect, long legs braced like a Viking atop an iceberg, with the wind blowing his mocha hair back with equal drama. I'm unable to see his eyes due to the photo-gray film on his glasses, but the subtle shift in the right side of his jaw already betrays how intense his silver gaze must be.

Holy. Freaking. God.

I stop for a second, visually pinned by him—until the ache of missing him is suddenly replaced by the need to be with him. Against him. All over him. The craving is so urgent, I don't even care about the camera strobes and excited shouts suddenly surging around me. Thankfully, airport security is part of that tsunami, and I dash through the narrow gauntlet the officers create in the throng for me. Racing toward my peace in the storm.

Toward my hero.

"Velvet," he grates into my hair, some of his volume stripped by my collision into him. I don't think Reece minds. His answering embrace is a crush, and he tightens it until I'm a breathless mess. I pull away for air, but he's already tucked his head in, lifting a hand to brace my jaw and position me for the kiss I've craved over every inch of distance between JFK and here. By the time his lips sweep down, mine are already parted, longing for the hot and heavy thrust of his take-no-prisoners tongue. He doesn't leave me bereft. My mouth is filled with him. Assaulted by him. Sighing in utter bliss as he groans, sucking at me, before pushing in for more of my surrender.

Around us, cameras still shutter in a frenzy, and bodies collide as reporters jostle for the best angle of our mutual mauling. I'm beyond caring. As exhilarating as the last five days have been, they were four and a half days too long. We haven't been apart for more than five *hours* since we finally decided to make this interesting relationship work—emphasis on the *interesting*. But that term came with its own definition in the world of Reece, who'd revealed to me that his bad-boy billionaire rep, while true at one time, had become the ideal disguise for his true identity as Bolt, LA's lightning-pulsed superhero savior. And the *oh, by the way* he piled on top of that? Just the small matter of the lunatic scientists who'd used him as their bio-electrical experiment to begin with and who were still hunting down their rogue Frankenstein.

Needless to say, our first few dates were slightly more eventful than grabbing a pizza and a movie.

But that's like another novel ago.

Right now, all I can think of is treasuring his muscular fullness in my arms, the powerful perfection of his mouth, and the feeling of his heartbeat next to mine again. Celebratory passion following what had to be the best business trip of my life.

The trip *he* made possible.

Thinking about it all—the phone calls he made, the emails he sent, the personal trips he took to shake hands with all the right people, to incite all the right kind of expediting—launches me to somewhere between giddy and euphoric. I funnel it all back into my kiss, showing him exactly how much joy he's brought to every inch of my heart. He responds with a darker groan, twisting one hand into my hair and the other into my T-shirt, which sets off a new frenzy of flashing cameras and a new surge of ecstatic reporters.

"Sheez, Reece," one of them finally shouts. "Give the woman a chance to breathe."

He's answered by one of the women in the throng. "Well, if a girl's gotta meet her maker, that's the way to do it."

"Not before getting bolted in a big way," a new female

quips. Or *is* she new? I pull back enough from Reece to glance her direction. Sure enough, it's Stall One Girl, now armed with a microphone and backed by a cameraman. My scathing scrutiny only incites her sorry-not-sorry shrug. Inwardly, I high-five myself for taking the icy professional path with her in the bathroom—not that it's made a difference, since she adds with a smirk, "And I do mean a *big* way."

Another reporter steps forward, seeming a little more on the sane side, until he taps his pen into the air and questions, "So what *does* comprise a Bolt-style homecoming for his best girl?"

"His *only* girl." Reece yanks me in tighter while correcting the guy, his tone edging toward censure. "And the rest of that's an irrelevant question because, as you all know by now, Bolt has taken an early retirement."

A round of groans is his instant reply. Some of them resound with disappointment, but the majority are expressions of skepticism, verbalized by the persistent pen tapper.

"Right. *Retired.*" A pen materializes in his *other* hand— imagine that—to assist his air quote emphasis. "Just like all his badass stunts were simply elaborate 'science experiments' used in a real-life testing ground."

"For which I've apologized to the mayor and made restitution to the city," Reece fills in. "None of the trials should have gone to the level of realism that they did, and for that I *am* regretful." His face takes on such somber lines, even I start to believe his ruse. "Of course, I'm also thankful. The DA has been lenient in not pursuing any charges in consideration of Richards Research offering to pay for all repairs to city property damaged in Bolt's escapades."

"Doesn't hurt that he helped put away some nasty bastards

in the process," the reporter counters, supported by a round of nods from...well...just about everyone. "Including the creeps who tried to assault Miss Crist in the train station."

"For which Miss Crist is deeply thankful," I interject. "Along with the other victims of the other crimes for which Bolt made the perpetrators pay—even though he isn't, and won't ever be, a paid law enforcement official."

I conclude by visibly squeezing Reece's shoulder, answered by his tender "yes, dear" glance. The moment sets off another flurry of flashbulbs, confirming we've done our job in convincing them the cover story is real. It helps that most of it is. I really *am* beyond thankful for what happened in the metro station a week after we first met, when Reece swept in and put down the scumbags who had me in a corner. He really did do it with nothing but six months' worth of martial arts and defense training under his belt, meaning the incident could've had a horrifically different result. And no, he's not going to attempt something like it again because Bolt's leathers *have* been retired for good.

The only thing the world doesn't know—or need to know—is exactly why.

"So." The declaration, issued from Stall Girl, all but lasers her question into the air. "What happens now, EmRee? Give us the scoop, you two. We've worked hard for it."

I grimace. "Paging understatement to the white courtesy curb."

She rewards my sarcasm with a cute wink, but isn't deterred from continuing. "Are we talking...what...a reality show? Maybe a scripted series? Endorsement deals? A book contract?" She tilts her head as if that one's rung a particularly loud bell. "Is that why you went to New York, Emmalina?"

Reece lifts one hand, almost looking like a Bible School Jesus about to multiply fish for the masses. "As stated in the press release from Richards Industries yesterday, which you all should've had time to read by now"—he hooks a brow her direction—"Miss Crist was in New York in her capacity as the supervising director of Richards Reaches Out, the new nonprofit arm of our company. RRO is focused on giving back to youth across the globe, especially in helping hardworking young leaders who haven't been given financial or social advantages to better themselves."

Another reporter sidles forward, bumping shoulders with Pen Tapper. "So you're actually contributing to social awareness beyond supporting the world's vodka industry, Richards?"

Rage clouds the edges of my vision. The prick is as smallminded as his gossip-rag readers. Can't they see that people can change when they really want to? That people grow up, man up, and want to take accountability for their lives? But the guy's smug smirk already gives me the answer, which should be my cue to summon my Zen side.

Impossible.

Thank God Reece has had a lot more practice with this shit, as he demonstrates with a diplomatic spread of his hands while offering, "Fair enough question, Quinn—but wouldn't you agree that turning over new leaves is a hell of a lot more interesting than digging through the worms beneath the old?"

The crowd buzzes louder as reporters order their cameramen to mark the time on their feeds. My man's zinger at the annoying Quinn will be tomorrow's leading soundbite—not that Stall Girl is going to rest on her laurels with that. Clearly, she's after juicier material here.

"So that's really just *it* for Bolt?" Her narrow face pinches into an accusatory pout. "We're not going to get the behind-the-scenes on those effects? The explanation of how your 'experimental' lightning pulses took down all those criminals—and about how *you* survived all those showdowns?"

Reece flashes an indulgent smile. "Come, come, Blair. You write for *Silver* magazine. You know a good magician never exposes *all* their secrets. Everything we have to reveal at this point was contained in yesterday's press release. When Richards Research has something new to share, you'll all be the first to be informed. Until then"—he caresses my back, captivatingly possessive, inciting yet another burst of camera shutters—"I'm just a guy running a couple of businesses, dating the girl he's crazy about, and enjoying life in La-La Land."

He punctuates that by unhooking a couple of his shirt buttons, just enough to reveal the distinct purple and gold of a Lakers T-shirt beneath. A new round of laughter fills the air.

"Just like the rest of us, huh?" someone cracks.

"More than you think." I snuggle closer to Reece, hiding any tells about my white lie by turning my face into his chest. Ironically, it's the whitest fib of the bunch. Like them, Reece has good days and bad. He puts on his pants one leg at a time, struggles to tame his hair in the morning, and has true cosmic dilemmas about what to binge next on the Roku. They don't have to know that between all that, he's formed Richards Research as a front for keeping tabs on the whack-a-doodle scientists who call themselves the Consortium. Keep your friends close and your enemies on at least three different monitoring platforms.

And, oh yeah—between all that, be sure to pleasure your woman like the ever-charged battery you really are.

As *that* erotic thought heats my gaze, Reece's nostrils flare. His gaze drops to my mouth—for the two seconds before he crashes another kiss on me, hotter and deeper and fiercer than his first. My balance falters. My world spins. He's the rock in my storm, sheltering and crushing me at once, turning me into a helpless heap in his brutal embrace.

At the edge of the tempest, I hear the same reporter chuckle out, "Yeah. Sure. *Just* like the rest of us."

Without breaking our contact, Reece deftly turns, trapping me against the car and deepening our kiss. The mob of media, receiving our messaging loud and clear, starts to dissipate. They've gotten what they came for—and with this hotter-than-hell kiss, we've probably even given my bathroom buddy *her* story—and are content to let us be just another couple indulging pent-up passions after being apart for too damn long.

I'm home.

**This story continues in Ignite
Bolt Saga: Volume Two!**

ALSO BY ANGEL PAYNE

The Bolt Saga:
Bolt
Ignite (July 31, 2018)
Pulse (August 28, 2018)
Fuse (Coming Soon)
Surge (Coming Soon)
Light (Coming Soon)

Honor Bound:
Saved
Cuffed
Seduced
Wild
Wet
Hot
Masked
Mastered
Conquered (Coming Soon)
Ruled (Coming Soon)

Secrets of Stone Series:
No Prince Charming
No More Masquerade
No Perfect Princess
No Magic Moment
No Lucky Number
No Simple Sacrifice
No Broken Bond
No White Knight

**For a full list of Angel's other titles,
visit her at AngelPayne.com**

ACKNOWLEDGMENTS

Where does a person start when trying to wrap gray matter around the concept that their dream book has finally become not only a reality, but the start to an entirely new romance fiction world? I think the answer is that they just don't—and perhaps just try to stick to the singular overwhelming emotion at hand. *Gratitude.*

It's the best word to describe what I feel when considering the incredible team—yes, it really does take a village!—who have taken the Team Bolt world from one little book into the start of a saga-length adventure.

None of this would be what it is without the diligence, dedication, and sheer brilliance of the Waterhouse Press team, starting with the stunning editing expertise of Jeanne De Vita and Scott Saunders. You two have not only caught every detail and nuance of this huge concept, but your insight has made my writing a thousand times better—and best of all, has made the hearts and souls of these characters shine. I could fill an entirely new novel with how much I love you two.

Just as importantly, to the entire "behind the scenes" team at Waterhouse: Not only have you believed in this project when even I had some doubts, but have proven so, over and over again, with devotion and passion that blows my mind and has moved me to tears on many occasions. From Meredith Wild's artistic vision to the marketing genius of David, Jon, Robyn, Yvonne, Kurt, Amber, and Haley, I'm simply blown away. And to the rest of the crew who help make every cog turn and every gear hum—Jesse, Jennifer, and Jeff Jones himself—I *thank you* from the very depths of my heart!

Additionally, I have to thank the beautiful and insanely talented Regina Wamba, along with her team (Yuli! James! Peter!) and cover models Anthony Kemper and Hannah Lundquist, who turned one *really* long, very blustery January day into beautiful images that have brought Reece and Emma to life in ways I never dreamed. Our cover shoot had to be one of the coolest experiences *ever*, and I'm so grateful for everyone's incredible enthusiasm. Here's to big things and amazing futures for all of you!

Special thanks to the goddesses of the Payne Passion force. I cannot begin to tell you how much your humor, love, and support, especially when a lot of the world wasn't "getting" this concept at first, have kept me going on a daily basis.

Last but definitely not least: No way would I be here now without the love and constant diligent support, which may or may not include hand holding, tear wiping, ass kicking, and general talking-down-from-ledges duty, of my incredible circle of friends. Victoria Blue, Martha Frantz, Meredith Wild, Mia Michelle, Chelle Bliss, Lauren Rowe, Carrie Ann Ryan, Jenna Jacob, Crystal Burnette...you're always there and always available, no matter how huge my meltdowns, and I truly, deeply appreciate you. Honestly, you ladies are the gold standard of friendship, and I love you so much.

Most importantly: Thanks to my incredible family. Tom and Jess, you are the rocks of my world. Mom: thanks for always telling me to strive for the special. And John and Sue: you're both still buttheads, but you're the buttheads I'm proud to call sibs.

ABOUT ANGEL PAYNE

USA Today bestselling romance author Angel Payne loves to focus on high-heat romance starring memorable alpha men and the women who love them. She has numerous book series to her credit, including the Suited for Sin series, the Cimarron Saga, the Temptation Court series, the Secrets of Stone series, the Lords of Sin historicals, and the popular Honor Bound series, as well as several standalone titles.

Angel is a native Southern Californian, leading to her love of being in the outdoors, where she often reads and writes. She still lives in Southern California with her soul-mate husband and beautiful daughter, to whom she is a proud cosplay/culture con mom. Her passions also include whisky tasting, shoe shopping, and travel.

Visit her at AngelPayne.com